BELOW THE BAY

Other Books by Edward Allen Karr

SERIES: Thrills N Kills in the Hills
(Racy, Comical Horror in Beverly Hills)
Dayzee Dazzle and the Kildare Killers – Book One
Dayzee Dazzle and her Manic Mansion – Book Two
Dayzee Dazzle and the On-Set Onslaught – Book Three
Dayzee Dazzle and the Cadaver Collectors – Book Four
* * * * *

SERIES: Socrates Lewis Stories
(Psychological/Religious Fiction)
Crosswinds – Book One
Crossovers – Book Two
* * * * *

SERIES: Fringes Of Infinity
(Contemporary Fantasy Fiction)
Lin Finity and her Mayhem Rising – Book One
Lin Finity in Holding On – A Novella
Lin Finity and the Words Unspoken – Book Two
Lin Finity and the Islands of Time – Book Three
Lin Finity and the Flights to Forever – Book Four
Tayo Tersoo and the Hunter of Souls – Book Five
* * * * *

SERIES: A World So Close
(Middle-grade Fantasy Adventure & Coming of Age)
Jayden Blue and the Gift to Imagine – A Prequel
Jayden Blue and the Sword in his Shadow – Book One
Jayden Blue and the Call of the Wings – Book Two
Jayden Blue and the Lair of the Iron Lions – Book Three
Jayden Blue and the Journey to Val ka'Yoom – Book Four
Jayden Blue and the Forest of Night Fallen – Book Five
Jayden Blue and the Wait of the Sun – Book Six
* * * * *

BELOW THE BAY

Risk and the Killers
Book One

Edward Allen Karr

LAKESIDE
LETTERS, LLC

Lakeside Letters, LLC
30628 Detroit Road, #247
Westlake, OH 44145

This is a work of fiction. Names, characters, businesses, events, and incidents are the products of the author's imagination. Any resemblance to actual persons, living or dead, or actual events is purely coincidental. Certain long-standing institutions are mentioned, but the characters are imaginary. The opinions expressed are those of the characters and should not be confused with those of the author.

Below the Bay
Risk and the Killers Book One
©2024 Edward Sechkar.   All rights reserved.

No part of this book may be reproduced in any form, stored in any retrieval system, or transmitted in any form by any means—electronic, mechanical, photocopy, recording, or otherwise—without prior written permission of the copyright holder, except as provided by United States of America copyright law. For permission requests, submit a written request to the publisher at the address shown.

First Edition, 2024
www.LakesideLetters.com

Cover design by JD Smith Design

ISBN-13: 978-1-950886-66-1

"Sissy's right. There's nothing in this stupid place that scares us."

She reached up and patted around on the basket's top rail.

"Oh, maybe just being so high up."

Risk grinned and tipped his head toward the ground far below them, where dead, abandoned buildings seemed to reach up for them.

"It's worse down there."

"We're not worried," said Sophia.

"We're killers," Marilyn said, petulant. "Nothing here is going to bother either of us."

He looked from one pair of blue eyes to the other, then back again. He gave their mostly bare bodies a quick glance, then shook his head.

"Alright. We'll see."

Risk and his lion turned away from the twins, then they both looked out over the dark, grim landscape shrouded in night deep below the San Francisco Bay.

From Chapter 3 – Below the Bay

Table of Contents

Chapter 1 – Up in Toxic Black Smoke

"Oh, those poor kitties! Sissy, they don't deserve that!"

"No, Sis," said Sophia. "They sure as hell don't deserve it. Those were good cats."

Marilyn's long, wavy blond hair hung across her face, clinging to her skin from sweat brought on by the inferno so near. They'd paused their escape and stood in the recently discovered hidden chamber behind the back wall of the closet leading to Dayzee Dazzle's mansion in the Flats of Beverly Hills. They listened to the lions howling and watched the charring and curling and crawling flames that crept along the wall in every direction.

"Sissy, not past tense, please! Maybe they'll be okay?"

Beyond that burning barrier, two female mountains lions yipped and whined, but the path to follow Marilyn and Sophia was impassable. They'd helped the twins, whom Dayzee had named the Kildare Killers, and the rest of them put on a bizarre though thrilling performance in the hopes of luring someone or something through the portal to save them.

But major portions of the giant house's ceiling and floors above, along with furnishings in the rooms in the upper floors, had succumbed to the intense heat and had collapsed before the lions could rush through. The only remaining exit for them had become a raging oven.

Everything not already burning in Dayzee's luxurious house was being incinerated by bands of roaming Cadaver Collectors, whose flaming torch hands were touching everything, burning it all to the ground so that there would be no trace of them or the destruction they'd brought. The lions had tried lunging at windows and doors, but the heat and smoke had always driven them back.

Sophia looked away from the howling just beyond the fires and saw her sister's hair, then fluffed it back over her shoulders. It fell gently over her tight white dress, which was shredded down the front and worn more like a robe.

"Thanks, Sissy. I won't cry. I promise."

"I know you won't, Sis. I might, though."

Marilyn turned to her sister and gave her long, straight black hair the same treatment, lightly flipping it back for her. Then, she held her waist with both hands, just above the waistband of her short skirt, and looked into her eyes.

"I just want to go back to Kildare," said Marilyn. "We never had demented Collectors sucking up dead bodies and blood and guts, no headless guys looking for head, and—"

"Dead Firemen, too, Sis. Don't forget them."

"Yes, them too. And burning mansions, and all of our Earth friends dying, and such sweet lady lions about to—"

"They're not dying," said Kenzie, who joined them from one side and placed an arm around each's waist. "Not my cats."

The twins turned enough to look at her and in unison, each gave her long brown hair a gentle brush back over the shoulders of her tight, mostly unbuttoned blouse.

"Your cats?" Sophia with a smirk.

Kenzie didn't smile, and she was about to defend her statement when Dayzee screamed up at them from the bottom of the ancient, circular stone stairway that they'd found only recently.

"We're down here, girls! Come on already!"

Sophia didn't break up the group hug, just leaned over the railing and yelled.

"We made it, Dayzee! Kenzie, Sis, and I are safe!"

"Alright, well, hurry up—there's a bomb ticking down here, remember?"

"We remember!" Marilyn yelled. "We're coming!"

Her eyes blinked heavily when she said to her sister, "Damn bomb."

"Well, Sis, it was the only way to stop more of those damn Collectors from coming through, right?"

A loud, frantic lion howling got them all to look at the long fingers of twitching flames.

"They're not dying," said Kenzie. "I'm keeping those cats. Somehow, I'm not letting them go."

"Kenzie, you can't get through there. It's not like we could take them with us through the portal anyway."

"Sissy's right, Kenzie. Those cats will just have to—"

Kenzie broke free and took a few steps toward the shadows and smoke blanketing the walls of the dark room. She looked around, tipping her head, then strode away from the twins, her high-heeled shoes giving sharp strikes to the old stone floor.

"Kenzie?"

"Where's she off to now, Sis?"

Marilyn looked up, Sophia joined her, and they both studied the small square of light high above them. At the sound of smooth leather stamping on old metal, they tipped their heads back to focus again on Kenzie, who had begun to climb the wall with the crude rungs built into it.

"Oh, Sissy, that can't be good."

"She's going up to that skylight?"

They looked up again and saw flames high above them, darting out from the walls and sometimes blocking the view of what they all thought was a skylight in an attic that even Dayzee had never visited.

Sophia rushed over and grabbed Kenzie's ankle, stopping her ascent.

"Kenzie, no! You can't go up there!"

"Fifi, let me go!"

Marilyn had followed close behind her sister, and she spoke just loudly enough to be heard over the roar of both the burning house and the panicky lions.

"She's still calling you Fifi!"

Sophia looked back briefly and said, "That won't matter if she roasts herself, Sis!"

Still holding her ankle, Sophia yelled, "Kenzie, there's too much fire. Don't go!"

Kenzie shook loose of Sophia's grasp and continued her climb and said, "Those cats! I need those cats!"

Only seconds later, she'd been mostly swallowed up by smoke and shadows.

The twins stood side by side, arms around each other's waist, and stared up at flames becoming more ambitious, sometimes reaching clear across the circular tower.

Sophia broke loose from her sister and started to climb, saying, "She's not dying today. No way in hell."

Marilyn grabbed at her lowest ankle and screamed, "Sissy, no! You can't go up there too!"

"Dammit, Sis, let me go!"

"She'll be okay," said Marilyn. "Sissy, she'll find a way. Come back down. Please!"

Sophia kicked her leg free and stayed up on the rungs, staring after Kenzie, but she climbed back to the dusty floor anyway.

They both looked toward the closet at the sound of a lion yipping like it had been stabbed. Another roar, high above them, caused them to look up again, and they saw that the flames had spread across the entire area, with Kenzie high above all of that and on her way to the skylight.

Sophia was still gazing upward when Marilyn laced her arms around her waist.

"We'll find her again, Sissy. And those lions will make it somehow too."

Sophia sighed and looked into her sister's blue eyes, bright from the firelight in a dim, smoke-filled room. Marilyn couldn't manage a smile as she wiped beneath each of her sister's equally piercing blue eyes.

"We have to go, though, Sissy. Before that telepathic bomb thing goes kaboom."

"Go where, Sis? We can't really just decide to go back to Kildare."

"Well, maybe we can ask him?"

"Ask who?"

"Whoever came to help us. Remember all that fun sex and danger stuff we just did, and how it sounded like somebody might be coming for us?"

"I remember. But I haven't seen anyone. And what makes you think whoever comes through would take us to Kildare?"

Marilyn sighed and looked down.

"I don't know, Sissy. But we have no choice. We have to go anywhere he takes us or burn to death."

Far below them, Dayzee screamed from the bottom of the stairs.

"Hey, let's go! Get your gorgeous Kildare asses down here already!"

Marilyn giggled, softly and briefly, and said, "You do have a gorgeous ass, Sissy."

Sophia didn't offer anything close to a giggle or even a smile.

"Yours is gorgeous, too, Sis. We're twins. And, uh, so was Kenzie's."

"Sissy, she's not gone. I promise, we'll see her again. Oh, and those lady lions have very nice asses, too, in a lion kind of way."

Sophia offered a quick grin and said, "Yeah. Those gorgeous she-lions. Alright, let's go, Sis."

She took Marilyn's hand, and they began a careful descent, placing their pointy heels in the few remaining stable areas of old stone stairs that been mostly destroyed by the Cadaver Collectors.

* * *

"Girls, you're starting to sweat."

Dayzee grinned and shook her head at the sight of them, which caused her wild, wavy blond mane to sway behind her too. She'd managed to place her own high heels on one of the few remaining areas of unbroken stone floor, and she stood with her hands on her hips, just above her short skirt which was taking on a layer of soot and ash. She'd kept her blouse unbuttoned low, and none of her exposed skin showed even the start of a bead of sweat.

"Oh my goodness," said Marilyn, fanning herself with her free hand. "It's so much cooler down here."

"Oh yeah," said Dayzee. "It's way cooler so far underground."

"Not for long," the Boss said as he pointed up. "Besides a hungry inferno that wants to snack on us, we—"

"Sis is quite a tasty snack," Sophia said with an unenthusiastic smirk.

Marilyn said, "Hmm, not if I'm roasted, Sissy. You neither."

"Girls, let the Boss finish."

The Boss, a handsome middle-aged fellow with graying hair, who appeared quite human, was the manager for the team of Dayzee, Marilyn, and Sophia for their mission on Earth. He'd only grinned during the interruption, then turned toward Dayzee after she'd cleared some time for him to continue.

"Thanks, Dayzee. These twins, huh?"

"More gorgeous than Earth deserves."

"You too, Dayzee," said Marilyn. "You're the hottest."

"Thanks, Mare. Fia, too, you know. I'm still astounded that no one ever knew that neither of you are from Earth."

"Earth is just too easy sometimes," said Sophia. "Uh, until it all burned."

"Well, Sissy, it's not all—"

"I thought I was allowed to finish?" the Boss said, smiling at each of them for a second. "Like I was saying, besides that fabulous mansion of Dayzee's going up in toxic black smoke, we have a newfangled bomb from the lab back home. Things are about to blow, and we—"

"Oh, we're back to blowing again?" said Dayzee. "Even at a time like this, all you can think about is—"

"No! I mean, yeah, all the time. But what I mean is that the bomb's about to detonate, and it'll wipe out that portal when it does. Don't you think we should probably get going?"

"Wait," Dayzee said, tugging on his sleeve. "Girls, where's Kenzie?"

Sophia looked down, frowning, and kicked at the dust and chips of old stone. Marilyn gave that a glance, then looked back at Dayzee.

"She, um, she's trying to save those lions."

"What? Those two that joined in all that sex and danger stuff up there?"

"Yes, Dayzee. Those two kitties. She, uh, climbed up to that skylight way up there. Remember that?"

"Oh, wait," said the Boss. "Dayzee and I wondered if that might be another portal."

"What is with this house?" said Dayzee. "We keep finding stairways we didn't know about, it's so big we can't find the elevators half the time, some rooms are—"

"Stocked with really sweet lingerie," Marilyn said with a nod.

"Oh, and trapezes. Don't forget that room with a trapeze too," said Sophia.

"Mare. Fia. Yes, all of that. So, that barmaid from the Prism is climbing—"

"She's an actress, Dayzee. She told us so many times."

"Thanks, Mare. Yeah, and a damn good one. So, she's climbing up for that portal?"

"She doesn't know it's a portal," said Sophia. "She's just desperate to save those big cats."

The Boss tapped his wristwatch and said, "As for Kenzie, we'll have to hope for the best. Unless you all want to be gorgeous, tasty, *toasted* treats."

"Not me."

"Me neither. Okay. We should go."

"Yes, we should, Mare. Boss? Lead the way."

"Because it's my job?"

"Not so much," said Dayzee. "Mostly because you like me bossing you around."

"Aw," said Marilyn to her sister, "they're so cute together."

"Yeah, Sis. Yeah. Not just them—so were—"

"You and Kenzie. I know, Sissy."

"Girls, we're all cute together. But we really have to—"

High above them near the top of the circular stairway, two lions screamed, and they all looked up. Thick arms of flames were reaching across the stairway, smacking the railings on the opposite side.

"We really have to move!"

"Finally," said the Boss, and he started picking at the shattered remains of the old wooden door that led to the tunnel that led to the portal room. "Damn Collectors, always wrecking everything that they—"

Dayzee used both hands to shove him through, knocking loose many of the splinters.

"No time, Boss! Get your ass moving and lead the way, alright?"

"She's quite a boss herself, Sis."

"Oh, Sissy, she's a hot boss. She can boss me around anytime."

"When we're all back in Kildare, you mean?"

Dayzee gave them both a smile before turning and following the Boss through the doorway and into the tunnel.

"Yes! Whoever the kind thing is that comes through that portal to save us, we'll just ask politely."

"And if they refuse?"

"Well, Sissy, we're killers. We'll just burn him up!"

Chapter 2 – Delirium of Sex and Death

Dayzee held the Boss's arm as they stood in the dark room that housed a portal through which the mansion in the Flats had been invaded by the Cadaver Collectors, dozens of them. All had followed the scent of dead bodies, most of those without heads, and satiated themselves, sucking up every last bit of gristle and slime. Then, satisfied, they'd ignited everything to burn to ash the house, themselves, all of the dead bodies, and many of the loose heads.

With her free hand, Dayzee brushed at the dust that she and the Boss had acquired, then helped Marilyn and Sophia clean themselves up too.

"That little thing is going to somehow destroy the portal, Boss?"

"Yes, Sophia," he said, stooping down to pick up the compact briefcase.

After brushing dust and soot off of it, he flipped it open and showed them the flat screen inside, much like as if it were a laptop.

"It's telepathic," he said. "Some ungodly mix of sorcery crystals and irradiated brain cells."

"Sounds wonderful."

"Yeah, Dayzee, those lab boys, huh? It's made to pick up on the thoughts and emotions of anyone close enough."

They gathered around to look at a grouping of four images.

"Aw, that's almost as cute as you two in real life," Marilyn said while clapping her hands silently.

On the screen, there was an image of the Boss and an image of Dayzee.

"You're both just thinking about each other?"

"I'm sure thinking of her," said the Boss, and he leaned enough to kiss Dayzee on the lips, then gave her a chance to speak.

"Huh," she said. "The thing's malfunctioning. It should show me in my sadistic prison guard costume from that film."

The Boss grinned and said, "That's the image up here," and tapped the side of his head.

"It'd be an X-rated image, too, you know."

"I hope so!"

"Oh, those kitties are mine," said Marilyn. "It's not fair what happened to them. Not fair," she said and stomped her white high heel on the dusty stone floor. "Oh, but look at that."

She pointed to the fourth image, which was only a luscious pair of lips.

"Uh-oh, Sissy. I think we all know who that is."

Sophia finally looked up and at the screen.

"Good memories, Sis. Even just that."

"We'll find her again. I know we will."

"She knows we're from Kildare, right, Sis?" said Sophia. "I mean, if we talk whoever came to save us into taking us there through this portal, Kenzie will know?"

"She'll know, Sissy. She knows we're the Kildare Killers."

"She used to call us the Killer Kuties."

"She will again. Oh, she called us Kool Killer Kuties once too."

"Okay," said the Boss, "as fun as this is, there's not much time left. You girls have to follow right after us, alright?"

"Before that thing goes kaboom?"

"Yeah, Marilyn. Right. But more importantly, you'll have a better chance of taking the fast lane to the same place as Dayzee and me."

"Wait," said Sophia. "You don't know where any of us will end up, do you?"

"Uh . . . no, but—"

A crash from parts of the house falling in on itself sent a thick puff of smoke into the portal room.

"Oh, boy," said Dayzee. "Just wonderful. Girls, we have no choice."

She accepted the Boss's embrace, his arms around her waist, and she put hers up over his shoulders. "Promise you'll follow right away?"

"We promise, Dayzee."

"Good, Mare. Fia?"

"Uh, yeah, Dayzee."

Sophia turned to look again back through the tunnel, then faced Dayzee again.

"No reason to stay, I guess."

"Alright, good. See you gorgeous twins on the other side."

She locked her lips on the Boss's, and they fell sideways into the shadows, making not a single sound and scattering up no dust.

"Alright, Sis, we have to—"

More crashing, louder than the last time, preceded a dusty, ashy wind that swept past them and swirled around in the room before clearing.

And closely following the smoky gust was the sound of agitated growling.

"Uh-oh, Sissy. Those big kitties aren't so happy anymore."

"Well, would you be, Sis? They've been through a lot."

"Oh, true. It's a bit much for such nice—"

They stopped at the sound of more growling, closer.

"Sissy, wait. Did the kitties get through? Did they make it down the stairs?"

"Uh, let's hope not, Sis. Those are some angry lions now."

"Oh. That's true. Maybe they—"

"Hey, Sis!" Sophia screamed while pointing down at the clock on the bomb. "There's only three seconds before—"

"Kaboom!"

"Yeah!"

The sisters hugged each other close, then turned to scan the shadows to locate the portal with their cheeks touching.

"Sissy, we'd better just jump into the shadows where Dayzee and—"

The entire room shook from a soundless wave of unidentifiable energy that drove the girls back a step. They fought to not fall, and they held each other even more tightly.

"Oh my goodness," Marilyn said when a tall, muscular man stepped out of the shadows and swirling smoke, his fists firmly planted on his hips.

He wore his wavy black hair shoulder-length, and the black whiskers on his chin were neatly trimmed. He rarely blinked, letting his black eyes study first one, then the other.

Blue jeans, faded, ripped, and stretched over powerful legs, ended in gouged and scraped black work boots. His arms were uncovered, crowded with lean muscles, and with not a single tattoo visible.

His black leather vest had never had buttons, and it hung open, displaying ab muscles harder than the stone floor on which he stood.

Without a smile, he focused his unblinking black eyes on Sophia's. "Who are you?"

The Kildare Killers only stared and squeezed each other more tightly.

He shifted only his eyes to drill them into Marilyn's.

He leaned toward her and said, "Why did you call me?"

The girls did nothing but stare, never looking away from his intense eyes as he gazed from one to the other repeatedly.

Softly, Marilyn said, "Oh, Sissy, I don't think—"

"You're sisters?"

Sophia cleared her throat and said, "Yeah. Twins."

He gestured with both hands and said, "Face me."

They turned toward him but kept their arms around each other.

He looked at both of them repeatedly.

"Yeah. I see it."

He leaned in closer, examining each for a few seconds.

"Mostly the same. Different too."

After his black eyes had stayed fixed on their blue eyes for a few more seconds, he began a detailed study of Sophia, first her breasts squeezed into a tight red blouse, then across the meager cloth of her short black skirt, then he slowed more to scan along her bare legs.

He focused on her high black heels, tied around her smooth skin with tight, thin black ankle straps. He offered a satisfied grin which faded almost immediately.

But it reappeared when he shifted his gaze toward Marilyn, her high white heels first.

He let that grin vanish, then let his eyes trace a leisurely path up along Marilyn's legs, then all around the torn white cloth of her dress, held together by the Boss's belt, then lingering for a few moments on each of her breasts.

He snapped his eyes up to again look into her bright blue eyes, then Sophia's equally bright eyes.

With a grim smile, he said, "This can't be Hell."

His meager smile vanished, and he said, "I asked who you are."

He was staring at Marilyn, so she said, "I'm Marilyn."

He did nothing but gaze into her eyes, then he nodded.

Then, he leaned his head and met Sophia's unblinking gaze.

"You?"

"I'm Sophia."

He squinted for a few seconds, then nodded to each of them.

"I'm Risk."

With more crashing from the mansion burning above them, and the wild howling of two terrified mountain lions, Risk looked down at the suitcase bomb near his boots. The girls looked too.

And they all saw its timer start up again, paused only due to Risk's arrival, as it counted from three seconds to two.

"Uh-oh, Sissy."

"Dammit, Sis."

Then, from two to one.

Risk scoffed and said, "Fuck."

Its clock showed zero, then it fell over without a sound, chasing up wispy plumes of dust.

"Don't tell me," he said.

"Uh, yeah," said Sophia. "That took out the portal."

Marilyn said, "It was our only hope to—"

Seemingly before the lion behind Risk had roared, he'd spun himself around and held his arms out to shield the girls. A single mountain lion with crazy eyes and bloody, bared fangs, crouched and stared up at Risk.

Risk crouched, too, and the twins held him around his waist, all eyes on the lion.

"Don't," he said to her, his voice calm. "You don't have to."

The lion stared only at Risk, her snout twitching and showing her sharp teeth as she continued a low growl.

"Just don't," he said.

She growled and leaped, and Risk just as quickly lunged at her. The girls had to let go of him, and they watched as two savage beasts tumbled in and out of smoke and shadow, both growling and both showing glimpses of fangs and claws.

After the battle had gone silent, the smoke began to clear, and Marilyn and Sophia saw Risk, on all fours beside the dead lioness, his mouth still closed on her bleeding throat.

He stared back at them as he released the lion to slump to the floor, then stood, blood dripping from his fingers and dribbling down his chin. He held their gaze for only a second, then started looking all around them.

Sophia leaned toward her sister and said, "Sis, who the hell is he?"

Marilyn embraced her sister and said to her, "Oh, Sissy, *what* the hell is he?"

A commotion caused the smoke clouds in the tunnel to wave and scatter with the sound of more cautious growling.

The second lion revealed her worried eyes as she crept out of the smoke-filled tunnel. She looked first at her fallen friend, slaughtered and bloody on the floor, then up at Risk.

She hid her fangs and panted. Then, she began a low whimpering.

Risk held his palms toward her and said, "It's okay."

She kept whimpering and whining while looking toward her fallen friend, then back into Risk's eyes.

"Shh, now," he told her. "It's okay."

She didn't flee when he stooped near her and held her head in both hands. He tipped his head back once toward the dead lion.

"She didn't leave me a choice."

The lion relaxed with a single, raspy sigh, and Risk reached farther along with his right hand to pat her side.

"You, though, would have killed all of us."

The lion looked into his eyes and panted quickly, as if laughing.

"Thanks for being kind."

She gave his hand a quick, wet swipe with her long tongue.

Risk stood and faced the Kildare Killers, and his lion stood beside him, both gazing calmly at Marilyn and Sophia.

*   *   *

Risk shook back his wavy black hair as he gazed at the blond Kildare Killer and said, "Marilyn."

She held his gaze with her eyes open wide.

"We can't stay here."

Marilyn nodded but didn't speak.

He focused his intense eyes on Sophia, the blue of her eyes shining even as smoke engulfed them all.

"Sophia."

She only tipped her head and kept hugging her sister.

"Show me the exit."

Sophia shook her head, cleared her throat, and said, "There isn't one. Not anymore. The bomb got it."

With one hand, he scratched around the ears of the lion beside him and with the other, he raked his fingers through his unruly hair. He looked all around the portal chamber, then up.

"Not good."

To Marilyn, he said, "Where are we?"

Marilyn said, "We're, um, underground in a room that—"

He held out the hand not fussing with his lion.

He let a few silent seconds pass, then pointed up.

"No. Up there."

"Up there used to be Dayzee's mansion."

Risk noticed Sophia giving a quick glance to the flames and thicker smoke that had begun trapping them, blocking any escape back through the tunnel, and he gave it a quick look too.

He turned back toward Marilyn and said, "No. The place."

Marilyn said, "It's Beverly Hills."

He nodded and said, "Good. I'll remember."

The twins looked at each other for just a second, didn't say a word, and looked back at Risk.

"Are we going to die down here?" Sophia said.

Marilyn began taking quicker breaths while looking around their prison, then said, "We don't want to die here!"

He half-smiled at each of them.

"No one is dying here."

He held the gaze of the lion beside him as she tipped her head back, her eyes darting between his and the flames.

A few seconds later, he said to her, "No. Not you either."

She panted while looking into his eyes, then both of them turned again to Marilyn and Sophia.

"She wants a name," he said.

Sophia gave the lion a quick squinting look, then said, "Huh? The lion?"

He nodded and said, "She'll need one."

Marilyn sighed and shook her head, then turned to whisper to her sister, "Sissy, maybe Kenzie?"

Sophia blinked her eyes slowly and kept them aimed at the floor.

A moment later, she nodded, still not looking up.

Marilyn said to Risk, "Can we call her Kenzie?"

He looked down at the lion, and she looked up at him. She yawned and kept her mouth opened wide, displaying her white fangs for a second

Then, she snapped her mouth shut and leveled her gaze on the twins again.

"Kenzie Cat," said Risk.

He tipped his head toward the lioness and said, "Her idea."

Marilyn giggled once nervously, then said, "Can Cat be with a 'K?'"

"Sis," Sophia said in a strained whisper. "You shouldn't—"

"Yeah. Even better," said Risk.

All of them turned enough to see the flames that had reached the tunnel's entrance to the chamber but went no farther.

"We have to go," he said.

"How?" said Sophia. "Everything's burning, and the—"

"And the portal is gone," said Marilyn. "There's no way."

He offered them the first true smile since they'd met.

"You must do as I say."

The girls looked at the advancing flames, which carried with them more choking smoke.

Marilyn nodded and said, "We will."

"Yeah. Both of us."

"Good. One of you, take out your knife."

They looked at each other before quickly looking back at Risk.

"Uh, we don't have knives."

He shrugged and said, "An axe, then."

They both gave their clothing a quick study. Marilyn's makeshift white robe was tight and barely hid her physical features. Sophia's short skirt and blouse didn't even demand any imagination from anyone.

Sophia scoffed softly and said, "Uh, sorry. Nothing."

Still scratching around Kenzie Kat's ears, Risk wiped the last of the dead lion's blood from his chin as he looked around.

"Oh, wait," said Marilyn. "Sissy and I are the Kildare Killers. We can—"

"You kill?"

"Yeah," said Sophia. "Easily too."

"How do you kill?"

Sophia relaxed her hold on her sister and raised up her other hand. She made it glow red hot.

Kenzie Kat yipped softly just once and pressed against Risk's leg.

Risk nodded and said, "Good. You too?"

Marilyn showed him her glowing hand and didn't try to stop her soft giggle.

"Good," he said. "Cool your fires."

Their hands instantly returned to normal.

Risk held both arms out, hands together, then slowly spread them to the sides.

The girls gave each other a quick look, let each other go, then took a step to each side.

Risk looked first at Marilyn, then Sophia, then Marilyn again. He focused on Sophia for a few seconds, then looked down at the big cat.

He scoffed and said, "Yeah. Either one."

Kenzie Kat gave him a laughing snarl, then they both looked again toward the twins.

An explosion high above shook even the floor and walls of the underground room, and a wave of flames invited itself in, then branched to begin flowing around each way, encircling them.

Risk looked each way and said, "Dammit."

"Can we get the hell out of here already?"

"Sissy, he knows how, he just—"

"Too close," he said while scanning the hungry flames creeping along the perimeter.

"Can't do it right."

He rubbed around the lion's ears as she looked up at him.

"It's never easy," he told her.

Then, he turned his eyes to Sophia when she said, "What do you mean, 'right?'"

He ignored her question and studied Marilyn when she said, "Then, let's do it wrong! We don't want to die!"

He grinned for just a second, then patted Kenzie Kat's head and said to her, "Wait."

He leaned closer to her and said, "Until."

He straightened up and said, "You," and took three steps to stand so close to Marilyn that she had to look up to see his eyes.

Quickly, he shot his left arm around her waist and held her head with his right. She'd only begun to open her mouth for a gasp, and he covered her lips with his own.

Sophia kept her distance and stared at them, and Marilyn groaned softly and struggled. Risk didn't release her from the embrace or the kiss, and she finally relaxed in his arms.

While still forcing her to kiss him, he began savagely tearing open her already damaged white dress. It came apart easily, and he snapped it back over her shoulders and down her arms, then tossed it to one side, where the flames welcomed it.

She'd started with her palms against his shoulders, pushing him weakly, but she reached up and cautiously touched his hair with her fingertips.

He used both hands to hold her by her waist and lifted her. Holding her up effortlessly, still kissing her, he waited the few seconds that it took before she wrapped her legs around him.

Breaking the kiss, he looked at Sophia and said, "You."

He pointed behind Marilyn and said, "Here."

Sophia only stared for a second, then she followed his demand and stood close behind her sister.

Still holding Marilyn with one arm, with her legs squeezing around his waist, Risk reached past her and began ripping at Sophia's blouse until he could peel it from her and let it drop.

She never fought him and didn't complain.

When he pointed at her skirt, she nodded and stretched it down over her hips and let it drop onto the dirty floor.

"Good," he said, looking at Sophia over Marilyn's shoulder.

Risk eased himself down onto his back and took Marilyn with him, freeing her only enough to kneel above him.

He made no effort to force her, but she leaned over on her own to continue their kiss with her hands on the stone floor.

He unclasped his belt and made himself ready for her.

Marilyn tipped her head up, still close and ready to resume the kiss, and he only looked into her eyes.

With minimal effort, she found the right place, right where he wanted her.

Sophia remained standing and watched the scene with her head shaking.

Until he held her gaze and tipped his head down.

"Um . . . I don't think—"

"Do it."

She cleared her throat, then knelt directly behind her sister, who had already lost herself to the pleasure of riding him, slowly and steadily, with her palms flat against his chest.

"Sex," he said, looking into Marilyn's eyes, and she never slowed.

He looked past Marilyn at Sophia and added, "And death."

She still only stared down at him as he crossed his right leg over his left between her bare thighs. When he grabbed her waist with strong hands, she looked down to watch as he wedged her onto that highest thigh.

Sophia began to breathe more heavily as he forced her down onto his leg, then let her relax, then drove her into it again. After a few times, he backed his hands away, and she kept up her steady thrusts on her own.

He got a hold on Marilyn's hips and said, "Sex and death. Same time."

Sophia was shaking her head, watching her sister mounted on a man or something else that had just come through the portal, while she kept herself more than busy behind her, her hands on her sister for balance as she kept rubbing on his leg.

He looked into Sophia's eyes and said, "There's no time. It has to be all of us."

"I . . . I'm already doing—"

"Touch her," he said.

She repositioned her hands on her sister's arms near her shoulders.

He scoffed and said, "Forget being sisters. Touch her."

Marilyn only smiled at that, her eyes closed as she kept moving.

Sophia looked into Risk's eyes as she reached around and held her sister's bare breasts.

Risk looked at Marilyn's breasts, each held by a hand with exquisitely manicured nails, then back into Sophia's eyes. Then, he watched her lips begin to curl into a smile.

He shook his head, smiling, too, and said, "Good, but it's not a game. You have to mean it."

Marilyn said softly, "Sissy, we're actresses. You can just—"

"No!"

Both pairs of blue eyes gazed down into a pair of insistent black ones.

"Feel it. Want it."

Sophia sighed and began gently squeezing Marilyn's breasts, and Risk nodded as he watched.

When he aimed his smile up to Sophia and nodded, then said, "More," she began soft pinching and pulling and leaned close enough that her face was in her sister's hair and her breasts were squeezed against her back.

All eyes looked to Risk's side as the mountain lion lay close to him, rubbing her snout against his exposed ribs where his leather vest had fallen open.

"It has to be more," he said. "All of you."

Marilyn gave her bouncing more energy, and she reached behind her with her left hand to play with her sister's black hair.

And she turned that way, too, just as Sophia leaned in closer, their noses touching as they gazed into each other's eyes.

No one looked at Kenzie Kat as she started a low wail, her jaws working against Risk's side.

"Do it," he said. "Or we all burn."

Their lips touched, and Marilyn kept up her steady gyrations on him. Sophia kept fondling her sister's breasts and riding Risk's hard thigh.

The flames had circled them completely and were trying to scale the walls.

"More," he said.

Sophia gasped softly, then they made their kiss as passionate as any in their lives.

The lioness snarled and snapped a sharp bite into Risk's ribs, sending streams of his blood down to form paste with the dust.

Marilyn kept her eyes closed and didn't break the kiss when Risk grabbed one of her wrists and moved that hand to a place over his heart.

She nodded when he tapped it and said, "When I say."

None of them stopped what they were losing themselves to.

The lion snarled and began a low growling.

Sophia quickened her pace, shifting her hips along Risk's thigh, and she gave even more attention to Marilyn's breasts, pinching, pulling, and rubbing them.

Marilyn was the first to moan when the girls heard Risk say, "Ah!"

Having found nothing to burn on the walls, the ring of flames began tightening around them, as if they sensed the only fuel left for them to digest.

"Ah!" Risk said while Marilyn sped up, jamming herself down roughly, and Sophia kept squeezing and pinching Marilyn's breasts while kissing her deeply and grinding on Risk's leg, and Kenzie Kat began sinking her fangs through skin, then sinew, then bone.

Risk, his eyes squinting, curled himself up and reached for both of them. Their kiss didn't end until they were close enough to take turns kissing him, then each other again while he awaited his next chance.

Marilyn gasped and stayed down on him, snapping her hips repeatedly.

Sophia kept up her short, urgent slides on his leg, her hands still grabbing and pulling roughly at the pair of breasts in her hands.

And they all kept kissing.

Until.

"Ah! Now!"

Marilyn didn't stop to look at her hand that had instantly become glowing hot, then began to sink into Risk's chest. She and her sister smiled at the smell of burning flesh, but the sex and violence wouldn't stop, and none had any intention of retreating from what they'd all started.

Marilyn broke the kiss only enough to say, "Mm, not just him. Me too, Sophia."

"God, yeah, Marilyn. I know your name, but I can't remember what—"

Marilyn stifled her with a kiss, and all of them stayed locked in a menagerie of sex and violence as Risk reached the peak of his own pleasure just as Marilyn's killer hand sank all the way through his heart.

Adding death to a room already ablaze with sex and flames.

"Damn," Risk said, and the girls and the lion paused to look at his face, which was contorted from both pleasure and the pain of Marilyn burning a hole through his heart.

With their cheeks touching and their hair tangled, they watched him smile as he lay back onto the floor. He tipped back his head, and it smoothly broke the surface of the stone floor like sinking into a frozen gray swamp.

A moment later, his entire head was lost in there.

Kenzie Kat resumed her savage biting, her wanton jaws snapping loudly through ribs while she shook Risk's torso from side to side. She paused only once to wail at the twins before renewing her attack.

And still, Risk kept sinking. And the girls sat up on him, neither one slowing as they still used him to keep their ecstasy alive.

They turned their heads only enough to resume their frantic kiss. Sophia roughly squeezed her sister's breasts, pulling their bodies together, and they both shifted their hips desperately on their own parts of him.

They paused only when a scream from the lion got cut off, and they watched as Kenzie Kat, with Risk holding the scruff of her neck, got pulled into the floor along with all of him from his waistline up.

"Sophia. Where the hell are we going?"

"Someplace with Risk and Kenzie Kat. Just don't stop."

"I can't. I won't. This is the strongest, sweetest one I ever—"

"Marilyn! Enough talk!"

Sophia groaned and forced her lips back into Marilyn's.

The Kildare Killers ended their time in Beverly Hills locked in a starving kiss, and their climaxes spiked as they sank with Risk and Kenzie Kat into a silent world of stone and darkness.

And flames just as insatiable as all of them—started by the torch hands of Cadaver Collectors that had ignited Dayzee's mansion in the Flats, then had eaten every floor and wall and ceiling, then had raced underground for any last prey to consume—claimed everything in that hellish pit.

Everything except the four who had escaped with their ravenous delirium of sex and death.

Chapter 3 – Below the Bay

Risk, his eyes barely open, gently rubbed the lion's ears as she lay sleeping beside him with her head on his lap, angled so that her long whiskers pointed straight up. She drew in a deep breath and expanded her lean body, then let it out, followed by licking her chops comfortably.

Risk smiled and said, "Good girl."

Kenzie Kat squirmed herself around to find a more comfortable position, then she lost herself to whatever dreams had gotten her paws twitching.

Risk studied those paws for a few seconds, then looked down at his worn black boots. The rough, dirty tarp where he sat added a welcome barrier above the cracked and stained wooden planks.

Just beyond his boots, part of a white high-heeled shoe extended out from beneath a thin burlap quilt.

He paused for a long, lazy yawn, then gave the shoe and foot a soft kick and waited. Nothing happened, so he nudged it around again, aiming for the sharp heel and sparing the expertly painted nails.

When the foot wearing that shoe slipped it out of sight, back under the blanket, Risk looked higher.

Marilyn, her wavy blond mane partly covering her face, yawned. But it never reached its full potential from her face being burrowed into the side of her sister's neck, so she only licked her lips instead. Sophia's black hair was mingled in with her sister's, and it all stayed lightly tangled when they both yawned together.

Marilyn opened her eyes first, then blinked them several times but still hadn't looked around them. Risk watched and listened.

"Oh, Sissy, what's going on?"

"I don't know, Sis. I just woke up, maybe because I felt you moving around."

They stayed close, blue eyes looking into identical blue eyes, and neither smiled.

"I'm so tired."

"Me too. Back to sleep for me," Sophia said, then squeezed her eyes shut again and flexed her legs.

Marilyn's legs were mixed in with her sister's, so she stretched hers too.

Risk grinned at the sight of four long legs held straight and flexing for a few seconds, then relaxed.

He watched quietly, looking away from the sleepy twins only when he saw one of Sophia's black high heels jut out from under their shared blanket, then tip lazily from side to side. He gave that a smile, then looked back up.

Marilyn took a quick look down, then back at her sister. The edge of their blanket was pulled up near their chins as the twins lay embracing against a collection of soft pillows.

"Thanks for the scratchy blanket, Sissy."

"Yeah, Sis, it kind of is. Glad we have it. I didn't put it on us, though."

"Who did?"

"No idea. I just need more sleep."

"The blanket's fine. Oh, I'm still so sleepy."

They both closed their eyes and yawned, and Marilyn began adjusting the blanket up even higher, keeping them both in the same snug cocoon.

After Marilyn had snuggled back in and stopped moving, Sophia said, "I'm sleepy, too, Sis. We need just another few—"

"Good. It worked," Risk said.

They both raised their eyebrows and began to look around themselves for the first time.

Marilyn leaned away from her sister and looked behind them. She reached between them and pushed against the pillows a few times, then looked higher. She touched the wall behind the cushions and pulled her hand back quickly.

Looking at her fingers as she rubbed them together, she said, "Wicker, Sissy? And it's oily?"

Sophia looked behind them, too, but didn't touch what she saw.

"Weird, Sis."

They both examined the low wall as it curved around them, forming a circular wicker enclosure around an area about the size of a spacious hot tub.

Their eyes fixed at the sight of Risk directly across from them, leaning against the far wall of the bowl that they shared. With a sleepy head resting on his lap, the mountain lion lay still save for her twitching paws.

He scratched between the lion's ears and focused his black eyes on the twins, then he tipped his own sleepy eyes once toward the tired lion.

"Remember her name?"

"I do," said Sophia. "She's Kenzie."

"Kenzie Kat, Sissy. Not the real Kenzie."

Sophia reached one hand out from under the blanket just enough to point at him and said, "You're Risk, right?"

He nodded and said, "Good. You woke up."

The twins looked again at each other, then back at him.

Marilyn said, "Um, you weren't sure?"

He closed his eyes and rubbed them for a moment, then he managed a meager grin.

"Nothing is guaranteed."

He let his eyes roam all over them for a few seconds, prompting them to lift the blanket and look at themselves too.

They saw that they were naked except for their heels.

"You'll get clothes," he said.

Sophia scoffed and said, "Burlap?"

"Sissy, shh. Don't make him mad," Marilyn whispered.

"I won't get mad," he said. "No, Sophia. Real clothes."

A whistling up above accompanied a shot of steam coming from a rusty metal tube, connected to something that could have been some kind of teapot. Following the puff toward behind the girls, the wicker basket rocked and moved slightly in the other direction.

The teapot was bolted to the side of a large metal pot, and a shadow of someone near it lifted its lid, sending flames and light straight up. Hanging by a chain from the bottom of the pot, another smaller container with no lid sent up its own modest flames, casting just enough light down into the basket to keep the shadows at bay.

The girls were craning their necks, staring intently, and the basket made a gentle move upward.

"Sissy. We're floating."

"How? What the hell?"

From the flash of light from the pot, they saw, above the flames, the open bottom end of a large balloon. All around its bottom opening, mismatched cables, ropes, and wires fed down and connected around the top ledge of their basket.

"A balloon, Sissy. This is so—"

"Weird. Yeah, Sis."

They looked at Risk but only for a moment, just long enough to see him indifferent to the workings of all of that as he flipped around the sleeping lion's ears.

Outside of the balloon, everything above them was black.

Not night because there were no familiar pinpoints of light.

Just the total absence of anything.

With another quick flash of fire and light from the pot, they saw that someone small, like a child, was hanging on up there. Tiny gloved hands held the taut wires and ropes and small, burlap-wrapped feet looked like they were reaching around and holding onto a narrow wooden plank.

"Like a little trapeze," Sophia said to herself.

"For that kid, Sissy. He probably came from one of Dayzee's neighbor's—"

That kid snapped his head to look down on them while prying up the lid enough to light himself for them to see. His round red eyes with centered black dots watched them intently and didn't blink. Between his staring eyes, a thick, tapered beak hooked down into a sharp point.

He let go of the wire with one hand and pulled forward the hood of his thin black jacket. His face merged with the darkness again but not before the girls had seen a face covered in tight feathers.

"Our navigator," said Risk, unconcerned.

They looked back at Risk but pulled themselves closer together.

"Good eyes," he said, shooting a quick glance up. "Important."

"Um," said Marilyn, "we aren't in Beverly Hills anymore, are we?"

Risk shook his head, holding Marilyn's blue gaze.

"It burned. Remember?"

"All of it?" said Sophia.

He shrugged.

"Not us."

"Sissy," Marilyn said, leaning closer to her sister, "I'm starting to remember all that. I remember the sex and—"

"And the violence, Sis. Yeah, then you killed him."

"Oh, yes. I remember that now."

They looked back at Risk.

"You're not dead?"

"No, Marilyn."

"That lion, she—"

"Kenzie Kat, Sissy."

"Yeah, Kenzie Kat," said Sophia. "Hey, let's shorten that, alright? How about just K Kat?"

"Good idea," Marilyn said. "Risk? Is that okay?"

He looked down at the lion whose mouth had lazily opened wide into a gaping yawn, showing rows of razors. She snapped her jaw shut and looked up into Risk's eyes for a second or two, then back at the girls.

He looked at them too.

"She said okay."

Marilyn shook her head slowly and tried unsuccessfully to laugh, looking first at K Kat, then at Risk.

"Sissy and I didn't pack any clothes."

Sophia chuckled just once, very softly, and said, "That's funny, Sis."

"There are crafters," he said, his eyes blinking slowly. "Or from friends."

"Where?"

He tipped his head up toward the edge of the basket, which was about chest high for the twins when standing, and said, "Down there, Marilyn."

Sophia took in a deep breath and let it slowly rasp back out.

"Not Beverly Hills shopping, though?"

"No, Sophia."

Marilyn frowned and started breathing more quickly. She pulled the blanket up under their chins.

"Where the hell are we?" she said.

Risk gave them a smile for a moment, then said, "That's what I first asked you."

"He's not wrong, Sis. He did ask that."

To Risk, Sophia said, "Seriously, though, where the hell did you take us?"

He stood and stretched, which opened his leather vest enough to show undamaged skin stretched over hard muscles, then leaned back with both hands out to his sides to hold the top rail.

K Kat sat up, close enough to rest her head against his leg.

"We all took us."

"Oh. All four of us. Together."

"Yes, Marilyn. When you called, I was here."

Sophia scoffed and said, "And here is—"

He tipped his head back quickly, then said, "Look."

The girls shared a momentary stare at each other, then reached up and behind them for the rail, using it to help themselves up onto their heels.

They held each other, still wrapped in their blanket, and looked out over the edge.

"Oh my," said Marilyn.

"Sis, what the hell?"

Far beneath their basket floating from a balloon piloted by a small fellow with the face of a hawk, a dark city sprawled out to dim horizons in most directions.

Crooked streets, devoid of traffic of any kind, crisscrossed all of it with no set pattern. Between the streets, there were buildings, some short and some taller, open fields, expanses that were still and smooth and black, and small groups of things with wings flapping over the low structures and around the higher ones.

Dotting the tops of some buildings and along some of the streets, pinpoints of light flickered, dancing. And from each of them, a slender thread of light smoke snaked high up into the blackness, barely moving in the still air.

"Fires?" said Sophia. "Just fires?"

They didn't turn toward Risk when he said, "Electric's out."

But they both got big eyes, looking at each other, when he said, "Damn reactor."

Sophia shook her head slowly and whispered, "Don't say 'damn lions,' Sis."

"Never again, Sissy."

The twins studied their surroundings again, looking out away from their basket and not at the perplexing sights far below them.

Directly ahead, a good distance away, a large fire burned, and clouds of things with wings were circling silently. Or they were too far away to be heard.

Far to the left, they saw another fire, low and wide. Spikes like fiery lightning cut up into the blackness slowly, like they were being painted upward one at a time.

To the right, near the horizon, the world ended in a jagged cliff, with a sea of flames burning all the way to that horizon.

The girls held each other close, arms around each other's waist, as they studied a world that laughingly, horrifyingly, could not have been Beverly Hills.

"Risk," Marilyn said while her eyes tried to see all of it, "what is all that down there?"

They didn't look at him when he said, "There's no name."

Sophia turned to see him, and she saw that K Kat was standing up next to him, also studying the world that she'd helped bring them to.

"Well," she said, "what kind of place doesn't have a name?"

He pointed up and when Sophia looked up at the unbroken black, Marilyn did too.

They heard him say, "Far above, there's water."

"Okay," said Marilyn, still looking up, "there's water. What water? Like rain clouds?"

"No. San Francisco Bay."

"What the hell?" said Sophia.

She looked around and swept her arm both ways.

"All of this is—"

"Below the bay."

"That's what you call it?"

He shrugged and said, "We can, Sophia."

Marilyn blurted out, "How do we go home? I want to go home."

"Sis is right. We don't belong here. How the hell do we go back home?"

He laughed once and said, "You already know."

Marilyn looked at her sister and wiped at her eyes.

"Sissy?"

"Sis, we do know. Think about it."

She nodded and said, "I remember sex."

"And violence, Sis. No, it had to be death."

"Oh. Yes, I remember when Risk said that."

They turned, still holding each other, when Risk said, "Remember it."

The twins stared at him for a moment, then faced each other, their arms around each other's waist.

They gazed into each other's eyes, like seeing their own blue eyes in a mirror, as seconds passed and they floated over the dark city under a bay.

Marilyn almost grinned and said, "I remember all of it, Sissy."

Sophia tipped her head and said, "I remember that acting doesn't work."

"Oh, no. It has to be real."

"We have to feel it, Sis."

"Yes, Sissy. Both of us. All of us. Even a lion if she's with us."

"It wasn't just for fun."

Marilyn sighed and said, "Not just for the cameras or some dumb reality show."

A few seconds later, they shared their modest smiles with Risk.

"Good," he said. "Don't forget."

From far behind the girls, the sound of a sharp explosion roared past them and echoed off into the distance behind Risk. The girls turned to look. A massive fireball was rising from the far edge of the landscape and convulsing toward the black sky.

It began to fragment and fade when it struck that ceiling, and swarms of black dots flew away from the impact site and raced around it. And their screeching, like voices of men impatient for death, was loud enough to reach their vessel.

"Oh, Sissy, I don't know about this."

"Sis, we'll get home soon and—"

"Come here," Risk said. "Not much time."

They turned toward Risk and saw him waiting with his arms wide. K Kat was huddled close, standing next to him.

"Really," he said. "It'll hit soon."

"Sissy, what is—"

"No time, Sis," Sophia said as she grabbed her sister's hand, and they ran the few steps toward Risk while holding the blanket over themselves.

He turned away and lifted his arms out as they rushed toward him, and each found a safe place, their arms around him, as he held the blanket around all of them. Even K Kat was wrapped in there and standing with them.

Then, a sudden blast of hot wind shook the basket and jerked the balloon with it, causing the hawk boy navigator to squawk madly.

Risk's hair got snapped around, and Marilyn's wavy blond hair and Sophia's silky black hair fluttered out over the landscape beneath them. They all stayed pressed together under the blanket with bright sparks racing past and spiraling until they died in the dark.

Risk held the basket's rim, and the Killers held him, and all of them, even K Kat, looked out at the dark lands waiting for them Below the Bay.

* * *

The basket shook, then swayed, then settled and continued its steady float. The girls still held Risk around his waist, Sophia to his left and Marilyn to his right, and he held the blanket over all of them, including K Kat to the right of Marilyn.

They'd watched the last straggler sparks drift past them then become part of the night, all while the hawk boy above them squabbled, his cursing more squawk than words. As the basket and balloon floated so smoothly as to feel motionless, he let out one final hawk-like call, then gave the teapot a chance to answer with a quick whistle.

In their arms, they felt Risk take a deep breath, laugh just once, then say, "Huh. Hawks."

The girls leaned forward to see each other, and Marilyn shook her head quickly and looked over the edge.

"Oh my goodness," she said and quickly turned back toward her sister. "Sissy, I hate this place."

She looked up toward Risk, whose eyes were scanning side to side, and said, "Risk, I hate this place!"

She started wiggling to get free, but she couldn't slip away from under his arm.

"Risk, let me go! I don't want to be here!"

He released her, and she flailed her way out from inside the blanket, evoking an amused grunt from K Kat as she got nudged to the side.

Risk, Sophia, and K Kat turned, still under the blanket, to watch Marilyn, naked except for her high white heels, hurry back to where she lay with her sister just moments earlier.

She hurried to immerse herself in the pillows, using several to cover herself before she saw them all watching her, all amused. Even the lion.

"I hate it! I'll do anything—all that sex and death stuff, I don't care—just take me home!"

Sophia said, "That's my Sis," causing Risk to look down at her where he still held her close under his arm. He waited.

She finally looked up at him and promptly lost whatever small traces of a smile that she'd had.

"She isn't wrong, though. Me too."

She scowled and fought to get free, and Risk didn't hold her back. He only looked her up and down as she defiantly strutted toward her sister, taking her time though wearing nothing but her high black heels.

Risk got the blanket around just himself and K Kat, and they both watched, charmed and grinning, each in their own way.

Sophia wiggled herself in close with Marilyn, and they both used strategically placed pillows to conceal key regions of their anatomy.

Sophia, satisfied with the arrangements, held Risk's gaze again. She was about to speak, but she stopped to look at K Kat, gave the lion her own scowl, then looked back up at Risk.

"We both want to go home. Sex? Death? Fine. Let's go."

"No."

"What?" said Marilyn. "You said that if we would—"

"Later, Marilyn."

"Well, why the hell not now?"

"I was busy when you called me, Sophia."

"Oh, so you're saying that you—"

"Yeah. There's work to do."

Marilyn shook her head and Sophia smirked while they both stared at him.

"You're scared," he said.

"Not on your life," Sophia said with a sneer.

Marilyn whispered, "That's kind of funny, Sissy," but she was ignored.

"We're the Kildare Killers," Sophia continued. "We can handle anything."

Risk held his eyebrows up for a second, then looked to Marilyn and waited.

"Sissy's right. There's nothing in this stupid place that scares us."

She reached up and patted around on the basket's top rail.

"Oh, maybe just being so high up."

Risk grinned and tipped his head toward the ground far below them, where dead, abandoned buildings seemed to reach up for them.

"It's worse down there."

"We're not worried," said Sophia.

"We're killers," Marilyn said, petulant. "Nothing here is going to bother either of us."

He looked from one pair of blue eyes to the other, then back again. He gave their mostly bare bodies a quick glance, then shook his head.

"Alright. We'll see."

Risk and his lion turned away from the twins, then they both looked out over the dark, grim landscape shrouded in night deep below the San Francisco Bay.

The twins studied his broad shoulders and his protective arm around K Kat, then looked up at the sudden whistling from the teapot, an eruption of flame and light from the giant pot, and the perfectly understandable, well-articulated announcement from a boy with the face of a hawk.

"Ham! Ham is here!"

* * *

Risk turned to his right and looked where their navigator was pointing. K Kat leaned enough to look around him.

Sophia whispered in her sister's ear.

"Ham? Ham who?"

"That would be funny, too, Sissy, if we weren't trapped in this awful place."

"Alright, I'm curious."

She stood and tried to take with her the pillows that she needed, but Marilyn wouldn't let go of two of them.

"Sissy!"

Sophia stopped, halfway up, and let her sister keep the pillows.

"Not like you have a problem with being naked, Sis."

"Well, that's certainly true. Just not here, Sissy. This is too weird."

"Oh, yeah. I get it. Well, I'm looking."

She rose up onto her heels, her skin picking up stray light from the burning pot above them, and looked for whatever was coming.

Without looking down, she fumbled around a hand, trying to find her sister but snagging only some of her blond mane.

"Sissy, stop that. You're being silly. Fine. I'll look too."

They stood side by side, and their reflexes got arms around waists without thinking about it. Their free hands held only the tiniest of the pillows, allowing anyone in the basket to see major expanses of smooth Kildare Killer skin.

They didn't care. Not right then.

They were watching a shadow, only somewhat lighter than the night it swam in, as it rose quickly with a glow, then drifted lower again repeatedly as it drew near.

"Risk," said Sophia, "are we being attacked?"

He gave her a cursory glance, then resumed watching Ham approach.

"Not right now," he said.

The twins looked at each other, then back out into the night.

Marilyn whispered, "Um, I know we're killers, Sissy, but—"

"I know. This is just too weird. What the hell is a ham, and why is it about to attack us?"

"Oh, no, Sissy. Risk said we'll be attacked later."

She giggled softly, which got Sophia to smile back at her.

"He didn't exactly say that, Sis."

"Oh, I know. He kind of did, though."

"Yeah, I guess. Wonderful, as Dayzee would say."

"Maybe you should fill in for her, Sissy?"

"I could. Alright. Hey, you know what else?"

"Uh-uh. What?"

"She never called us Marilyn and Sophia."

"No, it was always Mare and Fia."

Marilyn waited, and her sister paused a few seconds, then looked toward Risk, who was still watching Ham coming out of the dark.

"Oh, Sissy, really? Would he?"

"Sure. Why not?"

"Because he's something that killed a lion? Remember that? He bit through her neck!"

"Oh. Yeah. That's not such a cute thing. But I'm still going to ask him."

Marilyn sighed and said, "Okay. But it'll be weird if he ever meets Dayzee and they're both calling us that."

Sophia shook her head softly while scanning the night above and the ruins and fires below, then she held her sister's gaze again.

"We might never—"

"Sissy, no, don't even say that."

Sophia sighed, then looked toward Risk.

"Hey, Risk. Who or what is a ham?"

"It's a who. His name is Ham."

"You were meeting him when we, um, called you to Beverly Hills?"

"Yes, Marilyn."

He kept watching the approaching vessel until Sophia said, "Why?"

"Hawken won't go any higher."

Marilyn said to her sister, "Here we go again."

Then, to Risk, she said, "Who or what is a hawken?"

Risk didn't look their way, just pointed a finger up and said, "Navigator."

Sophia said, "So, another word for navigator, here, is—"

"No, Sophia. It's his name."

"Because he's a hawk?"

"Not entirely. Part."

"The eyes," said Sophia, nodding at Risk, who wasn't looking.

"Oh, the beak, too, Sissy."

"Yeah, Sis. And feathers. But Risk, what's a hawken?"

Risk finally turned toward them, looked from one pair of blue eyes to the other, then said, "Not long ago, he was Ken. Just Ken."

"What the hell are we talking about here?" Sophia said while frowning and shaking her head.

Risk scoffed, pointed up, and said, "Ask him."

The twins looked up, and Marilyn said, "Mr. Hawken? Could we—"

"Sis, too formal. Try again."

"Oh. Okay. Hey, Hawken, can we ask you something?"

He got a wider grip on a wire and a rope, then leaned closer to them as they stood below him in the basket. The darkness inside the hood fled when he flipped the cloth back onto his shoulders, revealing the feathers covering all of his head.

"Mutant," he said with his eyes locked on Marilyn.

He blinked them twice, then rotated his head enough to stare directly at Sophia.

"Uh," said Sophia, "what do you mean? You're a mutant?"

She pointed up at him but when he didn't respond quickly, she dropped her hand back down and searched around until she found Marilyn's.

He swiveled his head and studied the region where abrupt cliffs led to a churning sea of fire. With no other reaction, he spun back and faced the girls.

"The reactor. It . . . does things."

"Turned you into a bird?" said Marilyn. "You used to be human, but now you—"

"No. I can't fly."

Hawk eyes stared down.

Two pairs of blue eyes stared up.

"But you," said Sophia, "are kind of sort of a—"

"Not afraid of heights anymore. Yeah."

He trained his eyes on Risk, and the girls looked that way too.

Risk was looking up when he said, "Eyes are good too."

He looked at the twins, then, and said, "But he won't go any higher."

Sophia said, "Wait a minute. He just said that he's not afraid of—"

"It's not the height. Something else."

"Okay," said Marilyn, "something like . . . what?"

Risk held up a hand, the girls got quiet, and he said, "Hold onto something. This isn't easy."

"What isn't?" said Marilyn.

Still watching the rapidly approaching craft, Risk said, "He has to come in hot. The balloons are big."

"Uh-oh. Okay," she said, and both twins reached up to hold the top rail.

Ham's balloon softly squeezed into theirs, tipping their basket just as a decidedly more oil-stained basket bumped into theirs. Risk quickly grabbed a hook on the other basket and dropped it over his own basket's rim.

Then, he got busy hooking more of the many ropes and began tying their vessels together.

Chapter 4 – Here's Enough

Ham, still standing in his vessel's basket, waved to Risk and called out, "Permission to board your goddamn boat?"

With his long blond ponytail looped around to hang over a shoulder onto his chest, he smiled big enough for his perfect teeth to catch some of the firelight from above. A subtle sheen of sweat gave life to his clean-shaved face.

His short-sleeved t-shirt stretched over a solid chest, and his right shoulder was bare from that sleeve having been ripped loose and discarded.

Risk scoffed and said, "It's your goddamn boat."

"Which you're fucking borrowing, which makes it fucking yours. For now."

"Yeah. For now."

"So?"

Risk scoffed and barely nodded, and Ham laid his left hand on Risk's basket, then stopped when he saw Marilyn and Sophia.

He turned toward Risk, grinning, and said, "Well, what the fuck? The new arrivals are getting sweeter all the time."

Sophia and Marilyn glared at him but made a better effort to hide themselves behind whatever pillows they could grab without looking.

"New," said Risk. "Yeah."

"Fuck, I'd like to have watched them do whatever the fuck they did to get here. Shit, sweet things like that? They must have—"

"I brought them."

"So," Ham said, laughing, "that means you must have—"

"Yeah. I did."

"Well, fuck."

He turned toward the twins and said, "Ladies, I'm Ham Sledger. Risk and I are running some operations together up here. Who the fuck are you and how soon before I take your fine asses home?"

He smirked and waited, his eyes all over them.

Sophia whispered to her sister, "What a creep. I'll show him."

"Uh, Sissy. Maybe, um—"

"Sis, shh."

Sophia let her pillows fall as she got up on her heels, still totally naked, and strutted to within burning distance of the man in the other basket. She got her hand and part of her arm burning hotter than any fire tended by a mutant hawk.

Ham let go of Risk's basket and stumbled back, smeared the smile from his face with a dirty left hand, and said, "Shit, just what the fuck is that?"

"I'm a killer," said Sophia. "That's what the fuck that is. You got any more smartass comments for a killer?"

She stared, waiting for an answer from a man who only stared back.

Behind her, Marilyn giggled and held up her own deadly hand.

"We're the Kildare Killers," she said. "Oh, and we're twins. And don't you forget it."

"Easy, now," he said, holding both palms out toward them. "Didn't mean anything. Just, uh, messing the fuck around. Easy, alright?"

Sophia froze and let her fire fizzle.

She didn't even look when Marilyn gasped behind her. She was too busy staring.

Ham had a normal left hand, but his right was ten times that size. And it didn't appear fleshy and soft and likely to ever hear laughter from anyone. It was more a blunt force weapon than any kind of hand.

He lowered his hands, and his eyes, and said, "Really, I'm just kind of an asshole most of the fucking time. Ask Risk."

The girls turned toward Risk, and he nodded and said, "Most of the fucking time. Yeah."

He grinned at Risk's comment, then looked again at the twins.

"I wish I could say I wasn't always an asshole, but you know what? Coming to this fucked up dump didn't fix my, uh, assholiness?"

Sophia tried to hide a slight grin, and Marilyn popped her eyebrows up. He gave each of them a genuine smile.

"Is that even a word? Making up stupid-ass words—just one more way to be an asshole, huh?"

Sophia broke, smiling and shaking her head.

Ham didn't take his eyes off of her hand, which appeared normal again, and said, "Hey, uh, Risk. This is the dame that killed you? With that whatever the fuck it was?"

He kept watching Sophia but managed a grin when Risk said, "No. The blonde."

Sophia turned and teased him with her best strut as she took the few steps needed to sit with her sister. She took her time in arranging pillows, with both Risk and Ham watching them.

Then, the twins stopped fussing with pillows and turned their attention back to the men flying their vessels around in a pitch-black sky lost somewhere beneath an expansive bay.

* * *

Risk shook his head once before looking away from the girls, then said to Ham, "Come on over."

"Don't mind if I do. Ladies? Sure you don't mind? I sure as fuck don't want to piss off either of you."

"We don't mind," said Marilyn.

"Just watch yourself," she added with a giggle.

He nodded and gave them another view of his white teeth.

"Oh, I certainly will. I'm too young to die."

Sophia scoffed and said, "No one is."

Marilyn giggled softly and said to her sister, "Sissy, you like to be cruel sometimes."

"You too, Sis. When we have to be."

Ham laid both hands, one normal and one gigantic, on the rail of Risk's basket, then hopped over the wall and landed softly on the plank flooring.

With his eyes wary and focused on Marilyn and Sophia, he sat with his back to the wall near Risk, who also sat.

Sophia leaned toward her sister, snickered softly, and said, "This one, jumping like that? Part chimpanzee, Sis?"

Marilyn let out a single loud laugh, causing Risk and Ham to look their way.

Marilyn then whispered to her sister, "Oh, Sissy, that's no monkey hand, though."

Sophia snorted once, softly, then they turned and watched from behind their protective pillow blockade.

Ham squinted at the twins for a second, then turned, about to speak. But he met the resolute stare of a mountain lion just on the other side of Risk.

K Kat didn't blink, but she licked at her whiskers once, then resumed her gaze at Ham.

"Just how many fucking ways can I die today?"

Risk scoffed silently, then said, "Pick a number."

"A lion? A fucking lion? I've never seen one here before."

"I brought her. Meet K Kat."

"Nice fucking name."

He reached his left hand across to shake her paw, but she only bared her fangs, very quietly. Ham withdrew his hand slowly and carefully.

"Brought her from where?"

"Twins said Beverly Hills."

"You've been there? How was it? I heard the women are absolutely fucking gorgeous."

Risk tipped his head toward the twins.

"Oh," said Ham, grinning. "There's the fucking proof. But why a lion?"

"Cat didn't want to burn."

Ham studied Risk, who offered no change of expression. Then, he looked at the twins.

Sophia stared back, and Marilyn shrugged once.

"Uh, yeah," Ham said. "And neither did those Kildare Killers, I'm guessing. Sure would be a shame for them to burn up."

Risk had no response, but K Kat closed away her sharp teeth, still watching the man with one giant hand.

Ham leaned to each side, aiming his eyes around the pillows, then looked up at them.

"Hey, even killers need clothes. I have a couple of shirts I can loan you."

"Sissy, a shirt is better than nothing."

Sophia elbowed her sister gently, then grinned at Ham while she said, "Sis, you do have some very nice high heels."

Marilyn said, "Oh, I do. Yes. They are very high."

She slipped one out from behind the pillows, then the other.

"You too, Sissy. I think yours are even higher."

"Maybe. Yeah. You really have the legs for them, Sis."

"Well," Marilyn said with a soft giggle, "so do you. We're twins."

Sophia displayed hers for Ham, too, and he stared even when Risk said to them, "Hey, easy. He's already crazy."

Sophia kept her grin and Marilyn giggled as they both hid themselves more completely.

"Alright," Ham said to Risk, "Shirts. We'll talk biz in a second. Don't go away."

He stood and vaulted himself easily into his own craft, rummaged around low, out of sight, then stood with wrinkled rags in each hand.

"Here. Try not to burn the fuck out of them."

He snickered and added, "They're custom tailored."

He tossed them toward the girls, who each held one out to examine.

Sophia smirked at hers, and Marilyn shook her head and said, "Oh, of course."

Both button-down shirts were missing not just their right sleeves, but wide portions of where those sleeves should have joined the rest of the shirts had also been ripped away.

Ham laughed and said, "Well, fuck, what did you expect?"

"They're fine," said Marilyn. "Sissy and I are truly grateful."

Still seated, they put on the shirts and buttoned them partway up.

"You'll get more soon," said Risk.

"Uh, I don't know," said Ham. "The last crafter down there that I knew of got herself eaten—I mean, uh, she isn't around anymore."

Risk showed no surprise and said, "Pauline, then."

"Right. Fucking black leather everything."

"Almost everything."

The girls had finished but still held pillows close as they watched the two men and a lion across the basket.

"We'd better get up there," Ham said, "before the next storm. Can't predict those fucking things."

"We do need them, though."

"Well, fuck, yeah. Those few of us that want to keep on living, that is."

"Storms?" said Marilyn. "This place has storms?"

"Just the one kind," said Risk.

Ham, not smiling, said only, "Kaboom."

The twins stared from one to the other.

Ham said, "There was one just a minute ago. You must have seen it."

"That explosion, way over there?"

Sophia pointed behind her and her sister and waited for Risk to answer.

"Yes, Sophia. We call them storms."

"For fun," Ham said with a grin. "The only fucking fun to be had around here. At least before you two showed up to bare and share some of your sweet—"

Risk's hand was a blur before it rested on Ham's chest. The claws jutting out from each finger lingered a moment, two of them poised over Ham's throat.

And the hand was more like K Kat's paw than anything else.

Ham held his breath and stared up at Hawken until Risk let the claws retract, then he backed his hand away slowly.

Still looking up, Ham said, "Hey, Hawken, how come you haven't been ripped the fuck apart yet?"

Hawken squawked once up into the mammoth balloon, then said to Ham, "Simple. Don't fuck with Risk's stuff."

Marilyn said softly to her sister, "Sissy, we're his stuff? Who said so?"

"Could be worse, Sis. Would you rather be Ham's stuff?"

"Oh. No. No thanks."

"Storms clear the air," Risk said to them.

"Oh," said Marilyn, "because of all the fires."

"Wait," said Sophia. "It's just more fire. How the hell does that clear anything up?"

Ham said to Risk, "Allow me."

He turned to the twins and said, "Ladies. Those explosions send up tons of fresh air from somewhere underground. If it wasn't for—"

"My turn," Marilyn said with a giggle. "We're already underground. Right, Risk?"

He nodded and said, "Below the Bay."

Sophia snickered and said, "So, this hellhole gets its air from somewhere below Below the Bay?"

"That's just silly, Sissy. Sounds like it's true, though."

Ham and Risk shared a look, then faced the girls again. Both nodded.

Sophia addressed Risk.

"So, just what the hell is down *there*, then?"

Risk blinked a few times, then said, "Here's enough."

Sophia leaned forward, squinting at him.

"He means," said Ham, "that you have probably zero chance to survive, especially looking so fucking fine, all the fucking—"

He stopped abruptly with the sharp point of a claw at the side of his neck. Risk grinned and waited, then bounced his eyebrows once after Ham had turned to give him a friendly snarl.

The claw stayed while Ham cleared his throat, then he said, "It's just that, uh, there's enough here to keep us busy."

Behind Marilyn and Sophia, the sound of flapping wings and one short, sharp shriek zipped past. They turned to look, but all they saw was the same landscape below as before, with the same blazes raging farther away, and the same totally black underside of a bay far above.

They turned back and listened as Ham said, without a smile or even a grin, "Like that."

$$* \quad * \quad *$$

"Alright," said Ham, "why don't we just get the fuck up there already?"

"Sure. How many?"

"Just one. The boys can't handle more than one at a time."

"One of what?" said Sophia.

Marilyn said, "And what boys are you talking about?"

Ham shook his head and said to Sophia, "One of those fucking things that just scouted us out."

To Marilyn, he said, "Lab boys, we call them. Took them a while to build it, but they have a pretty good fucking cage. They pay alright for a complete unit."

Risk turned to him and said, "Pieces sometimes."

"Well, fuck yeah. If that's all that's left."

"Sheesh."

Marilyn giggled and said, "I've been wondering how long that would take, Sissy."

"What kind of pay is worth anything in this place?" said Sophia.

"Food, for one," said Ham. "Fresh stuff. Like fucking stuff for my navigator."

"Oh, you have some kind of hawk too?" said Marilyn.

"Ziggy isn't no fucking hawk. No, little ladies. Uh-uh."

The girls leaned forward and tried to look high up into the rigging above Ham's basket, but they gave up after a few seconds.

To Risk, Ham said, "Maybe you should wait to do your fucking shifting, you know? Spare the women folk that trauma?"

"They've seen it."

"What? Just that fucking claw at my throat just now? Which I didn't fucking appreciate because—"

"No. In Beverly Hills."

"Risk killed a lion to save us," said Marilyn.

Ham pointed at K Kat and said, "But . . . the lion is still—"

"Another lion."

He looked at the twins, shaking his head, and said, "Lions? In Beverly Hills?"

"All day, every day," Sophia said, nodding back at him.

"They weren't dancing, though," said Marilyn. "Not them. Just attacking people."

"Oh. Yeah, well, that happens."

He turned toward Risk and said, "So, they, those Kildare Killers, can wait here, and we can—"

"No. We all go."

Ham shrugged, whipped his ponytail behind him, and said, "Whatever you say."

He stood and pointed up at Hawken with a grin and got a happy squawk in return.

The girls stood and let the pillows fall, revealing their bare legs spanning from the bottom of Ham's ripped and soiled shirts down to their heels. Their right arms were bare too.

"So, it's like I'm fucking keeping those shirts after all," Ham said. "They're just wrapped around some living dolls."

He reached out to grab his basket's rim, then made a silent, acrobatic leap into it. He'd just turned when Risk's basket shook and Hawken squawked.

"Fuck," Risk said as he jumped up and toward two sets of sharp black claws hanging onto the rim of his basket.

The girls sat back down quickly, grabbed as many pillows as they could find, and hugged each other close.

Chapter 5 – We Hate this Place

As he took several strong steps toward their clawed attacker, Risk's arms grew a dense layer of short brown fur, and they swelled with twice the muscles there before.

His animal arms were already reaching out, and sharp white claws sprang out on every finger.

His chest and back and shoulders bristled with new, tight muscle, all wearing a sleek coating of fur much like K Kat's. His black leather vest had been stretched to its limit.

And his head, with an open mouth and bared fangs, could have been one of K Kat's distant ancestors, one more savage and from a time when its world demanded all the savagery any surviving animal could muster.

Marilyn and Sophia gasped and kept embracing with their cheeks pressed together. Before either could say anything, Risk had snagged the uninvited beast, digging his claws into its paws and causing a mad shriek from over the side.

He roared once at the balloon or Hawken or maybe the black ceiling above, then yanked the beast up for all to see.

Its head appeared first, like a bat's. But hungrier. Less kind. Much more of a monster—something carved of granite and snarling atop an ancient building.

But still, it said, "Wait! Before you kill me, just—"

Risk rushed one set of claws to grasp the animal by its throat just as its wings, wider than the basket and blacker than the sky, spread out and flapped madly. The wind from its wings blew around the twins' hair and Ham's shirts, anything loose in the basket, and the balloon above, giving the hawk up there another reason to squawk.

Another two sets of black claws appeared on the basket's rim, and the thing's sinewy, leathery legs tried pushing away. With the wings snapping and its legs pushing, the basket jolted every which way.

And Hawken, high above it all, squawked nonstop, sometimes articulating a very clear "Fuck!" as he spun around and blasted the hot spout.

Risk roared and swiped his other set of claws across everything that was trying to push against his basket, and blood erupted like a row of whips had slapped into a puddle of red slop.

The beast screamed, and Ham appeared next to Risk, where he balled up that swollen, mutant hand into fleshy hammer. He cocked it back and waited, timing the mad creature's erratic path back and forth, then swung once.

Another scream erupted, but one wing hung limp, causing the battle to descend into further chaos.

Risk grunted something, and Ham rushed to his other side. He timed his strike perfectly, and the scowling bat thing hung from Risk's grasp around its throat, its crippled wings beating slowly and pathetically.

"Oh, my."

"I really do hate this place, Sis."

* * *

The girls huddled behind pillows small and large and watched Risk drag the thing quickly toward him, aiming perfectly to strike its head on the basket's top rail. It went limp, but its eyes still blasted hatred and hunger, and its mouth might have cussed or screeched or laughed insanely if it didn't have claws perforating its throat.

Risk tumbled it roughly over the edge and pinned it to the scarred floorboards with a knee on its chest.

Ham positioned his bludgeoning hand directly over the thing's head, and it calmed itself and looked up at what could easily splatter its face into a pancake of bloody mush.

Risk roared, up close and in the thing's face, then stood and dug into its chest with one of his black work boots.

He sighed with a softer roar, shook a few times as his natural features returned, then twisted his foot into the thing's chest, causing it to howl and Hawken to laugh at it.

Risk put his human hands on his hips and said, looking down at the snarling face, "Talk."

"Then die," said Ham. "You know you're going to fucking—"

Risk held a hand out.

"It knows."

"If I give good info, I can live?"

"No."

"A little longer," said Ham. "Keep us interested, you son of a bitch."

It snorted toward Ham, then focused on Risk.

"There's a madman down there."

"More than one," said Risk.

"Fucking dump is full of them," said Ham. "So?"

"But this one has a plan. He wants to kill everyone and everything down here."

"Why?" said Ham.

It turned its head enough that its solid black eyes could aim at Ham.

"Crazy needs a reason?" said the thing.

"Where, then?" Risk said, looking at the beast.

It looked back at Risk and said, "Somewhere. Not much time."

"You're already dead. What the fuck do you care?"

Risk looked up at Ham and gave him a very slight grin, to which Ham only shrugged, then they both looked down again.

And Risk twisted his boot again. Hawken laughed at the sight of it, but the winged freak was losing its resolve.

"We'll find him. Risk and I. And the Kildare Killers."

The beast tipped its head to look all around and fixed its eyes on Marilyn and Sophia for only a second.

"The lion too," said Risk.

"Give me a chance," said the bat thing, "and I'll eat that stupid cat like—"

Risk stomped his boot onto its throat and stared down at it.

"Where's the opening?"

It gurgled and struggled and its eyes turned up to the ceiling that held a bay of water high above all of them, then looked again at Risk.

Risk backed his boot away enough for it to answer.

"There's no—"

Its neck almost snapped at so much weight bearing down on its throat. Risk waited, and the thing stared up at him.

He relaxed the choke just enough.

"Only some know where. Not me. I'm not special,"—it spat some bloody sludge to the side—"enough."

"You're fucking right about that," said Ham. "Just another fucking bat freak, stealing people from up there, then enslaving them at the reactor. You're a bunch of sick fuckers."

The thing chuckled, with blood leaking out of its mouth both ways and adding to the stains on the wood floor, and said, "Fuck yeah. Fuck all of you."

Risk clamped its throat and neck, grinding it into the floor, and looked to Ham.

"Just a body, then?"

"Sure. They'll pay. Even though it's a goddamn fucking ugly body."

Risk scoffed and said, "The head's worse."

He moved his boot, leaned over quickly while growing one hand full of claws, and swiped left to right several times at a blinding speed. Each stroke sent a spray fanning out and with one final slash, the head tumbled that way, rolled over, and faced upward. Dead eyes staring.

Risk picked it up, never looked at it, and tossed it over his shoulder.

Only then did he turn toward the Kildare Killers, who looked like they might never blink again.

"What?"

* * *

"Sissy," Marilyn whispered, "we still don't know what he is."

Sophia scoffed, then whispered, "A killer, Sis, obviously. Hey, maybe he's the best and most famous Below the Bay Killer."

"That's funny. But not really."

More loudly, to Risk, Sophia said, "We hate this place."

His claws had retreated, but they hadn't taken the bat's blood along, so he shook his hand over the dark city below, shedding what still coated his fingers.

The blood on his face got no such attention.

He shrugged and said, "Huh. It hates you."

Marilyn popped her eyebrows up, and Sophia scowled at him silently.

A second later, he said, "Well, all of us. Not just you."

"It hates the absolute fuck out of me," said Ham. "Every fucking minute of every fucking day."

Risk gave him a glance and a quick grin. Ham rolled his eyes and looked back at the twins.

"Alright, it's not always that bad. But still . . . this place is fucked up. If you can get your fine asses home, get the fuck going already."

"K Kat too," Marilyn said with a giggle.

"The goddamn lion?" said Ham. "Oh, sure, what the fuck. Risk, they don't belong here. Take them home."

Risk gave them both a smile, one that fled quickly, then said, "He's right. Tell me when."

He wiped at his cheek, smearing around some of the bat's blood, unaware of it.

"Um," said Marilyn, "that would mean, uh, Sissy and I would, I mean—"

"What she's trying to say is that we, uh, we do want to go, but uh, you know, there's always . . ."

"Tomorrow?" said Ham. "Don't bet your fucking life on it."

"Today. Tomorrow," said Risk. "We do it right."

"Oh," said Marilyn, "you said something about that at Dayzee's house. You said we had to do it wrong."

"Yeah," said Sophia. "There wasn't enough time."

"Well, no, Sissy. We were going to burn all up."

Sophia said, "So, what's that all about? What's right and wrong about doing what we all did?"

"K Kat, too, Sissy."

"The right way," said Risk, "is just one."

"Wait just a fucking second," Ham said with a hearty laugh. "You're saying that you and,"—he pointed at each of the girls several times—"both of them? Altogether at the same fucking time?"

Risk grinned and said, "Same time."

"The lion too," said Sophia. "Never thought I'd get pulled into some weird act like that."

"Well, Sissy, you're an actress. Maybe that lion is too?"

Sophia looked down and got quiet.

"Oh. Sorry, Sissy."

"So," said Risk, then he wiped more blood around on his face. "Who's first?"

He looked at each staring twin for a second, then looked down as he reached for his belt buckle. He stopped quickly at seeing his exposed abdominal area streaked with blood, some of it drying where thin lines of it had begun to drip over and between the well-defined muscles.

He looked up at Marilyn first.

"Oh. Um . . ."

He focused on Sophia, who was shaking her head and smirking. She said, "Uh, maybe we'll stay."

They all looked toward Ham when he said, "Whenever the fuck you all do it, I'm there."

Risk felt K Kat nudging the side of his leg, so he looked down at her, and she gazed up at him.

"You don't mind the blood?" he said to her.

She seemed to laugh.

"Good girl."

He patted her head and rubbed around her ears.

Ham said, "On second thought, if that lion's in on it . . ."

*　*　*

"Ladies," Ham said with a polite bow, "my chariot awaits."

"Not so fast," said Sophia. "That guy up there, that—"

"Hawken, Sissy."

"Yeah, him. He won't go higher because of things like that?"

She pointed at the headless remains of a bat as large as Risk, if it didn't have wings.

Risk nodded and said, "With heads. Most."

"Sissy," Marilyn whispered, "Everywhere we go!"

"Uh, almost, Sis. That thing isn't looking for head."

To Risk, she said, "What was all that talk about holes up there and taking people?"

"They take people," he said and pointed straight up.

"We want to know where the fuck they go through to get up there. Not everyone can screw two fine Kildare Killers and a goddamn lion and—"

"She bit," said Risk.

Ham squinted at him and said, "That counts? She didn't have to fuck you too?"

"Feeding. Killing. Kinda like sex."

Ham nodded and said, "Oh, right. Yeah, I get that."

Again addressing Marilyn and Sophia, he said, "If there's a goddamn way to the top, we all want to know where it is."

"And there must be?" said Marilyn. "Because these gross things snatch people and . . . what, exactly?"

"Reactor slaves."

"Risk means that they get put to work at that fucking toxic power plant. Things like piling dirt, trying to block some fucked up form of radiation."

He noticed that the twins were looking at his enlarged hand, so he held it up and studied it too.

"Sure, I shoveled dirt, too, like a fucking slave. I ran my ass off just when this goddamn thing started itching real funny one day. You can see how the fuck that turned out."

"One more thing," said Sophia. "Bats? Giant bats, and they talk?"

"Timing," said Risk.

"I'll expand on that for him too," said Ham. "The freakin' reactor sometimes gives out blasts of some god-awful bullshit radiation. If someone's downwind of it, they kind of, uh, get tangled up with things around them."

"Oh," said Marilyn.

"All that DNA crap gets spun together like bloody fucked up spaghetti."

"Sheesh."

"So true, Sissy."

Marilyn turned to her sister and said, "Think about Hawken, Sissy. He got blasted when a hawk was flying by."

"Is that for real?" Sophia said to Risk.

"Or it fucks you up," he said.

Ham held up his giant hand and grinned.

"Alright," said Sophia, "what about the bats, then? Some bat was flying past a dictionary, and the reactor sprayed radiation, so now they can talk?"

Risk shrugged and said, "Who knows?"

"Maybe they were already here," said Ham, "before anyone moved into this place and built all this shit. I still think it had to be military."

Sophia nodded and said, "And they moved out when—"

"When they started growing extra heads. Yeah," said Ham. "Or maybe that was okay, but when the fucking extra heads started fucking complaining and trying to take over, maybe it was just a bit much."

He grinned while they all stared for a few seconds.

"Well," Marilyn said with a pleasant smile, "it could be worse. Your hand is pretty useful, actually. And Hawken seems nice. Oh, I don't know about those bats, though."

"So, there's some weird shit," said Sophia, "but it doesn't sound all that bad.

Risk stared at her for a few seconds, then shook his head for a moment.

"Give it time."

"Well, we can't even imagine," said Marilyn.

Ham, without any sign of a smile, said, "You won't fucking have to."

Chapter 6 – One Sinister Fucked Up World

Ham snatched the headless bat body by an appendage and dragged it up and over the adjacent basket rails. He grunted as he forced it to splat near the center of his basket.

"Fucking bats," he said, then he grabbed Risk's top rail with his left hand, then swung his right hand, using that heavier weight to assist in a graceful jump over the edge.

The girls looked at Risk, and he only shrugged.

Then, he swung one dirty black boot over and into Ham's basket and climbed in.

He extended a hand back toward Sophia, held her gaze, and waited.

She started reaching for it while looking to each side and down.

"Oh, God, that's high up."

Risk held Sophia's hand as she paused to look down from the basket at a city with no lights but dotted with fires. As the two vessels traveled slowly above the landscape, thin streams of smoke from the fires passed by them like spindly ghost columns.

Risk and Ham stood in Ham's basket, and Ham took her other hand.

"I don't think I've ever—hey!"

They lifted her high enough for her heels to clear the top edges and set her down between them.

"Fun?" said Ham.

She smirked and said, "Sure. Why not?"

Marilyn was next, and she stayed out of their reach.

"No, wait! I only go up high in private jets!"

Her sister laughed and said, "Fine. Stay. Tell the next bat we said hi."

"Ooh. Um, okay."

She walked close enough, got lifted and set beside her sister, and they both straightened out their borrowed shirts, trying not to laugh at the missing right sleeves.

"They never asked," Ham said to Risk, who only shrugged. "So, I'll just tell them."

He looked straight up and said, "That's Ziggy."

The girls looked, but Risk didn't bother.

"Oh my goodness. He's, um, he's—"

"Some kind of lizard?" said Sophia.

Only the angular head of a reptile looked down on them from its perch above the big pot, which had no fire at all, unlike Risk's vessel. But its hanging lantern was about the same.

"Hey, that's not so bad," said Sophia. "But where's the big fire?"

"You're looking at it," Ham said with a big laugh.

He looked up and said, "Ziggy! Climb!"

The lizard boy tipped his head up and breathed out more flames than they'd even seen from Risk's ship.

"How is that even possible?" said Sophia. "I'm trying to figure what kind of weird shit was close by when some poor sap—"

"You'll never figure it out. He doesn't even know."

He used his normal hand to unhook the baskets from each other, then yelled, "Clear!" up to Hawken and pounded on Risk's basket.

"Okay, Ham!"

Hawken fed fire up into his balloon, tooted his spout, and the two balloons began drifting apart.

Ham looked up again, into his own balloon, and said, "To the shack, Ziggy!"

He breathed more fire into their balloon, then blasted his hot breath to the side, like his own teapot spout, and got them scooting along through the night.

*   *   *

Marilyn took a place at Risk's right side, and Sophia to his left, where he stood at the wicker wall and looked ahead. They watched in silence for a few minutes, then a faint, twinkling light appeared higher than their ship.

Behind them, they heard Ham call up to Ziggy, "Higher! Then, hold and slow!"

They didn't look at the sound of fire burning up into the balloon, but they felt that they were climbing.

"Ham lives on a mountain?" said Marilyn. "Sounds kind of cozy."

Risk gave it a few seconds, then said, "Cozier than the ground."

"You said we'd get some real clothes there?"

"Yes, Sophia."

"From someone named Pauline?"

"That's right, Marilyn."

"Hey," said Sophia, "I have no idea when would be a good time. But Sis and I have a request."

He turned to her and waited. She studied his serious look with intermittent light from Ziggy's fiery blasts above them.

"We, uh, we had a dear friend who—"

"She's not dead, Sissy."

Sophia leaned forward to look past Risk.

"We don't know that, Sis. Who knows where that portal took her? It might have planted her in a brick wall or something."

"Well, Sissy, that's just too negative. I think she's having a lovely drink right now at the Prism."

"Oh, maybe. With the Boss. She said—"

Risk cleared his throat.

"Oh. Uh, yeah. So, we were wondering about shortening our names."

"Just to save time," said Marilyn.

"Right. Yeah, Sis. Anyway, Risk, our friend used to call us Mare and Fia."

He squinted at Sophia for a second, turned to look at Marilyn, who gave him a pleasant smile, then he turned back to Sophia.

"It saved time?"

"Uh, no. Probably not. We, uh, we kind of liked it, though. So, what do you think?"

"Good idea."

He held her steady gaze.

"You're waiting?"

She nodded.

"Fia."

He heard Marilyn's clapping hands behind him and turned to look.

"Mare?"

"That's me. Yay!"

He shook his head and looked forward again, and the girls leaned back to smile at each other behind him.

Until he said, "I'm still Risk."

* * *

"There," Risk said and pointed straight ahead and up at what appeared to be a single, dim light.

Sophia pointed, too, and said, "Up there? That little light?"

"Yeah."

He paused, then said, "Fia."

Marilyn saw her sister's self-satisfied grin and pouted before looking again toward Ham's home. As they all watched, the pinpoint of light faded, then seconds later reappeared but as three distinct lights.

"What just happened?" said Marilyn. "Someone switched off the light then turned on three of them?"

"Clouds."

Risk looked ahead, but the girls turned mostly their eyes to watch him. It took a few seconds before he spoke again.

"Mare."

She refocused ahead and clapped her hands silently a few times.

"Storms and now, clouds too?"

"Good question, Sissy. Risk, does it ever rain here?"

"Not water. Rock sometimes."

"What? It rains rocks?"

Ham had been listening but mostly monitoring Ziggy and their flightpath.

"Those fucking bats burrow in up there like the fucking rodents they are," he told them. "They sometimes break shit loose. Pray that a sharp fucking piece doesn't hit our balloon."

He walked over and stood to Marilyn's right, nudging K Kat farther to his right and eliciting an annoyed growl.

"Easy, big cat," he said, then waited for the attack.

K Kat only nuzzled around his massive right hand.

"Yeah, I know," he told the mountain lion. "I'm a fucking freak. Be kind to the freak."

Sophia leaned forward to see Ham.

"Uh, Sis and I aren't much for praying."

He scoffed and reached his left arm over the basket's rail, sweeping his hand from side to side.

"You might reconsider that if you ever have a reason to walk those fucking streets."

"Ooh, maybe not in the dark," Marilyn said as she leaned over barely enough to look too.

"Almost there," said Risk.

All eyes focused on a compact set of buildings, connected to each other and built into the side of a steep slope. Higher up, the mountain's top blended into the darkness leading to the underside of the San Francisco Bay.

"Easy now, Ziggy," Ham called up to his navigator. "Careful of the spikes."

Ham grinned at the loud hiss from his part-lizard navigator, and the girls leaned to stare at each other when they got lit up by a brief, roaring blast of flames above them. With that, the balloon started to rise, and they saw, level with them for a moment, the tall wrought iron fence and barrel fires beyond.

"Like Dayzee's fence, Sissy."

Sophia scoffed and said, "Sure. Except for there being no headless guys walking around."

She grinned at Marilyn until she tipped her head back.

"Flying, though?"

"Oh, Sissy, yes. Flapping around, maybe."

"Flapping around for bat head," Sophia said with a soft snort, which caused Risk to turn toward her without a smile.

"Oh, um, Sissy's joking about when we were at Dayzee's, before things were burning, when all of these headless—"

Risk had turned toward Marilyn, still not smiling.

"Sis, let's talk about that later, alright?"

Risk sighed and looked straight out from the vessel, just as the bottom of the basket cleared the points of the fencing and sailed soundlessly into the courtyard.

"Easy, there, Ziggy," said Ham. "I don't want to have to patch the fucking balloon again. Easy."

Ziggy hissed and gave out a few sideways blasts of fire breath, bringing the craft to the middle of an oily stone patio. He jerked a few times on a rope leading somewhere high up, and something up there whistled a few times, bringing the basket down for a soft landing.

"Nothing to it," said Ham, then he picked up the looped end of a rope near his boots and tossed it around a heavy iron hook embedded in the patio's floor.

Risk had turned and taken a step toward the dead bat lying on the floor, where he kicked it a few times lightly.

Ham repeated his tethering on the vessel's other side, then yelled up, "Alright, Ziggy. Tighten it up."

The girls looked up and saw Ziggy's hot breath burning up inside the balloon, which swelled and groaned enough to try to pull the basket up, and the ropes complained as they were pulled tight.

Looking down again, Marilyn said, "Um, why are you kicking that dead thing, Risk?"

He scoffed, gave it one more kick, on a different part of it, and said, "Some things need to be killed again."

Marilyn turned to her sister with her eyes opened wide.

"And again," he added.

Sophia's eyes matched her sister's, and she mouthed the word, "Sheesh."

Risk didn't ask, he just lifted Sophia with hands up under her arms, then set her outside of the basket. Marilyn watched, then grinned when he turned toward her, and she lifted up her arms.

He quickly hid away his smile, then lifted her while looking into her bright blue eyes. She tried not to giggle as she feigned a struggle to balance on her high white heels, causing him to not release her as quickly as he had with Sophia.

"Why, thank you, Risk."

"Watch your step."

She looked down, as did her sister, and they frowned at the streaks of oil on the smooth stone surface. Marilyn looked up first.

"Sissy, this place is so dirty. Not like Dayzee's mansion."

"Well, Sis, at least it's not burning."

"Oh. Good point."

Risk held the rim and jumped over, then looked back at Ham. K Kat had bounded over the rail right after Risk and stood by his side.

"You coming?"

Ham was crouched down near the dead bat. He popped his head up at Risk's question.

"I will. I just want to get going on this first."

He lowered his head out of sight but raised a cleaver high enough for everyone outside the basket to see. He swung it downward sharply, causing a squishing sound as it struck the basket's wooden floor.

And something rattled around, twitching and scraping.

The girls stared at each other, neither saying anything.

"Damn fucking bats," he said, still out of their sight.

He swung it again, and it made only the sound of squishing and sharp steel hitting wood.

"About fucking time."

Sophia shook her head slowly, and Marilyn held a deep breath before letting out a heavy sigh.

Risk said, "Let's see Pauline," and started walking toward a heavy wooden door.

The girls gave each other a quick glance, then followed after him to the sound of a cleaver slicing and chopping.

*　*　*

Risk pounded on a thick wooden door bearing deep dents, sets of parallel gouges, and splatters of red stains. The girls studied it all, then looked up at him, but he was only waiting for the door to open.

A few seconds later, there were sounds of bolts sliding at different levels, then the door swung in, revealing a woman with striking but not model pretty facial features and long, tangled red hair.

Her black t-shirt's short sleeves weren't long enough to hide defined arm muscles, and its lower hem reached only to just above a thick black belt looped around a trim waistline.

Black jeans, fashioned of some leathery material, were tight over strong legs and ended at a pair of scuffed black western boots.

She looked at Risk for only a second, then peeled her eyes open wide at the sight of a mountain lion sitting next to him and sniffing in different directions inside the building.

"Huh," she said. "That's a big cat."

"Yeah. She is."

Risk only shrugged when she looked at him again and raised her eyebrows for a second.

Then, she examined each of the Kildare Killers, scoffing at the sight of them wearing one-sleeved button-down shirts and high heels.

Before speaking, she looked into each pair of blue eyes for a few seconds, holding Marilyn's gaze.

"Well, this is different."

She looked down at Marilyn's white high-heeled shoes and grinned.

"Yeah. Practical."

Her eyes took in Sophia's high black heels next, then traveled up along her bare legs, then quickly focused on the blue eyes staring back at her.

"A bad place to be caught almost naked, Sweetie."

"Marilyn," Risk said with a tip of his head.

"And Sophia."

Pauline smiled at each while Risk said to the twins, "This is Pauline."

She looked at Risk and said, "Just Pauline, right?"

Risk snorted a soft laugh but didn't answer her.

"Hi," said Sophia. "Nice to meet you."

"Me too," said Marilyn, who then looked up and around at the outside of the structure. "Quite a nice place."

Pauline grinned and said, "Like hell. Nice of you to lie, though. Come on in."

She turned and walked away with her hips swaying, and the girls watched until Risk gave them each a modest shove inside, took a step inside himself, then boomed shut the stout door.

Pauline led them all toward a fireplace with folding metal chairs arranged around it, saying over her shoulder, "It's Ham's place. I rent."

She dropped onto a chair, looked at Risk, and said, "So, what's the story with you this time?"

The twins found seats, and Risk kept standing.

"They're new. They called me away to get them."

She grinned and looked first at Marilyn.

"You called him, huh? How?"

"Um, our friend's house was getting destroyed and burned by these creepy things, and we knew that we needed some kind of help, so we—"

Sophia said, "We all used sex and danger."

Pauline trained her eyes on Sophia and said, "Ooh, sex and danger. How fun."

She tipped her head and held Marilyn's gaze.

"Sex always gets somebody to come."

She laughed once and added, "At least, if it's done right."

Marilyn smiled with a quick shrug, so Pauline looked again at Sophia.

"But that's not what brought you to this oily, fiery slice of Hell, is it?"

"Oh, no. Well, almost. It took sex and—"

"Death," said Marilyn.

Pauline held her gaze without smiling, then pointed at her.

"Those two go together in ways you can't even imagine."

She stood and kicked some charred wood back into the struggling fire, then turned back to the twins.

"Alright, you're wondering how I got here. I'll tell you. Death on a motorcycle."

She pointed at Sophia again, smiled, and said, "What else? Quick!"

"Uh, sex?"

"Yep."

Marilyn tipped her head and said, "Um, moving or sitting still?"

"Moving, of course. I got class. Hasn't Risk explained anything to you?"

She looked toward him, and he only shrugged.

Marilyn said, "He's very, um, kind of—"

"Economical," said Sophia. "You know. With words."

"Oh, damn right. Yeah. Alright, here's the deal: if you or the one you're fucking dies during sex, and I mean, at that best fucking time, you—"

"Good pun," Sophia said with a grin.

"Funny, too, Sissy."

"Oh, fuck," said Pauline. "I knew there was something about you two. Sisters?"

"We're twins," said Marilyn.

"Yeah, it's right there. I should have seen it. So, anyway, if one of you dies at just that best time, you'll probably find your regretful asses here."

"Below the Bay," Marilyn said with a serious nod.

"Yeah, it's up there somewhere. Good luck finding it."

"Clothes," said Risk.

Pauline looked first at Risk, then she examined the twins again.

"Yeah. Naked looks good on them, but it won't be much help around here. That just brings more trouble."

"We don't want to be any bother," Marilyn said.

"Sis, she's offering. And we can't wear just these shirts."

"Listen to your sister," Pauline said as she reached into a cloth bag on the floor, then pulled something out.

She held up something like a black leather bikini and addressed Marilyn.

"For you. I insist."

Marilyn giggled and said, "Oh, not for me. Maybe Sissy, though. She wears black all the time."

Pauline let her hand drop to her side as she focused on Sophia.

"Sure."

She looked down at her black heels.

"To match those shoes."

Looking back up at Sophia, she continued talking to Marilyn.

"This is one sinister fucked up world, though. Maybe she's ready for a change?"

Sophia stared for a second, then said, "Uh, I like black. Always have. Maybe not just a bikini, though."

Marilyn reached for it and took it from Pauline's hand.

"What is this? Is it leather?"

Pauline snorted and said, "About as close as we can get here."

She looked at both of them, then said, "I'm just messing with you. I have some real clothes for both of you."

"Good," said Risk. "I'm helping Ham."

He got up and stretched his arms to his sides, opening up his leather vest and showing his lean, muscular physique.

"With what?" said Marilyn. "Oh, I think I know."

"Chopping up bats, Sis. Hey, maybe Kenzie would—"

Sophia looked down when Marilyn said, "K Kat, Sissy. Yes, she might want to help too."

Risk shrugged and walked toward the door, the lion close by his side. While the door was open, Ham's blade struck again, then Risk and the lion went out, and Risk pulled the door shut.

Chapter 7 – Everything Died to Get Here

Risk leaned on the edge of the basket, and K Kat stood beside him with one of her paws touching his hand. Both watched Ham give another hard chop on one of the bat's limbs that were still intact.

Ham looked up and said, "Pauline's about to fix some dinner, right?"

"Hope so," said Risk.

Ham reached to one side, toward a small pile of swollen, sealed bags, and grabbed one.

"Doesn't get any fresher. Unless you were to fucking eat it raw."

Risk laughed and said, "Sometimes. Sure."

"Fucking animal."

He wiped both sides of it across his jeans, then held it out.

Risk took it and said, "Thanks."

"Don't tell those fine ladies what the fuck that is. They'd never give it a real chance."

Risk laughed once quickly and said, "Should we?"

"Fuck no. But we do have to fucking eat."

He held the bat's leg, gave it a few chops, then threw a wet piece of it high. K Kat watched it closely, then snapped it during its flight and swallowed it whole.

"Fucking lion likes it."

"She's more."

Ham stopped and stared, then said, "You mean, she wants more? Yeah, I bet she fucking does."

"No. She *is* more."

"More than just a lion, you mean?"

"Yeah."

"Like what?"

"I think a girl."

Ham frowned at Risk, then looked at K Kat. A smile grew as he nodded at the mountain lion.

"Oh, I get it. A *pussy* cat."

When Risk laughed, he looked back at him.

"Speaking of that, which one of them did you actually fuck?"

"The blonde."

"Why that one?"

"Had to pick. Either."

"Damn right," said Ham. "So, next time it's that black-haired one?"

Risk shook his head and said, "Not that way. We had no time."

"Oh, that again. You know, Risk, there's no fucking way to be a saint in this goddamn wasteland. You're—hey, this is funny—*wasting* your time."

"Not a saint. I told you."

"Whatever you're trying to be. It isn't going to work Topside either. That's almost as fucked up."

"Not your problem."

"I know. Just fucking with you. I wish you well, my friend."

He noticed that K Kat was staring at him, sometimes swiping her rough tongue around. So, he chopped off another piece, which caused the bat body to spasm just once. He plopped down his hammer hand on its chest, then threw the gristle to the lion, who choked it down.

Risk rubbed around her ears and said, "Good girl."

"You mean," said Ham, "good pussy . . . cat."

"We'll see."

"Yeah. You should give it a try sometime. Whatever else she is might be even finer than those two, uh, what did you call them?"

"Kildare Killers."

"Right. The kind that can burn a man down to fucking nothing."

* * *

"What did you mean by 'just Pauline?'" said Sophia.

Pauline shook her head, snorted once, then said, "He teases me sometimes. Calls me Tramp Pauline."

"Oh, that's not very considerate," said Marilyn. "Why would he call—"

"Well, shit. Because I *am* a tramp. It's actually a damn accurate name. He says I'd let just about anything bounce around on me."

"You must mean 'anyone,' right?" said Sophia.

"Sometimes 'ones,' sometimes 'things.' You two will see. This world can fuck you up in so many ways."

"Like, how?"

"Because you might find you like a fucking 'thing' the best. Take Risk, for example, Marilyn. He's got this big, glorious goal to be some impossible good man. He always—"

"He's really a man?" said Sophia. "We, um, we saw him sort of, uh, change a couple of times."

Pauline scoffed and said, "Yeah, he does that when he fucking has to. But didn't he always go back to being a man? That's his fucking baseline. Anyway, that's not the point. The thing is, he always talks about trying to do the right thing. But really, girls, in this world? No one has a fucking chance."

"Oh, Sissy, remember when we first met him?"

"Yeah. He wasn't happy about the fires. He said he didn't have time to do it right."

Pauline scoffed and said, "A good excuse to fuck you both, I'd say."

"The lion too," Marilyn said with a soft giggle. "Not really, though. She only bit him."

"She ripped up his side, Sis. I thought he was dead."

"Not until I burned him, Sissy."

"Huh? Burned him how?"

Marilyn held her hand out and quickly got it glowing hot, causing Pauline to wince and step back.

"Holy fuck. What the hell is that?"

"We're killers," said Sophia. "From Kildare. Sort of. It's complicated."

"You too?"

Sophia displayed her burning hand.

"Shit. Don't let me ever piss off either of you."

They cooled their hands, and Marilyn said, with a pleasant smile, "Oh, yes. You'd better not."

Pauline looked at Sophia and said, "Your sister would fry me in a heartbeat. Not you, though, right?"

Sophia squinted at her and said, "Even quicker."

Pauline tipped her head and looked into Sophia's blue eyes for a few seconds, then said, still holding her gaze, "Right. So, Risk and I travel sometimes when he's around."

She finally looked away toward Marilyn and spoke to both of them.

"I'm his travel buddy."

"Wait," said Marilyn. "You and him? You mean that you—"

"I kill his ass. At just the right fucking time. And I do mean 'fucking time.'"

She looked at Sophia and waited.

"You and him, you go back to the real world?"

"No way. He always wants to come back here, and I wouldn't be any good to him up there. He'd just have to find someone else."

"So, where do you go with him?"

"Never Topside," she said. "Just around town."

"Topside. That's kind of funny," said Marilyn.

"Yeah, Sis. He, um, he never kills you, though, right?"

She shook her head and said, "Wouldn't work. I'd just be dead. Risk is . . . different."

"But couldn't he take you 'Topside' and leave you there?"

"You seem to forget—I died up there. Remember? You two, as far as I know, are the only actual living things here."

Marilyn said, "Oh my goodness. I never thought of that. Everything died to get here."

"No, that isn't right. My brain is fucked sometimes. Those boys are trying to figure out how they're stealing actual living people and dragging their miserable asses down here."

"Oh, we heard that," said Marilyn. "Reactor slaves."

"Yeah," said Pauline. "They're truly fucked. Can you imagine that? You're drifting along, somewhere in Frisco, then—"

"That makes sense too," Marilyn said. "They catch them up there in San Francisco."

"But other than that," said Sophia, "everyone else is dead?"

"Hold up again," she said, wincing and hitting the side of her head. "There are some that were never really alive. Herds of them. Don't catch those fuckers on a bad day."

"We hope not," said Marilyn. "What are they, then?"

"They're nice, then they're not. I think they're just alive enough to be a special kind of fucked up evil. Stay the fuck away from them."

"Okay. Good advice. The rest, though? All died?"

"Yeah. Pretty pathetic, huh? So, if Risk somehow got back up top, he'd just have to find someone else to get him back here. Where the hell is he going to find anyone to have sex with him and kill him?"

Marilyn giggled and looked at the floor.

"Oh, Sissy. Maybe just us."

At the sound of something heavy dragging across the floor above them, they all looked up. When something up there let out a loud wail, then an insane cackle, the girls looked at Pauline.

She hid her grin quickly so that it was barely noticed, then looked at each of them.

"Uh, there's always something trying to break into this place. This whole damn world is full of freaks."

Marilyn said, "That sure sounded like it was—"

"A goddamn freak. Yeah. So, you two could probably leave this place for good, right? Risk could find a way to take you back. Or are you going to stick around?"

Sophia scoffed and said, "What, like some kind of vacation?"

"Shitty vacation," said Pauline.

"He offered," said Marilyn. "Just a little while ago. But he, um, he was—"

"Covered in bat blood," said Sophia. "Sheesh."

Pauline grinned at each of them.

"Good luck catching that one without some murdered freak's blood on him."

*　*　*

The solid wood door swung in, and Risk and Ham walked inside. Risk carried a package close by his side and tried to keep it away from K Kat's sniffing snout.

"Hey," said Pauline, "we were just talking about you two."

"Probably about how goddamn handsome we are," said Ham. "I mean, what else could it be?"

"That you're covered in blood all the time? How about that?"

They looked down at themselves and saw that it was true.

Pauline faced the twins and said, "These two. They're always convincing something to bleed, and they don't ever bother to get out of the way."

"Sheesh."

"Yes, Sissy. Very true."

"It's done," Risk said and wiped his hands together, mostly just smearing it around.

"Until the next time," Ham said with a satisfied grin.

"Well," said Pauline, "your new friends, the Kildare Killers with the fucking hot hands, are—"

"Not just the hands," said Sophia.

"All over if we want," Marilyn said with a pleasant smile.

Pauline stared for a second, then shook her head and said, "Nice. That'll get you some dates. Anyway, you're probably hungry, aren't you, girls?"

"Itchy too," said Sophia.

"Damn itchy," Marilyn said, nodding.

"Oil will do that," said Ham. "The fucking clouds up here are practically dripping with it. You'll get used to it."

Sophia turned enough to give Marilyn a modest smirk, and Marilyn replied with a shrug and a sigh.

"Forget the oil," said Pauline. "I'll get some kind of dinner going, then we can—"

"Oil?" said Risk. "Huh. That reminds me. We're thirsty too."

Ham pointed at him and smiled, saying, "Oh, you're right. You're so fucking right."

Risk shot a quick point and a grin at Ham, then faced Pauline.

"Crude wine. All around."

Pauline smiled back at him, then smiled at each of the twins.

"Perfect. Yeah, let's all have a drink. It's not every goddamn day we have Kildare Killer visitors."

She pointed at the twins.

"The lion too," said Ham. "K Kat, wasn't it?"

"Yeah."

"We all need a fucking drink," said Pauline. "Especially you new girls. Nothing gives you the true flavor of this damn place like a glass of crude."

"Uh, not to be rude," said Marilyn, "but I'm not so sure Sissy and I want to drink some kind of oily stuff."

"It's refined," said Ham. "Kind of irradiated, too, in a way. Thing is, it's just fine for sipping."

He slapped Risk's back and added, "Maybe not chugging, though."

"I'll get it," Pauline said as she got up and started toward the kitchen. "Be right back."

They watched her sway her leather-clad hips as she vanished into the kitchen, then they heard bottles and glasses clinking and clunking on a table.

Sophia leaned toward her sister and said, "I could kind of use a drink, Sis. Even if it's some oil crap."

"It isn't crap," Ham said, laughing. "It's actually damn good. You'll see."

"I don't mean to be rude either," said Marilyn. "But didn't you tell us we'd get some real clothes?"

"I say we leave them naked," said Ham. "As a matter of fact, I want my shirts back. Right now. I'll just fucking take them."

He took a step toward the twins, and Risk laid a hand on his shoulder, which stopped him. He looked down and saw that it had already sprouted a dense layer of fur, but no claws had yet sprung out.

Looking at Risk, he said, "Tell me you don't want them naked. Just them and their fucking heels."

Risk shook his head, and Pauline said from the kitchen, "Sounds good to me."

Risk kept his soon-to-be claws on Ham's shoulder and turned his head to call toward Pauline.

"Clothes would be good."

Ham muttered, mostly to himself, "I say the goddamn heels are enough. As soon as I can, I'm going to—"

Risk didn't look when he sprouted a few claws, the points of which embedded in Ham's skin through his shirt. Each point quickly had its own soaked spot.

Ham didn't cry out, just grimaced. Then, he nodded.

"Yeah. Clothes. Uh, right fucking now."

He grinned at the twins and added, "Told you I was an asshole."

"Clothes are next," Pauline said as she rejoined them, balancing five full glasses on a square of oil-stained cardboard.

Risk retracted his claws, and he offered a rare smile as he looked at the relieved faces of Marilyn and Sophia.

"I sure don't want to get ripped apart," Pauline said with a smirk, seeing the line of blood spots on Ham's shirt. "So, how about a drink, then we'll get them some kind of wardrobe?"

She handed a glass to each and kept one for herself. She held hers up and aimed it toward the twins.

"To new . . . adventures."

She quickly drank half of hers.

Ham said, "Gotta be better than the fucking old ones," then chugged all of his.

The twins looked at each other until Marilyn shrugged and took a sip, so Sophia took a taste of hers too.

"Alright," said Pauline. "Finish those, then let's get something for you two to wear. And then, goddammit, let's have some dinner."

She left for a closed door across the room, and Marilyn leaned toward her sister.

"Sissy, we need clothes. Drink your drink."

"Sure, Sis. It has a funny taste, but what the hell."

They clinked their glasses, drained them, then got up to follow Pauline.

Ham gazed intently at their leisurely strut and mumbled, "Never should have given them those goddamn shirts."

Risk, also watching, scoffed and said, "Live and learn."

Chapter 8 – Just a Touch of Prettiness

Pauline pushed the door, getting it to squeal lightly into a dim room.

"It isn't much," she said, "but it's good enough for a dead biker chick living in some burning, oily, fucked up place."

"Not exactly a travel brochure," Sophia said, smirking as she looked around.

"She isn't wrong, though, Sissy. Oh, maybe about living here, though."

Before walking in, the girls scanned around with the little amount of light from outside barrel fires that came through a cracked glass block window covered with a tight pattern of metal rods. A single candle burning on a dresser helped.

The room had a comfortable level of disarray, with old, worn furnishings mixed with stacks of cardboard boxes. On the dingy bedspread, an odd collection of mismatched pillows congregated near the headboard, and a few soiled stuffed animals lay nearby, some facedown and others missing limbs.

The wide dresser with the candle had been left with several of its drawers pulled out varying amounts, and the top surface was cluttered with jewelry boxes and figurines, most broken, some only cracked and fighting for survival.

"Well, let's see what we can find for you two."

Pauline led the way in, and the twins followed, still studying the odd refuge of a self-admitted tramp living as a renter in an abandoned compound high on a mountain.

"Anything is fine, Pauline," said Marilyn. "Anything but this old ripped up shirt."

She stopped to look at what the girls were wearing and scoffed.

"Ham's a freak. With a big fucking hand. I'll tell you, there's no limit to the freaks around here. Yeah, Marilyn, I think you're easy to pick for."

"And I'm not?" said Sophia.

"No. Not as easy. I'm good at reading people. Maybe I got a spike of radiation down here myself, something that messed with my brain."

"Sure, but I'm with Sis—just anything. We can't wear just these stupid shirts."

"No. And we'll have to find you some better shoes too. For now, though, you're stuck with those heels."

"Stuck with pointy heels," Marilyn said with a giggle. "That's kind of funny."

Sophia didn't laugh, just looked around the room more, so Marilyn cleared her throat and said, "So, should we just pick something ourselves, or should we—"

Pauline had already pulled a pair of jeans out of a dresser drawer, along with a fairly clean white long-sleeved blouse. She tossed it all onto the bed close to Marilyn, pointed at it, and said, "How's that?"

"It's almost too nice. Sissy and I aren't planning to stick around this place long anyway, so I plan to return it soon. Thanks, Pauline."

"You're welcome. Should fit."

"Yes, probably. I'll try to keep it all very clean too."

Pauline turned to rummage around in another drawer, pushed it closed, and pulled open another. Sophia watched her, waiting, but Marilyn picked up the offered wardrobe.

"Is there any way to clean up some of these oil streaks I picked up?" she said to Pauline.

"Yeah, there's water in the kitchen. Not running, though. Just a bucket. If you're ambitious, you can heat some over the fire."

"Okay, thanks," she said and started walking toward the door.

"Sissy, I'm going to wipe some of this oil off first so I don't get this blouse all dirty. Hurry up, and we can help each other change."

"Funny, Sis. Alright, I'm right behind you."

Marilyn started to exit, but she leaned back into the door frame instead and held a hand to her forehead.

"Sis, you alright?"

"Oh my. Just, I don't know, like a hot flash or something."

"Probably the wine," said Pauline. "You're just not used to it."

"Oh, yes, that could be it."

She shook her head and blinked a few times.

"Well, I'm starving, too, so let's get moving, Sissy."

"Sure, Sis. Yeah. I'm right behind you."

Marilyn left, and Pauline said, "You feel anything like that yet from that wine?"

"No. Should I? It really isn't all that bad."

"No, you'll be fine. You should probably have another glass. I mean, you haven't even seen just how fucked up this world is yet."

"Huh. Maybe I'll have to if Risk doesn't take us back right away."

Pauline walked over and leaned her back into the door while looking around her room and saying, "There was something special. I just can't remember . . ."

The door latched, and she walked over to the closet, swaying her hips on the way, which Sophia noticed.

Pauline opened the door and took out a box, which she set on the bed after swatting aside a few of the sad stuffed animals.

"Ah, yeah. Here we go," she said as she lifted out a pretty dress with a floral pattern and trimmed in delicate lace. Its short sleeves fell loosely from puffy shoulders, and patterns of fine lace edged where it was cut low in front.

Sophia stared at it in Pauline's hands.

"Hey, uh, jeans are good enough. Really."

Pauline walked over and held the dress up to her, ignoring her comment. They both looked down at how obviously short it was.

When Sophia looked up again, so did Pauline, and she said, "I think this is perfect for you."

"Not my style. I don't mean to seem ungrateful, but—"

"Look," Pauline said as she lowered the dress but stayed close, looking into Sophia's eyes, "it's an ugly fucking world out there. What's wrong with adding just a touch of prettiness to the whole fucking nightmare?"

"With that dress? How the hell is that going to help your fucked up world?"

"Sweetie, it's kind of your world now too. At least, for a while. You don't always have to dress in black, you know."

"I like black."

Pauline held it up again.

"And you're stunning in black. It's a pretty little dress, though, right?"

Sophia lowered her eyes and examined it again. Then, she swayed slightly and rubbed at her forehead.

"Oh, like Sis," she said. "Damn. Must be that wine."

"Must be," Pauline said with a short laugh. "Look again. Short is good, right?"

Sophia leaned her head forward, still blinking her eyes from the hot flash, and studied how much of her legs would be left uncovered when wearing the dress.

"Uh, yeah. I do like short."

Pauline laughed and said, "Good legs. You must like showing them off, right?"

"Uh, yeah. I guess I do."

"How about how pretty it is? I bet you kind of like pretty things, too, don't you?"

"Well, sure. Yeah, it's pretty, but—"

"I see it, even if you don't."

"You see what?"

"That inside, you kind of like it. You'd like to try being pretty for a while. You know, I bet you'd love how it feels to be just a little girl again. A very pretty one too. Um, just for kicks."

Sophia sighed, looking at it and rubbing her forehead again, then she reached out and pinched some of the lace.

"It's kind of soft, isn't it?" said Pauline. "Nothing wrong with soft, right?"

"Uh, yeah. Sure. Soft is . . . kind of nice."

Sophia looked up when Pauline touched her long black hair, slowly brushing it back over her shoulder. Once it was out of the way, she touched her cheek gently, then took her hand back.

"Aren't you kind of soft, too, sometimes?"

Sophia laughed and said, "When I'm not burning someone up?"

Pauline laughed, too, and said, "Yeah. Times like those. Times when you're just . . . soft. And pretty."

Sophia looked down at the dress, then took it from Pauline with both hands.

Pauline said, "Times like these?"

Sophia sighed and looked into Pauline's eyes.

"Oh, fine. This place is so fucked up, it'll be good for a laugh."

Pauline nodded and said, "We sure do need a laugh around here. It's a fucking grim kind of place."

"Yeah. I can see that."

"Okay," said Pauline. "We're off to a good start."

Sophia held the dress against herself and leaned forward, seeing just how much of her legs would show beneath its short, lacy hem. She didn't notice that Pauline had looked around, then returned with something else, and she was grinning about it.

"Oh, no way. You can't be serious."

Pauline held up pair of stretchy panties that looked appropriate for a very young girl. They weren't cut high, and the smooth pink fabric was trimmed around the waist and legs with delicate white lace.

And the backside was covered completely, top to bottom and side to side, with rows of frilly lace of varying lengths, puffing out like a short bunny tail.

"It's all I could find. They'll be tight, but you should be able to wiggle yourself into them."

Tipping her head and studying all of the lace and frills, Sophia said, "This is all your stuff? For a, um, dead biker chick? Can't be."

"No, this was all here. I don't know what kind of family lived here before. It doesn't matter. But I think these would be just about right with that dress."

Pauline held the panties up and gave them a whiff, then smiled.

"I don't think anyone's ever worn them. And they're clean. Not much around here is. See?"

She held them toward Sophia's face, who only looked into her eyes. When Pauline didn't take them back, she scoffed and leaned enough to inhale too.

"Hmm. Yeah. Like a little girl's perfume. But—"

"Look," said Pauline, "it's up to you. I think you should just say what the hell."

She laid the panties on the bed, smoothed the fabric out, then looked back at Sophia, who was still holding the dress against herself.

Pauline nodded with a grin, then began the short walk toward the door while Sophia said, "I, uh, you must have other stuff."

Pauline stopped before opening the door.

"Let's just say that that was all I had. That'll be our story, alright? Nothing wrong with being a pretty girl just for fun."

She opened the door and took a step, then turned back to Sophia to say, "Of course, being a pretty girl could get you into trouble too. You're not afraid, are you?"

"I'm not afraid of anything. I'm a killer."

"Yeah," she said and gave her a sweeping glance from bottom to top. "And a pretty girl too. On the inside—not so obvious to most."

Sophia stared back, not speaking.

"Maybe it's time to make it just a little obvious? It might lead you into a whole new kind of adventure."

She bounced her eyebrows a few times and pulled the door shut as she left Sophia alone in the room. Then, she leaned against the door and held up a small two-way radio.

"You there? Yeah. I did my part."

She waited a few seconds, listening.

"Yeah, strong doses of Key-S. There are two of them. We'll see just what they're all about now. Everyone has something they're tired of hiding, especially the hot blond and brunette Risk brought here."

She waited a few seconds, then said, "Yeah, one of each. They're twins too."

She paused again, then laughed softly before speaking.

"Oh, I'm kind of sure one is for Widow. Widow's going to love that one to death. The other is probably good for Mortimer, if they go where I'm telling them to go. If she isn't exactly right, he'll make sure she is pretty damn quick."

She laughed after a few seconds and said, "Shit, you'll know when you seem them which is for which."

Another few seconds passed.

"No, Risk doesn't have a fucking clue. Just take this one the same place as the others."

She listened, then said, "No, you get my blood only through Widow. We got a good fucking thing going here, asshole. Don't mess it up."

She nodded while listening, then said, "Oh, no, the one for Widow is fucking special. Both of them are. If it all works out, you owe me a fucking lot. So do Widow and Mortimer."

She waited, smiling, then said, "Yeah. A bite would be payment enough. About fucking time."

A few seconds later, she laughed softly and said, "A trampire? That's what I'd be? Oh, for fuck's sake. I have to go."

She tapped the device, jammed it into a pocket, and left to join the group.

* * *

"Oh, really, you two," said Marilyn. "You should turn around."

Risk scoffed and kept looking at her.

"Oh, I know," she said with a giggle. "You've seen everything already."

Ham had turned himself around, and he laughed while saying, "He did more than see it, from what I hear."

"Well," said Marilyn, "this is just different. Somehow. Now, turn around, Risk!"

He grinned and spun himself until he was shoulder to shoulder with Ham.

Marilyn hummed while she unbuttoned Ham's mutilated shirt and slipped it off, which caused her bare breasts to jiggle.

She wiped at a streak of oil on one, then rubbed the shirt around on her breasts a few times, saying softly to herself, "God, I'm so damn itchy."

"What's that?"

"Nothing, Ham. Just give me a few seconds."

She bunched the shirt up as a cushion to lift both breasts, then she rubbed the cloth across herself a few more times.

"Mm," she said too softly for anyone to hear. "So itchy."

She watched the men turned to look away, rubbed her breasts some more, and said very quietly, "Mm, that does feel good."

With the shirt pulled away, and with her arm primed to throw it, she noticed the unmistakable perkiness.

"Mm. That's a sight."

She gave the shirt a toss, and it landed neatly over Ham's head, covering it completely. He made no effort to remove it. Instead, he only inhaled a lung-busting amount several times, then laughed and pulled it off of his head.

"Thanks for the shirt, Ham."

"Anytime, blond killer from Kildare."

"Don't you forget it, big guy."

Marilyn giggled and pulled on the tight jeans first, then strapped her white heels back on, then slipped on and buttoned up the shirt partway.

"Okay. You can turn around now."

Pauline walked into the room and stopped to look at Marilyn.

"Looks good. Better on you than on me."

"Oh, thanks. Where's Sissy? I thought she was right behind me."

"Getting dressed. She'll be out in a few. You're putting on a show for these two thugs?"

Risk shook his head and Ham laughed a few times.

"I would for food. I'm so hungry, I'd kill for some food."

Pauline snickered and said, "This place will do that to you. Yeah, you need to eat. A fucking lot."

* * *

Across the room, the door to Pauline's bedroom opened, and the rest of them turned to see as Sophia walked out, then turned herself enough to pull the door shut.

"Oh, that's something," Marilyn said softly to herself.

Sophia had put on the dress that Pauline had offered her, and the bottom hem's lace, held away from her thighs by its soft bell shape, hid very little of those thighs. She showed smooth skin, more even than when she was wearing just Ham's shirt, all the way down to her high black heels, which were held in place with thin straps around her ankles.

The door latched, and she turned to face them.

She said, "What? I'm trying something different, alright?"

Marilyn softly said, "Mm . . ." to herself at the sight of her sister's breasts promising to squeeze themselves out above dainty patterns of lace.

"Nothing, Sissy. You look good, that's all."

"Eh. I figured what the hell. And besides, it was—"

"It was all I had," said Pauline. "All that's clean, anyway. It'll have to do."

While Sophia was taking graceful steps toward her sister, not her usual strut, Marilyn said, "Sissy, I've never seen you like this. It's, um, you look, uh, kind of like a—"

"A little girl. I know."

"Do you like it, Sissy?"

Sophia grinned and said, "Yeah, Sis, I kind of do. Different can be good, right?"

"Especially with that world out there so fucking dark and dismal," said Pauline. "What do you guys think?"

Risk and Ham had begun staring when Sophia made her entrance, and they hadn't yet stopped.

"Different," said Risk. "Yeah. Good."

"Shit," Ham said with a scoff, "all you need is a braid in that hair of yours."

"No, Ham," Marilyn said while holding up two fingers. "Sissy needs two braids."

"Sis, let's not get crazy, alright?"

She threw Ham's shirt toward him, and he never looked at it as it fell near his boots.

"Alright, everybody," said Pauline. "Enough with that. Leave the little girl—"

Marilyn spat out a single laugh.

"Ha! She said 'little girl.'"

"Well, Sis, I guess I'm kind of pretending, just for the hell of it."

"I like it, Sissy. You can always go back to your usual style later."

"Yeah. Yeah, I can."

"Anyway, let's leave her alone. Who's hungry?"

"I'm starving," said Marilyn. "I'd eat just about anything."

"I bet. Risk? Ham? You guys want the usual?"

"Sure," said Risk.

"Like we have anything else," said Ham.

"Good enough for me. I'll get cooking."

Chapter 9 – I Was Born Here

Risk sat at one end of the large wooden table, and Ham took the opposite end. Sophia and Pauline shared one side, and Marilyn sat across from her sister.

Pauline had just placed a steaming platter of food on the table, then took her seat. The girls looked around but didn't see any side dishes of any kind. Just a large plate of cooked something that looked like thin slices of steak.

Marilyn stared at the plate with big eyes, while Sophia was busy examining herself, leaning each way and seeing hints of pink and lace beneath the hem of her flowery dress. She grinned at the sight and tried pulling her new dress down to hide it, then joined her sister in studying the impending meal.

"What is it?" said Marilyn.

"It's, uh, steak," said Pauline. "This whole place down here had all kinds of provisions stored up. Or so I've heard. That was before I got here."

"On a motorcycle," Sophia said with a smirk.

Pauline turned to her and said, "Oh, yeah. Some sweet sex too."

"Tell us," Marilyn said while picking up a fork.

"Sure. Nothing too radical. Just sitting on a mad biker's, um, lap, racing down the highway. We both got there at the same time, and that son of a bitch lost control. I survived only long enough to see the sloppy streak his brains left on the asphalt."

"Brains?" said Marilyn. "Oh, that's terrible. So, he's here too?"

"Was."

She turned her eyes to the steaming tray and said, "Goddamn bat got him. Ripped him inside out and had itself a hot meal."

Looking again at Marilyn, she said, "Too bad his chopper didn't end up here too. That would have been sweet."

Marilyn laughed and said, "Sweet. That's my Sissy now."

She held her sister's gaze and said, "Sissy, I'm glad you had nothing else to put on except for that dress. It's quite pretty."

Sophia looked down and blinked her eyes a few times.

"I'm glad, too, Sis. I mean, at least she still had this for me."

She looked back up and said, "I look sweet like this?"

"Mm-hmm. Oh, yeah. You're hot in your usual stuff, but sweet is nice too."

Ham grunted and said, "I still say heels are enough."

He pointed at Pauline and said, "You too. Just those god-awful greasy boots of yours. That'd be damn hot. Right, Risk?"

"Sure. All of them."

He held the smiling gazes of Marilyn, then Sophia, then looked and pointed at Pauline.

"Wouldn't be the first time."

"Right. Because I'm a tramp. Thanks for reminding all of us. At dinner, no fucking less. Alright, who wants to eat?"

"Steak," said Marilyn. "I do like steak. Sissy?"

"Well, sure, Sis. Um, Pauline, are there any, I don't know, napkins?"

Before Pauline could answer, Marilyn snorted and said, "Right, Sissy. Don't want any food on that pretty little dress."

"Well, Sis, yeah. It's not even mine. As soon as I get—"

"Consider it yours, Sweetie," said Pauline. "It's just too right for you to have to give back. And yeah, I'll get some kind of napkins for all of you."

She got up and swayed her hips back to the kitchen, with all eyes on her.

"I can't wait," Marilyn said as she reached out and pinched off a piece of steak and quickly ate it.

"Mm. Not bad. Maybe a little oily."

"Every fucking thing here is," said Ham.

"Hey," Pauline said from the kitchen, "that's getting a little goddamn personal."

"Deny it," said Risk, causing Ham to give him a thumbs-up.

Marilyn cleared her throat, then said, "Is that what everyone is burning down there?"

"Yes . . . Mare," Risk said, causing her to smile. "When the reactor is out."

Ham said, "Damn reactor."

"Will it come back on soon?" said Sophia.

"Uh-oh. Sissy's afraid of the dark now too."

"No, Sis. Well, maybe a little. It's just that—"

A fresh storm sent its billowing roar toward the house on the side of the mountain, and the leading edge of it slammed into the walls, rattling everything and shaking the whole structure.

"Dammit," Risk said as he jumped up.

"It's always fucking something," Ham said, and he left the table too.

He and Risk hurried everywhere, checking shutters and doors, then Ham leaned out the front door and yelled, "Ziggy?"

Amid crackling of his hot breath, Ziggy called out, "Good!"

Ham slammed the door, and they rejoined the dinner party just as Pauline came back from the kitchen, a mess of rags in one hand.

"Goddamn storms. Why don't we eat already before some other calamity hits us? I swear, this world . . ."

She stabbed a giant fork into the pile but stopped when Ham said, "Hey, some more wine would be good."

"Oh, yeah, that's an idea. I'll get it. I insist."

She left for the kitchen again.

"So, Risk," said Sophia, "we got Pauline's story. What's yours?"

"Huh," said Ham. "Might take more than just a few fucking words, huh, Risk?"

Risk shook his head and sighed.

"I was born here."

Ham held four fingers up and aimed them first at Marilyn, then at Sophia.

"Four words. Fucking progress."

Risk ignored him and said, "My mother got sent here the usual way."

"Killed during sex," Ham said, nodding.

Risk glared at him for a second, then said, "She got raped right after she got here."

"Oh my goodness," said Marilyn. "Is she, um, still around?"

Risk and Ham shared a look for a few seconds, then Ham said, "People don't last long here."

He pointed at Marilyn's generous cleavage from where she'd chosen to not use many buttons, then at Sophia, wearing a frilly dress.

"Especially the way you two characters dress."

"I'll take my chances," Marilyn said, then pointed at her sister. "Sissy will too. We're killers."

"Yeah, so we've heard," said Ham. "From Kildare. Well, guess what? There are worse fucking things around here than killers."

From somewhere on the roof, a loud pounding began, followed by an insane wail.

Risk turned his eyes up and said, "Like that."

Ham stood and said, "Excuse us, ladies. We have to—"

Marilyn laughed and held up one finger and said, "One lady."

Then, she giggled and said, "And one little girl."

"Sis, that's not—"

"Oh, Sissy, I'm just having fun. We all know you're just pretending for the fun of it."

"You girls figure it out," said Ham. "Risk?"

Risk stood, and the two of them began a walk toward the stairs.

Marilyn lost her smile, looked down at the plate, and said, "Are we ever going to fucking eat?"

"Sis, you're a riot. You can't be that hungry."

"I can't? Are you sure? I think I fucking am."

"You're getting harsh."

"Well, maybe compared to a little girl."

"Stop, Sis, I—"

"You two need another drink," Pauline said as she returned with the cardboard tray.

She placed the twins' drinks in front of them, then the rest for Risk and Ham and herself.

"Drink up."

*   *   *

Ham pulled open the hatch in the second level's ceiling and unfolded the stairs. His normal hand rattled the assembly around a few times, then let it go.

"Huh. Should hold. After you," he said, and Risk grunted and started the climb into the attic.

Ham followed, saying, "That went over well. I could see it."

"What?"

"Actually talking to those two. I know you're focused on other things all the fucking time. But really, they'd like to hear more from you."

Risk sighed as he looked up at a fresh hole and some kind of paw reaching through, grasping around and scratching whatever it could. Ham stood by his side.

"They're leaving soon."

"Maybe, maybe not. And that will literally be a fine fucking time for you, my friend."

Risk grunted his agreement, then looked down when he felt the mountain lion nosing around, bumping his leg.

"Good cat."

"No. No way. Not with that one too."

"I told you. She bit."

Ham blew out a deep breath and said, "Yeah. I heard that. Weird shit, that's all I know. Alright, which one of you is dealing with that?"

"Lion's turn."

"Yeah, probably, but what'll she do? Eat the fucking thing?"

"Huh. Alright. Hammer it, then."

"And make a bigger fucking hole in my roof? I don't think so."

"That bad every time?"

Ham held up his enormous fist and said, "There's no stopping this fucking thing."

Risk sighed then looked to one side of the large, dark attic at a shuttered window opening without any remaining glass.

"Yeah, Risk. Go outside and play."

Risk grinned, then he walked over, pried loose a few of the boards, and climbed out and up onto the roof.

Ham stood waiting with the lion by his side, both looking up. Both pairs of eyes followed the soft thumping of black work boots on the outside and approaching the invading beast.

He tipped his head toward the cat and said, "Maybe not right under the fucking thing, huh?"

K Kat stepped to one side, and he joined her.

Still looking up, he said to the cat, "Not like we can hose down your fucking hide."

Then, he looked down and she looked up into his eyes.

"Tell me the truth. Somehow, he fucked you, too, right?"

The lion began panting, still holding his gaze.

"You think it's funny? Goddamn cat."

They both looked up at the sound of a horrifying shriek, and a gooey substance, a swirl of colors, streamed through and splattered on the floor.

"Told you we had to move. You owe me, goddamn lion."

* * *

Marilyn had just set down her emptied glass when Risk, Ham, and K Kat came pounding down the stairs.

"Everything alright?" said Pauline. "We heard something scream."

"It's dead," said Risk.

"He means that it's ripped apart and thrown down the mountain and he'll help patch up the roof later."

"Right."

"Sit," said Pauline. "Time to eat."

She looked next to her at Sophia, who held a half-full glass.

"Finish your drink, Sweetie. There's more."

Sophia said softly, "Okay," then finished her glass.

Risk and Ham reclaimed their seats at the table, and Pauline jabbed the pile of meat with the big fork.

"Who's first?"

Above them, something screamed softly or maybe laughed.

"Wait. What did I just hear?" said Marilyn.

"I didn't hear anything," said Ham.

Pauline said, "Me neither. You thought you heard something?"

"Uh, yeah. Maybe it was thing that just got killed."

"Could be," said Risk. "Sure."

Pauline added a few slices to each plate, then stabbed the fork back into what was left. The fork waved around before coming to a standstill.

Then, it shook just a little bit more.

Marilyn froze, her eyes on the platter, then she looked at her sister. Sophia stopped with her fork in the air, a chunk of steak skewered on it. She only shook her head.

"Well," said Marilyn, "I'm starving, and that's all that matters. I just need some of this in my stomach already."

She took a bite and began to chew, making a face as she chomped down and ground her teeth into it. Everyone watched until she swallowed it.

"Eh, not bad. Sissy, try some."

Sophia took a cautious nibble and chewed, her eyes looking around the table as they all watched her.

She grimaced and swallowed, blinked her eyes a few times, then picked up her empty glass.

"Oh, here," Pauline said and poured more from the bottle. "Just the wine."

"Huh?"

"Oh, I just mean, we don't have anything else here. Wine. Just wine. See?"

Sophia squinted at her for a second as her fork dragged around blindly on her plate until she guided it into a piece of steak.

"So, Ham," Marilyn said while chewing, "what's your story? Were you born here, too, like Risk?"

"Oh, fuck, no. I've been here so long I can't even recall it."

He pointed his fork, held in his left hand with a piece of meat pierced on the tines, at each of the girls.

"That's another thing about this fucking place. It fucks you up, then it gets so that you can't hardly remember who or what the fuck you were. You just get kind of fucking lost in some weird dead-end bullshit. Isn't that right, Risk?"

"I remember."

"Yeah, well, you're different. Soon, you,"—he jabbed the fork toward Pauline, who scoffed—"won't even remember the name Pauline."

She scoffed again and said, "Let me guess: all I'll remember is that I'm a tramp, like Risk wants to call me."

Risk laughed with his mouth closed, chewing and stabbing around for more.

"That's what you're saying, you big fuck?"

"Yeah," said Ham, "exactly that."

He rested his hand on the table, having forgotten to jam the piece of meat into his mouth.

The girls watched it.

Ham's next bite moved on its own. Curling and twisting. Trying to escape the fork impaling it.

"Um," said Marilyn, still staring at it. "Did that, uh, meat just move?"

"I thought so, too, Sis."

Pauline watched it, biting her lip.

Risk let out a deep breath as he watched the meat on the fork too.

No one saw the windup, but they saw a massive hammer hand drop gingerly down and crush the hand and fork and grind the alleged meat into the table.

Then, Ham looked at each of them while he worked everything in slow rotations with his giant fist, none of it making a sound.

"What? I, uh, do this with all my food. Isn't that right, Risk?"

Risk was looking at his plate, shaking his head and laughing to himself.

"Yeah. All of it."

"Sometimes for sex too," said Pauline, shaking her head. "You and that goddamn freak hand."

"Never heard you complain. Sometimes you even want those fat fingers to—"

Something heavy rammed one of the shuttered windows with a frantic screech. Then, another hit at the other side of the room. Then, two more.

"Back up!" Risk said to the girls as he pointed toward a corner. "Go! Now!"

Chapter 10 – What's Going On With Us?

Risk jabbed a finger toward the far corner and yelled, "Get back!"

He turned and yelled to Ham, "Not yet. Move the rug."

Ham looked down at the worn and oil-streaked area rug near the large shuttered window which was taking most of the hits.

"Oh yeah. Good thinking. That fucking blood doesn't wash out."

Risk laughed once and went to join him.

Sophia jumped up, dumping her chair backwards, and grabbed Marilyn's hand.

"Sis, he did say we'd get attacked later. Well, here we go."

She pulled, but Marilyn stayed seated until she'd grabbed a slice of meat, folded it, and stuffed it into her mouth. She tried to laugh up at her sister with her cheeks like balloons.

"Huh. Someone has quite the appetite. Imagine that," Pauline said, then she laughed and ran for the kitchen.

"Sis, seriously, that crap isn't even that good! Come on!"

Marilyn stood up but remained beside the table, and she reached out for the platter of meat.

"You can't be serious!"

"Mm, I'm starving. Just a second."

Marilyn picked up the tray, then said, "Okay, Sissy. I'm ready now."

Then, she allowed herself to be dragged to the corner, where they stood behind a couch and watched.

"You're that hungry?"

Marilyn giggled and said, "You're that little?"

"No, I'm only pretending. What is going on with you?"

"I don't know. Oh my goodness, Sissy. It's crazy. This world is crazy."

Across the room, Risk and Ham had grabbed the large rug and were about to take it where blood wouldn't soon be splattered, but they stopped at Pauline yelling from the kitchen doorway.

"Move the goddamn furniture off of it first! Come on, you guys. We went through this last time!"

They shrugged and scoffed at each other, then started moving the two upholstered chairs and a table with a lamp just as two more bats shrieked and pounded their bodies into the shutter.

Marilyn kept eating and said, "I like your new style, Sissy."

She ripped a bite off of another slice.

"It's not like it's my style, Sis. I'm just . . . I don't know. Just dressing up."

"You're just having fun. I get it. But you really are pretty, Sissy. No reason you can't dress like a, um . . ."

Sophia grinned and said, "You really want to say it, don't you?"

"Oh, yes. I sure do."

"Go ahead, then, Sis. Say it."

"Hmm. You want to hear it, don't you?"

Sophia looked down, smiling, and said, "Uh-huh."

Marilyn giggled and said, "You're dressed like a little girl. A very sweet little girl."

She took another bite and watched her sister smoothing down the dress, looking all around at it, then touching softly the lace near her breasts.

"The lace is nice," said Sophia. "It really is cute. It's kind of fun to pretend."

Marilyn stopped chewing, leaving one cheek puffed up much more than the other.

"Sissy. Uh-uh. Wait a second. Maybe this is more than just you having fun?"

Sophia looked into her sister's blue eyes with her own blue eyes.

"Um, maybe. Yeah. I, um, kind of sometimes thought maybe I could, you know, try to—"

"Dress like a little girl? You thought that before?"

"Uh, I think so. Yeah, I think I must have, but I'm not sure."

"I'm all for it, Sissy, but it might not be enough."

"What do you mean?"

They stopped at the sound of Ham yelling, "Hey, easy with that, Risk! Not like we can go fucking shopping for a new one!"

Risk set the table back down and steadied the lamp that was going for a ride on it.

Sophia returned to fussing with her lacy new dress, and Marilyn leaned out to try to look into her eyes.

"Maybe you should, I don't know, try to seriously see yourself as a little girl too? How fun would that be?"

"You mean actually see myself as just a little girl? Like that?"

"Mm-hmm. Yes. Just for fun. Convince yourself that you're a pretty little girl."

"Oh, God, I don't know, Sis. Already, this is making me so itchy I can't hardly stand it."

"Ooh, dressing like a little girl?"

"Yeah. Crazy, huh?"

"Just from that dress? Really?"

With both hands, Sophia tried to smooth down the dress all around her hips.

"Uh, yeah. Just the dress."

She pinched the hem and wiggled while pulling it down and added, "What else could it be?"

"Well, I say, don't fight it. I'm so itchy you should have seen me before you came out of that room. I was rubbing Ham's shirt around on my nipples, and those two guys could have turned anytime and watched. I probably would have like it too. I wouldn't have stopped."

"Well, you're stunning. Who wouldn't want to watch that?"

"Aw, thanks, Sissy. And I'm so hungry. I never told anyone, but—"

Ham yelled out, "Hey, Pauline! Get some fucking mops ready!"

She leaned out again just enough to say, "Try not to fuck this place up too much, alright? This isn't some goddamn slaughterhouse!"

Risk laughed once and said, "The fuck it isn't."

The twins ignored them and focused on each other again.

"Like I was saying, Sissy, it hasn't been easy to not pig out most of the time. There's something about this world. It's just getting harder to fight it."

"Well, Sis, you should eat all you want. You do that, and I'll—"

"You'll be the most precious, sweet little girl ever. Mm-hmm. Oh, yeah."

"Pauline said the dress was soft, then she said I was soft too."

"You're a killer, Sissy, but you sure are soft too. You're a soft little girl."

"Sis, what's going on with us? It's this world, right?"

"It has to be. But we're not going to be here long. We'll be back at the Prism in no time."

"I hope so."

"And you'll be the cutest baby girl at the bar!"

Sophia nodded slowly, then said, without a smile, "I, um, I'd like that."

"Oh. Maybe you won't be old enough to get in."

"Funny, Sis."

Marilyn watched Risk and Ham and K Kat about to open a thick wooden hatch over a window.

"Let's just watch them, little girl."

Marilyn waited a few seconds, then stole a glance at her sister. She saw that Sophia was watching the impending attack and just nodding, nothing else.

* * *

"I bet it's those fucking bats," Ham said with his left hand on the shutter's iron handle.

"This high up?" said Risk. "Yeah. Probably."

"They haven't hunted up this fucking high before. Not in a goddamn group."

"First time for everything."

"Yeah. What's it going to be for you? The usual fucking wolf monster thing?"

"Eh, maybe. Maybe just me."

"Yeah, that's goddamn dangerous enough. Ready?"

"Yeah."

Ham yanked open the slab of wood and three large, angry bats crawled enough to get their heads in, scraping their long black claws on everything. The lead bat paused, and its head bobbed left and right as its beady black eyes darted at everything in the room.

"Holy fuck," said Ham. "Goddamn bats."

It took less than a second before it shrieked, flapped its wings one last time just beyond the outer wall, then tried to launch itself inside.

"Ha!" Ham said as he swung his bloated fist, and that lead bat found itself with a broken neck and a head leaning to one side from a vicious strike from a freaky hammer hand.

"Fucker."

It was still alive.

"It's still alive," said Risk.

"Stupid fucker. You want some more?"

He raised his hammer and crushed the creature into the lower sill, which was old but metal and still sharp, sending detached wings fluttering down the mountainside and freeing up an ugly bat head to fall inside and thump on the floor.

"He's laughing at you," Risk said with his own laugh.

"Not for long," Ham said as he kicked the head toward the lion, who snarled and sank her fangs into it, then wrestled it around on the floor.

Risk was holding another of the bats by its throat, low enough that it was fighting to get its arms and claws inside, and he turned toward the lion first, then Ham.

"Is that safe to eat?"

Ham looked back at the twins, safe in the corner and watching them. And listening.

He leaned closer to Risk and said, "Uh, we'd better hope so, right?"

"Right. The head, though?"

"That I don't know. The fucking lion likes it."

Ham turned to look again at a mountain lion eating a bat head, and Risk used an extra hand to strangle his bat, then twist its head completely off.

But he threw it back outside just in time to punch the third bat in its face. With blood flowing from rips all around its mouth, it shrieked and leaned back, ready to attack with a bite.

But Ham gave it another punch, with his normal fist, and said, "They're pissed. They know it's us that have been selling them to the lab."

"This won't stop us."

"These fuckers must think it will. Dumb fucks."

Risk gave the dazed creature another punch, and its wings went limp behind it.

"Nice one."

"Thanks. I might quit this war against bats."

Ham reached behind himself and fumbled around until he found a lamp. He started to lift it when Pauline yelled from the kitchen doorway.

"Goddammit, Ham! Find something else!"

He frowned and set it back down.

"The tramp is always watching. Always fucking watching."

In those few seconds, the beast had breached the perimeter and spread its wings inside, then started beating them against everything close enough. The lamp got caught up in the oily web of a wing and was flung against a wall near Pauline, and it shattered while she screamed and rushed back into the kitchen.

Ham yelled over his shoulder, "Should have let me break it!"

Risk grabbed the marauding bat from behind, and Ham wound up for a punch with a monster fist, then planted it somewhere around the thing's midsection.

Promptly causing a vomiting of oily, bloody slop.

"Sorry!" he yelled toward the kitchen. "I'll clean it up!"

Risk laughed and said, "No. Fuck no, you won't."

He grabbed its head with both hands, spun it completely around to face him, then spit in its face. Not waiting to be certain that it was dead all the way, he dragged it toward the window and heaved it outside.

Free of attacks for the moment, he leaned on the windowsill and looked down, listening to the thing tumbling down the chaotic rock surface like a snapped umbrella.

Still leaning out and looking each way, then up, he said, "Well, good. That's it for now."

He came back inside and checked on K Kat first. She was gnawing on the bat head like it was rawhide chew toy.

"Good cat."

"How about 'good fucking Ham,' too?"

Risk laughed once and said, "Sure. Good fucking Ham."

"Thanks. I like to hear that sometimes. You're not seriously quitting this fight, are you?"

"Is it good to kill so much?"

Ham didn't answer right away. He just scratched at his chin with his left hand.

"Shit. You're damn good at it."

"Yeah. I guess."

"Besides, I already died. Maybe I'm not the best son of a bitch to answer that."

Risk grinned, then looked at the girls in the corner.

"What the hell is going on with you two?" he said.

Ham leaned toward him and said, "Nice. You used lots of fucking words. Try to keep that up, at least for them."

Then, he turned his head, and he and Risk observed a blond Kildare Killer, wearing jeans that appeared painted-on and keeping her white blouse unbuttoned so low that she could spill out at any time. She was shoveling in sliced dinner entree meat and didn't appear to have noticed any of the battle.

"That's a hungry dame," said Ham.

"Yeah. The blond one."

Beside her, so close that they were pressed together, the brunette Killer was caressing the lacy hem of a pretty dress with one hand while she watched her other hand tugging at the lace barely holding in her generous breasts.

"What's with that one, though?"

"In this fucking world?" said Risk.

He grumbled and added, "Could be anything."

Chapter 11 – A Plan to Kill All

Risk held the shutter behind him with one hand and kept staring at the twins, who still hadn't looked his way. One was looking down at her dress, and the other was staring at a plate of meat.

"What the fuck?"

"Something isn't right with them," said Ham. "They're still damn hot, though."

"Yeah."

Pauline was peeking around the wall from inside the kitchen, heard them, saw where they were looking, and looked herself.

Without the slightest look of surprise, she said to Risk, "What's wrong? You told them to hide over there, right?"

"Yeah, but she—"

"Dinner got interrupted by a goddamn bat attack. What the hell do you two savages expect?"

Marilyn looked up, chewing on a slice of meat and not bothering with a thin track of juice sliding down her chin.

"Sure," said Risk, "she's hungry."

"She's damn hungry," said Ham. "Looking damn good, too, though. But hungry. Yeah."

Her sister smoothed down her short dress with both hands and looked up, too, while still fussing with the lace.

"And that one, she—"

Pauline said, "Hey, it's a pretty dress. Of course, she likes it. You guys done playing around with bats for a while?"

Risk started swinging closed the hatch, still not looking, and said, "Yep. Done."

Then, it got rammed by another, more determined bat.

"Not done. Those fuckers," said Ham.

He saw Pauline hide herself away in the kitchen and yelled, while laughing, "Hey, it's only one of them! Come back and help!"

"Yeah, one," said Risk. "A big fucker, though."

Its spindly black arm was flailing around inside, and it hooked onto Risk's vest and wasn't letting it go.

"Dammit."

With a low roar, K Kat jumped up and sprinted to his aid, which caused the bat head she was chewing to spin across the floor toward the twins.

"Uh-oh, Sissy. Heads. Everywhere we go."

"It's the only thing normal about this place."

"Good one, Sissy. True too. I'm not even normal anymore."

"Nope. Me neither. But you know what?"

"Yes, I do. We kind of like it!" said Marilyn. "Oh, and I feel like biting into that head too."

"Sheesh, Sis."

K Kat jumped up and sank her teeth into the thing's arm, then hung there long enough to pull it down and rest her paws on the floor again. She started jerking it each way, digging her claws into the floor to back away. She tugged and pulled and growled, then, with a loud snarl and a vicious shake, she stumbled back with just the arm to the sound of mad screaming outside.

Risk said, "Fuck," then reached up quickly for the thing's other arm and dragged what was left of it inside.

As soon as Risk slammed it to the floor, Ham began beating all of its remaining limbs until it was thrashing uselessly around, without enough energy to wail with any real gusto.

"Damn fucking,"—he raised his heavy fist high for the last hit— "bats."

"Damn fucking humans," it said with its faced knotted and twisted from Ham having hammered everything.

Ham raised his massive, fleshy fist and aimed it for a decisive strike to the part of the thing that could still cuss at them.

"You'll be a damn fucking puddle in just about—"

"Wait," said Risk. "Hold up a second."

"You know," said Ham, "we should make this quick. I'd kind of like to finish that fucking dinner."

He looked over at Marilyn, who stared back and took another bite.

"If there's any left."

"I'll just fry up some more," said Pauline. "Let the poor girl eat. She's fucking famished."

"Fine," Ham said and lowered his pounder.

Risk was stooping down next to the bat, and they stared at each other in silence for a few seconds.

"You hate humans."

"Yes," said the bat thing. "But some hate everything else."

"Some humans hate everything else?"

"Yes, hate. A plan to kill all."

"What? How?"

"Some human. Has a plan."

Risk looked up at Ham and got only a shrug from him.

"You're talking about someone."

"Yes. The someone I'm talking about."

"Goddamn smartass freak," said Ham. "I swear, I'll clean it up. Just one good—"

"Hold it," said Risk.

To the bat, he said, "Who are you talking about?"

"The one I'm talking about."

Risk scoffed and pointed at the shoulder that had lost its arm, and it got pounded even before Ham could laugh about it, which he did.

The thing grimaced but had lost too much strength and gooey blood to make an energetic effort. It kept looking up at Risk.

To Ham, Risk said, "Yeah, that's funny."

"We like to laugh," he said to the bat. "Maybe you'll make us laugh some more."

"Laugh? Not for long," it said.

"How long?"

"Not."

"Just let me beat the shit out of this fucking—"

"Hang on," Risk said, holding a hand up.

Ham kept his bulbous hand poised to pulverize.

"Who?"

"Where."

"Risk, this stupid fucker is—"

"Soon," said the bat.

"Say where," he said to the crippled thing on the floor, oozing from every rip and tear and smash.

"I have a reason?"

"To live a few more seconds."

The bat considered it, its eyes blinking slowly.

"Hot and cold."

"What's that?"

"A place."

Risk looked up at Ham, who only shrugged again and said, "This fucker thinks this is some kind of—"

"Wait."

To the bat, he said, "That's the name?"

The bat spat some slop out to the side and said, "Call it that. Sure."

"But that's not its real name?"

"Nothing here has a real name. Hot and cold. It's all I fucking know."

"You're sure?" said Risk.

"All I fucking—"

"You don't know anything else?" Risk said as he pointed at the thing's snarling head.

"No! I don't fucking—"

Risk snapped his fingers, the hammer dropped, and Pauline yelled from the kitchen, "I'll get the goddamn mop for you."

* * *

Risk scoffed at the gooey puddle exploded out from under Ham's massive fist, which Ham ground from side to side several times while laughing at the sight of it.

"Bats," said Risk.

"A fucking inconsiderate bunch," said Ham. "Never clean up after themselves."

Ham raised his fist and wiggled the thick fingers around, keeping the dripping of them over the already established mess site. He fumbled around with his other hand and found some rags, which he used to start cleaning it up.

"That mean anything to you?"

"No," said Ham. "Hot and Cold could be anything."

He looked toward the entryway to the kitchen, where Pauline was watching from a safe place around the corner.

"Could even be her," he said, tipping his head that way.

Risk chuckled and said, "Not at the same time."

"True. Damn close, though. Alright, hot could be just about anywhere. But where's cold?"

Risk stood and locked his fists to his hips, then looked around the room. His eyes lingered on each of the twins for several seconds, both of them absorbed in either eating from a tray of meat or fussing with a lacy dress.

"Not on your mountain."

"Yeah. Nothing cold up here."

Risk looked up toward the ceiling and said, "Nothing higher either."

Ham chortled and said, "Maybe that goddamn bay, if we could get to it. That puddle,"—Ham pointed and Risk snorted a single laugh—"wasn't talking about the bay."

"No."

"So, let's figure out what kind of plan would kill everyone down there."

He hooked a thumb toward the door, which led to the patio, which led to the steep side of the mountain.

"A human with a plan to kill everyone else? That's what he fucking said?"

"Yeah, Ham."

Risk walked toward the couch, stopping long enough to rub around K Kat's ears while she enjoyed chewing on the bat head near the twins.

"Good cat."

He kept going and dropped down into the cushions. Ham had followed and stood nearby.

"Let me guess," said Ham. "You're going to hunt down that madman, aren't you?"

"It's either that or hunt bats."

"Which you wanted to stop doing anyway."

"Yeah."

"Because you're trying to be a goddamn saint."

"Not a saint."

"Whatever. You're not even coming close."

Risk sighed and raked his fingers through his unruly, wavy black hair.

"Yeah. I know."

"What about that fucking opening Topside? You don't care about that anymore?"

"Won't matter if everyone here is dead."

"Hey," said Ham. "Hawken."

"What about him?"

"He might know where the fuck that Hot and Cold place is."

"He might. But he's across town."

"Which means running through fucking fires, sneaking around fucking monsters, dodging fucking death traps, hiding from fucking—"

"Organized bats."

"That's a good goddamn observation," said Ham. "Yeah, that's new. You're not sure you can be monster enough yourself to handle a platoon of those bastards?"

"Huh. Maybe not. Numbers."

"Yeah. So, what are your options? How you going to get to Hawken?"

Risk looked up at Pauline and gave her a modest grin.

"Sex and death would do it."

"No fucking way," she said, frowning at both of them. "And that wasn't a goddamn pun."

Ham laughed and said, "Shit. You're afraid of—"

"Afraid of waking up naked and recently fucked, in a basket surrounded by homicidal bats? Yeah," she said, holding fingers out to show a small gap, "maybe just a little fucking bit."

Risk and Ham stared at her while she smirked then flipped back her red mane with both hands.

"You two do it," she said, grinning. "I'll make some goddamn popcorn."

Risk and Ham looked at each other, and Ham said, "Uh, would that even work?"

"Huh. We'll never know."

Risk turned to look at the twins, who'd been listening while still eating and playing with a dress.

He pointed in their direction and said, "One of you."

Marilyn stopped chewing and Sophia stopped fussing long enough to look into each other's eyes.

But they turned back toward Risk when they heard him laugh, then say, "Or both."

Chapter 12 – It's My Ass to Risk

Marilyn took another bite and said softly to her sister, "Maybe there's food there. Wherever Risk is going, we should go too."

"We? Go if you want. Go get a free meal."

Marilyn giggled around the steak she was chewing and said, "Maybe you're too little to leave home."

"Funny, Sis. I'm still a killer."

"Yes, and a very pretty one. It's just not safe for such a pretty girl to be out in the world."

"Uh, thanks. I think."

Risk called across the room.

"No whispering. You both in?"

Marilyn frowned when she looked back at him, then she pointed.

"You still have some, um, there's some . . ."

He wiped at the goo splattered across his forehead, frowned at the sight of it on the back of his hand, then wiped it on his jeans.

"That's a good start," she said. "Sure, that's—"

He wiped around on his cheeks, mostly smearing it around.

Marilyn elbowed Sophia, who said, "Sheesh."

"Thanks, Sissy. I still like hearing that. You still have to pay attention."

To Risk, she said, "Uh, maybe we'll pass this time."

Ham said, "You didn't like all of that fun and games that got your asses here? Sounded damn good to me."

"I bet," said Marilyn. "Maybe we, uh—"

"Maybe we like it too much," said Sophia.

Marilyn giggled and said, "That's my Sissy. She's always so itchy."

"You too, Sis. All day, every day."

"She's not wrong."

All four again looked at Pauline, and she gave each one their moment of her full attention and a raised middle finger.

Ham snorted and said, "I think that means fuck no."

Risk said, "Or no fuck."

"All the same."

"The lion," said Sophia.

"Oh," said Marilyn, "Sissy's right. Yes, use K Kat."

All eyes turned toward the mountain lion who froze, looking back at them with the bat head hanging from her mouth.

"Sexy as fuck," Ham said with a laugh.

Pauline cackled and said, "You already bought her dinner."

"Good one, Pauline."

"Thanks, Marilyn. Ready for more wine? You and your twin sister?"

"Okay, yes. More wine would be nice. But you'll have to check Sissy's ID because—"

An insane wailing mixed with laughter pierced the ceiling above them. Everyone looked up until it finally subsided.

Marilyn said, "Another bat?"

Risk shook his head.

Sophia smirked and said, "Just its head?"

"Good one, Sissy."

Risk shook his head again.

"You might as well tell them," said Ham.

Risk looked from face to face, each of them waiting for his answer.

"It's my mother," he said.

"She's upstairs? That was her?"

"Yes, Marilyn."

"It's Mare, remember?"

"I do now. Yeah, Mare."

Sophia said, "Is she alright?"

"Maybe right this second," Ham said while shaking his head. "Give it another fucking second."

"He's right. Fia."

Marilyn leaned toward her sister and whispered, "He remembered, Sissy."

Sophia whispered back, "But does he like my new dress?"

"It's yours?"

"Oh, yeah. I'm keeping it."

"She changes. Quickly," Risk said while pointing up.

"Uh, changes how?"

Risk held the back of his hand toward the girls and gave everyone time to focus on it. Then, he let it flash into a massive, furry paw with pointy white claws.

He looked from face to face then, satisfied that they'd all seen it, he let it return to normal.

"She has a paw?"

"No, Mare. Not like that."

"What Risk means," said Ham, "is that she changes all the time, into all kinds of things. And she usually has no fucking control over any of it."

"Or what she does," Risk added.

"Sheesh."

"Yes, Sissy. Very much."

"I'm helping out by keeping her chained up here at the house."

"No, I don't believe it," Marilyn said. "You keep her in chains?"

Ham laughed and said, "No. Uh-uh. Probably should, though. That was just fun to say."

Sophia said, "So, how did that happen to her?"

"A drug."

"Okay, Risk. A drug," said Marilyn. "What drug?"

"It's called Zoojoose."

* * *

"I was born here," Risk said, then he pointed up. "After that."

Ham laughed and said, "Uh, now's the time."

Risk turned to him and said, "For what?"

"Lots of fucking words. Don't be shy. Just grunting isn't going to make it."

Marilyn giggled softly, and Sophia rolled her eyes.

Pauline said, "I'll believe it when I see it."

"Hear it," said Ham.

"Smartass."

Risk looked around the room, then cleared his throat.

"I was—"

"Hold it," said Ham. "Everyone, take a seat. Risk, get over there where you can explain this to all of us. I don't want to miss a fucking bit of it."

"Me neither," said Pauline. "You got some explaining to do."

"I do?"

"Shit, look at you! You didn't just fucking happen. Let's get to the bottom of this right now."

"Yeah," Ham said while the twins were finding places on the couch. "Start with your name. What the hell kind of name is Risk?"

"Sure," Risk said as he walked to a place where he could stand and face the couch, which was where all four of them were seated.

He cleared his throat again while nodding at Marilyn, who had set the plate, almost empty of meat, on her lap. Sophia, next to her, smoothed down her dress over her bare thighs, which drew Risk's stare for a second.

Until he heard Pauline cough. He looked at her and grinned at her smirk and shaking head.

"Before the next wave of goddamn bats, alright?"

"Sure, Ham."

He coughed once to the side.

"She came here the usual way. She died during sex."

"How did she die?" said Pauline.

"Drug overdose. Not long after she got here, she got raped."

"Oh my goodness," said Marilyn. "That's terrible."

"Yeah. So, that's how I got here."

"Any idea who the, um, who the—"

"I don't know my father. But I do know what he is. Or was."

"What's that?" said Ham.

Risk smiled and started to speak, and Pauline said, "Must have been damn good looking."

Risk looked down with a light scoff, but he didn't say anything.

"Your mother has a name?" said Ham. "All this time I've had her chained up,"—he paused to point at Marilyn, getting her to giggle once—"you never said."

"Lucy."

"Oh, wait," said Ham. "I did hear that from someone. They even made a joke about that drug, called her Lucy—"

"But you don't think that's funny."

Ham coughed and looked down.

"I'm curious," said Marilyn. "I bet Sissy is too. How did you get a name like that?"

"She was already messed up from the Zoojoose, and she thought she was filling out a birth certificate. But it was just scrap paper. She wrote the word 'name,' then a line to fill in."

"She made her own birth certificate?" said Sophia. "Wow, pretty ambitious."

Risk squinted at her.

"Sissy, let him finish, alright?"

"Sure, Sis."

They focused on him again.

"This is what I heard. She wanted to write a lot about me, all about her hopes for me, everything to come in the future. And she saw that there wasn't enough room."

He had everyone's attention.

"So, in that space, she wrote . . . an asterisk."

The room was quiet.

"She was going to write it all somewhere else on the form, where there was room."

"On the form, huh?" said Ham.

Risk shrugged back at him and said, "She thought so."

The room went quiet again, and there wasn't any shrieking from upstairs either.

Risk shrugged again and said, "So the story goes."

"And you got stuck with the name Risk?"

"Sissy, saying 'stuck' isn't very polite. You're a bad little girl."

Sophia grinned and hung her head.

"She didn't mean it that way, Risk. I think Risk is a good name."

Ham laughed and said, "Of course. You two are the Kildare Killers. Why the hell not?"

"Well, Mr. Ham Sledger," said Pauline. "Or should I just go ahead and call you Hamilton?"

"Hey. Not fucking funny."

"Relax," said Pauline. "It's a good name. I have kind of a fun name too."

Risk smiled and said, "Yeah. Tramp Pauline."

"Aren't we leaving someone out?" Marilyn said, her eyebrows up high as she looked at each of them.

"Oh," said Risk. "Yeah. The mountain lion. K Kat."

Ham said, "Let's not start naming all the dead fucking bats, too, alright?"

"Risk?" said Marilyn. "You've lived your whole life in this place? That's horrible."

"No. I left when I was little. I only came back when—"

"Uh, wait a second," said Sophia. "Just . . . no way. Sex and death? When you were—"

"No, Fia. Remember the lion?"

"Oh, yeah. Killing to eat is kind of like—"

Marilyn said, "You killed something? That's how you left?"

Risk blew out a deep sigh and looked around at all of them.

"Hey," said Ham, "don't fucking stop now. I've never heard any of this shit either."

"Alright. The short story. I got fed a drop of Zoojoose, changed into something, killed something, and ended up Topside."

Marilyn was shaking her head, and she said, "Who gave you the Zoojoose? What did you change into? What did you—"

"Short story, Mare, alright?"

"Oh. Okay. And you never came back until—"

"No. I've been back."

"Sex and death, though, right?"

"Yeah. It has to be."

"You always find someone to kill you during sex?"

"No, Fia. It—"

"Risk," said Ham, nodding and gesturing, "come on. This is one of those times."

"What times?"

"More words. Really, just fucking spill it out."

Risk laughed and said, "Alright."

Addressing Marilyn and Sophia, he said, "Getting out of here is easier. Lots of things here want—"

"People too," said Pauline. "Shit, I'm about ready to call it quits."

Risk pointed at her and said, "Not yet."

"Will you fucking let him finish?" said Ham.

"Fine."

"So, to get out of here, I just need a volunteer. We do it, and I . . ."

He looked at the twins staring at him and listening.

". . . kill myself. At the right time."

"Oh. Oh, my."

"Sheesh. What happens to the other person or thing?"

"They live Topside. For a while. Then, they're done. They died up there, remember?"

They nodded, but no one spoke.

"To come here is worse. I can't always find someone suicidal for me to kill. Sometimes. Not always. So, the same deal: I kill myself.

They come here with me and wish I'd killed them instead. They usually don't last."

"That's supremely fucked up," said Ham. "One more detail. Tell them."

"Alright. For everyone else, it's a one-way trip here. No going back unless they're with me. I'm, uh, different."

"Different how?" said Marilyn.

Risk looked down and said, "I don't know."

"Shit, that's crazy," said Pauline. "No wonder you'd never talk about it."

"Until they showed up," Ham said, pointing at the twins.

Pauline scoffed and said, "They didn't just show up, Ham."

"No. It was a goddamn sex and death orgy. Hey," he said, pointing at K Kat, "maybe it's because of her. That fucking lion."

The outer wall shook with the impact of something heavy and bulky slamming into it. Something that howled.

Ham grinned and said, "Not that fucking thing either, whatever the hell it is."

"I'll get it," Risk said as he began walking toward the door. "It's big. Could cause some damage."

Everyone noticed the claws that had already started to grow.

"Don't go," said Marilyn. "That was way bigger than those bats, I think."

"Sis is right. It can't get in, right? Why risk it?"

"That's funny, Sissy. It's a fair question too."

Risk was about to open the door, but he stopped and looked back at all of the concerned faces.

"I have to say it," he said, grinning. "You want me to."

"Say what?" said Pauline.

"I think I know," said Ham. "Fucking say it, Risk."

Risk nodded to each of them, then said, "Hey. It's my ass to risk."

He grinned and left before anyone could answer.

Sophia whispered, "Damn. Good one, Risk."

"Uh-huh. Yes, Sissy. Quite true too."

Chapter 13 – Damn World's Full of Surprises

"He can talk more when he wants to, Sissy."

Sophia didn't look up from the lace edging around the hem of her short dress as she gently pulled it down all around, hiding what she wore underneath it.

"He can be funny, too, Sis. 'His ass to risk.'"

"You know what his problem is?" said Ham.

They waited, then he said, "First, Pauline, can you guess what my problem might be?"

They stopped at the sound of a heavy body slamming into the wall outside, then a loud shriek.

Pauline said, "You don't know if that scream was from Risk or whatever else?"

"No, that's not a problem. I need some wine. I bet these killers do too."

Pauline scoffed and said, "While Risk is out there risking his—"

"Ass," Marilyn said with a giggle.

"He can handle it like no one else you fucking know. And we're all thirsty."

"Oh, right. Yeah, more for these two girls too. Could only help."

She stopped at the door to the kitchen when Sophia said, "Help with what?"

"Oh, shit, girls. All kinds of stuff. This damn world's full of surprises. That's all I meant. I'll be right back."

Something got slammed into the shutter again. One animal growled, then another. Then both.

The girls looked at Ham, concerned, and he only shrugged.

"Happens a lot. A fucking lot."

Marilyn said, "When he, um, is an animal, does he eat things like that, that he kills?"

"First," said Ham, "we don't know who will win. Second, we—"

"And you let him go out there anyway?" Sophia said, looking up from her dress.

Ham scoffed and said, "You want to try to stop him sometime? No. You sure fucking don't. Now, second, who knows about what he eats when he's like that? He might rip off a juicy chunk and swallow it real quick just for fun. Not tell anybody."

"Ooh, that kind of sounds good," said Marilyn.

"It does? Do you even know what the fuck that is out there?"

"No, and I don't care. It just sounds good. That whole ripping a juicy chunk part of it."

"Sis, you're losing your mind. You can't be that hungry."

Marilyn giggled, her stomach growled, then she said, "And we can't really be twins, Sissy. You're too young."

"I, uh, kind of am. Yeah."

Pauline walked in with her cardboard tray and five drinks, three on one side and two on the other.

"Here you go, Kildare Killers," she said and turned the tray to give them the two. "One young and one not as young."

"Guess which one you are, Sissy."

"I'm the youngest," she said without hesitation or a smile.

"Ham, guess which one."

He laughed and took the biggest glass from Pauline, which was really a jar.

"It's a good start anyway."

While the twins were sipping their drinks, and after Pauline had taken a separate seat with her own, Ham downed half of his.

"I'll tell you that name, if you want. While Risk is risking his ass."

"Damn asterisks, Sissy."

"That's funny, Sis. Yeah, Ham, tell us. What's the name?"

"Lucy Joosie. Because she's messed up from that goddamn Zoojoose shit."

"Ooh, yeah," said Sophia, "Risk must not like that name too much."

"His claws can be pretty goddamn sharp. Yeah."

"Hey, Ham," said Marilyn, "could that juice drug change—"

"Zoojoose. Zoo. You get that?"

"Oh, I do now. Oh my, yes. Zoo. Okay, can that change K Kat into a person?"

Sophia looked up first at her sister, then at Ham, who said, "You want to mess with the goddamn lion?"

"Oh, I was just wondering. I bet Sissy is too."

She elbowed Sophia, who then said, "Uh, yeah. That would be something."

"We'll never know," said Ham. "Nobody's got any of that shit anymore."

"What about Lucy—I mean, Risk's mother?"

"No, Sophia. All she has is a messed-up brain."

"That makes sense," said Marilyn. "Oh, what about this? If we had some, we could give it to Sissy, then she could change herself into a lion. Would that work?"

"Fuck, I don't know. If we had any. Maybe."

"Sissy, if we find some, we could—"

"Sis, I'd probably just be a baby lion, right?"

Marilyn stared at her sister for a few seconds, then said, "Oh, uh, yes. That's probably quite true, Sissy. A little one anyway. Maybe not a baby."

Sophia grinned back at her.

Marilyn said, "Aw, you feel like just a little baby, don't you?"

Sophia kept grinning and shrugged, then Pauline spoke.

"Don't let those drinks get warm," she said. "Come on. Drink up."

Marilyn giggled and said, "Um, because it's oil? It'll blow up?"

"You're a comedian," said Pauline. "No. It'll just pick up more fucking oil soot out of the air. Spoils the taste."

Marilyn's eyes got wide, and she finished it all. So did Sophia.

Ham pounded his empty jar onto the table and belched at Pauline, who scoffed and took it for a refill.

"Soot or no fucking soot, it still gets you drunk. Which I like. Oh, here's something fun: that fucking drug will—"

"Zoojoose!" said Sophia. And when they only stared at her, she said, "Just showing that I'm paying attention."

"You can still play with your new dress, Sissy."

"Okay."

She looked down at her lap and started flicking the lace hem around.

"Okay, what, Ham?"

"I've heard that that drug could make you change your sex, too, if you tried hard enough."

"He said 'hard,' Sissy," Marilyn said with a giggle.

"Funny, Sis."

"Intriguing, too, though."

"Good word. Keep them coming."

"And just like that, we're right back to 'hard.' But I don't know how anyone could keep that going."

Sophia snickered softly and said, "Yeah. Who wouldn't want an endless orgasm?"

"Sign me up for that, Sissy!"

"You two," said Pauline as she handed them fresh drinks. "I think you're feeling that crude wine. It'll get you rocking."

It sounded like a rock hit the shutter, then two things growled in sequence.

"What's taking him so long?"

Sophia looked up from her dress only long enough to say, "Maybe they're mating."

Marilyn elbowed her and said, "Good one, Sissy. Could be true too."

The door swung in with a brutal kick, and Risk stood there with blood on his hands and face, and he'd leaned a dripping portion of some beast up over one shoulder.

*　*　*

"Took long enough," Ham said with a grin, then he tipped back his drink again.

"Fine. The next monster is yours."

"Oh, uh, no thanks. Take all the fucking time you want."

Risk kicked the door closed behind him, propped the fleshy leg bone against the wall, and started cleaning up with a rag.

"Your drink's right there," Pauline said, tipping her head and sending her thick red mane swinging.

He nodded, then looked at the twins.

"You're both still drinking that stuff?"

Marilyn hiccupped and said, "What other stuff you got?"

He saw that her eyes were on the haunch near the door and laughed.

"Uh-uh. It's for the lion."

Her stomach growled, and Sophia said, "Sheesh, Sis. You've never been so hungry before."

"And you've never been so little, Sissy."

"Hmm."

"What was it?" said Ham.

"Something new. Mean."

"Goddamn radiation changes all the time. Always some new goddamn freak to deal with."

"Yeah."

"It didn't fuck with Ziggy, though, did it?"

"It tried. Half its head was burned."

"That's my Ziggy. This world's full of goddamn freaks. And they're not all such pleasant, sophisticated guys like me."

"Right, Ham."

K Kat somehow kicked the bat head, getting it rolling a few times, then began a slow padding toward Risk.

"Hey, lion," he said, then stooped down and held her head in both of his hands.

"You're hungry?" he said to her.

"Yes!" Marilyn answered.

Sophia elbowed her and said, "Sis, you can't be that hungry."

They both watched Risk tip his head, and K Kat began a series of low growls.

"Good," he said and patted her side. "I thought so."

She yawned, showing her teeth, then snapped her mouth closed.

When she'd finished, Risk nodded and looked their way again.

So did K Kat.

Chapter 14 – K Kat Isn't Just a Lion

"What the hell you doing with that lion?"

"Talking, Ham. Mostly listening."

"You took more of a beating out there than we thought. You must have hit your head a few times."

"Come drink your wine," said Pauline. "Leave that goddamn lion alone. All she wants is food."

"Me too," Marilyn said along with her stomach growling.

Risk stood and took a few steps closer to the couch, leaving K Kat behind him and beginning to gnaw on the fresh chunk of animal.

He stopped and placed his bloody hands on his hips.

His first gaze was at Ham, who only smirked up at him then took a deep drink from his jar.

Pauline smiled and brushed back her red hair, then held out his glass, which he took.

He studied Sophia next, and she didn't notice because she was fussing around with the hem of her dress, trying to keep it covering more of her thighs.

When he looked to Marilyn next, she only shrugged, then grinned.

"K Kat," he said, and everyone waited.

"Isn't just a lion."

"What the hell you talking about?" said Ham.

Pauline leaned and squinted at Risk's full glass.

"It isn't the wine. He hasn't touched it yet. Maybe he did fucking hit his head out there."

Sophia had started ignoring her dress and said, "She, um, she's someone else too?"

"Yes, Fia."

"Who?"

"I'll ask her, Mare."

He walked back toward K Kat to the sound of Ham and Pauline laughing softly, and with the twins watching him and the lion closely.

Risk stooped down and looked into the cat's eyes, her mouth still closed around a meaty bone.

He gently took it from her and set it on the floor.

She yapped a couple of times, then went silent with her head tipped and looking into his eyes.

"Good girl," he said as he rubbed around her neck with both hands.

Then, he turned toward the listening group.

"She said she's Kenzie too."

"Huh?" said Ham.

No one else spoke, and Risk stood to face them.

He pointed at the twins and said, "You wanted to name her Kenzie. Who's Kenzie?"

*   *   *

"Kenzie's a barmaid that we know," said Marilyn.

Sophia elbowed her and said, "She's an actress, Sis."

"Oh. Yes, that's true too."

"From Beverly Hills," said Risk.

"Yes. Oh my, we got into so much trouble with her."

"Like what, Mare?"

"Like too much to explain," said Sophia. "But she was with us when the house was burning, when we, uh, when you—"

"When you came to save us," said Marilyn.

"Yeah, like Sis said. But she got trapped by the fires. She was worried about the two lions because they were trapped for a while too."

"Yeah," said Risk, hanging his head. "There were two."

After a few seconds, Marilyn said, "She didn't leave you any choice, Risk. That other one."

He nodded but kept looking down.

"There were two before all that wild sex?" said Ham. "Sex with one of those lions?"

While Risk was nodding at him, Pauline said, "What happened to the other one? Fucking fire got it?"

"No," said Marilyn. "She attacked Risk. Risk didn't want to, but—"

"He killed her to protect us," said Sophia.

Pauline pointed at K Kat and said, "This one made it, though?"

Risk said, "She chose not to attack."

He focused on Marilyn and Sophia.

"That bomb. What was it?"

"Oh, that thing," said Marilyn. "Some kind of telepathy stuff. At least, that's what we were told."

"The Boss," said Sophia. "He said it was kind of experimental, though."

Risk looked down at the lion, who had resumed chewing on her bloody body part, then back up at the twins.

He pointed at K Kat and said, "She was scared."

Marilyn nodded.

He looked into Sophia's staring blue eyes.

"So was Kenzie?"

"Oh, yeah. Yep. And she said she loved those cats."

"She wanted to keep them," Marilyn added.

"And the cats. Did they like her too?"

Marilyn laughed and said, "Oh my goodness, yes. We set up this sweet little scene where both of them were trying to get her."

"To eat her, Sis."

"Hmm, that might have been someone else's goal, Sissy."

Sophia grinned and looked down at her dress.

"All of them were scared," Risk said.

Marilyn nodded.

"All of them wanted each other."

Sophia looked down quickly and said, "Yep. Yeah."

Risk said, "One lion survived."

Every eye in the room was on Risk.

"Kenzie survived too. When the telepathy bomb went—"

"Kaboom!" said Marilyn.

* * *

"I told you, Sissy. I knew Kenzie would get out of there somehow."

"Yeah, Sis, but as a lion? What the hell?"

Marilyn shook her head and looked again at Risk.

"Risk, Kenzie told you she's in there with the lion?"

"No. K Kat said she's there."

Sophia said, "Can we get her out?"

"Aw, you miss her, Sissy."

"Well, yeah. Of course. And shouldn't we get her back if we can?"

"Why, yes, Sissy. Of course."

Risk had walked over to the shutter and faced it, head tipped back and looking up.

"Hawken," he said.

"What about him?" said Ham.

Pauline said, "That hawk navigator of yours?"

Risk turned around and said, "Not just a hawk. Ken too."

"Oh," said Marilyn. "Ken was a friend. If we can get Kenzie back, maybe Ken can come back too?"

Risk ran his fingers through his hair, then let out a deep sigh.

"Ken got mutated," he said. "Probably not. I think that's a one-way street."

"Forever?" said Sophia.

He shrugged and looked down, then said, "He'll probably always be Hawken."

Risk continued.

"Dammit, we got distracted. Hawken might know. He's all over this place."

"He might. He fucking might," said Ham.

"He might know what?" said Pauline.

"Pay attention," said Ham. "Hot and Cold. Some fucking place called Hot and Cold."

He turned back to Risk and said, "Ask that bastard. I bet he knows something."

Risk turned back toward the shutter and said, "He's traveling. Past the city."

"Little freak is always flying around," said Ham.

Risk turned back around and shrugged again.

"Yeah. He's part hawk. Let's take your ship."

"Can't. Ziggy's down."

"Sick?"

"Out of gas. He needs to fucking recharge. Tomorrow, he'll be back up to fucking speed."

"Too late. We—"

"Hey," said Marilyn, "how can you tell time down here?"

Ham grinned at Risk for a second, then turned to her.

"We can't. We're just so fucking stupid that we keep talking like we can."

"Oh, I see. So, tomorrow means—"

Ham put his normal hand up to stop Risk from answering.

"Yeah. It means some other fucking time. Not fucking now."

Chapter 15 – Some Kind of She-Lion Crush

"Maybe you should go on foot. I'll go with you," said Ham, then he looked at Pauline. "Maybe the—um, Pauline will too."

"You're a funny fucker, Ham. You're always so fucking close to calling me a tramp. No. No fucking way am I walking through that goddamn city."

"What if the lights were on?"

"They're not, Ham. And even if they were, I'd just have a better view of all the death coming at me. You and Risk run along and have some fucking fun."

Ham looked at Marilyn and Sophia and said, "We could use some killers, you know. Interested?"

"Oh, um," said Marilyn, "Sissy and I, we, uh, we—"

"What Sis is saying is that she and I, we, together, as sisters, think that—"

"Nobody's going through the city."

They stopped their discussion and looked at Risk.

"You think I want that?"

"Nope," said Ham. "You're too fucking smart. Do you even know about every fucking freak disaster hiding down there?"

"No. No one does."

"Damn right. So, you're really going to fuck and die and hope that you end up in that hawk boy's basket?"

"No other option."

"You could try riding a bat."

"Sure, Ham."

Risk gave a slight grin for Ham to see, and Ham started smiling and pointed at him.

"You like that you have no other option."

Risk shrugged, gave him a grin, then turned toward the twins.

"Mare. Fia. Your last chance."

Sophia whispered to her sister, "Sis, maybe we should help because—"

"Hush," Marilyn whispered with a giggle, "you're too little to even think about sex. You're just a little baby."

* * *

"Alright."

He looked again at Ham and Pauline, and both of them only shook their heads. So, he half turned himself to look at the mountain lion, who was contentedly digging sharp teeth through flesh and into bone.

"Oh, you can't be serious," said Ham.

Risk pointed at Sophia and said, "It was Fia's idea."

"Bad little girl," Marilyn whispered to her sister.

"Funny," said Pauline. "That's a big goddamn pussy cat."

Ham watched Risk walking toward K Kat and said, "He's fucking serious. He's going to screw the goddamn lion."

Risk leaned over toward the lion and said, "No, keep eating."

She did, but she turned her eyes up toward him.

"Want to go for a ride?"

Ham snorted out a laugh and said, "Damn lion doesn't know just what kind of ride!"

"Wait," said Marilyn. "I want to hear her answer."

"Will she sound like Kenzie, Sis?"

"Who knows? Maybe."

They watched the scene near the door to Ham's house.

K Kat set down her feast and stood, her eyes level with Risk's.

Then, she nodded her head so slightly that no one could be sure.

"I saw her nod," said Sophia. "You see that, Sis?"

"I think I did. Yes. That was the Kenzie part of the lion, I bet."

"You two," said Pauline.

"Wait a second, Sissy. Kenzie's got some kind of she-lion crush on Risk?"

"Looks that way. Yep. Remember at Dayzee's?"

"Oh, I get it. Maybe that's why this lion didn't attack. Because she was kind of Kenzie too."

"Yeah. And she was already crushing on Risk."

"Hey," said Pauline. "Pay attention."

Risk patted K Kat on her side and said, "Thanks. Good girl."

He stood and looked at the staring faces, then focused on the girls. "You two can watch."

* * *

"What about us?" said Pauline.

"Yeah. I want a seat at that fucking spectacle. Literally."

"No fucking."

"Oh, that's right," said Ham. "Just bloody feeding time. Who's eating who?"

"Sis," Sophia whispered, "I'm so damn itchy."

"Me too, Sissy, but I'm not biting a lion."

"Even if she's Kenzie?"

"Sissy, Kenzie wouldn't bite back!"

"Sure she would. You'd like it too."

"Quiet, you two," said Pauline. "It's show time. Drink your goddamn drinks."

"Good plan," said Ham, and he joined the twins with his own drink.

Risk looked over at all of them and said, "I'll have to change."

Pauline said, "Since when do you need the right goddamn clothes?"

"No. Not that."

137

"Oh, right," said Ham. "Something for that lion to chomp down on."

"Why?" said Marilyn. "She gave you some good bites before, back when—"

"When we almost burned up. Back at Dayzee's."

"Yes, Sissy is correct."

Risk looked into the eyes of each of the twins and said, "There was plenty of sex then. No sex this time."

"Oh, okay. That makes sense."

"Carry on," said Ham. "Do your fucking or biting or chewing or whatever the fuck."

K Kat had been ignoring the chunk of animal that she'd been chewing and sniffed all around in Risk's direction. He turned back to her, then lay down near her.

He turned his head to look at the crowd, then his face transformed into that of a wolf showing its fangs.

Everyone gasped, and Ham said, "Fuck. Lions don't eat wolves."

Risk changed back to himself and said, "Just kidding."

"Oh my, what a relief," said Marilyn. "So, what are you really—"

He went blurry for part of a second, then a tiny lamb lay there looking first at them, then at K Kat. He lay on his back, kicking around his hooves and crying out softly.

"Uh-oh, Sis. Get ready for it."

"I don't even want to watch, Sissy."

"Don't, then," said Ham. "I sure as fuck will."

"Just one thing eating another," Pauline said, softly chuckling, then she held Sophia's gaze to finish. "Could happen to anyone, especially in this goddamn burning corner of the world."

Sophia only squinted back at her and shook her head, then focused again on the lamb and lion.

K Kat froze, her eyes big as she watched the lamb within biting distance. A second later, she pounced, closing her jaws on the neck of the shrieking lamb.

The lion lifted up the lamb and shook it around, spreading its blood all over its neat white coat. K Kat rushed it into the floor but never let it go as all four legs kicked.

"Oh my, Sissy."

"That's Kenzie? No way."

"More lion than barmaid," said Pauline. "Apparently."

Ham laughed and said, "I heard she was an actress."

Marilyn and Sophia ignored the bloody lamb for just a second to stare at each other, their eyes wide.

When they looked back again at K Kat and Risk, their eyes didn't relax and they didn't speak. No one did.

Still biting into the lamb's neck, the lion's hind quarters began to sink into the rough wood floor.

K Kat whipped around to look, then focused again on her kill.

More of her body sank until she was in up to her chest. She pointed her snout up as high as she could, holding the lamb up and causing the blood to flow down onto the short brown fur of her head in wide streams.

She snorted and gave the lamb another hard shake, and it went limp.

The floor claimed K Kat's chest, and she kept sinking.

Her eyes darted everywhere until the floor covered them and most of the lamb hanging in her jaws like a bloody white rag.

She let out one loud snort before all of her snout vanished, and the only parts of them still visible were a few of her whiskers and the head of the lamb, its eyes staring and lifeless.

Then, it all sank into oblivion, leaving the room dead silent.

A quiet half of a minute passed.

"And there's no fucking basement right there," said Ham. "Weird shit."

Chapter 16 – Sis, Play Along, Alright?

"I didn't bring a blanket."

Risk lay entwined with K Kat in a familiar wicker basket with a familiar hawk-like face looking down at him from beside a large iron pot.

"I threw that over the two of you," said Hawken.

Risk sat up, nudging aside the sleeping lion, then stood and looked over the side. They were floating along the coastline where dark city met burning sea but far enough inland to not be consumed by erupting flames.

"I wasn't cold."

"Not here, no. Lots of fire."

"Why the blanket, then?"

"She was still kissing you. It was awkward."

Risk scoffed and looked down at a lion lying on her side, licking her chops then stretching out her limbs, which were mostly still covered by Hawken's blanket.

"She's a good cat."

"Hey," said the hawk boy, "don't kiss and tell."

"Funny. Why are we here?"

"I was going to make a stop at the Pitching Point."

"Criminal or far-gone?"

"Way far-gone. No butcher can fix this one."

"Two heads again?"

"Three."

"Radiation's worse?"

"New mix of it. Record levels too."

"Huh. Damn reactor."

Risk sat back down, and K Kat flopped over to lay her head on his lap.

"Tourist run," said Hawken. "Wants to see the catapult from up above."

"You're sailing out over the fire?"

"No. Too hot to stay low enough. We'll hug the coast. What brings you here? And I don't mean the sex."

"It wasn't. It was just a kill."

"I hope," he said and cackled up into the balloon.

"A bat confessed something."

"Voluntarily?"

Risk looked up and held Hawken's gaze until he said, "Right."

"He said there's a new madman. A leader."

"I heard that."

"Bat said he has a plan."

"Oh. A plan. What kind?"

Risk wiggled out from under the lion's head and stood, his hands on the top rail as he looked out at a dark city with pinpoints of flickering light abutting a sea of nothing but fire.

He pointed toward the sprawling urban landscape in the grip of the endless night underground.

"A plan to kill all. Everything not human."

"I'm part human," said Hawken.

Risk shrugged and said, "Then, he'll part kill you."

"Not even part good. You believe he can do it?"

"Who knows? Maybe."

"How?"

"I don't know. I need to find him."

"Where?"

"Hot and Cold."

"That's a name?"

"No. A place. You know it?"

Risk looked up and waited, watching the hawk boy look all around at the city on the edge of fire.

"Plan to kill all? Like me?"

Risk laughed once and said, "Not all are as good-looking."

Hawken still looked around quickly, his eyes darting from one location to the next before he had time to focus.

"I can't stay out here, then."

"Hot and Cold. You know it?"

"The plan might work."

"Maybe, sure. Where's Hot and Cold?"

His hawk face fixed on a destination beyond the dark city, toward a house high up on a mountain that was buried deep in the thick night.

"Ham's mountain," Hawken said, pointing.

"The madman isn't there."

"No. But I should be."

"Oh. Yeah. Safe there?"

"Yeah. Maybe."

"What about Hot and Cold?"

"I'll tell you there. When I'm there."

Risk nodded to his navigator, then nudged the lion, rousting her from her lingering sleep.

"We're flying back to Ham's," he told her. "Keep those teeth sharp."

She yawned, then panted, looking up into his eyes.

"Good lion."

Looking up again at Hawken, Risk said, "What about your tourist?"

"Fuck that. He can watch from the ground like everyone else."

* * *

"What the fuck did we just see?" said Ham. "That's how that shit works?"

Pauline, shaking her head, said, "I've never seen it from the outside. That's fucking bizarre."

"You've always been on the 'getting fucked' side of it?"

"Yeah, Ham. It isn't all that bad from that side either."

"You two," Ham said, pointing at the twins. "You only did it that one time, right?"

"Yes," said Marilyn, "and it was two for the price of one."

"Good one, Sis."

Ham flipped them off, then added two fingers.

"Three for one. Don't forget the fucking lion."

"That's fucking actress Kenzie to you, Mister," Marilyn said with a giggle.

"Right. Yeah. What the hell was I thinking?"

"Too weird for me," said Pauline. "You girls, wasn't that the weirdest fucking thing you ever saw?"

"Not me," said Sophia. "Headless guys looking for head. That was kind of weird."

"Sissy's right. We've seen all kinds of creepy things. But that, actually, I, um, kind of liked."

"You what?" said Ham. "What the fuck exactly did you like? Seeing them both sink into a goddamn basement I don't have?"

Marilyn's smile faded and she said, "Um, just the way that lion, she, uh, kind of took what she wanted."

"You mean, she bit the fuck out of it," said Pauline.

"Yes, she did!"

"And your thought was . . . what? Cool?"

"I don't know, Ham. It was just, um, something. Sissy, wasn't K Kat something, the way she dug those teeth into—"

"Sis, I think I liked that little lamb that used to be Risk. Oh, maybe it's Risk again? If it worked?"

"If not, it's just a bloody little meal right now, wherever they are."

"Not in the basement," said Pauline.

Ham pointed at her and said, "Exactly."

"But that lamb was so cute," said Sophia. "Like a little baby."

"Until he got bit in two."

Ham nodded, listening to them, but he was mostly just looking at their curves, one of them in tight jeans and the other with the tiniest bit of lace as a boundary to nothing but bare legs.

Sophia noticed.

"Sis," Sophia whispered softly, "play along, alright? Let's mess with that big Ham guy."

"I'm in, Sissy. You lead, and I'll follow."

Sophia coughed a few times, glanced in Ham's direction, then continued.

"Well, it was more of a nibble, Sis. And she was still cute. Maybe even cuter because she was getting nibbled."

"The little lamb was a she, Sissy?"

"Uh-huh. Yep. Just a cute little baby lambie."

Ham and Pauline were taking regular drinks from his big jar and her glass, looking from one Kildare Killer to the other, who were sitting close and squeezed together on the couch.

"You're cute, Sissy," Marilyn said with a grin. "Maybe you'd be cuter if something horrible nibbled on you?"

"Hey, K Kat isn't horrible. She's damn good-looking herself, you know. For a lion, I mean."

"Oh, and that makes it all okay?"

"Well, if you're going to get consumed by something, it might as well be a fine-looking something. Don't you think?"

"That's exactly right," said Pauline. "What you just fucking said."

Sophia stared at her with her eyebrows up, then looked back at her sister sitting up against her.

"Anyway, I don't think I'd mind if the one doing the nibbling was cute and hot. It'd be kind of flattering."

"Sissy, I've been told that I'm cute and hot, so—"

"You are, Sis. Oh, yeah."

"—so maybe I should try taking a little nibble on you. Let's see if you feel even cuter then."

"What in fuck is wrong with them?" Ham said softly.

Pauline never stopped watching them, and she didn't hide her grin.

"Oh, they're just having fun. Maybe it's the wine. It's probably the wine."

"I already feel very cute and pretty with my new dress."

"You look so delicious in that dress. It makes me want to bite you."

Sophia smiled, looked away, and tipped her head, exposing more of her neck.

"Oh, hmm, maybe I'd love to feel even cuter and prettier."

She gave her black hair a few flings, clearing her neck more.

"I think you're teasing me," said Marilyn, "so that I'll have to bite you."

"Hmm. I am. Because I'm sure I'd feel even cuter and prettier. That's all I want."

Marilyn started leaning toward her, her mouth open and her lips back to expose her teeth.

"I might not be able to stop at just a nibble, Sissy. Oh, no."

"I might not be able to stop you."

Marilyn slipped her arm around her sister's waist.

"You won't *want* to stop me."

"Mm, I think you're right. One nibble might not be enough."

Sophia paused for a couple of deep breaths, each giving her breasts a chance to break loose from the frilly lace. They were getting close.

She tipped her head a little more and said, "That little lamb wasn't wearing anything, was she?"

"Oh, no, not a thing," Marilyn said, her breath hot on the soft skin of Sophia's neck. "We should get you out of that pretty little dress, shouldn't we?"

"Mm-hmm."

"Would you like to be my pretty little thing that's not wearing a dress?"

"Mm, yeah, I'd sure be your pretty little thing, then, with no dress to cover me."

"You'd be just like that lamb. Just a pretty little thing, not covering all of that soft, smooth skin."

"I'd be nothing but soft, smooth skin everywhere. Helpless."

"Mm-hmm, just helpless, waiting for me to take that first, tasty little—"

"Hey!" Ham yelled as he got out of his chair to stand in front of the twin girls thinking they might be a lion and a lamb.

They didn't stop, and Marilyn was getting close to the first tiny nibble on the soft skin of Sophia's neck.

"Mm," said Marilyn, "so soft and tender. One little bite, then we'll get you undressed, okay?"

"Okay. You're forcing me?"

"Mm-hmm. Oh, yeah."

Ham shook his head and pointed, then turned to make sure that Pauline saw too: each of them was caressing the other's thigh, Marilyn's wrapped in tight blue denim, and Sophia's bare below the hem of her very short and lacy dress.

"Damn wine," Pauline said with a snort.

"Oh, no fucking way," Ham said, then he pushed them apart enough that he could turn around and wedge himself in to sit between them.

He gave Pauline a frown and a shrug, then turned toward Marilyn.

He flinched at seeing that she was close to biting his neck, so he pushed against her forehead until she was sitting up straight.

She only giggled softly and stared at his neck.

He felt a hand on his thigh, looked down, and saw Sophia gently touching his leg. A look higher showed that she'd kept her head tipped, offering him her neck.

When Pauline said, "Eh, they're from Beverly Hills," he turned his head to hold her gaze.

She said, "They probably do this kind of shit all the time there."

He pried himself loose and began walking away from them, shaking his head at the sight.

"Maybe it's the damn wine?" he said.

"No way, Ham. I'm sure it's not the wine."

*　*　*

"Do you like them?"

"Who, Hawken?"

"Those girls that you screwed to get here."

"Hey, they called me."

"How?"

Risk said, "It must have been with sex and death."

"Who died?"

"I never asked."

They sailed in silence for a few seconds, passing a thin column of smoke as it sought out the ceiling high above them.

"Which one?"

"Huh?"

"If you had to choose."

Risk scoffed and said, "They're twins."

"Oh. That's right. So, either one."

"Or both."

"Both," said Hawken. "Yes. They've seen you shift?"

"Yeah. They know my mother's a shifter."

"She's still chained up in Ham's attic?"

"Something like that."

"What are the twins doing now?"

"Probably sitting somewhere, bored."

"Yeah."

A loud thunk got Risk to look up at the arrow that was stuck in Hawken's platform.

"Arrows, Risk!"

"Take her up. Up!"

While Hawken was sending flames into the balloon and getting it to lurch upward, another arrow pierced the basket's wall, near K Kat.

"Not the fucking cat," he said, then reached over, pulled it out, and sent it downward, point first.

"Fuckers."

"Who's shooting?"

"Does it matter?"

"If it's the madman, then he—"

"He won't use arrows. Not for his plan. Alright, we're high enough."

"I'll keep us up here, then. Let's go wake up those bored twins."

"Yeah. Okay."

*　*　*

"Oh, Sissy, what was that all about?" Marilyn whispered.

"Sis, I told you: we were messing with that Ham character, right?"

Marilyn shook her head a few times, then blinked even more times.

"Okay, sure, but I don't know, Sissy. I almost bit you!"

Sophia nodded and said, "Oh, yeah, that sure did get carried away. I'm sure I would have loved it, though."

Marilyn giggled a few times and said, "And you would have felt even prettier?"

"I'm sure of it. Don't ask me why, though."

"I won't."

"Stop whispering over there. You two just need some more crude wine," said Pauline. "I'll get it."

She got up but stopped her jaunt to the kitchen when Ham said, "Maybe there's something wrong with that wine?"

"How the fuck do you feel, Ham?"

"Like I'm getting drunk. Why?"

"Sounds about normal to me."

"I guess you're right. Hey, a refill for me too."

Pauline gave him a friendly sneer and said, "Is that it? Anyone else?"

"Juicy Lucy," Marilyn said, then giggled.

"Sis, it's Lucy Joosie, and you'd better not say that when Risk's around."

"I won't, Sissy. I'll have my mouth full. Of your neck."

"Is that juicy, too, Sis?"

"Mm-hmm. Oh, yeah. Not just your neck," she said, then giggled.

"There they fucking go again," said Ham. "Better get that wine already, Pauline."

"It's on its way. I'm sure it'll help."

She slipped out of sight into the kitchen, and Ham turned when the twins kept talking to each other.

"You know what else would help, Sissy?"

"What?"

"If you had a braid. Didn't we plan to give you one before?"

"I think so. Sure. Oh, I remember. You said two braids."

"Sissy, I'm getting too drunk. I'd never get them the same, and you'd be out of balance."

"You'd have to tie me to something, somehow, so I don't fall over?"

"Hmm, or get away."

"Funny, Sis. Probably true, too, though, like you always say. How about just one, then?"

She pointed at Marilyn's lap.

"May I?"

Marilyn laughed softly and said, "Why, yes. You need to sit right here on my lap."

"Okay."

"Like a good little girl."

"You're funny, Sis."

Sophia smiled as she stood, then sat herself down on Marilyn's lap, with the help of two hands on her hips, gently guiding her to find just the right place.

* * *

Hawken tended the fire in the heavy iron pot, feeding hot air into a giant balloon as it floated over the dark city. In the suspended basket, Risk sat with K Kat, rubbing her ears, sometimes telling her that she was a good girl.

"Did you feel that?" Hawken whispered down to the passengers. "That wasn't from you?"

"No. Something tipped the basket."

Risk eased the slumbering lion completely off of him, then stood and held the rail as he looked over the side.

"Be careful," said Hawken.

"Helpful."

Looking up but still leaning out over the landscape, Risk said, "Nothing. Couldn't be wind. Maybe—"

A large, scaly hand got hold of his throat and tried to yank him up and out of the basket. But he held on with one hand as he grabbed at the thing's wrist.

"Hey, Risk! Watch out!"

Risk jerked the hand off of his neck, dragging sharp claws across his skin and leaving thin red lines that quickly dripped and merged.

After one quick laugh, he said, "Good plan, Hawken."

The thing sent another hand up, and that one found Risk's throat too. But by then, K Kat was standing beside him, and she roared and bit through the limb.

She remained standing next to Risk, a dripping severed hand in her mouth.

"Good girl!"

She spat it over the side while Risk started to lift the offensive thing up. But that only caused it to spread magnificent black wings that began to flap and snap and shake around the basket and the balloon.

Hawken screeched, high above and fighting to keep the vessel steady.

"Risk! Kill it!"

Risk glanced at K Kat quickly, and she seemed to laugh.

"Another good plan," he called up to the half-hawk navigator.

He finally raised the beast high enough to see its face, something part bat, part snake, and part human.

"That thing's ugly, Risk!"

K Kat roared out a low laugh, but Risk didn't have time to join her. He hurried to hold it by its throat, then punched it repeatedly with his still human fist. Multicolored blood, thick like paste, splashed out and around and rained down onto the city.

And still it flapped its wings madly, gurgling through a squeezed throat as Risk pummeled it nonstop and K Kat bit at it and swiped her claws at it whenever it swayed close enough.

"It's enough," said Hawken, tugging on ropes while shooting hot blasts from the teapot's spout. "Let it go before it sinks us!"

Risk yelled, "Fine!" then gave it one more solid punch, causing its eyes to roll up, then close.

But still, he held it out from the balloon, and its wings, though more slowly, kept unsettling their craft.

"Let it go, Risk!"

"In a second."

He pulled the beast in closer, and K Kat got her jaws open wide and sank all of her fangs into its head. Then, she growled and wrestled it from side to side to the sound of Risk laughing and Hawken screaming.

"Let it go! We're sinking!"

"Sure."

K Kat let out one last vindictive growl then released the thing's mutilated skull, leaving its thick black skin shredded and flapping loosely all around.

To the lion, he said, "Had enough?"

She barked.

"That's different. Alright."

Risk released it, and it quickly sank into the night below the basket.

"Kill the next one quicker!" yelled Hawken.

Risk looked up and said, "Lions need fun too."

"Any idea what the hell that thing is?"

Risk laughed once to the mountain lion and kept looking into her eyes.

"Yeah, Hawken. That thing is dead."

"If another one—"

The basket went dark, and Risk and K Kat both looked up, but it didn't help—they saw nothing but blackness.

"Hawken," Risk said quietly as they began to slowly sink. "How many?"

"Two," said the hawk, almost whispering. "Toward the sea."

Risk looked over the rail, and the mountain lion joined him. Between them and the relative brightness of the flaming sea, two round black dots were moving from left to right.

"Can they see us?"

Hawken said, "Not now. We're sailing dark."

"How long?"

"They're slow. Too long. I'll turn us and point the fire away from them."

"Good."

Risk watched only faint light and soft whooshing as Hawken pointed the teapot spout and gave it brief puffs, and the vessel began to rotate.

After a few seconds, he saw Hawken lift the lid on the hot iron pot, its opening facing away from the other two balloons and sending up minimal heat.

"We're holding," Hawken said.

"Who?"

"Don't know. Not a friend."

"Never is, Hawken."

"Soon, we'll go up."

"Good. You're a good navigator."

He looked up, but there wasn't enough light to see Hawken or anything else. Just an occasional escape of hot gas to keep the balloon inflated.

Chapter 17 – Whatever It Is, Don't

"Give it some fire," Risk called up to Hawken.

"I'm already higher than I want to be!"

"Crashing won't help you. Let's go up."

Hawken grumbled and stoked the fire, sending clouds of burning oil fumes up into the balloon, which groaned comfortably as it stretched and welcomed it like a hot meal.

Risk and K Kat stood side by side, holding the basket's rim with both hands and both front paws, and watched the darkness of the side of Ham's mountain approaching. Boulders were poised to tumble down toward the flatlands bordering the city, and smaller jagged rocks filled in the shadowy spaces between them. Any one of them could easily bite into the soft fabric of the balloon.

Risk looked higher along the steep slope and noticed several small fires scattered among the rough, steep terrain just below Ham's compound.

"What is Ham doing with fires? Signals?"

"I don't know, Hawken. Let's go closer."

"Too close already."

Risk pointed, drawing the eyes of both a lion and a hawk boy to one particular fire.

"Closer. Check that one."

"I don't like it."

Hawken gave the spout a blast, swaying the basket toward the mountainside and taking the balloon with it.

Risk said, "That one that's moving."

"Flames always—"

"No. It's more than just flames."

"No closer, Risk. Even higher is bad. There are always bats up there."

"Still. Take us up."

"Alright. Don't like it, though."

"There's wine at Ham's place."

Hawken scoffed, sending a few fine gray feathers floating behind the rising vehicle.

"Crude wine. Sure."

"It works."

"Yes. Alright, then. We go up."

Risk and K Kat watched the few fires close enough as the basket rose a safe distance from the jagged rocks.

"There's food too," said Risk.

"What kind?"

"You know what kind. The stored stuff is running out."

Hawken chattered out a nervous laugh.

"Say it anyway."

"Alright. Cooked bat."

Hawken scoffed and said, "Cooked, at least."

"It won't kill you."

At hearing nothing after a few seconds, Risk and the lion looked up and saw Hawken looking down.

He said, "Sure about that?"

Risk grinned and looked forward and a second later, so did K Kat.

"No. I'm not sure."

A few seconds passed.

"Don't tell the girls, Hawken."

More than a few seconds passed, then Risk heard, "Sure would like to meet a hawk girl."

Risk looked up again and said, "Yeah. You will. First, clear the fence."

Hawken blasted more fire into the cavernous balloon, and the basket rose higher than the thick metal fencing, then passed over it. He gave the spout a few brief toots, and their craft cleared the sharp points of the fencing and hovered over the patio, almost brushing against Ham's balloon.

"More fires," said Hawken.

"Makes sense now."

"Bats. Burning bats."

"Yeah."

Hawken began settling the basket into place near the mooring hooks.

Risk said, "No one messes with Ziggy."

*   *   *

"Careful," Risk said as Hawken gently maneuvered the balloon to set the basket between several smoldering fires on the patio.

From high above, Hawken laughed and said, "You did say cooked bats. Those are cooked."

"Yeah. I mean in a kitchen."

"I'll wait for that."

"Ziggy isn't a good enough chef for you?"

"Eh. Always well done."

"Yeah."

K Kat jumped over the rail and landed silently in a crouch. Then, she stood and arched her back in a casual stretch before padding over to the nearest smoking bat.

"The lion won't care."

"Tie us down?"

"Sure," Risk said, then jumped onto the patio too.

He fed out a thick, oily rope and looped it around one of the iron hooks embedded in the stone.

"Hang on," he said, then went and repeated that on the other side.

"Alright. We're good. Tighten it up."

Hawken stoked the fires, groaning the balloon out and adding tension to all of the ropes and cables.

Risk leaned against the basket and looked up, listening to the conversation above and the occasional snapping of a bat bone below, mixed with a few impatient yips from whiskers getting singed.

"Ziggy," said Hawken, "you cooked them."

"Damn right."

Hawken laughed and said, "Teach me that sometime."

"Huh," said Ziggy. "Try eating some spicy food."

"You're hilarious."

He looked down at Risk and said, "I'll keep the balloon up."

Risk didn't laugh when he said, "You'll have to settle for that."

Hawken sighed, then said, "Damn. Yeah. No hawk girls."

"Don't give up hope. The radiation never stops."

"Good. And new mutants are being born every day?"

"Yeah."

*   *   *

Risk turned and leaned his back into the basket, looking at the heavy front door to Ham's home. He glanced at K Kat, who was still dodging flames and ripping at a bat carcass, then focused again on the door.

Just staring and scratching his chin.

"Whatever it is, don't," said Hawken.

Risk tipped his head back, gave the hawk boy a grin, then looked at the front door again.

"I'm doing it."

"Don't. Doing what?"

"I'll pound on the shutter."

"Like a goddamn bat?"

"Yeah, Hawken. For fun."

He looked up again, waiting for the navigator's opinion.

"Fun to get hit with that mutant hammer of Ham's?"

Risk shrugged and looked at the shuttered window near the front door.

"Alright. That wouldn't be fun."

"No. Hey," said Hawken, "is that why he goes by Ham?"

Without looking up, Risk said, "His name is Hamilton."

"Oh. Alright, that's just weird."

"Yeah," said Risk. "Before."

"Before his hand. Alright."

A few seconds passed with Ziggy sometimes scoffing and K Kat almost constantly growling and ripping at burnt bat flesh.

Risk said, "I'm doing it. Hey, it's my ass to risk," then looked up.

Hawken stared down with no change in his hawk face's expression.

"Not funny?"

The hawk navigator shook his head.

Risk sighed and looked away from the window and toward the door.

"Right. You don't know my story."

"Tell me sometime."

"Sure."

"Front door is good, right, Risk?"

"Yeah. Alright."

Chapter 18 – That's a Zoojoose Brain

"You can knock," Risk said.

He looked down, and K Kat looked up. She tipped her head, but she didn't knock.

"You ate enough bat. Go ahead."

She snorted softly, rose up onto her back legs, then scratched at the door.

"No. Try knocking."

She growled low and briefly, then pounded a heavy paw on the door several times. A few seconds passed.

"Down. Or you'll fall in."

She dropped down to all four paws.

They listened to bolts unbolting and drawbars drawing back.

The door swung in, and Ham looked out.

Then, he belched.

"Risk. Figured. Bats don't fucking knock."

"Ham. Only on the shutters."

"When they're ready to fucking die. Yeah."

"We're back."

"We?"

He looked down.

"Oh, yeah. The lion. The lamb killer. Alright, get inside, then."

Behind Risk, Ham eventually got the door secured again after stopping a few times to sip the drink he still held.

"Mission accomplished?" Pauline said as Risk and K Kat walked into the room.

"Yeah. Sort of. Hawken's staying out there."

He focused on the twins while Pauline was saying, "I'll get you some crude. Be right back."

She left, and Risk looked from one twin to the other, then back again.

Marilyn still wore Pauline's tight blue jeans and a clean white blouse. And the tray on her lap was empty.

Sophia still wore her short dress and fussed with the lace. But he saw that she also had a single thick black braid.

"Huh."

Sophia downed the last of her wine, belched softly, then giggled.

"Sissy, that's not very grown-up."

"Uh . . . no."

Risk said, "What did I miss?"

Ham had joined them and sank into an overstuffed chair.

"Nothing. No fucking attacks while you were gone."

He pointed at Marilyn and said, "Except from that one," and waited for Risk to look where he was pointing.

"She attacked that one," he said, pointing at Sophia, and he waited again for Risk to look.

He did look at Sophia, then he looked at Marilyn, then at the ceiling.

He let out a deep sigh, then said, "Names, Ham. Try that."

Ham belched again and said, "Marilyn attacked Sophia. Wanted to bite her."

When Marilyn giggled and said, "It's her dress's fault," Risk leveled his gaze at her.

Sophia bounced her eyebrows once and said, "It's a little-girl dress. It's pretty. Can't blame Sis."

Pauline walked in with his drink.

"How much wine are you feeding them?"

"As much as they want, Risk. They're adults. They can—"

"Maybe not Sissy. She's just little."

The twins both giggled.

While Risk was staring from one to the other, and while they smiled up at him, Ham said, "Uh, yeah. So, Risk, you found that hawk character?"

"Yeah. Perfect shot."

"That horrible lion didn't bite the little lamb in two?" said Marilyn.

"No. Killed it, though."

"Maybe the lamb would like to be bit in two?" said Sophia.

Risk turned his squinting eyes to Sophia and left them there until she lost her smile.

Marilyn leaned toward her sister and whispered, "Sissy, maybe we should give that game a rest."

"Okay. But I'm still keeping the dress."

"Oh, I insist. Yes."

They both looked up at Risk again.

"So," said Ham, "what's the story? Did Hawken know anything about Hot and Cold?"

"He said he did."

Ham waited, didn't see any more detail coming, then said, "Well? Where the fuck is it?"

"He wouldn't say. Not until he was safe here."

"It's the safest place. Uh, safe from what?"

"The plan to kill everything not human."

"Could be a problem for a guy like me," said Ham.

He held up his massive hand and balled it into a killing hammer.

"I'll need this."

Pauline said, "Who's worried? Not me. I'm human."

Risk nodded, then looked at the twins. Sophia had gone back to smoothing her lacy hem back and forth, and Marilyn was dragging a manicured finger around on the tray, catching bits of gristle and juice.

They looked up, saw him waiting, then looked at each other.

"Um," said Marilyn, "No worries here."

After a few seconds of silence, she elbowed her sister, who looked up from her new favorite pastime.

"Uh, yeah. Me too. Besides, we're killers."

"The Kildare Killers," Marilyn said with a pleasant smile.

Risk let a deep breath seep out slowly.

"So?" said Ham. "He's here now, right?"

"Outside."

A few seconds passed quietly before Ham said, "Fuck, it's like pulling bones out of a bat one at a time."

"Sounds kind of yummy, Sissy."

"Sheesh."

Risk grinned and said, "I'll go ask him."

He walked over, pried open the heavy shutter, and leaned out.

"Hawken. Where's the place? Where's Hot and Cold?"

He tipped his head, trying to hear the reply, and all anyone inside heard was muffled chattering.

"What?"

More chatter, which stopped when Risk waved his hand around outside.

"Can't hear you. Come inside."

He slammed the shutter and blocked out laughter that came from Hawken and the cussing from Ziggy.

* * *

"I'll get it," Pauline said at the sound of knocking.

She unbolted everything, then opened it to reveal Hawken, who only gave her a stare with his red eyes.

"I didn't think you were that tall," she said.

"I'm not a boy. Kind of a hawk, though."

"Well, fine by me. Come on in."

He walked in, and Sophia said softly to her sister, "I thought he'd be just little, too, Sis."

Marilyn giggled and said, "Oh, like you, Sissy?"

When she didn't hear a reply, she turned to see. Sophia was only nodding quietly and still watching Hawken.

"Hmm."

"Thanks for letting me stay here, Ham."

"You're welcome. There's really nowhere else to fucking hide."

He approached one of the other upholstered chairs, his feet, hidden in wraps of burlap, scuffing across the wood floor. While walking, he tightened up the gloves covering each of his hands.

At the chair, he hopped and spun to land sitting with his knees pulled close. He tipped his head down to peck a few times around his chest, sometimes tugging at the black fabric.

Everyone watched in silence until he looked back up at Risk.

Ham said, "Are we fucking ready?"

Hawken trained his sharp eyes on him and said, "Yes. Hamilton."

Ham turned to Risk and said, "What the fuck? You weren't supposed to ever—"

Risk laughed and held up a hand, which was enough to cut him off.

"Fuck. Well, it is my fucking name."

Risk, still grinning, looked at Hawken and said, "Alright. Hot and Cold."

"Easy," he said. "At the reactor."

"Oh, fuck yeah," said Ham. "We should have thought of that. Cooling down the fucking steam."

Risk scoffed and said, "When it's running."

"Yeah," said Pauline. "Would be nice to have some fucking electricity. Hawken, you want a drink?"

"Yeah. Thanks."

Risk said to Hawken, "I'll need your balloon."

"Which means you'll need me?"

"Yeah."

"You can't get near that place with the balloon. They'll shoot it down too easy."

"Not going there. Just down the mountain."

"To the city, Risk?"

"Yeah."

"I'll drop you and leave. Sure."

"No. Stay over us."

"To get you the fuck out?"

"Yeah, Hawken."

"No, Risk. No city work for me."

"We'll be quick. Then, you hide. Here, at Ham's."

"I hide here now. How about that?"

"The plan is to kill you," said Risk. "It might be good to stop the fucking plan."

Hawken stared at him, then swiveled his feathery head enough to look at everyone else.

"Okay. To the city. But I won't stay long."

"Long enough. We'll try to find you something."

"What?"

"Zoojoose."

"You'll never find any. No one has any of the crazy drugs anymore."

Pauline coughed and took a long drink of crude wine, drawing the attention of Risk and Hawken. When Hawken spoke, Risk looked at him instead.

"I know where there's some."

"Tell me."

"No, Risk."

"You might get a hawk girl."

Hawken stared at him, then Marilyn said, "We need some too. Sissy and I."

Risk squinted her way and said, "For what?"

Marilyn only smiled while Sophia pointed at K Kat.

"Not worth it," he said to them. "That stuff's a nightmare."

Ham laughed and said, "This whole fucking place is a goddamn nightmare."

"Yeah," said Risk, then he looked again at Hawken. "That's your deal? I get the 'joose, and you and the boat will stay close?"

Hawken waved a gloved hand from side to side and said, "No. Make a hawk girl for me."

"We'd need a girl to start with."

Hawken nodded, said, "Yeah," and looked at Pauline.

"Oh, no fucking way," she said. "I'm not going to try to turn into some kind of bird babe for—"

"She said 'bird babe,' Sissy!"

"Sis, shh. Not now."

"—for some bird boy to fuck?"

"Even just some beak would be nice," he said, grinning as well as his beak would let him.

"Uh-oh," said Sophia. "Here we go again. He's looking for hawk head."

"Sissy, that's funny but kind of true too. He—"

She saw Risk looking at her calmly.

"Um," she whispered, "we're not in Beverly Hills anymore."

"No, Sis. Uh-uh."

Ham finished his drink and clunked the empty jar on a table.

"Just when I thought I heard fucking everything."

"For the team," Risk said to Pauline.

"The shit that got your mother chained up upstairs? That fucking shit?"

Ham mumbled, "She's not really chained. It's more like—"

"I don't give a fuck! No. I'm not going down on a goddamn hawk."

Risk sighed and looked at the twins.

Near him, Hawken was leering at them and bobbing his head around.

Marilyn said, "We, um, we're kind of new in town, and, uh . . ."

"What Sis means is that—"

A loud shriek tore through the ceiling, chased by a string of insane cackles.

After a few silent moments, Risk said, "It's not as bad as it sounds."

The twins stared at him, then at the hawk that wanted beak.

"Fuck," he said, pointing at the stairway. "Go look."

* * *

Pauline said, "You open the door, Ham. You're the fucker that chained her up."

Ham grumbled and said, "She isn't chained. I did fucking lock her in, though."

He twisted the knob, squealed the door in, and everyone stayed in the hallway.

Risk's mother's room had no furniture except for a four-poster bed scratched and gouged everywhere. A mound of dirty pillows was pressed into the headboard by an attractive woman with wild black hair and staring black eyes.

She wore a torn pink bathrobe and floppy pink slippers. No chains or ropes or any kinds of straps held her to the bed.

But the tight mesh of iron bars just inside the door, and all around the bed, along the walls and ceiling and floor, and over the single window gave Ham the confidence to walk inside the room.

"Come on," he said, waving his hand around behind him while keeping his eyes on Lucy.

After a few seconds, not hearing any steps behind him, he turned enough to look. Marilyn and Sophia were still in the hall with Pauline, and all of them watched the woman on the bed closely.

"She won't bite. No, wait. Yeah, she fucking would."

"She can't bite through goddamn iron," said Pauline, and she nudged the twins aside and walked between them to join Ham.

"She sure has tried, though. She just can't find the right animal for that kind of biting."

"So," Marilyn said as she took one step inside, reaching back to hold Sophia's hand, "she doesn't look so bad. She looks as human as Sissy and me."

"Sis. That's funny."

Ham turned and squinted at Sophia.

"Why is that funny?"

"I, um, I'm just trying to lighten the mood. That's all."

"Huh. Alright. Hey, something to do with those goddamn burning hands of yours?"

"Uh, maybe," said Marilyn. "That's Lucy, huh?"

Ham squinted at her for a second, then joined the rest in studying Risk's mother safely locked up in an iron cage.

"Lucy," Pauline said through the bars, "what do you want for dinner? How about a goddamn hawk roast?"

Ham turned to look at the twins, and they bit their lips and didn't comment.

Lucy scowled and said, "The usual. Always the usual. The usual is usually usual. Always."

Pauline scoffed and turned to the twins, one finger pointed at the side of her head.

"The brain. Goddamn it, that's a Zoojoose brain."

She turned back toward Lucy and grinned.

"Okay, the usual. Coming right up."

"I'm horny," Lucy said.

"Oh, fuck," said Ham. "Here we go. Girls, I dare you to watch."

"I've seen it too many times already," said Pauline. "My delicate fucking nerves can't take it."

She turned and pushed her way back between the twins and left the three of them with Lucy.

Ham took a few steps to one side.

"Don't want to block the view. Showtime."

Lucy cackled while looking from one pair of blue eyes to the other. And all of those blue eyes stared at Lucy's legs lifting up and shifting into deer legs, long and thin and strong, covered in short brown fur. Tiny hooves seemed to appear with a popping sound.

She held the shifted legs straight up with both hands, then with only one. The free hand was hidden behind her legs.

"It gets better," said Ham. "Give it a second."

Lucy kept watching the blue eyes and grinning, and the head of a snake appeared from behind her legs, its head poking out between her calves.

"She's kind of settled on this fucking arrangement. It's her goddamn favorite, we think."

The snake head looked everywhere as its tongue darted in and out.

"So fucking horny," she said.

The snake looked down, then began to slither tight against both of her deer legs, traveling to her knees, then past her knees, then sneaking in and out between her thighs.

"Uh-oh, Sissy. Like Dayzee?"

"Uh, no, Sis. That was a snake's tail, remember?"

"Oh, now I do. This is, um . . ."

"Something sick. Yeah."

"Girls," said Ham. "Quiet for the show."

Ham watched intently, and the girls tried to keep watching when the snake head wiggled its way behind Lucy's underwear at one side.

"I'm out of here, Sissy!"

"Oh, hell, me too!"

To the sound of Lucy cackling and moaning, the girls fled the room and took three stairs at a time to join Risk and Pauline and Hawken.

Ham didn't follow them.

*　*　*

"Not bad?" Marilyn said, her face twisted in a frown. "You said it wasn't bad?"

"It was bad," Sophia said, nodding her head.

Ham came pounding down the stairs with a big smile on his face.

"That never gets old. Yeah, your mother's horny as hell," said Ham, "but . . ."

He looked at Risk and waited.

It took a moment, then Risk shook his head and smiled.

"But the snake's hornier."

Ham pointed and said, "Damn right."

Marilyn leaned close to her sister and whispered, "Sissy, did Lucy get head, plus the usual?"

"Sis, somehow, she gave herself head. Plus the usual."

"This world is sure full of surprises."

"Oh, yeah. We probably can't even imagine."

"You won't have to imagine them," said Pauline.

The twins only stared at her.

"Uh, I mean, because you'll, um, be there. Yeah."

"Hey, wait a sec," said Marilyn to Risk. "Why doesn't your mom just shift into a really skinny snake?"

"Sissy's right. A skinny snake could get out of that cage up there."

Risk scoffed and said, "You wouldn't believe me if I told you."

Ham added, "And he sure as fuck doesn't like talking about it."

Marilyn looked from one to the other and said, "Well, now we just have to know. It's not fair to not tell us."

"Not fair!" Sophia said with a pout.

Marilyn giggled and said, "Cute little pout, there, Sissy. Such a cute little girl."

Then, they both looked at Risk and waited.

"Alright. She's tried that. It never works."

"Tell them why," Ham said, laughing. "Tell them why."

Risk let a deep breath flap his lips as it trickled out.

"She, uh, likes her breasts."

"I kind of do too," said Ham. "They're not some fake shifted bullshit breasts either."

"Do you mind?"

"Uh, no, Risk. Go ahead."

"Thanks. Her brain isn't quite right, and she—"

Ham laughed and said, "You think?"

He looked down at claws growing from the ends of all of Risk's fingers, then back up at his eyes.

"Sorry. Go on. Tell them."

"She can't find a way to leave her breasts behind. She won't shift those."

"It's something to see, I tell you," said Ham. "Ever see a long, long snake with two big, juicy, gorgeous—"

"They understand, Ham."

"Right. Fucking right. Yeah."

Risk sighed and looked toward Hawken.

"Zoojoose. Too fucking dangerous."

"Yeah," the navigator said. "No one wants to be like that. I give up on making my own hawk girl."

"Maybe you'll find one soon anyway?"

"Thanks, Marilyn," the hawk boy said, looking down. "Sure. Maybe."

"Fuck. You still want the 'joose," said Risk. "Which means a ride for us."

Hawken tipped his head and stared at each of them.

"Okay, fine. Here's the deal. I'll set you down near the city, then you—"

"Them too," Pauline said, tipping her head toward the girls.

"No. Too dangerous."

"They want to go," she continued. "Don't you, girls?"

Risk said, "Too dark. Maybe if—"

All of the lights came on.

He scoffed and said, "Damn reactor."

"You were saying?"

"Alright, Pauline. They can go."

"Who says we want to go?" said Marilyn. "I just want more dinner. And Sissy, she's—"

"Too little."

"Yes, she's right. She's too little to play outside."

"There's all kinds of good food to be found down there," said Pauline, and they all heard Marilyn's stomach growl.

"Food? Good food?"

"Uh-huh. Good things to eat. And you don't want to leave your little sister here, do you?"

Marilyn giggled and said to Sophia, "Even she's calling you a little girl, Sissy."

"Well?"

"Uh, no, Pauline," said Marilyn, "I don't want to leave her."

"I'm too little to be left alone," Sophia said with a grin and a bounce of her eyebrows.

"So, there you have it. Risk, the three of you—"

"K Kat too," said Sophia. "We need that Kenzie kind of lion."

"Alright," said Hawken. "Four of you."

Risk let out a deep breath, fluttering his lips. Hawken shook his head.

"Alright, that's set," said Risk. "What's your deal?"

"I set you all down and stay close and when you toss the 'joose up to me, I can—"

"Toss it up?"

"Yeah. Out of reach. Way, way up out of reach."

"Alright. I'll toss it up."

"Then," said Hawken, "I sail the fuck out of there."

Chapter 19 – Can't Stop the Killing Completely

"Don't put out the candles just yet," Pauline said as the twins and Hawken took their first real look around the inside of Ham's home.

In brighter light, with lamps and ceiling lights on again, the furniture showed its age and worn condition, and streaks and splotches of oil stains were crowded everywhere.

The floor was scratched and many boards were swollen and buckling. The cinder block walls showed chips and gouges and that haphazard attempts at painting had been attempted long before.

Ham mostly watched the expressions on the twins' faces, then said, "It isn't all that fucking elegant, but it does keep the bats out."

"Most times," Risk said, causing Ham to grin.

"Can we see the city now? Since the lights are on?"

"Yeah, Mare. From the patio."

"I want to see!"

"Is it safe out there?" said Sophia.

Marilyn shook her head, causing Risk to smile when she said, "Sissy's just a little girl. Maybe she should stay inside."

"Sis, I'm fine. That's all just for fun. I'm going out and to hell with those bats."

"Ziggy's got us," Risk said, then he walked toward the front door.

"Well, fuck. Me too," said Ham. "Pauline?"

"No thanks. I've seen enough of that nightmare death-trap fucking dump down there."

Marilyn giggled and said, "Another good line for the travel brochure."

Sophia elbowed her and said, "Sis, shh. She's probably right."

"Don't pay any attention to her," Ham said to the girls. "It's not all that bad. Not when you're way the fuck up here and only looking down at it."

Risk unbolted and unlatched the door, then swung it in and stepped outside. Hawken was close behind, almost tripping him up by walking so close. Marilyn and Sophia followed the hawk boy, and Ham followed them.

"There," Risk said, pointing down through the iron fencing and over the steep, jagged mountain slope.

Marilyn took a place to his right, and Sophia held the fence to his left, and they both looked down on what could have been a normal city seen from high above. Most of the streets had a nearly even line of lights to define them, and some of the windows in otherwise dark buildings showed that something was surviving inside.

Fires in barrels still burned, and the electric lights illuminated their strands of smoke that snaked upward with no wind to deflect them.

"It's kind of beautiful," said Marilyn. "It's like we're looking down at Beverly Hills, Sissy."

"Uh, sure. Except for those," Sophia said, pointing.

They watched in silence as a dense group of moving black points circled around one of the taller buildings, then all converged at a point lower, near the street surface.

"Hunting," said Risk.

"Even bats have to eat," said Ham.

"Those are bats?"

"Yeah, Marilyn. If the electric keeps up, they'll scatter soon. Right now, though, they caught someone or something out in the open."

"Sheesh."

"Yes, Sissy. Very much."

"We should go," said Hawken. "Right now."

"We will," Risk said as he continued watching the twinkling lights below with the twins.

"No. We can't wait. We need to—"

Risk turned his head enough to look at the face of a hawk, whose eyes were trained directly on his.

"You're in a hurry. Why?"

"Um, while there's light. It's better. We should go."

"No. It's not better. Anything could see the ship."

"Okay, yeah. But still, we should—"

"Tell me."

Hawken blinked several times, then looked down.

"I know the madman's plan."

"Talk."

"It's happening. Soon."

"Dammit. Everyone, inside."

* * *

The girls reclaimed their seats on the couch, Ham and Pauline sank into threadbare chairs stained with oil, and Risk and Hawken stood, facing each other.

"You knew the plan when we were at the Pitching Point?"

Sophia cleared her throat quickly, then said, "There's baseball here? No way."

"No. No way," said Risk.

"Pretend we don't know anything," Marilyn said with a pleasant smile. "What's the Pitching Point, then?"

Risk grumbled, then looked toward Hawken.

"There's time?"

"Not much. Maybe enough."

To Marilyn, he said, "In the city and—"

"You'll need a few extra words," Ham said with a big smile. "Lots of fucking words. Go on. Don't be shy."

He sneered at Ham, then focused again on Marilyn.

"In the city and all around it, there are all kinds of dangerous things. Even zombies that—"

"They don't like that name. You know that."

"Yeah, Ham. I know. Zombies that are okay some of the time."

"Not all the time, though."

"No. There's a pact. Unspoken. Leave each other the fuck alone."

"Except for those fucking bats," Pauline said, rolling her eyes. "Those fuckers never did care about any fucking pact."

Ham snickered and said, "He's on a roll. Just let him go."

Everyone got quiet and waited for Risk to continue.

"The bats are outlaws. It's part of why Ham and I hunt them."

"And kill them. I like the goddamn killing part. We want to find that goddamn door Topside too."

"Are you done?"

"Uh, yeah. Sure. Proceed."

"Thanks."

Risk shook his head at Ham for a second, then managed a modest grin.

"Everything else should follow the pact. When something doesn't, and it's worse than killing just a couple of—"

"Wait," said Sophia. "This pact. It's okay to kill a couple of people or things? That's allowed?"

"Can't stop the killing completely," Risk said. "Not here."

"But when someone or something crosses that fucking line," said Ham, "then they—"

"Get pitched. At the Pitching Point."

"And we're back where we started," Marilyn said with a sigh.

"It's a catapult on the shore of the Hot Sea. It can—"

Sophia said, "What's a—"

"Allow me," said Pauline.

Addressing Sophia, she said, "It's what you can see way the fuck out there. You must have seen it. Nothing but fire? Looks like it fucking goes on forever?"

"We've seen that, Sissy."

"Alright. Just checking. Trying to keep up."

Risk coughed into a hand, then said, "They're loaded up, soaked in oil, then—"

"Oh, that's just mean!"

"No, Mare. It's merciful. It's a quicker burn when they hit."

"Enough schooling," Ham said with a sweep of his arm. "Let's get back to—"

"Sissy's a little schoolgirl," Marilyn said with a giggle. "She just needs a plaid skirt uniform."

"You know, Sis, I think I'd kind of like—"

Risk coughed again, got them to look his way, then said, "Not Beverly Hills, remember?"

"Oh. Yes. Now, I do."

"Yep. Me too."

"Like I was saying," said Ham, "enough of that bullshit. The plan, remember? The madman's fucking plan?"

"Yeah," said Risk. "Back to that."

He took a step and looked down at the twins, then held both hands out toward them and moved them apart. The girls started shifting away from each other.

"Uh-oh, Sissy. Remember what happened last time he did that?"

"Oh, yeah. First, you—"

"Not this time."

He sat between them before there was enough room, then looked up at Hawken.

"The plan," he said to the hawk.

Hawken blinked a few times, looked at everyone quickly, then addressed Risk.

"The wolves. He's using the wolves."

"Real wolves?"

"No, Risk. The nearwolves. Starting only days ago, he sent—"

"You mean, werewolves?" said Sophia. "Those kinds of wolves?"

"Yeah," said Hawken. "Those. Some call them that."

"How did they get here?" said Marilyn. "Did they—"

Risk turned to her and said, "Yeah. They rape and kill. Same time. There's an endless supply of them."

"Oh my goodness."

"Hawken," said Risk. "Continue."

"The madman sent out posses and captured all of them. They're in cages all around in the city, places where they can see the sky."

Risk turned to Sophia and said, "Not really a sky."

He pointed toward the ceiling and said, "Just up."

"Yeah," said Hawken. "So, they're caged and ready to be set loose to kill everything."

"Don't they need a moon?" said Marilyn. "Everyone knows that."

"I leaned that in school, Sis."

Marilyn giggled and rolled her eyes, saying, "So cute," and Risk sighed.

"Phosphorous," said Hawken, shaking his bird head. "The bats helped. They're mounting a ball of it up on the sky."

Risk pointed up again, and Sophia said, "Alright. I get it."

"At the right time, they're launching a fireball up there. Boom. Instant moon."

"And unlocked cages?"

"Yeah, Risk. Nearwolves will hunt."

"Everything not human?"

"Human too."

"All except that madman?"

"Yeah. But the humans helping him don't know that."

"How the fuck do you know that?" said Ham.

He squawked once and said, "It's what I would do."

"If you were . . . what?" said Ham. "A madhawk kind of thing?"

"Exactly."

"He's making sense," said Risk. "That probably is the plan."

"Fuck that," said Ham. "We need more fucking shutters on everything, I'll sharpen the points on that fucking fence, and we—"

"When is it happening?"

"Soon, Risk. Very soon."

"We should stay here with Ham," Marilyn said with a nervous sigh.

"I'm with Sis. No way should anyone go out there."

Risk stood but didn't leave the space between the twins, his jeans still brushing against Marilyn's jeans and Sophia's bare legs. He looked across the room with his hands on his hips.

"I'm going. I have to go."

*　　*　　*

"Nonsense," Pauline said as she rose and took a few steps toward the kitchen. "Have some wine, enjoy the good company, and let those bastard wolves run wild down on the ground."

"She's making pretty damn good sense, Risk."

"You can all stay, Ham."

"Risk?" said Marilyn. "Why is it so important for you to go after that madman?"

"It's not just him, Mare. That plan must be stopped."

"But why you?"

He walked over to the shuttered window, sighed, then turned to face them.

"I'm here for a reason."

"Yeah," said Ham, "and we're going to keep catching and interrogating and killing those goddamn bats."

"After you take a break," said Pauline, "with some wine in a boarded-up house high on a fucking mountain."

"Not that. I don't know why, but I'm here to become a better man. There's right, and there's wrong."

"Oh, Risk," said Marilyn, "like when you were saving us, right?"

"Yes, Mare."

"I remember that," said Sophia. "You said there wasn't time to do it right. Even then, you wanted to do things right."

"Yeah. Yeah, Fia. Everyone should."

Ham said, "Oh, fuck. And that means—"

"Going to the reactor."

"Not in my goddamn balloon," said Hawken.

Risk shook his head and said, "No. You're right. It'll get shot down. We'll have to go through the city."

"At least there's light now that that fucking—"

Ham stopped when a shock wave from a distant explosion rattled the walls and shook the entire building.

"Oh, fuck."

Pauline laughed and said, "Wait for it. I told you not to put out those—"

The lights went out.

In a dim room with only a few candles flickering, Risk said, "Damn storms."

Chapter 20 – Screams and Cackles in the Dark

"Jeans are good," Risk said, looking Marilyn up and down. "Any other shoes?"

"Oh, Risk, these will be fine. I don't go anywhere without high heels."

"Don't get that nice white blouse all fucked up," Pauline said, pointing at her. "If you're doing something messy, take it off."

"She would anyway," Sophia said with a snicker. "For any reason."

"Sissy, that's not funny. True, though."

"Alright," said Risk. "At least take this."

He handed her a knife with a long blade in a sheath.

"On your belt."

"Thanks, but I don't think so," said Marilyn. "That's not really my style."

Sophia laughed and said, "Yeah, a knife with those heels. Uh-uh."

"Besides," said Marilyn, "Sissy and I don't need them. Remember this?"

She held out a hand that instantly burned hotter than any fire.

"I remember," said Risk. "Alright, you can cool it."

Marilyn smiled pleasantly and let her hand return to normal.

"You," he said, looking at Sophia. "That's, I mean, you look—"

"Like a little girl?" she said, smiling up at him.

"Yeah, that. Not the best for fighting zombies."

"Risk," said Ham, "they don't like—"

"I know."

He let his eyes roam all over Sophia.

"Heels for you too?"

"Always, Risk."

Marilyn snickered and said, "Even though she's just a little girl. How silly."

He sighed, looking again at Sophia, and said, "You won't take a knife either?"

"Oh, I suppose I could. Do you have a very pretty one?"

Marilyn giggled, pointed at her sister, and said, "A pretty little-girl knife. That's even sillier."

Risk said, "We don't have pretty knives here."

Sophia pouted and said, "Oh, well, then."

She held up her own glowing hand.

Marilyn said, "No knives for the Kildare Killers. Oh, but what about Kenzie? I mean, K Kat?"

"Fangs," Ham said. "Claws too."

"Oh. Okay."

"Good. Let's go."

"Wait a second," said Pauline. "I got a tip for you. Aim your crew toward the Royal Pub. You know of it?"

"Yeah. Why?"

"I heard it's easy to barricade and secure, if you need to. Could be a good safe house on the way."

"Alright. Anything else?"

"There might be booze there too."

She looked at Marilyn when her stomach growled.

"I don't know about food, though. Maybe."

"The Royal Pub. Got it," Risk said, then turned and began a determined walk toward the front door.

* * *

Risk held the door in and let Hawken hurry out first. The twins weren't moving too quickly, so he went next, with K Kat by his side.

181

Marilyn walked outside, holding Sophia's hand, and they stopped there after Ham said, "Safe travels," then shut the door behind them decisively without waiting for anyone to reply. They held each other's gaze as they listened to all of the bolts and drawbars being engaged inside.

"Um, that sounded good. That sounds safe in there."

"But there might be food at that bar, Sis, right?"

"Sissy, I'm so hungry. I hope so. You don't look ready for fighting, but it sure is a pretty little dress you have there."

"Oh, this little thing?"

Marilyn giggled.

"So innocent! Well, except for those sexy heels of yours. Those are kind of screaming for trouble."

"Hey, Sis, yours are just as sexy. Maybe even more."

"Hmm. Well, it's time to hit the city, and we're both dressed and ready for adventures. Back up in the balloon?"

"Ugh."

"Good, let's go."

They turned in time to see Hawken climbing up the ropes, his burlap shoes and gloved hands sure of every step and every handhold, like he'd done it countless times.

Risk was holding the rim of the basket with both hands and looking in, but he turned at the sound of their heels on the stone patio. Two outside torches seemed to dance their flames only to brighten their manes that swung behind them as they approached Risk.

"Who's first?" he said.

Neither answered quickly enough, so he held Marilyn high under her arms, causing her to giggle, then he lifted her without any effort and set her inside.

When he turned toward Sophia, she'd already lifted her arms straight up and was waiting.

"Should be easy enough," Marilyn said from inside the basket. "She's just a little thing."

"Funny, Sis."

"True, though. You forgot that part."

"Hmm."

Risk set her in the basket, too, and held her just long enough to be sure that she had her balance.

Before he could offer another lift, K Kat growled playfully and leaped up and over the rim, barely shaking the basket when she landed softly.

"Huh."

Risk looked up and said, "Hawken. Are we ready?"

He grinned as he sent a thin flame up into the balloon, causing the ropes and cables to vibrate and groan.

"Yeah, Risk."

"Good."

He unhooked one mooring line, then the other, then jumped himself in to join the twins and the lion.

And the hawk boy navigator lifted them off of Ham's patio and over the arrow-sharp points of the high iron fence.

*   *   *

On the descent, the girls mostly watched the smaller, sharper rocks on the side of the mountain as they gave way to larger boulders, some mounded together and others with spaces between them.

An occasional glance the other way showed them mostly shadows against darker shadows, interrupted only by flickering flames confined to barrels. Some of the taller shadows boasted of something existing inside by faint candlelight through windows.

But nothing was moving anywhere. The night revealed nothing of whatever things called that dark city home.

"Take us closer," Risk called up.

"Alright. Some," said Hawken, then he spun the teapot spout to point at the mountain and gave it a few puffs, sending the balloon on a smooth, slow coast toward the edge of the city.

"Lower," said Risk.

"No. Too many good jumpers."

The twins looked over the side and saw that they could have been looking down from the roof of Dayzee's three-story mansion.

"What the hell could jump this high, Sis?"

"The big bad wolf, Sissy," Marilyn said with a nervous giggle, which faded quickly.

"Good," Risk said as he looked at the dark structures just a short walk away. "Here is good."

"Alright."

Hawken pulled a rope which opened a flap at the top of the balloon, and the whistling of hot air rushing out accompanied their gradual descent. The bottom of the basket touched ground, bounced once, then hit again and began dragging slowly toward the city.

"I can't hold it," said Hawken. "Go. Now."

"Right."

He hefted Marilyn up and over, and she stood still, watching the city.

Sophia was next, and she stayed close to the basket, holding the top rail for balance.

"Go, girl," he said to K Kat, but the lion didn't jump.

She only began a low growl as she stood inside, near Sophia and looking past her.

"No time," he told the lion. "It's okay."

K Kat let out a disapproving growl and jumped out and to the ground.

Just as at least five separate voices began a chorus of screams and cackles in the dark.

Chapter 21 – Just Like That, a Thousand

"I'm going!"

Hawken hurried to throw wide open the lid to the iron pot. A giant flame invaded the balloon, then broke into smaller ones, each finger fighting for its own space to burn. All of the ropes and cables tightened and groaned, and the balloon snapped outward, growing from the hot air.

"No! Wait!" said Risk. "We—"

"Oh, no!" Sophia said as she held onto the basket and her heels left the ground.

"Sissy!" Marilyn yelled, watching her sister kicking as she was lifted into the air.

"Hawken," Risk screamed, "lower the craft!"

"We have a deal!" he yelled from high above the rising basket. "And that means I have to stay alive!"

Risk stooped down for less than a second, then jumped with a roar like a lion. When he was high enough, he wrapped his arms around Sophia's waist, which caused them both to drop. He landed lightly and shifted her around until she was on her back in his arms, with her arms around his neck.

"Dammit, Hawken!"

"Sorry!"

"Where's the goddamn Zoojoose?" he yelled up to the navigator.

"It's at the Royal Pub!"

"Huh? Is that why Pauline said—"

"She didn't know!"

"Then, why did she say to—"

Risk saw that Hawken had already floated too high to hear or respond anymore, and the boisterous, dangerous voices were drawing near.

Risk yelled one more time to the hawk navigator, "Come back for us when it's safer!"

Risk spun Sophia and himself around to face the approaching danger, then set her down to stand beside her sister. Then, he and K Kat placed themselves between the wild mob and the twins. They both began their own type of growling and crouched low, one with natural claws and one with rapidly growing sets of them.

"Maybe this was a bad idea, Sissy."

"God, I just want to go home, Sis."

"After you give Pauline back that dress, right?"

"Um . . ."

"Don't. Don't even think about it."

* * *

Marilyn and Sophia stayed close behind Risk and K Kat, each holding out a hand and maintaining contact. Their protectors were coiled springs, ready to pounce, and the savages in the dark kept closing the distance.

Then, a soft buzzing filled the air all around them. While Risk and the lion kept growling, never dropping their guard, the girls looked around each way, trying to determine the source.

But it came from everywhere all at once. Then, they noticed something.

"Sis, where did they go?"

"Um, maybe they're still there, Sissy. Hear those voices?"

"That's them? They're just having pleasant conversations now? What the hell?"

Risk and K Kat relaxed, stopping their growling and again standing tall. The lion began wagging her tail gently and panting up at Risk.

Laughter in the dark. Someone slapping someone else's back. More laughter, from both women and men.

Then, the voices faded as what had just been an attacking force retreated into the quiet dark of the city.

"Risk? Um, what the hell?"

"Not now, Fia. We have to move."

Marilyn said, "But we want to know what—"

"Later," he said and started walking toward the nearest structure, just a square of black against the blackness behind it. "Stay close."

They stayed close, and Risk and the mountain lion led the way, all of them silent and placing their steps quietly.

They'd reached the side of the building, a wall of crumbling masonry blocks that would have let light through if there had been any inside. And they walked along until Risk, at the head of the line, reached the corner and raised his hand.

They all stopped, and every one of them watched as he leaned to look around the corner.

He turned and whispered. "Clear. Come on."

They crept along the next wall until they reached a door built of rotting wood planks. Risk pushed it in carefully, opening up to them an interior even darker than the exterior. He waved for them to follow as he leaned to get through the compact doorway.

No one spoke as they filed inside, then he eased the door closed without a sound.

And the buzzing outside continued.

He struck a match and walked around with it, searching. From near his boots, he snatched up a couple of rags, then continued his hunt.

"Oh, good," said Marilyn. "You have matches."

"Match," he said. "Last one."

"Damn reactor."

"Good one, Sissy. Yes. You should have brought more, Risk."

He grumbled and nodded and kept searching.

Part of a broomstick was next, onto which he wrapped the rags. Then, he swept the thing around in a puddle of oil and lit it. He stabbed his torch into the soft soil floor near the middle of the small building.

"It won't burn long. Check the windows."

"These look good over here," Marilyn said. "I think."

"Test those boards."

Marilyn grabbed at one and tried to wiggle it, but it wouldn't move.

"Looks good."

"Good, Mare."

Sophia had been trying to move a rusty metal barrel over to block the door, but she wasn't making any progress, so Risk helped. And together, they blocked the door too.

"Is that enough?"

He looked around, and they did, too, all seeing that every window and door opening was blocked in some fashion.

"No, Fia. Never."

"That's not encouraging at all," Marilyn said with a pout.

"No. Still, let's give it a minute. Give them time to leave. Then, we'll go to the Royal Pub."

"Can't you just kill them?" said Marilyn. "There were only about—"

"Five. Yeah. Then, a hundred. Just like that, a thousand."

"Oh. Okay."

*　*　*

"What exactly are we trying to keep outside, Risk?"

"Anything, Fia. Everything. Like a storm, best to let them pass."

"What were those people that sounded mean, then were just kind of normal again?"

"Something we should avoid."

Marilyn said, "And that buzzing. What was that when—"

The buzzing stopped.

"Fuck."

Growling erupted outside the door, all mixed in with yipping and shrieking and maniacal laughter.

"Uh-oh, Sissy."

"It's never easy, Sis."

Then, cackling and wailing blew up along one side of the building. Then more, all around the structure.

"They won't stop," he said. "Wait here."

"Oh no, Risk, you can't go out there!"

"Mare, it's okay. Better me than—"

K Kat stood tall and put her front paws on his shoulders, looking him in the eye.

The girls watched as Risk and the lion looked into each other's eyes in a quiet, dark building surrounded by something. Lots of them.

Finally, Risk said, "Alright. Good girl."

Chapter 22 – She's Ripping Off Their Heads

"Good girl how?" said Marilyn. "Did you two somehow talk about something?"

"Yeah. She volunteered."

"Kenzie did what?"

"She's K Kat, Sissy."

"Right. What did I say?"

"The lion can be quiet," said Risk. "I wouldn't be."

"Oh, I get it. You'd just attract more of them?"

"Yeah, Mare. Quiet is better."

He walked over to the door, his lion by his side, then they both stopped and listened through the rough wood.

A few seconds passed, then Risk patted K Kat on her head, and she appeared to nod.

He rolled the barrel out of the way, then quietly pulled in the door.

And the mountain lion slipped outside, allowing Risk to close it all back up again.

He waited there, looking from one girl to the other, neither of whom was speaking.

At the sound of the first hints of claws scraping on pavement, then a stifled scream that turned into a gurgling, Risk smiled and walked over to them.

"Good. We're still on schedule."

* * *

"Goodness. More lions killing things."

"What's wrong with that?" said Risk.

"Before Dayzee's house burned, long before you came to save us, we—"

"It wasn't really all that long, Sis. It's just that so much crazy stuff happened, and it seemed like a long time."

"Oh. That's true. Anyway, we always had lady lions around, and they were always killing yard guys, and film guys, and neighbors, and—"

"Biting their heads off," Sophia said with a grin.

Another choked scream came through the walls, and they heard K Kat groaning repeatedly, like she was shaking her head to remove something else's head.

"There goes one now, I think," said Marilyn. "I think she's ripping off their heads."

"Good. She'd better."

They both stared at him, neither saying anything. He looked from one pair of blue eyes to the other.

He grinned and said, "So I don't have to."

"Yay, she's a good lady lion."

"It's Kenzie, Sis. Sort of."

"Kenzie wouldn't kill people, Sissy. That's the lion part of her."

Risk said, "Those aren't people."

"But there are humans out there, too, right?"

"Some. Even with humans around, too, it's a nightmare out there."

Marilyn turned so that the torch light gave her the best glow possible, then she shook back her blond mane.

"I don't mind living in a human's world as long as I can be a Kildare Killer in it."

"Good one, Sis. First one in this Below the Bay place."

"Thanks, Sissy. I knew there would come a time for that one."

Risk had been squinting at one, then the other. He ended up focused on Marilyn.

"Yeah, you're a killer. Still, watch yourself. That might not be enough for this place."

K Kat growled, something gagged before it hit the ground, and the three smiled at sounds that they were sure belonged to a lion decapitating . . . something.

"You," he said, pointing at Sophia. "You're a killer too."

"Even though she's kind of a little girl now," Marilyn said with a soft giggle as she still looked at the walls protecting them.

"Sis. That's just for fun."

"Oh, Sissy, I know. But you sure are a sexy kind of little girl."

Sophia held one leg out, very little covered by her short dress, and rotated a few times her very high-heeled black shoe.

"It's not just legs and dresses and stuff, Sis. My sexiness is from everything within me."

Marilyn clapped her hands without a sound and grinned at her sister.

"Sissy, that was such a good one! The first one for you too!"

They both shared a look, then turned back to Risk.

"Inside you," said Risk. "Yeah. Try to keep it all in there."

Sophia's eyes got wide and she looked down at the dirt floor.

Marilyn shook her head and said, "Damn Below the Bay world."

K Kat scraped her claws around again from outside of a different wall. She repeated her rhythmic grunting and low growling, and the three of them smiled at each other and listened.

And they all nodded at the sound of something heavy dropping onto the pavement.

"Good lady lion."

"Good Kenzie, too, Sis."

"What about you two?"

"What about us?" said Marilyn.

"You're good too."

"We are?"

"Yes, Fia. But be ready. Things here are clever and deadly."

"Not you, though, right?"

Sophia elbowed her sister and said, "Sis, of course, he's deadly. I'd say clever too."

"Oh, I agree. But never deadly to Sissy and me, right? That's all I meant."

"Never."

A quiet moment passed with just them looking into each other's eyes.

Then, K Kat scratched at the door.

"Oh," said Sophia, "um, that must be Kenzie."

"K Kat, Sissy."

"Both."

"Don't be so sure. I'll look."

*   *   *

Risk moved the barrel, opened the door, and laughed when the lady lion rushed in and jumped up so high that he had to hold her like a child.

"Oh my goodness! Kenzie!"

"Wish you would have tried that with her before she was a lioness, Sis?"

"Sissy, shh."

"Good girl, K Kat," Risk said as the lion licked his cheeks, causing him to laugh again.

He let her drop, then turned toward the girls.

Sophia said, "You, uh, you got a little, uh . . ."

"What Sissy means is that your, uh, cheeks are, um . . ."

He smiled at them both as he wiped off blood from a lion's kisses.

"Better?"

"Much," said Marilyn. "We could probably just leave K Kat kind of messy. She is a lion, after all."

"It's safe, thanks to K Kat. We should go."

"To that bar?"

"Yeah, Fia."

He tipped his head toward the night crowding around the building.

"Stay close out there. Don't get separated."

"We won't," said Marilyn. "But don't forget, Risk, we're killers too."

"I remember. You killed me once."

Sophia grinned as she pointed at him.

"And she could do it again."

"So could Sissy. Even though she's just little."

Sophia elbowed her, bringing out a giggle.

Chapter 23 – They Got My Sis!

Risk lightly held an arm of each of the Kildare Killers, getting them to stop before they all set a course for the Royal Pub. He leaned back and quietly pulled the door shut.

"Why close it up again?"

"To keep things out, Mare."

Sophia pointed down and said, "Like that head?"

"It's too dark to see, Sissy, but I bet he's winking at me."

"Even Below the Bay, Sis. Yeah."

Risk scoffed, snatched up the head, opened the door and tossed it inside, then closed it quietly again.

"Why?" said Marilyn. "Again?"

"To keep that part in."

"But it's dead, right?"

"Oh, Risk," said Marilyn, "Sissy's talking about how the heads back at Dayzee's would most times still be alive. That became difficult at times."

He pointed at her and said, "Yeah. I bet."

Then, he pointed at Sophia, grinned, and said, "No, Fia."

The buzzing ramped up and became constant, and they paused to listen for a moment.

"It's not dead? That head came from a zombie?"

"Either way, it's better now. And they don't like that word."

"Who cares what they like?" Sophia yelled in a whisper. "Zombies are dead, then they're alive, then their heads are yanked off by lions, then—"

"Then, they wink at me, Sissy."

Sophia said, "You'd like some zombie thing flirting with you?"

"It's attention, at least. Risk, do the zombies have food?"

"Sis, you must know that what they like is—"

"This is fun," Risk said. "But we have to move."

With Marilyn to his right and Sophia to his left, and with K Kat leading the way, her ears listening in all directions, they began a slow hike down a narrow, dark street.

"Too bad there's no electric because there are streetlights here," Marilyn said. "Just our luck."

"Dark is safer sometimes."

"Oh," said Sophia, "so things don't see us?"

"Things. Yeah."

Right after a soft explosion in the distance, in the direction of the reactor, all of the streetlights came on.

"Dammit."

K Kat froze in her tracks, and her ears had stopped pivoting around to point straight ahead.

"Uh-oh. K Kat knows something."

"Yeah, Mare. Something."

They heard many footsteps, like a crowd approaching.

"A whole lot of somethings," Sophia said with a smirk.

Risk looked both ways, then said, "No place to hide quick."

"Sis and I can give Kenzie a break. Time for the Kildare Killers to pitch in a little."

"How fast can we burn things, Sissy? What if there are millions of them?"

"Millions, Sis? Isn't that a bit much?"

Marilyn looked down and kicked at a loose stone on the road.

"I suppose. But you know what I mean. We might need lady lion help. We always did at Dayzee's, remember?"

"I remember. They were always there for us."

"Wait," said Risk, touching each of them lightly.

The footsteps got louder, and they began to hear jovial conversations and laughter just around a corner ahead.

The first one came into their view, a very normal looking man, just kind of pale. A woman walked next to him, engaging him in a pleasant discussion of something.

More followed them, all very peaceful and happy to be in that street in a city below a bay. But all of their clothes were ripped and shredded, like they'd fallen into sticky rags, then stood up and got on with their business.

"They don't look so scary."

"Not now. No, Mare."

"When are they scary, then?"

"No telling, Fia."

"Well," said Marilyn, "if they get out of line, Sissy and I will save all of us."

She took her sister's hand and walked her forward, stepping on each side of the lion, until they were out front to confront the crowd if needed.

"Uh, Sis? There are a lot of them."

"Oh. Yes, you're right. I didn't stop to count."

"Too busy bragging about being a killer, huh?"

"Bad time, Sissy?"

"Uh, yep. I'd say so."

*　*　*

The crowd stopped about a dozen steps from the twins.

"Hello, there!" said the man in front. "What brings you out on such a pleasant evening?"

"Honey," said the woman beside him, "it's probably on account of the electricity. Things are all lit up so nicely."

"Oh, yeah, that's probably it."

He looked away from the woman and tipped his head to study Marilyn.

"You sure do look familiar. Do you live on—"

The woman elbowed him and said, "Try to make sense. While you can."

"Oh, yes, of course."

He cleared his throat and addressed Marilyn again.

"Do you spend time in this area of town?"

From behind him, someone said, "No, it's her. I think it's her."

Another voice: "It sure looks like her."

Marilyn whispered to Sophia, "Sissy, what are they talking about?"

"No, they can't be. Think about it, Sis."

"No! That other Marilyn? How would they even know about her?"

"They have electricity, so maybe they have TVs too? Risk, do they—"

She looked over her shoulder and saw Risk and K Kat facing a crowd coming from the other direction.

"Uh, Sis. Look."

Marilyn looked.

"Oh, that's not good. Millions, Sissy. I told you so."

"Sis, there aren't millions. Sure, there are a lot, but—"

"It's really her!" a woman yelled from back in the crowd.

"This is simply astounding!" said another.

"Uh, Sis. I'd say to run if we had anywhere to run."

"Oh, Sissy, they're being so polite. They seem like very nice—"

The buzzing all around them stopped in an instant.

So did all coherent voices that were speaking actual words.

Low growling rose like oozy swamp water in the crowds on both sides of them.

"Risk, um . . ."

"K Kat and I have your backs. You two handle them."

"What's with the buzzing?" said Marilyn. "Why did—"

A snarling adult male grabbed Marilyn's arm and spun her back around. His bared teeth were aimed at her head when Sophia's hand, instantly glowing hot, burned right through the side of his head.

He crumpled into a smoking heap, then his clothes caught, too, and it ended up being a compact, oily fire on the street.

"That was close! Thanks, Sissy!"

The closest ones were growling and grabbing at them.

"Don't thank me yet, Sis!"

Marilyn burned the nearest one the same way, then Sophia burned another. They didn't have time to look, but they heard two wild animals behind them growling and roaring and snapping among crazed voices yelling and screaming.

"Sis, stay close!"

"I'll try, Sissy!"

They didn't stay close. The crowd wedged between them and while they kept adding neat little fires on the road, the snarling, biting things drove Marilyn farther back toward the very middle of their mob.

"Sis! Come back!"

"I'm trying!"

She burned two more, one with each hand.

"I told you there were millions!"

Sophia got bumped in every direction, hands and open mouths reaching for her, and she burned as many as she could.

She was about to call for Risk, or K Kat, or both, when the buzzing came back.

Everyone around her, all biting and grabbing just a second earlier, stood tall and brushed themselves off, all smiling and some laughing.

"What the hell?"

Sophia looked back at Risk and saw that the crowd that they'd been fighting had calmed too. But he and the lion were maintaining a defensive line anyway.

When she turned around again, most of the crowd had departed. She heard their laughter and lively conversations as they snaked their way around the corner.

And Marilyn was nowhere to be seen.

"Risk! Kenzie! They took Sis!"

"We're coming," said Risk. "Come on, girl!"

They joined her and started to run toward the corner, but the buzzing sputtered and died, as did the congeniality of the folks around them.

"Stay back-to-back!" Risk yelled.

They kept up a fierce battle, K Kat as a lion, Sophia as a Kildare Killer, and Risk as nothing anyone could recognize, just a mad beast with bloody claws.

Ripped bodies fell, as did just pieces of those bodies. Some new fires were kindled. And the violence continued until a pop from hidden electronics positioned all around them led to a steady buzz.

They all calmed again and ignored the fallen and burning as they walked away. The other way. Not where Marilyn had been taken.

"Come on!" Sophia yelled and ran as well as she could in her heels and very short dress.

Risk and K Kat followed, and they all looked around the corner.

And saw nothing.

Just an empty street.

Then, the lights flickered and died.

"Damn reactor," said Risk.

"They got my Sis! Risk, where did they go?"

With K Kat whining softly, amid pleasant buzzing on a totally dark street, Risk sighed and said, "I've never found their hive."

"Hive? What hive? Why would people—"

"They're not people. I've looked before."

"But we can try again, right?"

"Yeah, Fia. We'll find her. It probably won't be too late."

Sophia wiped under each of her eyes as she stared at Risk.

* * *

"Wait!" said Marilyn, surrounded by so many and so closely that she could have collapsed and not fallen to the pavement. "Just stop, please!"

The laughing and rollicking crowd hurried away from Risk and Sophia and K Kat, first around the nearest corner, then halfway down the block, then through a wide double door.

"It's her," said one.

"How could it be?" said another.

"It's a gift! We deserve to have her!"

"Stop!" she yelled at them. "I want to go back!"

Marilyn groaned and wiggled her arms until she could pry them up and out of the bodies pressed into her, and she kept them raised as she was driven, taking short, shuffling steps on her high white heels, down a wide, dark hallway that sloped downward.

"Where are you taking me? Stop!"

She heated her hands, got them glowing, but everyone around her was smiling and talking pleasantly and sometimes pointing at her.

Their laughter and comments continued as the hallway transitioned into a tunnel with a ceiling of arched stones and bricks. Weak candlelight from infrequent wall sconces sometimes revealed odd, distorted faces, but all of them were smiling as the tide carried her farther underground.

A voice from the leading edge of the mob called out, "Only darkness after us! Only the dark!"

The stragglers in the rear laughed as they extinguished the sconce candles as they passed them, leaving the hallway behind the mob darker than night.

"Please, stop! Let me go!"

They'd reached an area where the tunnel widened, and rows of large doors lined each side, all of them identical. The few men in the lead brought them to just one of them, on the right, and they pulled both doors open.

The same voice, near the front, yelled, "Everyone, hurry! Let's go!"

They laughed as they ran into the darkness past those doors, and the crowd, with Marilyn pinned in so tightly that her heels never touched ground much of the time, followed.

The last one through pulled the doors closed, and the tunnel that they'd vacated filled with only silence and night and not a single sign that anyone or anything had passed that way.

* * *

"Come on!" Sophia yelled as she took Risk's hand and pulled him down the dark street.

He followed, shaking his head, and K Kat stayed close behind, scanning and sniffing all around as she followed too.

Barrel fires, staggered around them on rooftops and infrequent balconies, cast more shadows than light.

"Where's that torch? We need that torch!"

"It's gone, Fia. We left it."

She let go of his hand when they were near a set of doors, and she pulled one open enough to look in. The inside could have been a wall painted black.

"In here? Did they go in here?"

"I don't know."

"It's so dark! Sis must be terrified!"

She let the door swing shut.

"There! That one, maybe!"

She hurried along the street and squealed open the next door, which revealed nothing but darkness, like the one before.

"Risk, where is she? Where did they take her?"

"This part of the city is called The Maze," he said, shaking his head.

"What? What kind of maze?"

"Tunnels. Long hallways. All connected. It all goes deep underground."

"They took Sis underground? No! No, they can't!"

"We'll find her. But we need help."

"There's no time! Who were those people?"

Risk sighed and said, "You'd call them zombies."

She shook her head and said, "But—"
"But they don't like that. Yeah."

* * *

"No, no, no! Stop!"
Marilyn's heels sometimes grazed the wet stone floor as the enthusiastic mob laughed and flowed downward along the steeply sloping surface.
"No, please! Where are you taking me?"
"Home!" said one.
"You'll like it there!" said another.
"And we'll like having you there with us!"
The leaders of the pack pulled open two wide doors and led them all into a large, high-ceilinged room with evenly-spaced torches burning along every wall. Tall partitions divided up the area into many cozy rooms, most with upholstered furniture and candles on tables.
But they didn't stop at any of them. They pushed and shoved and mostly carried Marilyn along through the middle of it all, and she sometimes saw large TV screens mounted high on the walls, playing only reflections of candlelight. More of them, in their own residence areas, waved and cheered at the sight of her.
"Oh, please. Please, stop!"
They didn't stop, and she got bounced up high enough several times to see what might be their destination: a large jail cell, bolted into the far wall. Some of its rusty bars were bent but not enough for anyone to squeeze through. Inside, a cot with neat pillows and bedcovers waited with a small, clean nightstand.
The door was held open by two of them, both bearing silly grins. The crowd supporting her thinned and branched off to both sides, and those behind her kept up the pressure until she was squirted out from amongst them and into the cage.

Before she could turn around and scream, the heavy door was slammed shut, and its metallic ringing quickly got suffocated by the cheers and hooting and cackling of those who had imprisoned her.

As a tear tumbled down her cheek, she let the fire in her hands fizzle away.

Chapter 24 – Her Most Enraptured Fans

Risk took Sophia's hand and tried to look into her eyes, but it was too dark for either of them to be sure.

"What? You mean, they call themselves something different?"

"Yeah. They don't like that name."

"I don't even care what they like! How do we save her?"

"There's one who knows The Maze. A little."

"Where? Who?"

"He's sometimes at the Royal Pub."

"Dammit, we don't have time for bar hopping!"

She groaned and pulled her hand free, then ran, clattering her heels on the quiet street, to the next set of doors.

"Maybe through here?"

She jerked it open and leaned in, trying to see through the thick night inside.

"We have to pick one and look. We have to!"

She started taking a step in, then stopped when Risk got a strong grip on her upper arm.

"You'd die in there."

"No, I won't. Because you and Kenzie are coming with me."

"We won't be enough. And it's K Kat."

"Dammit, Risk, let me go!"

She tried to break free, shaking herself and her long black hair around, but his hold was too strong.

"We'll find her. Not like this. This is suicide."

She snarled, turned, and tried to run into the dark building, but Risk pulled on her arm, snapping her into himself, and he held her there with both arms.

"Fia. We'll find her."

"No! We never will because they—"

With one hand, he took the back of her head, gently, and pressed it into his chest. And he held her there as her breaths raced in and out and she tried to squirm herself free.

But she couldn't, and he didn't relax his hold until he heard and felt her sobbing.

Then, he let her look up at him and returned that hand to her waist along with the other.

"Risk!" she whispered as they stood in the dark on a dead-silent street aboveground, above The Maze.

"I know," he said. "I know. I can't explain, but we have time."

"How can you know that?" she said with tears flowing quickly enough to drip onto his chest.

"I just know. We need to go."

She kept looking up at him, trying to focus on his eyes, and didn't answer him until she felt K Kat's furry, whiskery snout flipping one of her hands up and around.

That hand got diverted to wipe at her cheeks, and she managed one weak chuckle.

"Kenzie says we should get going too."

"K Kat," he said, daring a kind smile.

She didn't smile back.

"I'm burning to hell every one of those goddamn zombies."

He let his smile go, too, and said, "They don't—"

"Yeah. So, I'll burn them twice. I swear, Risk, I'll burn every fucking—"

He pulled her in close again, and she allowed that for only a few seconds. Then, she leaned back and looked up at him.

"Let's go, dammit. We're wasting time."

He grinned and said, "Okay, Killer."

* * *

Marilyn spun around to see a friendly looking older man turning a big key to lock her in her cage. He wore a long white shirt like it was a lab coat, despite its many stains and streaks of oil. Small round glasses magnified eyes that showed good cheer along with a generous dose of confusion. His mop of wavy gray hair was teased up, hinting that he spent much of his spare time combing oil and grime out of it.

While he was struggling with the key in the lock, and laughing at himself for having such difficulty, she sat on the bed and looked out at the hundreds of them surrounding her prison.

All were dressed in shabby clothes, ripped and hanging and smeared with old oil stains. Their skin showed some kind of damage, like cuts and wounds that had never even tried to heal. And there was just enough light to see that almost all of them had skin hanging in loose folds, much more that simple aging could ever do. Others, though, appeared somewhat normal.

Past them, over their heads, giant TV screens were mounted to the walls left and right. But they were offering no images or sounds, unless the incessant buzzing that saturated that room and every other street and vacant structure in that city was being emitted from them.

Most of the faces were smiling, looking at her as many hands pointed toward her. She heard the name "Marilyn" more than a few times, always followed by spirited outbursts of debate.

Near tears, she focused on the elderly man who had just accomplished his single-minded task: to lock that door.

He looked up with a satisfied smile, and he tipped his head at the sight of Marilyn shaking hers.

He cleared his throat, and many around him quieted down.

"Aw, it's okay. We're all very happy to finally meet you."

"Finally meet me? How the hell would you know me at all? I just got here."

"Yes. Yes, you did. And we're all quite thrilled."

"I want to go home!"

"We don't want you to go home!"

Sobbing but not touching her hands to her face because they'd begun a steady climb in temperature in preparation of burning anyone she could reach, she looked down at her lap and listened to what could have been her most enraptured fans ever.

She didn't look up until the man, still holding the key in his hand, said, "I'm Mortimer."

He laughed and said, "And you can call me . . . Mortimer!"

More laughter erupted behind him, Marilyn cooled her hands, and used them to cover the tears that she could no longer hold in.

* * *

"Wait," Risk said, hushing and holding Sophia by his side with both of their backs to a wall.

K Kat, on his other side, leaned slowly to peek around the corner. She snapped her head back around when they all heard grunting and heavy clatter on the oily brick street surface.

"What the—"

Risk squeezed her arm, then pulled her in close, his arm over her shoulders. He leaned to check the lion and saw that she'd become a very quiet and still version of herself.

The stomping grew louder, and they waited in silence, watching in almost nonexistent light, just the weakest of flickers from distant barrels, for whatever would round that corner.

And when the first one did, Sophia started to gasp, but Risk quickly covered her mouth while pulling her in closer.

The three of them watched as quietly as they could as a boar as big as a small bus trotted past, twitching a tail too small and horribly mismatched with a body so full and bloated and slick all over with crude oil.

And it wasn't alone. Three more followed it closely, the sixteen hooves clacking as they continued on their way, all of them showing more grace and balance than should be possible for beasts of that size.

Risk relaxed his covering of Sophia's mouth, and she remained silent. All eyes watched, waiting for the herd to pass.

Then, the buzzing, persistent and everywhere, staggered and stopped, and the lead bore squealed like he'd been struck with an axe. He began a brisk gallop which seemed to drift the others with him, but the buzzing returned almost immediately. And the four bulbous bodies huddled together, not moving, as each looked in a different direction.

No one moved. No one dared to breathe.

Not the boars.

Not Risk or Sophia or K Kat.

They watched four pairs of oiled-up ears twisting and twitching, turning in every direction. And the eyes that could be seen were probing into every shadow around them.

But the buzzing continued, didn't flicker again, and the lead boar snorted softly. He resumed a careful, quieter trot than earlier, and the others followed.

The last they saw of them was a silly little tail stuck to a wide body as it meandered out of sight around another building.

Sophia didn't try to get free, but she did tip her head back to look up at Risk.

She didn't smile when she said, "This isn't bad, here with you, but we have to go."

"Right. Yeah."

She did smile, barely, when she said, "Now that the bacon is gone."

Risk scoffed and shook his head.

"They're hunters. Smart too. They hunt in packs."

"Sure, but it looks like they fall down a lot. They're all oily."

"No, Fia. They do that. Makes it almost impossible to kill them."

She made a face and said, "They probably taste like crap too. You could kill one, though, right?"

"Maybe. If it's just one. Still, maybe not. They're meaner than bats."

She scoffed and said, "Can't even take one to that pitching place, I'd bet."

"Uh, no. Too heavy."

She blinked slowly and said, "I really do hate this place."

He nodded once, said, "You should," then tipped his head in the direction that brought them the boars.

"Royal Pub. Right around the corner."

"Dammit, that guy we need better be there."

"No guarantees," he said.

"You said that when we all woke up in that basket. When Sis and I first got here."

He held her gaze, nodded, and said, "It's still true."

She held up her glowing hand, still looking into his eyes, and said, "I guarantee we're getting Sis back."

Risk turned his eyes toward her burning hand, then back to her eyes.

"Let's do it. Killer."

He took her other hand, she cooled the hot one, and they rounded the corner. Ahead of them, just enough firelight crept down over a weathered wood sign that read "Royal Bar."

Sophia tightened her grip on Risk's hand as she looked the place over.

"It's a dump. It doesn't look like anyone's in there."

"Yeah. But it's our best chance."

She started backing away, retracing their steps and still holding his hand.

"No. It's no good. Let's go back and try another door. Oh, and bring a torch. We can—"

The buzzing stopped. K Kat gulped, then looked up at Risk.

"We can what?"

"We can get our asses inside the goddamn place," she said. "Damn buzzer. Let's go!"

Chapter 25 – We've Been Watching You

"Aw, don't be upset," Mortimer said with a giant grin. "You're too famous to be upset. Pretend you're on the red carpet somewhere."

Marilyn looked up at him and wiped at her cheeks.

"I want to go home. Can you please just let me go?"

"We certainly cannot. You're our absolute favorite. And I hope you don't get offended, but your body looks even better in person."

"What are you talking about?"

She heard more of them saying her name, sometimes laughing, often exclaiming their love for her.

"How do you all know my name?"

"Well, we've been watching you. A lot."

"Watching me how? I just got here."

His eyes got big, then he hooked a thumb over his shoulder. She looked and saw that most of the crowd had joined him in pointing at one TV or the other as a low murmuring flooded the big room.

"Oh my goodness. *That* Marilyn?"

"Uh, what? You're not her?"

"No! I just have the same name!"

"We like that TV Marilyn so much. We watch her all the time."

"How? There's cable down here? This doesn't make any sense."

"Cable? Uh, no. Recordings. Sure, there are some other films, with horribly lesser stars, but we like Marilyn the best."

"Oh, okay. I get it. You watch her movies all the time. Nice. But I still want to go home."

"Oh, no, no, no. Stop that. We've all wanted a, um, taste of your, uh, talents for so long. We're absolutely famished for you."

An outpouring of agreement and laughter filled the room.

"Well, I sure am flattered. I, uh, have to say that I'm actually more accomplished than that other one anyway."

"You are?"

"Why, yes. Of course."

"Yes, I can see. Especially in the flesh. Oh, that counts for so much."

Many heads were nodding all around Mortimer.

"I really am very flattered, but you've met me, and we've had such a nice chat, but now, can I please just go home?"

He rubbed his chin and furrowed his brow, then turned each way to see what his congregation thought.

"Maybe," said one.

"Sure. Uh-huh."

One pointed at Mortimer and said, "After. She should prove it."

Marilyn didn't wait. She yelled out, "Prove what? What are you all talking about?"

Mortimer turned back around, grinning and nodding.

"Heh. He's right. Yes, of course. Why, *Marilyn*, what you just said. That's what he's talking about."

"I don't understand. You're all crazy! Just open the door, get out of my way, and let me—"

The buzzing stopped.

And so did the pleasantries.

Eyes went blank, faces sagged more, and a lot of lips got stretched back to reveal mouths full of broken teeth, dirty and rotten like they'd been grazing at an oil field.

"Oh, boy. Um . . ."

The key dropped from Mortimer's shaking hand, and every arm covered in ragged cloth, every one close enough, reached between the bars, swiping at Marilyn.

"Uh-oh. Um, no. I changed my mind. Leave the damn door locked!"

* * *

Risk jolted in the splintered wooden door, and K Kat leaped inside with an eager growl. He held it open until Sophia rushed past him, then he looked each way along the street before entering and pushing it shut.

Sophia and the lion were still close, and he took a second to see what locks could be used, but there weren't any. Everything had rusted through or been pried loose.

He turned and leaned his back into it.

Sophia whispered, "Was anything coming?"

He shook his head said, "Shh. Wait."

She stepped in closer to put her arms around his waist, and he put one of his around her. The mountain lion leaned into his torn jeans on his other side.

After a few minutes of keeping themselves quiet, the buzzing stuttered, then evened out.

When Sophia sighed, Risk said, "It's for those . . . zombies."

"Uh-uh. They don't like that."

"Funny, Fia. No, they don't. Because they're not. Not completely."

"Huh? What does that mean?"

He let his arm drop off of her and looked around.

"Buy you a drink?"

She scoffed and said, "Yeah. Me and my lion."

"Yeah. Kenzie."

Sophia looked down, past the short skirt with a lacy hem, past her bare legs ending in high black heels, and used one of them to kick at the dusty floor.

"Sorry," he said.

"It's alright. Yeah, a drink would be good."

"Are you old enough?"

"Close enough," she said, shaking her head. "After all that. They took Sis."

Her hand in his, and with a mountain lion's tail sometimes slapping them from behind, they walked toward the long bar that still had a few stools lined up while others lay dusty on the floor.

Sophia spun one to face the bar, then took a seat.

"Running from zombies, or whatever you're going to explain they are, is tiring. Not fun either."

Risk walked around the bar and stopped, both hands on a smooth but gouged surface wearing alternating messes of dust and oil.

"Getting caught is worse."

"Oh. Yeah. You do have a point."

She patted the seat next to her, and K Kat leaped up onto it, circled around expertly on the small surface, then found a way to sit there too.

"Huh," said Risk. "Never saw that before."

"Oh, come on. All the crazy shit you must see down here."

He smiled and said, "*You* have a point."

He stooped down, out of sight, and clinked and rattled bottles around. When he stood, he held a bottle to the side and blew at it, sending a small cloud out to settle somewhere else.

He frowned while looking around, then turned back toward Sophia.

"Out of the bottle."

"Fine by me. It's actual alcohol, right? Not that crude oil stuff?"

He cleared his throat and said, "Crude rum. You pass?"

"Hell no."

He twisted off the cap and handed it to her. While she was tipping it back, he began the explanation.

"Sure. They're dead. The flesh part of them."

"What other part is there?"

"Mechanical. Electronic."

He shrugged and added, "Who knows? Something."

"Uh, cyborgs?"

"I guess."

He pointed up and said, "They came from up there."

She clinked down the bottle, and her eyes stretched open.

"They build them in . . . what? The attic of this place?"

He grinned and shook his head, looking into her eyes.

"No, Fia. Somewhere Topside."

"Then, what? They sent them here?"

He took a deep breath and let it seep out.

"Complicated."

"This is one of those times."

He tipped his head and said, "What times?"

"A time to use a lot of fucking words."

"Alright. Some factory made a bunch of them. Brain chips planted in cloned flesh."

"And they all decided to vacation here?"

"They gave them all an upgrade. Gave them feelings . . . sexual feelings."

He took a long drink from the bottle.

"Go on. Don't stop now."

"Alright. Their chip brains became obsessed with sex."

"Not a surprise."

"Hey. You're too little," he said, then leaned over the bar to see her legs.

She giggled and pulled down on the hem, trying to cover more of her thighs. Then, she leaned each way, checking what was visible, then looked at Risk again.

"It's a pretty dress. I like it."

He looked up and said, "Yeah. It is."

He straightened up and put one hand on the bottle.

"While their brains were raging with thoughts of sex, they glitched out."

"Glitched? How?"

"That flesh wasn't alive. Not really. Never was."

"Oh, no, no, no. Don't tell me: that upgrade threw them all right into some kind of instant cyborg sex and death dance, and they—"

"They probably weren't—"

"I know they weren't dancing! Neither were the dead guys at Dayzee's. I'm just saying. And they all ended up here? Just like that?"

He snapped his fingers, looking into her blue eyes, and said, "Just like that."

"Sheesh. Hey, we'd better find that guy. The one that knows The Maze."

Risk tipped his head to one side and said, "He's here. Sort of."

"Oh, God. Dead?"

"Sort of."

"I hate this place. How did he sort of die?"

"Bit. In the neck."

"Oh, no fucking way. This place has vampires too?"

He looked at the dead body behind the bar.

"Lots of things here bite."

"Sheesh. Two holes in his neck?"

"Yeah. So, at least one vampire. Vampires aren't sexy?"

"Ugh. I used to think so. Maybe kind of in a weird romantic way. But not when they're killing the—"

"Sort of."

She shook her head and glared at him for a second.

"Not when they're *sort of* killing the guy we need to find my sister."

"Alright. We'll go it alone."

"Now, you're talking."

Sophia took a long drink, then thumped the bottle onto the bar.

And all three turned their heads at the sound of a door creaking, then stopping, then creaking some more.

It opened all the way, and a handsome young man, wearing a polo shirt and short pants and sneakers, tried to look around while rubbing his eyes.

He dropped his arms to his sides and stared at Sophia first, then Risk, then the lion.

"I'm minding my business," he said with a strong British accent, "sublimely knackered, and you,"— he winced and pointed at the lion—"*three* decide to have a celebration?"

Chapter 26 – You Asked for It

Marilyn had pushed herself as far up against the wall as she could, then dragged all of the blankets up to her chin.

"Stay away from me! Leave me alone!"

Arms raked dirty fingers at her through the bars in front of her and from each side. While she was watching, one of them reaching through dislocated his shoulder with a sickening pop, giving him just enough arm length to hook a nail in her clean white blouse.

"No! Don't you dare!"

She heated her hand up without a moment's pause, and she got a burning grip on his wrist. With a puff of smoke and the stench of charred flesh, she burned almost completely through. The guy wailed and withdrew his arm, his hand dangling from just a few threads.

"You'll all get the same! You don't know who you're messing with! That other Marilyn could never—"

The buzzing resumed at a steady pace.

"Oh, that's not ideal," said the man with a dangling, smoldering hand.

He shook it around, puffing smoke out like from an incense burner, and said, "Mortimer. Really. Come on already."

Mortimer looked at the other guy's hand and said, "It's a challenge, Winslow. I'm on it."

Then, he glanced down at the floor by his own feet.

"Huh. I don't even remember dropping that."

He bent over to pick up the key, and several of them led away their damaged companion, leaving a trail of sooty smoke above the crowd.

Who had all refocused on Marilyn.

Mortimer brushed off his clothes, sending a few tatters to the floor, then gave Marilyn his full attention.

"What was . . . oh, I remember. Yes. You,"—he pointed at her and bounced his eyebrows twice—"made a claim that we will require you to validate. If you can, then—"

"What claim? What is wrong with you people?"

He turned one way and snickered at the crowd, saying, "Wrong? Where would we even begin?"

They all snickered back, some shrugging and others nodding their heads or laughing while counting their fingers. He looked at Marilyn again.

"Continuing? Thank you. Now, if you can in some observable way *prove* to us that you are, as you have professed, 'more accomplished' than the Marilyn on our screens, who we absolutely adore . . ."

The crowd behind him roared their agreement.

". . . then, we will seriously consider having you stay only for a very nice dinner. Then, we can—"

Marilyn's stomach growled, loudly enough that Mortimer stopped to listen.

She said, "Oh, um, I really am kind of hungry. But I'd rather just—"

"Prove your claim, then," he said, shrugging. "Prove it. Then, we'll all enjoy the most delightful dinner imaginable. After that, if you still want to leave, well, you will be free to do that."

"You promise?"

"Oh, yes, I do. It will surely be the most delightful dinner you ever—"

"No! Not that! You'll let me leave?"

"After the delightful dinner?"

She squinted at Mortimer, who held the key up and shook it, a silly grin on his weathered face.

"Hmm. You're not leaving me much choice."

"We're not known for leaving anyone a choice."

He turned his head to look at all of the obsessed faces behind him.

"We're kind of a headstrong—"

They cheered and laughed and clapped.

"—lot."

"Okay. Um, I'll show you just one way that I'm so much better than that fake Marilyn on your TVs."

Holding his gaze, she reached up with both hands and took her time with the top button of Pauline's white blouse, then she fluffed the material out to the sides.

Mortimer rubbed his hands together, staring at her chest. Everyone around him got quiet, some holding the cell bars, others holding the old man's shoulders, and all watching every move she made.

She took a deep breath, expanding her lungs, and there were murmurs of approval, which made her grin.

She whispered to herself, under her breath, "Well, it's some kind of attention, at least."

Looking around at the staring faces, she slowly undid the next button, pulled the shirt apart some, and held it. The smooth skin, the fullness, the tempting roundness of her breasts was on display for her adoring captors.

Her stomach growled again, and she didn't mean to, but she giggled softly.

Then, she opened another button, again pulling it apart and leaving the blouse that way.

"So far," said Mortimer, "you're so much better. You understand that we need complete proof, though, don't you?"

Marilyn nodded and giggled, then looked down.

"Oh my goodness," she mumbled to herself, seeing the clear points of her nipples through the thin fabric. "I can't believe I'm so excited from this!"

"We like excited! We are too!"

"And damn, I'm so, so itchy."

"So are we! Whatever that means!"

Her stomach growled.

"Mm, and hungry too," she said.

The murmuring got louder, and Mortimer said, in a serious tone, "We sure know what *that* means."

She delayed popping the final button just long enough to take a breast in each hand, and she sighed and batted her eyes as she lifted them several times, easing them down and feeling the soft cloth of Pauline's blouse rubbing in such a nice way.

"Go on. Go on!" said Mortimer.

"You asked for it."

He nodded like a dilapidated bobble-head doll with a delirious grin.

She unfastened the final button, then held the blouse with both hands.

"You got it."

She pulled it open all the way, displaying her large, milky white and very smooth breasts. Then, she took another very deep breath, smiled, and let it out slowly.

Mortimer said, "You are so much better than—"

A young man beside him, staring and not at her eyes, said, "And she has such perfect . . . she has such, such—"

Marilyn giggled and said, "Perfect nipples? Hmm."

"Yeah, that. Say that again," said Mortimer.

"What? Nipples?"

He giggled and many hands slapped his back.

"You have such perfect . . ."

He waited with his eyebrows way up.

Marilyn giggled and said, "Nipples. I have perfect nipples."

She slipped the blouse back over her shoulders and let it fall.

"Skin," said someone in the crowd.

"Such smooth, soft, living skin," said another.

Some in the crowd shook noticeably, others had thin streams of drool leaking onto their chins, and others pointed with one hand and got busy on themselves with their other hands. Male and female.

"Ooh, you even like the sound of that, don't you? Nipples. Oh, and they're so very excited. See? See my excited nipples?"

Her stomach growled.

She groaned and reached up, pinching both of them and looking at all of the dazed faces.

"Ooh, my nipples are so much better than hers. Don't you think?"

Mortimer, staring at her breasts, only nodded.

The men flanking him pointed and drooled and felt themselves with shameless vigor.

She let both of her breasts go, then turned herself from side to side, getting them swaying.

"Mm, such nice nipples."

Her stomach convulsed. Everyone stared. And drooled.

"I touch my nipples all the time. Just like this."

Her stomach roared and churned, and she grabbed her midsection with both hands.

"Oh, this is crazy," she whispered to herself. "I'm getting even hungrier."

"Hungry. Yeah. More," said Mortimer. "More!"

She reached up again, squeezed them, and said, "They feel so good when they're pinched. Bet you'd like to pinch them, wouldn't you?"

"I'd bite them," said one man in the crowd.

A woman said, "I want to bite them too!"

All through the crowd, both men and women proclaimed their sincere desire to bite Marilyn's breasts.

"Oh, maybe just a little nibble for me. No, some big nibbles."

"I'd sure like to bite them. Can I bite them?"

"Well, you'd all have to get in line, wouldn't you?" she told them. "Then, you'd all get a turn."

"More, more, more!" said Mortimer.

"Then, dinner? You promise?"

"Yes! We'll prepare a special dinner just for you!"

"Oh, okay."

She took a few seconds to unstrap her heels, then set them beside her on the bed.

"You haven't seen anything yet."

She carefully unbuttoned Pauline's jeans and started wiggling her hips.

"Ooh, so tight. I simply must wiggle," she said, giggling as her breasts shook around. "Hmm, what kind of goodies might be in here?"

A chorus of groans came from the crowd.

She shimmied, keeping her breasts in motion, until the waistband was halfway down her thighs.

Giggling again, she said, "Uh-oh. Panties too. Well, we'll just have to get rid of those too."

"Say that again," said Mortimer. "Again!"

"What? Panties?"

The crowd cheered, and hands on crotches got even busier.

"Panties!" Marilyn said. "Uh-oh, I have panties to take off too!"

She turned herself around to give every direction a good view.

"I'd bite that ass."

A woman called out, "Wow, I want to bite that delicious ass."

"Well, all I really want is dinner," Marilyn said, "then we—"

The buzzing ground to a silent stop.

Mortimer and the rest ended any intelligible speech and started snarling, grabbing at her through the bars.

"Oh, my!"

She reached for the blouse, but it was too close to a hand which snatched it out through the bars.

"Hey, I want that back!"

Without planning it, she took a few steps toward the stolen shirt, but other hands, lower, grabbed at her ankles, toppling her to the floor.

"Hey, stop!"

More hands snaked between the bars, grabbing at her pants. She kicked and groaned and tried to back away from them, but they wouldn't lose their grip. Her jeans got peeled away and dragged first through two spaces between the bars, then there was mad growling, then the pants flew through just one opening and were gone.

"Hey, this isn't funny!"

Up on the bed, wearing only her panties, Marilyn put back on her high-heeled white shoes and watched the mob around her cage salivating and snarling and growling.

She pulled the sheets and blankets up again, not noticing the thin streaks of oil staining her skin.

"Oh my goodness, what is going on with me? And them!"

*   *   *

"Who the hell are you supposed to be?" said Sophia.

The bottle went flying and crashed on the floor and in the next instant, Risk was at the man's side. He had one set of long claws at his throat, the points ready to rip in deep. Two from his other set of claws were poised to take out his eyes.

"He killed our contact."

"Hey, wait just a second!" said the stranger. "I can explain that!"

"Talk."

"Uh, how about if we get those nasty claws stowed away somewhere safe first?"

Risk snorted and let his hands return, but he stayed closed, staring into the man's eyes.

"My, oh my. Such a forceful, virile thing you are."

He looked away from Risk.

"And one of the fairer sex who are so seldom fair. It's almost a pleasure to—"

"Hey," said Sophia, rising from her stool with both hands glowing. "I can fry your ass at least as quick as he can remove your throat."

"Hmm. I do believe you. Quite the little tart, you are."

"Tart?"

The man scoffed, looking her down then up, and said, "Let's just say tease, then. Dressing up like a sweet, innocent little girl, when you're probably—"

"I like this goddamn dress."

He snickered and said, "Girlie, you're not the only one."

"You?"

"Oh, heavens, no. I don't have a taste for your kind at all."

He hissed in a laughing kind of way and bared a set of white teeth with two modest, pointy fangs.

"Still, biting a tart might be a fun way to while away the gloomy hours around here."

"Don't even think about it."

He gave Sophia an elegant smile, fangs obvious, and said, "Sorry. Kind of a reflex. Blame it on the environment?"

She snorted her reluctant acceptance and sat back down, just as the pervasive buzzing sound dwindled and stopped.

"Fuck."

Risk left the man and hurried to the front door, where he opened it enough to look both ways. A moment later, he closed the door quietly and returned.

"Quiet from all of us is good."

"Uh, yeah," said Sophia. "Alright."

Risk looked at the man from the basement again.

"We needed him."

He glanced toward the body behind the bar.

"As did I. Different reasons, of course. I'm Bentley. And with whom do I share this disreputable establishment?"

"Risk."

Then, he tipped his head and said, "Sophia."

"An unparalleled pleasure. I'm at a loss to explain why, but it sounded, in my slumber, like there were,"—he smirked at K Kat— "four of you."

"Some damn good ears you have there," Sophia said with her own smirk. "My sister. She was with us, and now we're looking for her."

"Oh, well . . . oh, my. What, pray tell, has happened to your dear big sister?"

Sophia leaned toward him, squinting.

"Who said she was my big sister?"

"Well, no one. It's just a British thing to say that."

"No, it's not," said Risk.

Bentley leaned out farther from his doorway, examining Sophia's legs, bordered by high black heels and a lacy hem.

"Oh. I know. It's that little-girl style of hers. That must be it."

"Forget her style," said Risk. "We needed your last meal to guide us around The Maze."

"Oh, that dodgy place. Not exactly a highly-rated vacation spot. Um, may I sit?"

He tipped his head toward the line of barstools.

Risk looked toward Sophia, and she only scoffed and rolled her eyes.

"Go," he said.

"Thank you, indeed."

He placed one hand on the stool next to Sophia, and she said, "Uh-uh. Try again."

He touched the next one over.

She smirked and said, "Just take the last fucking one already. We don't have time for this."

"Oh, well. I think I'll just take this last one, then. Only because there's no 'bloody time.'"

He swiveled it around and sat.

"Perfect. Now, listen up, kids. I most assuredly have no interest in biting any of your kind,"—he pointed at Sophia—"and you're far too strong and dangerous,"—he smiled at Risk—"so I will simply—"

"Wait," said Sophia. "What's wrong with 'my kind?' Women, you mean?"

"Oh, are we sharing secrets? Very good. I'll begin. It was a woman that got me here, wherever the bloody fuck this place is. I was—"

"Wait again," Sophia said, shaking her head. "You're a vampire, right?"

He nodded.

"British?"

"Why, yes. You've noticed the accent, I'd wager."

She looked at Risk and said, "A vampire that says 'bloody' all the time? Is this place a joke?"

Risk grumbled and said, "Wish the fuck it was."

Loudly, Bentley said, "As I was saying . . ."

He waited until he had their attention.

"So, I was about to have a delicious little tramp meal, in the delightfully darkest and most dismal alley in San Francisco, when—"

"This isn't a goddamn poetry class," Sophia said, snarling. "Just get to the point, will you?"

He coughed, then said, "You're not so delightful. No, not a bit. I would think that you'd much rather behave as a good little girl, the way you're dressed. I dare say, you could at least admit that, hmm?"

Sophia rolled her eyes and scoffed.

"Close enough. Now. I was a professor before I found my, uh, true calling? Let's call it that. Excuse the hell out of me if I wax poetic now and again. Now, I was about to feed off of this little harlot, and I decided I might as well fuck her first. Who wouldn't, right?"

He waited for an answer, but Risk and Sophia only glared at him.

"Hmm. Well. The key to that brilliant idea was to keep things in order. Fuck first, bleed later. Key, I tell you. Simultaneous was an unfortunate, um, menu option, let's say, and it led to a dashing, haunting kind of fellow like me being transported to this fiery pit."

"You bit her while you were having sex with her?"

"Yes. Now, you're catching on. And in the excitement of a most unholy and unforgettable orgasm, I forgot to *not* take too much of her blood."

Sophia nodded and said, "Bloody right."

He scoffed at her and continued.

"So, she died while I was at a relative peak of pleasure, and, well, you know the rest."

"So," said Risk. "No more women?"

He scrunched up his face and said, "Uh-uh. Oh, no. Male blood is so much spicier. Oh my, there's so much violence and impetuousness in it. Such powerful but all too brief and fleeting sparks! Mm, to taste it at its peak. You could say that I have a sweet tooth for homoglobin."

They stared at him.

"Oh, come on. Give an undead one-time English professor a break. That's funny."

He paused, waiting, and still got not even a grin.

"How about this, then? I'd do some very satisfying biting if I could find a tasty little homo *goblin*. Funny, right?"

Sophia was smirking and shaking her head, and Risk was frowning.

So, Bentley sighed and looked down and said, "It's bloody funny."

Sophia lifted her red-hot hand off of the wooden bar surface but not before it had begun to char and smoke.

"I've had enough of him. In record time."

"Wait," said Risk.

He looked at Bentley and said, "Do you know The Maze?"

Bentley looked up, smiling enough to give a good hint of his fangs.

"Eh. Some. What you really want to know is where their hangout is."

Sophia cooled her hand and said, "You know where the zombies took my Sis?"

"Ew," said Bentley, shaking his head and frowning. "They find that appellation rather crude and decidedly inaccurate. No, young lady."

He grinned at her colorful and lacy dress.

"*Very* young lady. Childlike, I'd say, in a teasing, voluptuous, grown-up woman, come fuck me kind of way with all the—"

"Hey!"

"Sorry. Language just kind of all sticks together when it gets flowing sometimes. No. They consider themselves zombeings. And there is significant justification for that term. They *are* actual beings of a sort, after all. Sort of. Sometimes."

"Enough of this!" Sophia yelled, one hand again heating up. "Do you know where they took Marilyn?"

"Marilyn is her name? Huh. That's something. Why, yes, I have a fairly good hunch, and it has nothing to do with my back."

He looked from one unimpressed face to the other.

"Gee. You'd think that someone of my rare and, to some, mythical demographic would elicit some modest praise, even if just out of pity."

"Take us there," said Risk.

"Huh," he said. "No pity?"

"Or die," Sophia said, her hand fully heated.

"No," she added. "Probably both."

Chapter 27 – Still, Who Would Know?

"Who's responsible for this lion's behavior? Who will I sue if I get bit?"

Risk had just closed the door to the Royal Pub, and all four stood outside. Bentley clutched a full bottle, and K Kat watched him closely and growled softly.

"Maybe she wants that blood," Sophia said, pointing at the bottle. "And who the hell are you to complain about being bit?"

"Oh, you're as witty as your little dress is short. Well, she'll have to find her own blood, the savage thing."

"Hang on," Risk said, then went back inside.

"He could certainly be an overpowering sort of man, couldn't he?"

"Huh. He's not always just a man. Better watch yourself."

Bentley tipped his head back and laughed at the featureless black sky.

"Oh, that's rich. I can almost see past your unsavory femaleness if you continue with wit at that enviable level."

"Huh?"

"You told me to watch myself. Ponder that for a second in that pretty little head."

Sophia scoffed and said, "Oh, right. Mirrors."

"Yes! That's a bit of a problem. Next, you'll be telling me to bite my own throat. And I would if I could because that's kind of like . . ."

He waited, bouncing his eyebrows.

"What? Just say it."

He grinned and said, "Masturbation. Oh, yeah. You have no idea."

"Sheesh. I'm sorry I asked."

The door got snapped open, and Risk stomped out, letting it swing shut behind him.

"What's that?"

He held the small bottle out and said, "Zoojoose."

"Yuck," said Bentley. "Horrid stuff."

"Are we ready?" Sophia said. "Can we get going already?"

Bentley bowed, straightened up, then frowned.

"Times like these . . ."

"Oh, God. What, now?"

"It's a good time to have a sinister black cape. I'd swing it around, maybe hold it across my face, just looking over the top, and say, 'Hugh vill now follow me.'"

"Just bite him, K Kat. We'll find Sis on her own."

The lion notched up her growling and looked ready to pounce.

"Okay! I'm done!"

He turned and started walking, saying over his shoulder, with a laugh, "You will now follow me!"

Sophia looked toward Risk and scoffed, and he shook his head, then patted K Kat's head.

"Come on, girl. Let's find Mare."

They hurried a few steps to catch up with Bentley, then followed close behind him as he led them down dark, narrow streets. He turned corners seemingly randomly and after the next one, they stood and looked along a drab road lined with shabby wooden structures close-in on both sides.

"The entrance, I think," he said, "is not too far along this fine avenue."

"Well?" said Sophia. "Show us."

"Oh, you must have seen those frightening bat creatures. The ones that roost way up there in the spires and stalagmites that crust up that ceiling. You've seen them?"

"I've seen them," said Sophia.

Risk grunted, barely nodding his head.

Sophia tipped her head toward him and said, "He's killed them. Viciously too."

Bentley turned enough to look down along Risk's abdomen, not hidden by the buttonless black leather vest, then down along his legs in worn blue jeans, and ending at his torn and gouged black work boots.

"My, my. Such hot, hot blood."

He looked at Sophia and said, "Those horrible bat things do a lot of swooping in these environs. I'd feel safer if this very intimidating, breathtaking, and tantalizingly bite-worthy creature here,"—he pointed at Risk—"leads the way. Oh, and with that shaggy carnivore that you so oddly have adopted into your little tribe."

Risk scoffed and started down the street, K Kat by his side, and Bentley followed, so close to Sophia that he sometimes bumped into her.

"How far?" Risk said without turning around.

"I'll give you sufficient notice. I haven't forgotten about you. Not with jeans that tight. Mm."

Risk grumbled and kept walking.

And Bentley, with Sophia by his side, gradually slowed his pace. Risk and the lion were three steps ahead, then five, then seven.

Bentley looked down and said, "I do adore those sexy shoes of yours. Can I have just a very quick better look?"

"You can't have them. Just . . . no way."

"Silly, girlie. Not my color. Come on. Just a quick look."

Sophia stopped and held one leg out, then tipped her foot each way as Bentley leaned closer, studying it.

"Well, that's monumentally alluring. A little higher, please?"

She scoffed and lifted her leg higher, then reached a hand for his shoulder to keep her balance.

"Oh, that's nice. That's sweet how that little strap around your delicate ankle holds it right there."

He looked up at her, still leaning over, and said, "No matter what kind of gymnastics might occupy you."

She snarled at him quietly, then looked ahead with her leg still raised.

"Hey, we're falling behind. We'd better—"

He stood too quickly, almost tipping her over, and she staggered back a few steps.

"Oh, I'm so sorry!"

He hurried to stay close to her, reaching for her arms and shoulders but doing nothing more than keeping her off-balance and backing up.

"Hey, just stop trying to—"

"A little girl needs help, that's all."

"Just stop. Quit—"

"Such a pretty little girl too. All I want is to—"

She'd backed close to a dingy wall with a heavy plank door, which he jerked open quickly and shoved her through. She'd just started a protest, not exactly a scream yet, and he dropped a thick wooden post across it to prevent her opening it from the inside.

He stood near, grinning and wiping his hands, and tipped his head to listen.

Faint screaming, having no chance of reaching through the thick boards, flared for just a second, then stopped completely.

Bentley looked ahead, saw Risk and the lion walking toward their destination, then scurried himself out to the middle of the road.

Where he fell to the ground and screamed.

"Help! Come back!"

He tipped his head enough to see that they'd heard and were running back to him. Then, he laid an arm across his face and sobbed.

"Help me! I've been attacked!"

* * *

"Hey, what are you—"

The wooden door closed quickly from the outside.

"You goddamn vampire! You wait till—"

A small man with an extra, non-functional head, was lurking above Sophia, clinging to the rotting boards. In his hand was a wet cloth that he held as far from either of his faces as he could.

He saw her hand starting to burn, so he frowned and launched himself. Hitting her back like a loose sack of dirt, he wrapped one arm around her neck and with the other hand, he held the cloth over her face.

She wobbled, and he hung on. Her feeble attempts at pulling the cloth away only caused her hand to start burning into his sleeve. But that heat, like her consciousness, faded quickly.

And when she collapsed, he still held on and took the ride down with her.

He unwound his arm and patted at the smoldering cloth, all while keeping his rag tight over her face.

"Dammit. Always some kind of goddamn complication."

He hit the fabric of his sleeve again, chasing a few weak sparks onto the cold stone floor, then he gingerly backed the cloth away from her face.

"Oh, you're a pretty one. Very pretty. I can't wait to deliver you."

He wiggled free the parts of him that she'd pinned to the floor, then stood to observe his catch.

"Very pretty."

It took strenuous effort and almost constant grunting, but he managed to roll and shove and tug her up onto a low, flat, wheeled cart. He started at her head, feeding a coarse burlap sack over her, but he stopped when it had just passed her shoulders.

"Oh, so pretty. So very pretty."

Sophia, lying on her back, partially covered with burlap, never moved when he held her breasts, one hand on each.

"Oh, just lovely. So soft. So nice in lace."

He squeezed them around for a few seconds, gave the locked door a quick glance, then pulled down the lacy dress that could hardly contain them, working it lower until he could tuck it under Sophia's breasts.

"Oh. Oh, those are nice. Too nice for me! I'm just a slave!"

He licked his lips, staring at them, then giggled as he began to lean toward them.

"Still, who would know? Mm, just a nice private tasting for me. No one will ever know! I won't tell!"

But he stopped at the sound of Bentley screaming where he lay in the dusty street just beyond the barricaded door.

"Dammit!" he said, still dragging his wet tongue around on all the sores on his lips.

He stared at Sophia's bare breasts for a second, then said, "Oh, fuck it."

He leaned over and closed his dripping lips on one of her nipples, then moaned softly while tugging at it before letting it pop back out.

"Do the job right, slave! Do it right!"

He giggled then spent a few seconds sucking on her other nipple, seeing how far he could stretch it up and keep it stuck between his lips.

"Mm, so nice. So pretty and so nice."

He stretched out the pretty cloth, letting her breasts settle back, then froze, staring at them.

"Oh, all wet. She'll know! She'll know!"

He wiped across her breasts several times with his sleeve, then he stretched her dress back in place, barely covering what he'd been delaying his escape just to suck for a second or two.

"Always something! No one will know! I won't tell! I won't!"

He dragged the sack down over her, grunting from the effort, until at last he could push first one high black heel, then the other, into the bag, which he tied off quickly with a built-in cord.

He walked to one end of the cart, grabbed the handle, and started pushing his cargo out of that room and into a darker room.

"Oh, so pretty. A good catch. A very good catch."

He whistled a cheerful tune as the cart's wheels squealed softly and he pushed her farther into the shadows.

He stopped the cart. He stopped his whistling.

"Maybe there will be some left for me? Even a little? No, don't be stupid. You're just a slave!"

He shrugged and resumed his transport duties.

And his whistling.

* * *

Risk towered over Bentley where he lay in the road, an arm still covering his face.

"It was terrible! They came out of nowhere!"

"Who? How many?"

He looked up at Risk, then turned only his eyes to see K Kat's sharp, shiny teeth, close and ready to snap on his head.

To Risk, he said, "Well, I don't know! I got hit in the head, and I fell, and when I could finally look around, she was gone!"

Risk and K Kat both growled and looked around them.

Bentley reached up a hand.

K Kat took a snap at it, and he pulled it clear just in time.

"Good girl," said Risk.

The lioness stayed close and kept her teeth bared. Bentley moved only his eyes between the lion and Risk.

"Later, you can bite the fuck out of him."

The mountain lion grumbled and took a few steps back.

"Strong as you are, you could easily help me up."

"I could step on your throat."

"Never mind, then. Brute."

Bentley got himself up onto his feet and swiped at the dust his clothes had picked up. Risk and K Kat looked in every direction, with the big cat sniffing with her snout up.

She stopped moving, snorted a few times, then ran toward the door through which Sophia had been shoved. Risk followed so closely that he could have held her tail.

"Who barred this door? You?"

Bentley was walking toward them, still dusting his arms.

"Me? What? Why? Maybe it's been like that forever."

Risk grumbled and threw the post aside and jerked open the door. Before he could take a step, K Kat brushed past him and into the dark room. He followed.

Bentley stayed outside, where no one could see his smile.

"Fuck," Risk said with a slow groan.

It was a large, cluttered room with a dozen doors leading out of it. All were closed and looked like no one had used them in a long time.

Risk pulled open one of them and looked inside.

K Kat growled at the absolute darkness.

Another door. The same thing. He tried them all.

Risk ventured back out of the building, with a lion by his side, and walked up to Bentley.

He grabbed his throat with a human but still unstoppable grip.

"Talk."

Bentley gagged, and K Kat swiped at Bentley's kicking feet which weren't touching the ground.

Risk helped him hit the street more quickly than if he would have only let him go. Bentley sprawled out, and a small two-way radio bounced away out of a pocket.

K Kat sniffed it a few times, then brought it to Risk, who held it close and studied it.

"This works?"

Bentley, holding his throat, said, "Static, sure. Who the hell is there to talk to?"

"Why do you have it?"

"Oh," he said as he stood, "just in case somebody radars in some pop music. British, preferably."

"Now, K Kat."

She leaned back, ready to leap onto him, and he said, "Oh, go ahead. I've been wishing I was dead ever since I got here."

The lion held back, tipping her head and only watching.

Bentley bared his throat and said, "How appropriate. Yes, dearest girl lion, bite the vampire's throat. Rip it the fuck apart."

She was about to comply when Risk held a hand out.

"Not yet."

"Oh, come on," said Bentley. "Death by girl. A right proper end."

K Kat snarled and snapped in Bentley's direction, then sat calmly.

"Marilyn. The Maze."

"Ah, yes. You need me. How utterly foolish of me to think either of you would dare kill me."

"I can be foolish."

Bentley lost his grin, then turned his head when K Kat bared her teeth and snarled at him.

"Her too."

Bentley blew out a deep breath and looked down at the dirty street.

Risk chuckled silently and said, "Good girl."

Chapter 28 – Such a Precious Little Girl

Sophia yawned and tried to keep it going much longer than normal. With her eyes still closed, she ended it with a comfortable sigh and licked her lips a few times. The feathery end of the braid Marilyn had given her tickled her nose, and she smiled as she tried blowing at it, which worked well enough to stop it from touching her anymore.

With her right cheek resting on a fresh and clean and puffy quilt, she lazily opened her eyes, only to have them drift shut again.

After a few seconds, she made another attempt, held them open slightly longer, and got a brief glimpse of the cushion on which she lay and a clean wood floor beyond it.

But no more than that. Her eyelids were just too heavy.

Another yawn came next, along with another slow, easy sigh. After a few lazy blinks, she was able to keep her big blue eyes open enough to look around more.

The floor was high, or maybe the cushion was low. No, the cushion was low, just lying flat on the floor. Farther along, tasteful antique furniture was all arranged neatly, including two high-backed upholstered chairs with dark blue fabric and a high wooden table between them, which supported an ornate candelabra with more dancing flames than she could count in such a sleepy state.

Beyond the candles and higher on the wall, the eyes of a beautiful but grim woman in a drab portrait studied her from behind years of dust.

To the right of that collection, a large, wooden square filled much of the wall, and its few thin gaps were like painted orange strips, teasing the existence of the weak firelight outside

But the braid fluff had flopped over and resumed its playful tickling. She tried blowing at it again, but it didn't help, so she reached up to flick it out of the way.

Except that her arm didn't move. Not even a little.

It couldn't.

Only then did she feel the soft cushion on which she lay facedown and her right cheek pressed into the fresh blanket.

And she felt her arms behind her back.

Tied. Tight. All the way from her wrists to as far up as whatever was used could be wrapped.

"Dammit," she whispered to herself.

She tried to pull them apart, or move the two of them together to one side or the other, or to even separate her wrists a slight amount.

She couldn't. And she knew that those bindings weren't going anywhere.

Not unless she burned through them.

She scoffed and started a slow burn in both hands, keeping it isolated in her palms, which she knew were both turned up.

With them glowing hot, she began a careful advance of her heat from her palms to her wrists, and from there, she would then—

"Oh, careful, my dearest little one."

Sophia stopped spreading the fire at the sound of a voice both feminine and syrupy, like someone had warmed it up then poured it into her ear.

It had come from behind her, so she picked her head up and rotated it, then laid it on her left cheek at feeling too weak to hold it up.

Several steps away, seated in a plush black chair with tangled streaks of white crisscrossing all over it, sat a beautiful woman with hair black like Sophia's but even longer.

In the faint light, her eyes appeared like small pits that had shooed away any color but black. And her long eyelashes were just as black.

When the woman offered a meager smile, Sophia looked lower, at her lips, which were full and red, even in the near darkness.

Her eyes were drawn lower, still, at seeing so much skin exposed below her delicate chin. The curve of her large, full breasts was assisted by a white blouse a size too small and buttoned not nearly high enough for any level of modesty.

Crossed legs, bare and dominating Sophia's view, were a blend of soft and smooth—unmistakably feminine—and the uncommon strength of lean muscles just beneath that softness.

She was kicking her crossed leg gently, calmly, like a metronome in a room without any sounds, even any that might invade from the outside. At the end of each kick, almost demanding Sophia's undivided attention, at least for a time, she wore a short black leather boot, crowded with tight black lacing in front and wielding a lethally sharp heel. A high one.

"Let's not burn anything, my sweet girl. It would be such a waste for you to be cooked."

Sophia stared without expression as she let the heat bleed out of her hands.

She watched the woman glance at her cooling hands, then smile as she looked into her eyes again.

"That's a good girl."

Sophia shook her head and blinked a few times, then struggled to say, in a still-tired voice, "Just who the hell are you?"

The woman barely smiled as she rose from her seat and to Sophia, from lying low to the floor, she appeared to be mostly legs. Long, strong, smooth legs with only a hardly-there black leather skirt to cover the very tops of them.

She walked over, her heels striking softly against the wood, then paused long enough for Sophia to turn her eyes down to study both of her boots.

After she'd tried to look up at her eyes again, the woman knelt beside Sophia. She leaned close, her black eyes now showing some white around the edges, and touched her hair softly, playing with it and moving it off of Sophia's cheek.

"I'm Widow."

"Widow? What the hell kind of name is that?"

"Hmm. So many have died and left me. All in my arms too."

"What are you—"

"I'm so happy you came to stay with me."

Sophia managed a weak snarl and said, "Stay?" then tried to free her arms again, causing Widow to smile and shake her head a few times.

"Oh, you're a precious little thing, aren't you?"

"I'm nobody's precious anything. You'd better just—"

Widow touched a finger to Sophia's lips, shushing her, then laid a pair of scissors on the cushion directly in front of her face. Sophia's eyes were pulled down to the metal, candlelight giving it some life, then back up to Widow's eyes.

"Such dreadful things can happen to a little girl if she doesn't behave."

Sophia continued to stare, even after the finger was removed from her lips.

"Now is a very good time to stay quiet for me."

She paused, smiled, and said, "I know you can do that for me if you try. Will you try to be a good girl for me?"

With the scissors back in her hands, still close to Sophia's eyes, she waited for an answer.

Sophia nodded.

"Mm. So nice."

She looked away from Sophia's stare and smiled.

"Oh, such a delightful dress for such a pretty little girl."

With Sophia lying still and quiet, her breaths slow, Widow began taking little snips at her flowery dress.

"What a shame to have to damage your pretty dress. But we can always dress you up again in something just as nice and pretty."

She cut up each sleeve to the neck opening, then through the lacy border. Then again along the undersides of the sleeves and down the dress's sides, making more cuts where necessary and taking her time to snip one lacy dress into just pieces of colorful cloth.

The large front piece of it remained underneath Sophia, held between her and the cushions.

And other pieces, above, held to her only by being snug under her bound arms.

"There we go. Almost there."

She gently lifted Sophia's arms and wiggled the top cloth pieces down and off of her.

"Oh, you're just a little girl!" she said at the sight of Sophia's frilly, lacy pink panties.

"No," said Sophia, "that's just, I mean—"

Flashing the scissors again, Widow said, "Don't be ashamed of your secret desires. I love little girls. And you are such a precious little girl."

She fluffed around the ruffles, tugging and tipping them to get them all standing up like a soft tail. Then, she patted Sophia's panties and her ass as she leaned in close and whispered in her ear.

"My turn. Be a good, quiet girl and just watch."

She set down the scissors and stood where Sophia could look up at her.

Holding Sophia's gaze, Widow unbuttoned her tight blouse, top to bottom, then pulled it open to reveal a tiny black bra that did little to cover nipples that were working on poking their way through the thin cloth.

She slipped the shirt back over her shoulders, let it drop to her wrists, then set it gently on the chair behind her.

Still smiling at Sophia, she pinched the waistband of her skirt and began shimmying it down over her hips. And Sophia looked away from Widow's eyes to see just how tiny the woman's black panties were.

Widow dropped the skirt, stooped down to get it, then set it neatly on the chair with her blouse.

"There we go. Now, neither of us has very much to cover us. You can see me, and I can see so much of you."

Then, she stood with her hands on her hips, a magnificent pair of legs dominating Sophia's view. And above them, the tiniest of panties, a trim waist, and breasts straining to escape their sheer confines, and a thick black mane framing a face of uncommon beauty.

Widow smiled.

"Mm. I have such a precious little girl."

* * *

"It might be the right time," Bentley said.

Risk stopped looking around at all of the buildings, which seemed to be all connected with dark hallways and probably tunnels too.

"For what?"

"The 'joose."

"I don't need it."

"Not you, you sublimely dangerous shape-shifting man," said Bentley. "The lion."

"Huh?"

"Look," said the vampire in a polo shirt, "even I can tell that this thing,"—he sneered and pointed at K Kat—"is more than just a big pussy cat. Oh, I think I might have revealed the secret. How about that?"

"You don't know what you're talking about."

"Oh, I dare say I do. She's something else, not just a lion. You know it as well as I do."

"I do?"

"Damn right. Give the lion some Zoojoose. Maybe she'll change into whatever or whoever else she is. If that happens, she'll have extra brain power *and* she might retain the cunning of a savage lion."

"Or she could die."

Bentley laughed and said, "We're all practically dead already. I mean, haven't you looked around at this fucking place?"

Risk looked around and grumbled.

"Not Mare. Not Fia. They're not going to die."

"Oh, you even have nice little pet names for them. Endearing. I'd say you have nothing to lose."

Risk rubbed around K Kat's ears, and Bentley said, "Well, maybe the monster cat. We shant shed any tears at losing her, I suppose."

"I'm not losing anyone."

"Oh, good, because I didn't really mean that I wanted to die."

"You, I'll lose. In a second."

Risk took out the small bottle of Zoojoose and dropped to one knee beside K Kat.

"Just a little," he said, and the lion held his gaze the whole time he tipped the bottle and emptied just a few drops into her mouth.

She closed her eyes tight and yipped, and Risk took a step back.

K Kat yipped again, aiming her cry at the black ceiling, and started shaking.

Risk looked at Bentley, but he only shrugged, so they both watched the lion.

Her shaking increased, and her growling sounded like it was rattling deep inside until it finally bounced out, causing occasional snorts.

With one big tremor, she fell onto her side and lay there panting.

Then, she got blurry.

Her tight brown fur got lighter.

Cat legs became woman arms and legs.

Her lion ears twitched as they were shrinking, and they seemed to grow into a long brown mane.

And Kenzie lay naked in the street, on her back, her bare breasts rising with every deep breath and jiggling as the last nervous tremors wracked her.

"Oh my," said Bentley. "Not what I want, mind you, but damn impressive all the same."

He reached for Kenzie's breasts, and Risk grunted and slapped his hand away, scowling at him, then looked again at Kenzie.

After a final tremor swept through her, she calmed and opened her eyes.

"You're Kenzie?"

"Who," she said, her voice a raspy whisper, "who are—"

Her back arched with a violent spasm, and her legs kicked as her arms flailed all around. With a high-pitched and very feminine howl, a brutal seizure snapped her around.

Bentley took a few steps back, but Risk knelt beside her and leaned over, covering her and holding her as she shook.

"It's okay. I have you."

She tried speaking, but it was only a mix of gibberish and growling, and Risk didn't let her go, even when Bentley chuckled and spoke.

"Told you it was despicable stuff."

Chapter 29 – Lick It Up, Hungry Girl

Marilyn looked out through the bars of her prison cell at all of the mindless stares, faces snarling, and hands grabbing. Her blouse and jeans had been dragged off somewhere into the crowd. And she huddled as far from all of them as she could get, on the bed and with her back to the wall.

Blankets pulled up high.

Wearing only panties and heels.

With a stomach that growled almost as loudly as the horde fighting to get at her.

And itchy. Feeling itchier than she'd ever felt before.

Even with countless pairs of dead eyes staring at her, she reached one hand down under the blanket. She let her fingertips caress her soft skin all the way down over her belly. Then, she smiled and closed her eyes after those fingertips had slipped inside her panties.

With her eyes still closed, she mumbled to herself, "Oh, what is wrong with me? Mm, but it feels so, so good."

She snapped open her eyes and stopped her eager fingers when the buzzing started up again.

The eyes that had been staring and vacant looked sometimes at her, sometimes at each other, and sometimes around the room. Like any other crowd.

"Well," said Mortimer, scoffing, "that was untimely. We're kind of a slave to that thing, you know."

"Uh, what thing? That buzzing?"

"Yes, that. Well, not the buzzing, so much, but what's causing the buzzing. It's a broadcast power source that animates our more reasonable selves. Without that . . . well, I think you've seen."

Marilyn laughed softly, got her fingers going again while trying to not move the blankets from it, and said, "Oh, yes, I did see. That was a little scary."

"And embarrassing for us. I'm sadly inadequate to make that whole thing more reliable."

"You made that? Whatever that is?"

"Yes. I believe I could keep it running with just a few upgrades. But you know what?"

He swept one arm back toward the crowd behind him.

"They kind of like all the silly antics that happen when the buzzing stops. Okay, you got me—so do I! So, there's not a lot of incentive to fix that blasted thing."

"Oh my goodness. You like how you, um, when that thing stopped and you—"

"You're still hungry, aren't you?" he said, pointing at her.

"Like you wouldn't believe."

"Huh. I might. I just might, at that."

He snapped his fingers to someone in the crowd, and Marilyn could see them shuffling around, making room and opening a pathway for someone approaching. They finally got close to Mortimer and stood to each side of him: a young man with short black hair, and a young woman with shoulder-length blond hair.

And both were as fit as any models on a magazine's cover.

He wore simple jeans and a t-shirt, all ratty and ripped.

She wore dingy khaki pants and a simple, stained flannel shirt.

And both wore old oil-stained sneakers.

Mortimer smiled at the two of them, then looked again toward Marilyn.

"We apologize for that inconvenience, and we hope it hasn't spoiled our time together."

"Well, as a matter of, I'd like to—"

"To show you that we're basically kind and not that different from you, I'd like to send in some meager assistance for you. You know, just to get you going in a good direction before that special dinner."

"Um, a good direction would be—"

"Clothes," he said, and pointed at the young woman holding up a clean blouse and jeans, "from Janie."

"My old ones, if you could just bring them—"

"Janie is short for Jane. Rhymes with . . ."

He bounced his eyebrows and waited, and the crowd around and behind him chuckled.

"Um, I don't—"

"She's my adopted daughter, you know. She insisted on being what she called 'in control' of your welcoming committee. Peculiar choice of words, I'd say. I wanted to send Melvin in there, but Janie is so incredibly perverted and sadistic. I couldn't tell her no!"

"Huh? Why would—"

"Oh, you'll see: we're all really just a bunch of perverts. Buzzing or not."

He shrugged and said, "We're just kind of built that way. Sorry!"

"Wait. You're saying that—"

"And Blaine, here,"—the crowd roared with laughter, then quieted—"has some modest canned goods to tide you over until we can deliver that very tasty dinner to you. He'll just carry those in for you."

"Uh, I sure am hungry, but I'd rather—"

"The key!" he said, holding it up like a trophy. "Yes, you're right!"

He inserted it into the lock, fought with it for a few seconds, then was able to swing out the heavy door.

"Um . . ."

Janie and Blaine walked right in, smiling.

And Mortimer slammed the door closed again.

When he looked up from clunking the locking mechanism, key still in his hand, he met Marilyn's alarmed gaze.

He shrugged and said, "Hey, it's better if it's only two of them, right?"

He waited. Marilyn stared.

"Right? With that unpredictable buzzing business?"

"Um, yes. Yes, better."

"Good! Okay, just let our ambassadors provide a thoughtful welcome, and we'll get things cracking,"—he paused to let everyone laugh—"for you very soon. And you just do exactly as dear Janie says, okay? Okay!"

He turned and blended into the crowd, all of whom were engaged in pleasant conversations, smiling and just being ordinary. But almost every pair of eyes was locked on whatever would happen in the cage.

"Oh, boy."

"Hi," Janie said as she walked toward the bed. "I'm Janie, which you already know."

She pointed with a big smile and said, "And you're Marilyn. The best Marilyn. Mm, you sure showed us that."

"Uh, I guess that's the deal, right? Then, I can go?"

Janie said, "That sure is what Mortimer said. Yep."

She gave Janie a quick smile, then watched as Blaine moved to a corner and was setting down what looked like cans of food. He noticed her watching and looked her way.

"I'm Blaine, and you already know that. Yes, there's a can opener too. I'll just set it all over here for now."

Janie looked around, then leaned in and whispered.

"Hey, I know you want to get out of here. Let me help, alright?"

"You'd help me?"

"Sure. But it won't be easy. They don't miss much."

"No, for sure. So, what do we do? How do I get out of here?"

"They're big on Marilyn. The one on the TVs. We just need some kind of show to get them distracted. Really, they'll kind of go numb, thinking they're watching that other Marilyn on TV. That's how they watch TV. Are you in?"

"Of course. Distracted, how?"

"Well, it doesn't take all that much. You'll see."

"Uh, how are you two in such good shape? I mean, if you're—"

"Zombies? Yeah, weird, isn't it? Oh, most of them don't like that word. They prefer zombeings."

"Oh, that makes sense. Okay."

"I'm okay with zombie, though. It sounds more cute."

"Okay. I don't want to insult anyone."

"Nonsense. You're fine."

Marilyn noticed the girl's kind smile and though her skin didn't look quite right, overall, she was very attractive. Her flannel shirt was unbuttoned enough to show that her breasts were generous, and she was fit and healthy everywhere.

When she finally looked back up, it was to see Janie grinning at her.

"They're pretty nice. I mean, if you were to get them out in the open. Oh, hey, you know what?"

She held up the blouse that she'd brought in for Marilyn.

"Before you take this, mind if I try it on? I don't usually get the pretty stuff like this."

"Oh, of course. Go right ahead."

Janie put one knee up on the bed, and Marilyn gave the girl's breasts another quick look, lingering just long enough to see two ample mounds hidden behind the soft material. They'd moved enough to make it obvious that the zombie girl wasn't wearing a bra.

And Marilyn was studying those breasts while her fingers were still busy inside her panties.

Janie smiled and said, "A little help would be nice."

"You mean . . ."

"You don't mind, do you?"

"Um . . ."

Janie tipped her head quickly toward all of the onlookers and whispered, "Just to distract them, remember? Play along. Pretend you're enjoying yourself."

Marilyn almost gasped from her hidden efforts, but she suspended that and said, "Uh, sure. I'm actually an actress too."

"Perfect."

Taking the blankets with her, she wiggled her way to the side of the bed, and Janie took just a step back, which gave Marilyn room to swing her legs over and sit.

Then, Janie stepped closer, and Marilyn, so close to some urgent ecstasy with her fingertips just seconds earlier, couldn't steer her eyes away from the girl's breasts.

Janie touched her cheek, and Marilyn, "Ooh, kind of cold."

"Eh. It happens."

She played with Marilyn's hair and stepped in closer, her legs outside of Marilyn's.

Marilyn popped the shirt's top button, using both hands, giggled once, and said, "Oh, just like that?"

"Mm-hmm. Keep going," Janie said over the satisfied murmuring from outside the cage.

"Um . . ."

Janie bounced her eyebrows twice, then spoke loudly enough for the onlookers to hear.

"You know you want to."

Marilyn stared up at her.

"I mean," she said in a loud voice, "you want to see my breasts."

Many in the crowd said "breasts" and "mm-hmm."

Marilyn sighed and reached for the next button. Then, the next, all while Janie fussed with her blond mane and sometimes caressed the smooth skin of her cheeks.

"There," she said after Marilyn had finished unbuttoning. "Now, what?"

Marilyn giggled and slipped one hand back inside the blanket. And inside her panties. And she gasped softly when she let two fingers sneak in a short way.

She looked up at Janie and said, "Your turn."

"Hmm. Yeah, it is. You can look into my eyes later. Not right this second."

Marilyn looked straight ahead.

Janie opened the shirt, showing Marilyn two perfect zombie girl breasts at eye level. And there was no doubt how excited the girl had become.

The murmuring all around the cage rose up, and a lot of them were making comments, some laughing. But Marilyn looked only straight ahead.

"Oh, wow. They're so perfect."

"My what are?"

Marilyn looked up, saw the zombie girl wink, then said, more loudly, "Your breasts are perfect."

Marilyn dared to look quickly to each side of the girl, and she had just enough time to see a lot of slack jaws dripping drool and a lot of hands rubbing crotches.

"Uh-huh, kind of perfect. Something else you wouldn't know: being a zombie like us causes an insane level of sexual hunger. Not just for the usual stuff. Oh, no. We like things dirty."

She waited, smiling at Marilyn, who only looked up at her.

"And my breasts . . . ooh, I want so bad for someone to touch them. I'd kill to have you to touch them."

"Me?"

"Mm-hmm. Go ahead. Mm, I'd love to feel warm hands touching them again."

Marilyn stopped caring if her left hand was moving the blankets, and she'd gotten herself to the same plateau she'd stopped at just minutes earlier. And she was about to jump off.

She reached out with her other hand and touched one of Janie's breasts.

Voices in the crowd called out, "Oh my God," and "Oh, yeah. Touch it. Touch it!"

"Ooh," said Marilyn. "Kind of cold."

"Cold is okay, though, right?"

"Yes. Just, I don't know, different."

"Squeeze my breast. I want you to play with both breasts."

Marilyn fondled the zombie girl's breasts, sometimes looking up into her eyes and seeing the pleasure she was giving her. No one around them was laughing, but they were making lewd comments about what they wanted next.

"Oh, that feels so good," said Janie. "Do you like touching my breasts?"

With her fingers busy, Marilyn moaned softly and said, "Oh, yes. They're so soft and they—"

"They need some lips on them."

"Yeah!" someone yelled, and another said, "Do it!"

Marilyn stopped fondling and looked up into Janie's eyes.

"They need that?"

"Mm-hmm. And a warm tongue. I need you to lick my breasts. Lick both of my breasts with that warm tongue."

"Do it!" said one, and another yelled, "Lick those breasts!"

Janie waited until Marilyn had looked straight ahead at her breasts again, then she leaned to one side and saw what she was doing under the blanket.

Marilyn's breaths had gotten quicker, and she gasped softly when Janie said, "Wouldn't you like a nice, soft zombie breast to suck on?"

She gave Marilyn just a second to moan.

"Especially while you're, uh, you know," she said, then tipped her head toward the busy hand under the blanket.

"You've always wanted to suck on zombie breasts. Isn't now a really good time to suck zombie nipples, while you're fingering your pussy?"

"She's what?" said a man in the crowd.

"I'd finger her pussy for her," said a woman outside the cage.

Marilyn stopped fingering and said, "I am not. What makes you—"

"Oh, come on. I bet you have a really nice pussy. I'd do more than just finger it. Go on. Get busy down there with your pussy."

Marilyn had reached the point of no return under the blanket, and she nodded and said, "I, uh, don't know if I've always wanted zombie breasts. Oh, but I do, um, I think, uh, kind of want them now."

She leaned forward, her lips about to touch.

But Janie touched her cheek and took a step back.

"Hold that thought, gorgeous. Keep playing with your sweet pussy a second."

She took the few steps needed to reach the bars, and Marilyn watched her moving from side to side before turning around and walking back toward her.

"Um, what's that?"

"You noticed that my nipples are wet? Oh, they sure are. Isn't that better for you to suck them?"

She stepped in closer, both of her breasts about to touch Marilyn's face.

"Suck them," she said to Marilyn as she played with her hair again. "Suck the wet zombie nipples. Mm, feel them between your lips. Touch the cold zombie nipples with your warm tongue."

"They sure are cold!" yelled a man.

"How do you know?" a woman near him said.

"Because she's a zombeing, that's why!"

Marilyn gave her fingers a decisive final set of soft strokes and slides, groaned, and parted her lips enough for Janie to lean forward.

"Mm, good. Are you still rubbing that sweet pussy?"

Marilyn, looking up, nodded, then she looked again at the breasts so close to her mouth.

"Taste it. Rub your pussy while you taste my nipples."

Marilyn sighed and closed her lips around the zombie girl's wet nipple.

Causing her stomach to growl madly.

She sucked it like crazy, then licked it until whatever was on it was gone. Consumed.

Then, she focused on the other one, licking and sucking with a growling stomach as Janie laughed softly and caressed her cheeks.

"Oh, good hungry girl. Yeah, suck those nipples."

Marilyn couldn't see it, but the smooth white skin of her cheeks had developed a pattern of jagged red lines, all emanating from around her lips and silently snaking out, covering her cheeks but going no farther.

She kept going from one breast to the other, and Janie said, "Hungry, aren't you?"

"Mm-hmm. What was that stuff? It's, uh, different. Tasty."

"Just something kind of special for you. Would you like more?"

Marilyn held a breast with one hand, a nipple covered with her own saliva close to her lips, and gave the finishing touches to the pleasure she'd given herself.

"Oh, wow. Yes, I'd like more."

"Blaine loves that answer," she said with a smile.

"Blaine?"

Marilyn looked behind her and saw Blaine grinning at her while loosening his belt buckle, then pulling down his zipper.

"I've been ready. Really ready," he said.

She looked back at Janie and said, "Oh, I don't know about—"

Marilyn saw just a flash of the same substance on Janie's lips as she leaned in and kissed her. And she didn't fight to get away.

She broke the kiss only long enough to lick the girl's lips frantically.

"Hmm, yeah," said Janie. "Just like that. Lick it up, hungry girl."

"I'm so hungry."

She turned and saw Blaine looking back at her while his very erect zombie male member, jutting out through the cell bars, was being brushed with the same mysterious substance.

"Um . . ."

They finished varnishing it, and he turned toward her. It was long and hard and something dripped from the very tip of it.

Her eyes still on it, Janie leaned enough to whisper in her ear.

"Zombie cock, Marilyn. Imagine zombie cock inside you."

"I'd take that offer," said a woman outside the cage.

"Shit, we all would!" said a zombie man.

Marilyn whimpered softly, still staring at it and still touching herself, and said, "Inside me?"

"Uh-huh. In your pussy. Just imagine a hard, cold zombie cock deep in your wet pussy."

She looked up at Janie and was about to speak, but stopped when Janie said, "No one gets a harder cock than a zombie. It's so fucking hard."

"Is that because it has—"

But Marilyn got forced into a deep kiss, leaving her no option but to moan and kiss the zombie girl right back.

* * *

Risk gently lifted Kenzie to sit, then sat behind her with his arms around her. Her head sagged to one side, leaning on his arm, and she sobbed quietly and held her eyes shut.

"It's okay. I have you."

Her breathing slowed, and she slumped completely into a deep sleep, causing Risk to pivot her around and get a better hold on her.

He looked up at Bentley, who was grinning down at them, sneering. Then, he adjusted one of his arms to completely cover both of Kenzie's breasts.

"Any advice?" Risk said. "Or should I just kill you?"

"I suspect you'd kill me anyway. Well, let's see. You know that those vile zombeings have someone named Marilyn. And her sister, whom you so affectionately call Fia, just got taken, and you have no idea by whom."

Risk nodded, gestured with a curling finger, and said, "Come closer."

"What? Why?"

"I don't want to talk too loud. She needs sleep. Come here."

Bentley walked up to them, then stooped down to listen.

Risk's hand was a blur, and it slapped against Bentley's throat before squeezing.

And shaking him a few times.

He hacked, leaning to one side, and managed to groan out, "We can't keep doing this!"

Risk let him go and said, "We won't. Not for long."

He coughed a few times, spit on the street while stepping back to a safer distance, and said, "Well, whatever was that for?"

"You said that I don't know who took Fia."

"Not true? I'd wager you don't know, do you?"

"You said it like *you* know."

Bentley shrank back, cleared his throat, and said, "Uh, I suppose it could sound that way. Sure. But I assure you that—"

A bright red light lifted off from somewhere far past the buildings, then a solid popping sound reached them.

Then, another, following about the same path.

"Oh, they are practicing, aren't they?"

"Who? For what?"

"Think about it. That madman's plan."

"You know of it?"

"I sure do. People talk."

Risk only squinted at him.

"Okay. Until I bite them and borrow their blood. Um, *keep* their blood. So, yes, I know of the plan. That must be their bloody target practice."

Risk watched another red light sail almost all the way up where the ceiling to the giant cavern would be.

"So, you don't know where either of them are. Perhaps you know where that madman is, though? Hmm?"

"I have to get the girls."

"If you don't stop the madman and his mad plan, there won't be any girls to get."

Risk grumbled and held Kenzie close.

"Except that one," he said with a smirk. "Your naked lion girl."

Chapter 30 – It Just Took a Little Key S

"Look," said Sophia, "you really haven't thought this through. Let me go right now. Maybe I won't kill you."

"Ooh, I like that."

She sat on Sophia's legs, keeping the frilly panties and upturned palms in plain view, and hugged her slender waist with her knees. Sophia grunted and tried rolling from side to side.

"Uh-uh. No playing with fire, little girl."

She pressed down on Sophia's shoulders, pushing her deeper into the soft quilt and the cushions below it.

"Stop. Just stop!"

"Oh, that's just silly. No, I have no reason to stop."

She leaned forward, lying on Sophia's tightly tied arms, and took her time in brushing aside a few stray hairs from her left ear and neck. Then, she leaned closer to whisper in her ear.

"Mm, so precious. You have such soft skin all over."

Sophia groaned and tried to escape, but Widow was too strong.

"Yes, fight, little girl. Ooh, such a petulant little girl."

She nuzzled in closer and kissed Sophia's neck.

Sophia snorted out a breath, then said, "You'd better think again about—"

Widow lifted her head, placing her open mouth where Sophia's desperate eyes could see.

Her smile allowed Sophia to see her perfect white teeth top and bottom.

And two long, slender, gracefully curving fangs spaced closely and descending from the top row.

"What the hell? What are you?"

Widow hissed out a soft laugh and said, "I'm someone that has something a girl like you so desperately wants."

"What? What are you—"

"You're such a pretty little victim."

She began kissing her way down Sophia's cheek, and Sophia groaned and tried to squirm her way free.

"Oh, do try to get away, little girl."

Sophia gave her best effort at thrashing around without turning up any heat.

"Such long legs you have. All so soft."

Widow stretched back her own long legs to lie flat on top of her. Their bare legs were woven together, skin rubbing all along their legs, and two pairs of black high heels rattled around from Sophia's kicking.

But Sophia couldn't free herself from Widow's superior physical strength.

"Such a soft little girl," Widow whispered in her ear. "Just a tender little thing. Mm, so tasty."

Widow sighed, then she bit into Sophia's neck.

Sophia's eyes stretched open and stayed open, and she stopped moving as she stared straight ahead, with two pointy fangs just barely piercing the skin of her neck.

Widow moaned softly but just for a moment, then she withdrew her sharp teeth.

After a few gentle kisses where she'd bitten her, she stayed lying flat on the almost naked Kildare Killer and said, "Mm, let's just lie here for a moment together."

"What did you do? You just bit me?"

"Yes, in your very soft skin. It was just a tiny nibble. Just a tiny beginning for us."

The weight of her body kept Sophia pushed down, and Widow's legs made it hard for her to even kick.

A quiet minute passed as Sophia's deep breaths gradually slowed but remained deep.

"There we go," Widow said, her voice warm and liquid. "So much nicer already."

"What . . . you seriously bit me?"

"You don't mind. Not at all."

"I sure as hell . . . um, I . . ."

Sophia paused, only breathing.

"Yes, my dear baby?"

"I think, um, you'd better—"

"You taste just as sweet as you look."

She kissed around Sophia's ear and whispered, "So sweet," then quickly sat up and off of her.

Sophia turned her head to look to her right and saw that Widow was pulling a strip of something out of a plain and unremarkable pottery vase on a small, simple table.

"Hey," said Sophia, "whatever you're . . . I mean, you'd, um . . ."

"Silly girl. Shush, now," Widow said as she sat back on her heels near Sophia's legs.

"Oh, those heels are adorable. Such sexy heels for a grown-up girl that likes to dress like a teasing little baby."

She played with the ruffles on Sophia's panties.

"A little baby girl that likes to dress for grown-up sex? What a wonderful tease of a little girl."

Sophia groaned as Widow lifted one of her calves, bending her leg at the knee.

"Don't. Just, whatever you're—"

"Shh, now, precious."

She lifted up Sophia's other leg, pointing both heels at the ceiling, and began winding the soft material around her ankles.

"Hey, don't."

"Shh."

She finished several tight windings, then reached to the canister for another length of her webbing.

"Hey, um . . ."

"Shh. You know you like this."

Widow looped the new piece around the last one, between Sophia's ankles. Then, she fed the other end through the part of her arm bindings closest to her wrists.

But she stopped abruptly.

"Oh, just one little thing. Before you're all trussed up like a tasty little farm animal."

Sophia groaned softly when Widow grabbed her panties' elastic band and began to tug it from side to side, revealing more and more of the smooth, white skin of her ass.

"Oh, such a sweet little thing. Pretty lace and frills to cover such smooth, tasty skin."

She pulled the panties down far enough to tuck the elastic in just below Sophia's cheeks, then she fluffed up the ruffles again.

"So much better now. You don't want to hide anything from me."

She pulled gradually on the band linking Sophia's ankles to her wrists, drawing her legs up until her pointy heels were near her hands. But she noticed, when tightening the link, that Sophia was resisting, though weakly.

Widow paused her work and placed both hands on one of Sophia's thighs.

"Strong but still, so soft."

She rubbed the leg up and down, then the other, touching Sophia's soft skin with her own soft fingertips.

Then, she snapped the strap suddenly, pulling her heels closer to her hands and causing Sophia to gasp.

"Hey, you—"

She smiled as she gave it another hard pull, folding Sophia's legs completely.

"Just delightful."

She tied a solid knot and patted her bare ass.

"And just like that, you're a very helpless baby for me."

She started near the bindings around Sophia's ankles, touching all around them, rubbing them. She felt her calves, squeezing them and caressing them. Then, she returned to her thighs, which were partially hidden by her calves tied down so tightly. But she still felt all along the sides, sliding her fingers up and down Sophia's long legs.

Then, she patted her bare ass.

"So precious. Such a delicious little girl who's not so talkative anymore."

Barely able to speak, Sophia said, "I'm just planning . . . planning how I, um . . ."

Widow grabbed Sophia's thick braid and pulled it back, tipping her head back and causing her to gasp.

"Hey, not the . . . hair."

"You're just about ready, precious girl, for our cozy time together. I adore the first, playful cozy time with a helpless little girl like you."

She gave the braid a harder pull and kept it back. Sophia faced straight up, unable to easily close her mouth or speak.

"Mm, yes. Just like that. So adorable."

Widow reached over for another band of her material and tied Sophia's braid to her wrists, keeping her without any possibility of moving.

Widow, after checking that every binding was secure, moved forward to kneel near and over Sophia, where she could be watched.

"Let's get comfortable together. My baby girl and I keep no secrets from each other."

She smiled, held the weak but steady gaze of Sophia's blue eyes, and unclasped her bra between her breasts.

"Mm," she said as she pulled it open, showing Sophia how round and full her breasts were. "That's so much better for us."

She let it drop behind her, then flicked her nipples gently, showing that they were stiff and springy.

"I can tell. You're the kind of little girl that likes being helpless. You can't believe right now how much you love being my helpless little lover girl."

She touched Sophia's hair softly.

"So helpless now."

She laid herself down beside Sophia, getting herself in close and rubbing her bare breasts all over her, then settled in with a sigh. A few stray black hairs were out of place, so Widow brushed them back and out of the way.

"So pretty now, Baby. I adore a pretty baby when she's bound so nice and tight."

She reached down and squeezed the closest ass check gently, and Sophia tensed it up as well as she could.

Then, Widow said, "Mm, you're tied up so nicely now. My little girl is ready for another tiny nibble."

Sophia whimpered softly and tried to squirm away until Widow's lips touched her neck, which made her hold herself still.

"Oh, so precious," she whispered, her mouth nuzzling Sophia's throat. "You know what's next, and you're lying here so calm and pretty for me. You might not admit it yet, but you want most to be a good little girl while I do anything I want with you. Mm, anything at all."

Widow gave her ass a gentle squeeze, held it, and let both of her fangs sink into the soft skin of Sophia's neck. And she stayed there, fangs in but not too deep, as Sophia only breathed and looked up at the ceiling.

After Widow felt Sophia relax more in her hand, she eased her fangs back out and gave her a soft kiss.

"There we go. Even just that little bit, and you're a much better baby girl for me now."

Sophia only moaned softly, not struggling any longer.

"We have to take it slow in the beginning, dear girl, or it'll be too much for you. Let's just lie here, so cozy together, and I'll give you another nibble soon."

Several minutes passed while Sophia only breathed and looked straight up at the ceiling, tied so completely that she couldn't even turn her head, and Widow caressed her bare ass cheek and sometimes kissed around her ear.

"Another for my sweet baby girl."

She wiggled her arm under Sophia, then held her close with both arms, a warm embrace that became still and unmoving after she'd rubbed her nipples around on her for half of a minute.

"We have nowhere else to go," she said, then kissed Sophia's cheek. "We have nothing but time for as many sweet nibbles as it takes."

She tightened up their embrace, bare skin rubbing bare skin, as she nuzzled in close to her throat.

"We're just two lovers, baby girl. I just love helpless baby girls. Mm, so tender."

Sophia held her breath until Widow had driven her two fangs deeper than ever into her neck, and she didn't take them out.

They lay close together in Widow's quiet room—a helpless Kildare Killer, wearing only pulled-down frilly panties and very high heels and tied up with no chance of escape, and Widow, wearing only very tiny panties and short boots with spiky heels and snuggled in close, her fangs again in Sophia's neck as she sucked gently and quietly.

Only seconds had passed before Sophia went even more limp. Widow moaned softly and continued sucking at her neck for several more quiet minutes.

Then, she backed away just enough to say, "Mm, you're such a soft little baby. So tasty and soft. You're probably shocked to see how much you like being my soft, precious little baby girl. You're starting to forget ever being anything else."

Sophia could do nothing but lie still and stare up at the ceiling as her breathing slowed even more.

"Mm, how about another fun little nibble? You must feel it by now. And even if you don't understand it, you're starting to like how it feels. Let's give you even more this time. I'm going to hug you tight and settle in for a nice, long bite. Such a good lover girl for me."

She bit into Sophia's neck again and tightened her embrace of the tied-up girl, who wasn't moving much, just taking slow, deep breaths. And Widow stayed there, occasionally moaning softly as she kept her fangs deeper in Sophia's throat than the last three times. She held Sophia close in her warm embrace, and they lay still together, mostly bare skin touching bare skin and with no sounds from the outside disturbing them.

After a full ten minutes of constant, gentle sucking at her neck, during which Sophia did nothing but breathe and stay very quiet, Widow sighed and pulled out her fangs, then kissed all around where she'd bitten.

"That's a good start for us, pretty baby. You're such a soft and juicy little girl."

Sophia only groaned weakly, then Widow kissed her cheek, and knelt beside her. She leaned out over Sophia's upturned face, giving a view of her own face beyond her bare breasts.

She saw Sophia's eyes tilt down to see them, and she smiled as she leaned closer, resting her breasts on Sophia's cheeks.

"Mm, you're right where you want to be, you delicious little girl."

She waited until Sophia's tired eyes again focused on hers.

"After so many of my patient little bites into your soft, delightful skin, we both have you ready for more of the sweetest gratification you can imagine."

* * *

Risk brushed aside some of Kenzie's stray hair when she began to stir. Before opening her eyes, she yawned, then picked her head up.

"Kenzie?"

She tensed up, looking first at the muscular arms around her, then she tried to turn her head enough to see whose arms were keeping her trapped.

When she started squirming, he said, "Shh, it's okay. I'm a friend."

She settled some but kept trying to see him, so he relaxed his hold enough for her to turn and see his face.

"Who are you?"

"I'm Risk."

"That doesn't tell me much. Really, who the hell are you?"

"Mare and Fia called me to a—"

"What did you call them?"

"They like those names. They called me to a place in Beverly Hills. It was burning."

She looked away at the dark streets and buildings, then up at the even blacker sky without a single star in it.

"I remember. I remember it all."

"The fires? The chamber underground?"

"Yeah, and me biting through your ribs."

"As a lion."

She nodded and said, "I was a lion."

"And Kenzie too."

"I remember. You saved all of us. I've been a mountain lion ever since."

He tightened his embrace, and she lay her head on his arm again.

"K Kat," she said. "A lion. Or I'd be dead."

He gave her a squeeze and a soft laugh.

She took in a quick breath and rushed it out even more quickly.

"Will I stay me? Or will I have to be a lion again? What if—"

"Shh, now. It's okay. We'll figure it out."

"I don't mind being a lion, but I'm not really, you know?"

Her breaths were speeding up, and she was trying to turn more to look at him.

"What if I can't come back next time? Will I always be—"

"Shh, Kenzie. It'll be okay."

She calmed some, but her eyes were darting around, looking at sinister, broken buildings and the absolute black of the sky.

"Where are we?"

"You already know."

She paused, the nodded.

"What you said when we first got here."

She tipped her head up toward the sky.

"Up there."

"Yes."

She managed a soft, nervous laugh.

"When I was a lion in a basket with all of you."

She sat up enough to look around more.

"We have to find them! I remember now. A mob took Marilyn. Then, Sophia vanished somehow."

She looked up at Bentley.

"You were there. You were the last one with her."

"Well, dearie, that's technically true. But when I got hit on the head, she—"

"I'll do worse than that. When I'm a—*if* I'm a lion again, you're the first fucking thing I'm fucking ripping apart."

"Oh, my," he said, taking a few quick steps backwards. "You're all so unapologetically violent."

Risk held her tightly to keep her from jumping up and attacking him.

He laughed and said, "Says the vampire."

Bentley coughed to one side, then smirked and said, "Perhaps you can delay your misplaced retribution until we've relocated ourselves someplace safer."

He tipped his head in one direction, still looking from Kenzie to Risk.

They all heard the rumble of a stampede of boars approaching from somewhere in the shadows.

"They won't even notice the cute, curious couple sitting in the street," he said. "No, they'll just make puddles of you both. Bloody puddles. That's not me being British, either."

"We have to move," said Risk. "Give her your shirt."

"What? No, this is my only reminder of the lifestyle I had to give up when—"

Risk rose quickly, Kenzie still in his arms, and looked down at Bentley.

"Or die."

Bentley scoffed and said, "Like every other 'if or' threat from you, I'm left convinced that I'll likely receive both no matter what. Fine."

He quickly removed it and handed it to Kenzie, who glared at him and didn't thank him. But she did put it on.

Then, she and Risk both looked at his shoes.

"No. You simply cannot take my trainers too. My feet are quite delicate—I mostly just creep around in the shadowy night. I mean, really, who ever heard of a barefoot vampire?"

Risk scowled and Kenzie waited.

"I'll run straight into that pork convoy coming for us. You'll have to pick through the slop for them."

"Fine," Risk said, then he lifted Kenzie into his arms without asking first.

"Let's go."

* * *

Widow reached for the knot holding Sophia's long black braid to the bindings around her wrists, and she loosened it enough that the hair slipped away. And Sophia couldn't hold up her head and let it drop silently into the soft quilt.

"There we go, pretty girl."

She loosened next the strap holding Sophia's heels up close to her wrists, then raised her bound calves straight up, pointing her black heels at the ceiling. She unwound the strap around her ankles next, then gently laid her legs straight out, one at a time, and caressed each of them several times.

"So soft and tender. You're such a precious little thing."

Sophia didn't kick or squirm or say anything. Until Widow started pulling back up her frilly panties, taking her time and wiggling the thin elastic band across her ass cheeks.

"Hey, my arms. My arms too?"

Widow laughed softly and said, "My sweet baby girl, you're silly. You'll never again have those arms free."

Sophia didn't protest further, and she only lay there breathing slowly as Widow took her braid and began to coil it up tightly at the back of her head and fastened it to stay there.

Still, Sophia hadn't moved, and Widow took her by the shoulders and started to roll her over onto her back, causing a slight groan. When she laid her down, it set her breasts swaying from side to side for a few moments before they came to a rest.

"Oh, baby, you're just a little girl, but you have such large breasts?"

Sophia only glared up at her and shook her head a few times.

Widow ignored the look from her and gave both of her breasts a few soft squeezes, one in each hand.

"Hmm, a baby girl with such very nice big-girl breasts. So precious."

She let them go and reached for the canister nearby and played out a length of her webbing strap.

"Hey, don't. Don't."

Widow smiled and touched a fingertip to Sophia's lips.

"This is special just for you. It's so sticky, and it hardens up quite nicely."

She started winding the material around Sophia's head, across her forehead, then lifting her head and working it all the way down in back to hide away her knotted-up braid.

"I'll . . . I'll burn you."

"Oh, nonsense, baby girl. Your very own soft bed beneath you will burst into flames. Stop being so silly."

Sophia grumbled softly, and Widow finished with that strand and smoothed the end into the layers below it, all of it covering Sophia's hair completely and ending just above her eyes.

"Wait till my sister . . . gets here. She'll . . . she—"

"Oh, a sister? Well, I'm sure she's delightful. I'd love so much to meet her, too, especially if she's as adorable as you."

She rubbed a few times at the webbing's end on Sophia's forehead, sticking it down more tightly.

"There we go. That'll set so nicely."

Then, she got a gentle hold on Sophia's chin and turned her head one way, then the other, then let her go. She placed a hand on each of Sophia's breasts, then leaned in close and gazed into the deep blue of Sophia's eyes.

"This will help you be a better girl for me. I know that what you want the most is only to be a good little girl. Just a sweet little girl for me."

She nuzzled in against her cheek, sighed contentedly, and said, "And we have nothing but time for each other, my dearest little baby."

She drove her fangs into Sophia's soft flesh and with her fangs deeper under her skin than with the previous bites, she released Sophia's breasts and lay atop her. She stretched back her long legs and used both of them to squeeze one of Sophia's bare legs, which allowed her firm thigh to press into Sophia high up between her thighs.

Giggling lightly, Widow pulled back her sharp teeth and looked down to watch as Sophia slowly eased her thighs apart, giving her more access.

"Already, you're such a sweeter girl for me. It feels so good to be my tender little girl, doesn't it?"

She kept watching as Sophia held her legs straight and tried, weakly, to spread her legs farther.

When at last she could go no farther, and her high heels were far apart on the cushion, Widow smiled and said, "Mm, such a cooperative little girl now. And I know you want to be even sweeter for me."

She drove in her fangs and held the sides of Sophia's head, sometimes rubbing her with her thigh as they lay together in the quiet, hidden room. Widow continued her quiet sucking for another ten minutes, sometimes moaning, and Sophia only stared up at the ceiling as her breathing slowed even further.

Widow finally withdrew her fangs, stopped caressing her captive, and pushed against the blanket with both hands, leaning herself up to look down at Sophia.

"Hmm, such a sweet little girl to share like that. Isn't it sweet to give yourself to me while I'm giving you such tender little bites?"

Sophia groaned softly, kept looking up with blue eyes more tired than earlier, and tried to squeeze her thighs around Widow's.

"Mm-hmm. Yes, dearest baby girl."

Neither of them closed their eyes when she leaned down and kissed Sophia's lips, then backed away only a bit and smiled.

"You're such a good little girl for me now. And you can't resist showing me exactly the kind of little girl you are."

She kissed the tip of Sophia's nose, then leaned back again with her hips and legs still resting on the bound woman beneath her.

"You're the kind of little girl that wants more than anything to be soft and juicy for someone to savor in any way they wish. It just took a little Key S for you to admit it to yourself."

Sophia only squinted up at her, moving her lips but struggling to form words.

"Key . . . Key S?"

"Yes and now, you can admit it to me. You see now that you've secretly craved being a helpless little girl and offering yourself completely, don't you, precious?"

Sophia only drew in a deep breath and held it, prompting Widow to glance down at their bare breasts squeezed together even more from that breath.

She looked back into her blue eyes and said, "Oh, so precious. You know it's true, and you'll admit it soon, my sweet little girl."

She gave her lips another quick kiss, then shifted off to her side, then wiggled down until her face was even with Sophia's breasts.

"You do like teasing with these delightful little-girl undies, don't you, sweet baby? Let's just get those out of the way. It's another thing you've secretly craved for so long: to lie there helpless, just a sweet little girl, while someone like me, somebody you just met, undresses you."

She tugged and pulled at the panties, first one side then the other, until they were strung tightly halfway along Sophia's thighs.

"No, you don't want to keep secrets from me. Not such sweet secrets."

Then, she reached across to Sophia's shoulder and started rolling her onto her side, facing her, and Sophia offered no resistance.

Widow slipped her right arm under Sophia at her waistline and held her with both hands, touching her fingertips all over the smooth skin of her back.

"Oh my, the baby girl has such very nice breasts. I know you'll enjoy a woman's lips on them. A woman's very soft lips."

Still holding Sophia, Widow parted her lips and gently suckled one breast for a minute before backing away and looking into her eyes.

"Isn't it wonderful that you can't resist this in any way? Mm, it's so much sweeter for you like this."

Widow sucked in Sophia's other nipple, spent another minute with it, and moaned softly the entire time before letting it go.

"Mm, so soft and tender. And you can't even pretend to not want it."

She gave each of her nipples a few slow, wet licks, then shimmied herself lower, using her tongue on the soft undersides of Sophia's breasts, forcing them up then letting them settle again.

"Mm, such a tasty little girl."

Widow wiggled herself lower, kissing Sophia all the way down until her tongue was at her navel, which she licked around and inside.

"Such a soft, tender little baby girl. You know now that it's all you want to be."

She kept shifting herself lower until she was rubbing and caressing Sophia's ass cheeks and the backs of her thighs.

"So soft. Such a soft little girl. A soft little baby that would never say no to me."

With a slow sigh, she nuzzled her face in deep between Sophia's thighs. Sophia tipped her head back, gasping softly, and Widow stopped only long enough to say, "Yes, it feels so good to be such a soft, smooth little girl for me. Mm, you're so very smooth all over for me."

Widow's head moved slowly and rhythmically as her tongue sought out every little detail, and she paused only to say, "My, what a juicy little girl you are, especially when you get sweet little kisses. I love sweet, juicy little baby girls."

Five quiet minutes passed, with Sophia unable to close her mouth and breathing steadily, sometimes moaning and sometimes panting. All the while, Widow kept her lips and tongue busy between the captive Kildare Killer's thighs.

She finally backed away, smiling, and said, "That was very nice. Such a very tasty little girl for me. Not even a peep of protest too. I knew you wouldn't resist my affections."

With the scissors, Widow gave the lacy panties a few quick snips, wiggled the cloth out from behind, giving it a series of short, quick upward tugs and smiling at Sophia again gasping, then tossed the remains to the floor. She also pulled the bottom half of her flowery little-girl dress out from under her and left it off to one side.

"Mm, so nice," she said, looking at Sophia wearing only her spiky heels. "You're so adorable in big-girl high heels."

She looked into a shaky gaze from two beautiful blue eyes and said, "Oh, but I still see just a little bit of defiance and denial in those eyes."

With another long strand of her webbing, she began another winding around Sophia's head, covering her eyes.

Widow glanced down at Sophia's chest and saw that she'd begun quicker, panicky breaths, but she grinned at the sight of her captive's nipples stiff and pointing straight up.

"Hmm, you like it. You like everything I'm doing with you, sweet baby."

She kept winding until it covered even her nose and chin, leaving only her mouth and her neck available.

"And just like that, my little girl is in the dark. Just a pretty little victim. So tasty and helpless."

She kissed her on the lips, then took another strand and wrapped it around Sophia's thighs just above her knees. Another length got wrapped around her waist, binding her already bound arms in place.

"Just like wrapping a sweet little present for myself."

She rolled Sophia over, facedown, then leaned over and held both of her hands.

"Shh, now, my precious."

She started clipping Sophia's long, manicured nails, taking them down all the way on each finger.

"We won't be needing these, my sweet girl, not for our long, quiet time together."

Sophia was only breathing deeply and not even trying to speak.

Widow finished after trimming all of them all the way down, then rolled her onto her back, sending her excited breasts swaying for a moment.

She gave each nipple a gentle touch, then said, "Oh, that's so sweet. You're becoming a very good little girl for me. And you love how all of this feels. You love more than anything to be just a helpless little girl. It was always your fate."

Then, Widow leaned over Sophia, nuzzled around her exposed throat, and said, "Now, let's see about that next fun little bite. You feel it already. I'm sure you want another. A longer bite, this time."

Sophia only panted, her chest rising and falling, her nipples stiff.

"Nothing to say, Baby?"

Sophia moved her lips a few times, and she said, "I . . . I . . ."

"Yes. You're just adorable. A little bit for you at a time, my precious girl. You're taking it all inside you and filling up so nicely. Just a tender little-girl sponge for my poisons."

Widow lay beside Sophia, one hand under her neck, lifting it, while she fondled a smooth round breast with a noticeably excited nipple. She gave Sophia a kiss on her lips, then aimed lower and sank her teeth into her neck, deeper than any of the other bites.

Sophia's lips stayed parted, and she started to go limp while Widow moaned softly, sucking at her neck and delivering more poisons.

She backed out of Sophia's throat to say, "Hmm, no more fight. Such a precious little girl for me now."

She studied all of the tiny bite marks in Sophia's neck, some with thin trickles of blood already beginning to dry.

"Just lovely. Let's get nice and comfortable. We're just two lovers, and we'll stay so close."

She rolled Sophia onto her side, snaked an arm under to embrace her and squeeze their breasts together, and settled in with a deeper bite.

A few moments later, she backed away and looked toward Sophia's heels. She saw that Sophia was slowly curling back one calf, and she held it there. She'd made no attempts to escape.

Widow gently patted Sophia's ass cheek and smiled at her, though Sophia had no way to see it.

"My sweet baby girl. You just accepted that this is what you've always wanted. And you love that you'll never again be anything else—just something that's sweet and juicy for me."

She nuzzled in close to her throat.

"And you feel the romance we share as I give you my sweet poisons. Oh, they feel so good, don't they?"

She slipped in both fangs, hugged Sophia close and rubbed her soft skin all over.

In a very quiet room, Widow gently sucked at Sophia's neck and continued a steady delivery of her poisons to her already weak and hopelessly bound prey.

Chapter 31 – So Much Better to Talk Dirty

Janie backed away and giggled when Marilyn's stomach growled loudly.

"Damn, you're a hungry girl. You're really starving, aren't you?"

Marilyn nodded and watched another slimy drop fall to the floor from what Blaine was pointing right at her.

"Say it, then."

"I'm starving."

In her ear, Janie whispered, "Starving for what?"

"That."

"Oh, that won't do. Talk dirty. Always talk dirty."

Some in the crowd laughed softly, and others spoke their agreement.

Marilyn moaned and said, "I'm starving for that cock."

"She's starving for cock!" someone cried out, causing cheering all around.

She kissed Marilyn's red-streaked cheek and said, "So much better to talk dirty, isn't it?"

"Mm-hmm. I guess."

"You know. Alright, so, what kind of cock are you starving for?"

Her stomach growled, she giggled, and she said, "Mm, zombie cock."

Marilyn heard only approving murmuring, so she looked. Every face was staring with big eyes while most were rubbing their crotches.

She touched Marilyn's cheek, still smooth and white but covered with jagged red lines, and turned her, then gave her a long kiss.

Their lips still close, Janie said, "Where do you want your zombie cock? Say it."

"Uh, I could. Okay. Um, I want that zombie cock in my pussy."

No one in the crowd spoke, so Marilyn looked again. Many were using two hands on their own crotches, and some were helping out their friends.

Janie laughed and said to Marilyn, "They'll quiet down. They won't want to miss any dirty talk from you. Forget about them."

Janie began soft, cold kisses around Marilyn's ear, giggling softly.

"Mm, and your pussy is wet, isn't it?"

"Oh my goodness, yes."

"You must have had at least one good zombie fucking before, right? In your very wet pussy?"

Marilyn laughed once and said, "What? No!"

"But you've wanted it. You've wanted it so bad."

"I, um . . . "

Her stomach groaned again, and she giggled and said, "Um, maybe."

"Such a bad thing to do, right? Didn't momma always tell you not to fuck the zombies?"

Marilyn giggled and said, "Well, that's just silly. No. No one ever told me not to."

"Momma never told her!" someone screamed, and the rest shushed her.

"Good. So, you're going to fuck a zombie. Right now."

"That's me," Blaine said, grinning at Marilyn. "I'm the zombie with the cock that's going way deep in your wet pussy."

Janie whispered, "He really likes talking dirty. And his cock is always so hard."

Marilyn nodded, staring at Blaine's stiff, slime-coated member. He appeared to be waiting for an invitation.

"Tell him," said Janie. "Tell him what you want."

Marilyn coughed once, while Janie was licking and nibbling around her ear.

"I, um, want my first zombie fucking."

"With the special stuff, too, right?"

"Uh-huh. Yes. Blaine? I'm so hungry. I want more of that,"—she pointed at the stiff pole pointing at her—"way, deep inside . . ."

"Say it."

"I want that so deep inside my pussy!"

Someone outside the cage handed Blaine a bowl of the stuff, and he dunked himself in it several times.

"Tell him to hurry, before it drips off of his hard cock," Janie said with a giggle. "That hard, dripping cock."

"Hurry!" said Marilyn. "Hurry up!"

"Hurry with what?" he said, his rigid rod aimed right at her.

"Hurry with that zombie cock!"

"Now, you're talking," said Janie. "Let's get you ready for a good zombie fucking."

She helped Marilyn to lie flat on her back, and she lay beside her, hugging her around her waist as Blaine walked toward the bed. When he was close enough, he grabbed Marilyn's ankles and pulled her and Janie around until Marilyn's ass was right at the edge of the bed.

"All the better to fuck you," he said.

"Good," Janie said to him. "She needs it. She'll need so much of it. Where?"

"Mm, in my pussy."

"Yeah," said Blaine. "In your pussy that's so wet for my zombie cock."

Marilyn nodded as she lifted and spread her legs while Janie hugged her and kissed around her ear and neck.

"Oh, wait," said Janie, then she quickly slipped Marilyn's white high heels back on and fastened the thin straps around her ankles.

"Might as well be even sexier for your very first zombie fuck."

With her head tipped up, Marilyn watched as Blaine lowered the head of it, sometimes dripping, close to where she wanted it.

"Watch his cock," said Janie. "Even watching it is so, so good. Where's that hard cock going?"

"In my pussy."

Blaine grinned and leaned forward enough to just barely touch the end of it, the slimiest part of it, to the softest part of Marilyn.

And she snapped her head back and gasped with her mouth locked open.

"Yeah," said Janie. "Now, you really feel it. So sensitive, that pussy of yours. Even more so now."

She covered Marilyn's gasp with a wide kiss, muffling the moaning that began when Blaine began to steadily delve deep into her, his zombie post like rock.

He kept drilling for a minute, then Janie broke their kiss to look down toward the action.

"Oh, Marilyn. You need to look now."

She tipped her head up and stared at maps of squiggly, crooked red lines emanating from between her thighs. Even as she watched, they zigged and zagged, cascading down along her thighs and sprouting up over the soft white skin toward her navel.

"What is that? What's happening?"

"You're just getting more beautiful. You want to be beautiful, don't you?"

She turned her eyes up to Janie's and said, "Well, yes. But what are—"

Janie touched her cheek and said, "Here too. On your pretty face. It's a good start."

"Um, if I wasn't so hungry, I'd—"

"And horny? You've never, ever been this horny, have you?"

"Oh, not even close. I'm starving in all kinds of ways."

Janie kissed her lips quickly, then said, "Your very first zombie fuck. How is it?"

She kept looking into Janie's eyes, but she heard Blaine saying, "I'm the zombie! I'm fucking you good!"

Marilyn tipped her head back and cackled for a few seconds, then looked again at Janie.

"I love it."

"You want more, right?"

Marilyn nodded.

Janie snapped her fingers, and Blaine pulled out and took a few steps closer to the bars to take again the bowl of sloppy something.

"Oh, you meant more of that? I don't know—it's making me so hungry!"

"And horny?"

"Yes! Whatever it is!"

Janie sat up, then straddled Marilyn, resting lightly on a belly being populated with pointy, meandering red lines.

Marilyn looked up at her, then lowered her eyes to the perfect zombie girl's breasts when Janie said, "Don't talk for a while. Here. Suck my nipples. You know you're starving to suck more on zombie girl nipples."

She leaned forward and Marilyn began suckling one, then the other, and Blaine returned with a fresh supply, which he drove in and left deep inside her.

With her stomach growling and with her moaning and sucking, Blaine spread the slop as deep as he could, laughing as he jerked her and Janie with every hard pump.

Janie touched both of Marilyn's cheeks, guiding her and directing her when to switch, and said, "Your cheeks look so damn good now. Did you like your belly and thighs? Kind of hot, right?"

"Mm-hmm."

"You want more, don't you?"

Marilyn stopped for a second, a zombie nipple still close to her lips and her stomach growled while she was saying, "More. Yeah, more. It feels so good to be so hungry and horny!"

"They kind of go together for us. For you too."

She backed away, and Marilyn tried to curl herself closer, reaching with her lips and tongue. Janie teased her with each one, bringing it closer, then leaning away before Marilyn's lips could close on it.

"You're ready for the next step? Wanna be even hungrier and hornier?"

"Oh, yes. I sure do."

"Good. You can't even say no anymore, can you?"

"Uh-uh."

Marilyn reached her lips toward a stiff zombie girl nipple, but Janie giggled and kept it out of reach.

"Let's get you set up, then."

Blaine slipped and slimed his way back out, having deposited all of the muck, and Janie swung her leg over and stood beside the bed. She and Blaine together maneuvered the bed, with Marilyn lying on her back on it, closer to the prison bars.

"What's this?"

"Your next step. You're gonna love this."

Marilyn's stomach roared and her eyes stretched open.

"Oh, my!"

With the bed pressed into the bars, the two fit zombies tipped Marilyn onto her side and together, they coaxed her bent legs up, leaving her ass end at the edge of the bed.

And her face was near the bars, with her mouth right between two of them and aimed at whatever anyone in the crowd might offer her.

* * *

"This way," Bentley said, pointing in one direction when they'd reached an intersection. "I think."

"The Maze is here too?"

"It's all over. Those cheeky zombeings have tunnels and passageways running every which way. You know what they like to do."

"I know."

"I don't," said Kenzie. "What's he talking about?"

"Let's just find her," he said, and they proceeded down the narrow, dark avenue.

But a nearby explosion, which launched another burning red ball into the sky, rousted scores of bats. They all screeched and scattered, becoming black shapes twitching against a blacker background.

"Over there!" Risk called out, but Bentley was closer to the other side of the street and ran that way instead.

He found refuge under a wide overhang, and Risk carried Kenzie to the relative safety of another low porch roof on the other side of the street.

Risk backed her into the wall, then turned to face the street with her behind him. He watched as Bentley, near tears, wailed and tried as many doors as he could, none of which opened.

"I remember those things," Kenzie said as she looked around him. "I ate them. They're okay."

"Not a lot to eat here."

"I don't suppose so."

They could hear the swarm circling above the buildings, and some of them would dive low, their wings kicking up dust as they raced past their hiding places.

"I remember other things too. About being a lion."

"Oh?"

"I have all of K Kat's memories too. I have a favorite."

Risk didn't respond, only watched, ready to shift and ready to rip apart bats.

"I'll tell you," she said. "I remember being in heat."

He took a deep breath and let it rush out.

She pulled up Bentley's polo shirt to expose her breasts, reached around his waist, and pulled herself into him.

"Hey," he said. "We could die out here."

"I'm in heat."

"No. You're not."

Two more bats dusted along the road, then angled back up and out of sight. Bentley had sat himself against the wall and put his arms over his head.

When Kenzie reached for his buckle, he didn't stop her.

"I am so in heat right now."

She unclasped it and pulled it open, then wiggled the zipper of his jeans all the way down.

"Just a girl in such heat. So much heat right now."

She reached in, found what she wanted, and used both hands on it. Risk only groaned softly as he scanned left and right, his hands up and ready to transform to whatever would be needed for battle.

She got him clear of his tight jeans and began slow strokes with both hands.

Across the street, Bentley was looking toward them from between his raised hands, and he lowered them.

"Oh, that's really helpful, innit? Now? Really?"

Still rubbing and stroking, Kenzie whispered, "I need it. So much heat. I'm so wet and ready from the—"

Risk grunted and spun around, took her waist with both hands, and lifted her up against the wall. She grinned as she first made sure that the polo shirt wouldn't slide back down, then she placed her arms around his neck.

He found the spot. Quickly. And the girl that was a lion not long before, and had said that she was in heat at the moment, tipped her head back and growled softly.

With her eyes closed, speaking only between his violent thrusts, she said, "I . . . need . . . such . . . a . . . good . . . fucking."

Risk groaned louder, and the sound of her back slamming into the cracked and weathered wood wall echoed up and down the street.

Behind Risk, they heard Bentley yell, "Are you daft, mates?"

Then, he screamed and they heard screeching from at least two bats.

"Tell me when you're about to cum," she said, her voice choppy from his sharp thrusts.

"Already. Yeah."

"Good. How?" she said.

"How what?"

"How do I kill you?"

He stopped and looked into her eyes, which were about level with his own.

"That's what this is?"

He saw the tears on her cheeks.

"I want to go home! Take me back! Tell me how to kill you!"

"No. Not without Mare and Fia."

"Then, let me the fuck go!"

He grinned and picked up where he'd left off.

"Stop it!"

She tried slapping him, and he grabbed her wrist. Then, the other, and he held her arms above her, pinned to the wall.

"No, I'm not in heat! Don't!"

From across the street, they heard Bentley laughing.

"No means no, you fearsome brute. Even here."

Risk scowled, then gave her one more violent thrust, cracking the wall behind her even more. Then, he gently set her down.

Then, he wiped her cheeks once each way.

She looked up at him and said, "You hate me?"

He let go of her wrists, then got his pants closed up.

It took a few seconds, but he gave her a smile.

"No."

She waited, her eyes wet with tears, then said, "Marilyn and Sophia won't be happy when I tell them how you—"

With blinding speed, he had the bottle of Zoojoose out and had tipped back her head, causing her mouth to hang open long enough for him to pour in a few drops.

With the bottle stowed away, he stayed close, holding her by her shoulders. The seizure began almost immediately, and she shook in his arms, her arms and legs becoming lion legs, her skin growing short brown fur, and her hair shrinking back and leaving only the ears of a mountain lion.

A familiar lion which stood near his leg and looked up at him.

He patted the lioness and rubbed around her ears.

"Good girl. No talking."

"Well, that's all very touching. But you, uh, might want to kind of turn around? Like, now?"

Risk spun enough to look, and he and K Kat saw several bats, on the ground and sneaking toward them.

Another explosion, closer than the last, sped a red fireball into the sky, and the sharp sound caused the bats to shriek and fly straight up and over the roofs.

"Now!" said Bentley. "For fuck's sake, let's go!"

"A quick fuck's sake," Risk said to the lion, and the three of them continued running down the street.

At the next corner, Risk waved for them to stop, and he took a quick look around.

"There's something. A fort."

"Why would there be a fort here of all places? That makes no bloody—"

"The madman maybe."

"Oh. Sure, that could be. Well, here's your big chance. Kill him real quick, then rescue your blond and brunette bimbo friends, then—"

Risk slammed Bentley up against the wall and held him there with both hands. His shoes had left the ground.

"Who said Marilyn was blond?"

"Lucky guess? I mean, is she?"

"You're dying soon."

"Oh, you wouldn't. You might still need me. And besides, you—"

Bentley heard the growling, looked down, and saw K Kat with her fangs out, ready for his throat.

"She might," said Risk, then he patted K Kat's head and tipped his own toward the fort, and they walked side by side toward the men guarding the door.

Chapter 32 – My Delicious Lover Girl

"There we go," Widow said as she smoothed down the end of another long winding of sticky material around Sophia's ankles.

She'd been careful to not cover the delicate straps that held her black high heels in place, and she gave a tug to the new binding, confirming that it was secure.

"Good. Nice and tight and already setting."

Standing, and still holding that strapping, she lifted Sophia's legs and turned her partway, which caused her head to tip back off of the cushions. Only her open mouth and the multitude of tiny bite marks in her neck and throat were visible—the rest of her head was an unbroken winding of material which covered everything, even her hair and nose and chin.

Widow walked with a slow, confident strut, her heels clacking softly in the silent room, until she could kneel on a folded blanket, then sit back on her heels near Sophia's head.

She leaned close to kiss one side of Sophia's lips for just a second.

"My sweet baby, I've given you so much of my wonderful poisons. They're swimming all around inside you, finding just the right places to settle in and become part of you—tight little places where they won't be found."

She backed away enough to lean down again and kiss the other side of Sophia's lips.

"Very soon, you and I will make sure that those delightful poisons are so permanent that nothing could ever take them from you. Mm, we'll both love doing that together."

She rose up, leaned over, and kissed her directly on her upper lip for a few seconds, ending it with a soft giggle, then sucking the lip in for a few more seconds.

"Before our little love affair here goes any further, it's time for honesty. I know you're a grown-up woman. But you've offered in such a deliberate and obvious way to be helpless for me. It's so clear by how you dressed yourself that you want to be just my sweet little baby girl. Have you changed your mind about that? Tell me now if you have."

Sophia's lips moved weakly, but she didn't speak.

"You must know how dangerous that could be. Such dreadful things could surely happen to a grown woman, even when she's just herself and not pretending. But things could become so much more dreadful if she chooses to be someone's helpless baby girl. But that is what you want, isn't it?"

Sophia barely moved her lips, making Widow smile.

"Mm, you would have told me if you'd changed your mind. No, this is exactly what you've always wanted. You love being helpless for all kinds of things, even if some are truly dreadful. You must know that being helpless often invites dreadful."

She leaned over and gave Sophia's wet lips a soft kiss, then backed away only enough to speak.

"Oh, I do adore you being so quiet like that. Even more dreadful things can happen to a pretend little girl when she chooses to be very quiet, too, and she doesn't protest anything that's forced on her. And still, you choose to be so quiet and not make a sound. I believe you want to be helpless and unable to save yourself from those dreadful things."

Widow rested herself back on her short black boots again and held Sophia's wrapped head with both hands.

"And do you know why, sweet baby? You want to feel utterly desperate for help to save you from the dreadful things you know are coming for you. And that desperation gives you a free pass, without any guilt, to do whatever it takes to please your abuser. You want to have to be a good little girl, and you want to do all the things you only dream about but won't ever let yourself do."

She brushed her lips on Sophia's, then kissed her for another half of a minute.

"My sweet, helpless, pretend baby girl, those wonderful poisons will completely stop almost everything going on inside you."

She leaned forward and kissed her on the lips once, then sat back up.

"Everything except for your lust for every bit of attention I give you and the unbelievable orgasms you're having for me. Oh, no, those parts of you will be stronger than ever. You already can't believe the wonderful orgasm that you're feeling. It'll only get more intense, and you won't want anything or anyone to ever stop it, no matter what else is happening to you. And you'll know exactly what else is happening to you. Something truly dreadful that just feels so much sweeter because you can't stop it."

She leaned over again, slowly, and sucked in first her upper lip, then moaned and wiggled it around.

"Still, you choose to be so quiet. Just a quiet little girl."

She then spent even longer with her lower lip, keeping it wet and sucking it in and out between her own.

"You love that contradictory thrill: you're playing at being just a tiny little girl, but you're having such big-girl orgasms. Mm, that's what you love because it just seems so wrong: how could just a pretty little baby have such big-girl orgasms? Hmm . . ."

She licked Sophia's lips and giggled at the lack of response.

"The longer you feel that new, unfamiliar kind of orgasm, the more it will set my poisons deep into you, everywhere inside. Nothing in there will ever work again All of it is getting so completely and hopelessly ruined. Just knowing that makes your orgasm even stronger, though, doesn't it?"

Sophia didn't move. She only lay with her bound head tipped back and her mouth still open, her lips wet from Widow sucking on them.

"Yes, you love it. You love play acting as just a little girl and helpless to whatever a selfish captor wants from you. You'll give yourself to anything your captor wants from you as long as you can be a sweet little baby girl. What kind of grown woman would pretend to be a precious little girl by wearing such frilly baby-girl panties?"

She kissed one cheek.

"Mm, and you're so helpless now. And it's all becoming so clear."

She kissed her other cheek, then she held her lips to just touch Sophia's.

"You're even more excited knowing that another *woman* has you. You love that you can't possibly get free from a woman that has captured you. And you adore that she's using you for her selfish sexual pleasure. Mm, yes, such sweet orgasms she's giving you."

Widow laughed softly and kissed her on the lips.

"But it's even sweeter for you because you know she's ruining you completely. You love all the things that can happen to you after you've offered yourself up as just a helpless little baby girl. Oh, you're so helpless!"

She gave Sophia's lips a long kiss.

"You love being helpless and in so much trouble."

She gave her just a brief kiss.

"But only for a woman. You crave being a helpless baby and giving yourself to a woman to use and enjoy. Not a man. Oh, no, not a man for you. Helpless for a man would never do for a sweet little girl like you. That's so obvious now. You know you want to admit it. It might be your last chance. You want to be a helpless baby girl, but only for a woman, isn't that true? Answer me."

Widow waited patiently, watching Sophia's open mouth, and she smiled at the sight of Sophia moving her lips to speak.

"Yes," she said softly.

"Mm. Of course. Such a good little girl to finally be truthful. That feels so much better for you now. The more you admit your secret desires, the sweeter the orgasm you feel."

Widow leaned over her and kissed her lips for a full thirty seconds.

"Yes, baby girl, I know. Yes, it has to be for a woman. It's just so glaringly obvious with everything about you. And do you crave being helpless for that woman, just a defenseless little baby girl, for whatever dreadful things that woman wants to do to you for her own selfish pleasure?"

It took longer than her first response, but Sophia said very softly, "Yes. I do."

"Oh, how sweet. Like a little vow for me too! And you knew that about yourself long ago, before the Key S, didn't you?"

"Yes."

"Oh, you're just the sweetest little thing. You didn't even need the Key S. Not really. If you would have met me before, you would have fallen in love with me and wanted desperately to be my helpless baby girl. It's all coming true for you, my precious little girl."

She kissed her wet lips for half of a minute.

"Such horribly dreadful things. That's what my baby girl wants."

Widow leaned over and kissed her on the lips again.

"You're already feeling it inside. Mm, such a quiet little baby now. And it's time that we hurry that process along to stop everything inside that we won't need anymore. This might feel a bit cruel to you, but you'll still be a good girl for me. Because you love the cruelty too."

Widow reached back for more of the webbing, and held the end to one side of Sophia's face and extended it out over and past her mouth.

"I love this part of it too. Every little bit of binding I add to you makes you more helpless."

She sighed and said, "And we both know that you adore being a helpless little girl. More binding excites you. You want to be so sure that you'll never escape all the dreadful things a woman is doing to you."

She held the banding material against Sophia's lips.

"Let's make sure your orgasm gets even sweeter. If you had the strength, you'd scream from that orgasm that you can tell won't stop.

I'll help you. Let's make your pretty mouth look like it's screaming from pleasure. Oh, it'll take just a bit of cruelty."

She worked the band from side to side between Sophia's lips.

"Oh, good girl for opening up. Yes, you want to try to scream. You want it all in between those pretty lips."

She kept jamming it down into Sophia's mouth until it stretched her cheeks down at both sides of her mouth.

"Mm, and you want so much to be a very quiet little girl for me. I'll help you to be a good, very quiet little girl that only looks like she's screaming. And I know that you want it to be tight. You want it so cruelly tight, my precious little one."

She held it with both hands and leaned forward, putting her weight onto it, driving it in deeper, then kept it tight as she looped it back around Sophia's head.

"Yes, it has to be brutally tight for my very quiet little baby."

Again, she tugged it roughly down inside Sophia's mouth, adding another layer as she wound it tightly around her head.

Widow paused to watch Sophia's chest rising and falling as she struggled to breathe past the bands in her mouth.

"Hmm. A few more would be so nice. We both want that. You'll be even more precious when we fill up that pretty mouth with it. Let's just fill it up completely."

She looped the material around three more times, leaving five strands of it crowded into her mouth, then she smoothed down the end, pressing it into the sticky layer below it.

"Mm," she moaned as she leaned over and kissed the wet lips that had been pulled until they were stretched almost flat and locked open. "Such tasty lips you still offer to me. Mm, not quite so pouty anymore. Not after that fun little bit of cruelty."

Widow touched a finger to Sophia's upper lip, then slid it across the layers of material that filled her mouth, then touched her lower lip, all of that mostly even.

"Mm, such pretty lips, even when the baby's mouth is packed to keep her so very quiet."

She reached back for more webbing and began another loop around Sophia's head.

"Let's just hide the pretty girl away even more. I love having such a quiet little girl to play with."

She placed the first layer just above Sophia's upper lip, overlapping the layer over her nose, pulled it tight around, then looped the next winding just below her lower lip, forcing her lips closer into a tight pucker that was still flattened from the tight bindings packed deep in her mouth.

Widow tore the material and got the end to stick to the rest of it.

She rubbed a finger across both of her lips several times, smiling at how taut and unyielding they'd become, no longer soft and full and able to bounce back.

"Yes, little baby girl, I'm having such delightful fun with your pretty lips. Oh, and your pretty mouth. Such dreadful things have happened to it."

Then, she paused to watch Sophia's chest struggling more than before as she fought to breathe past and around all that she'd done to her mouth.

"Oh, so sweet. My baby's big-girl breasts are teasing me so nicely, but her lips still want kisses. Okay, baby girl, we can kiss more."

With another soft moan, Widow leaned forward and kissed Sophia's strained lips, then sat back again.

"Mm, such a very quiet girl for me now. You probably would be by now anyway, but it's so fun to bind you all up in such sweet ways. Now that you have so many bindings filling up that pretty mouth, let's just cover that all up so it can't possibly come loose."

Widow took a wide band of the webbing and laid it over Sophia's bound lips.

"Yes, let's just cover up even those lips that used to be so soft. You have other lovable parts of you for me to enjoy, and they're all still soft and juicy."

She fed it around Sophia's head and snapped it tight.

"Yes, we'll just cover up all of that as it sets so nice and solid."

Widow lifted Sophia's head and fed the banding around.

"And you don't want any of my careful work to come loose either. No, my baby girl adores being helpless and bound up nice and tight to keep her so quiet for me."

She then covered her mouth with two more wrappings to seal her mouth shut. Below them, Sophia also had the two tight bands puckering her lips. And below those, there were five thick, tight bands stretched deep into her mouth and filling it all the way up.

Sophia's entire head, including her hair, had become just a tight mask of cocoon, each layer adhering to the ones below it, all of it quickly hardening. She'd left her with no possible way to speak or even breathe, and she'd had her mouth locked into a silent scream.

"So sweet. You probably don't mind that I don't even remember what you look like anymore."

Sophia barely moved. Only her chest shifted weakly, just enough to sometimes give her breasts a gentle shaking.

"And you must know by now that it's not your pretty face that I need from you."

Widow noticed Sophia's breasts and gave each of her stiff nipples a soft pinch.

"But you're still reminding me how sweet and precious you are. Such a sweet, teasing baby girl. Shame on you, teasing me with those adorable nipples. Little baby girls shouldn't tease with such perfect big-girl nipples that are begging for nibbles."

She pinched each one again and rubbed them lightly a few times.

"I really can't help myself sometimes. I know you'd love to have more bindings too."

She started another winding under Sophia's chin and fed it up and over the top of her head.

"That pretty mouth really has no chance. Poor little dear."

She wrapped several more loops around over the first, then smoothed down the sticky banding.

"Mm, so sweet."

Widow leaned over and kissed where Sophia's lips were hidden inside a cocoon that concealed every feature, rendering her head a just a ball of webbing.

"There, there, my delicious baby whose pretty face no one will ever see again. Use up the last of your resistance for me. So sweet to watch. Struggle, helpless baby girl, struggle!"

Sophia's chest was only sporadically moving, sometimes jerking softly, and Widow turned her head to watch the soft, smooth breasts bounce lightly, making two stiff nipples appear to be floating and growing even as she watched them.

"I think you liked that. Your unending orgasm got even sweeter when I said that no one will ever see your pretty face again. Mm-hmm, such a dreadful thing. So pretty and never to be seen again."

With her eyes on Sophia's nipples that were seldom moving, and with her mouth close enough to kiss her, if her lips weren't buried, Widow said, "This is what you've always wanted. Key S never lies. You decided to put on those darling little-girl panties, with so much lace and frilly things to pretend you were just a baby for me. You didn't know me at the time, but you were secretly hoping to be here with me or someone like me. You wore those frilly baby-girl panties just to offer yourself as a helpless little girl to a woman, one that would treat you just like this."

Sophia's chest came to a complete stop. Widow stared for a moment, watching for any slight movement, but there was none. Still, her nipples pointed straight up at the ceiling.

"Ah, there we go. Everything inside my baby has stopped except for her orgasm. Mm, you're such a perfect little girl for me now."

She watched Sophia's chest for another few seconds and confirmed that there was no motion at all.

"You're so close to being just a little doll of a girl for me. Just a pretty doll to play with."

Widow leaned over, took one of the excited nipples between her lips, and moaned softly while sucking it in and out. She let it pop out and when the breast stopped shaking, Sophia was again perfectly still. Just two hard nipples pointing up.

"Mm, just a sweet, tasty little doll baby. Every touch, every taste floods that orgasm through you."

Widow moaned and sucked on the other for a minute, allowing her saliva to leak out and trickle down, then let it go. Sophia still hadn't moved at all.

"Such a tasty little baby girl. A baby that's getting exactly what she's always wanted."

She shifted enough that she could check again the strap binding Sophia's ankles, then attached a shiny metal hook knotted to a thick rope threaded through an opening into a dark attic.

Back again, close enough to kiss her, Widow said, "Such a sweet girl. So very obedient now. Let's get you started on the way to our very quiet, very secret place. We'll be so close together for a very long time, and no one will ever find us."

She stood, then pressed a button near the bed. That started a motor whining and raising the straps around Sophia's ankles, lifting first her spiky black heels, then stretching up her long, snugly bound legs, then lifting her completely until she was hanging upside down beside the cushions with her black heels approaching the ceiling.

When her hips had reached the level of Widow's face, she hit the button, stopping Sophia there.

"Oh, I get so hungry sometimes. And you're such a tasty little treat. And you're only more tempting because you're packaged up so nicely. The wrapping is so important."

Widow took hold of the straps around Sophia's thighs to pull her in close. She then held both of Sophia's ass cheeks and inhaled all over, her fingers probing everywhere as she kissed her soft skin while spinning her around slowly, tasting her everywhere.

"Mm, such a perfect little girl now. So tender for me."

She reached for Sophia's masked head with both hands and pulled her face high between her thighs and held it there.

"Oh, that's nice too. We should have found time for this before we hid away your pretty face."

She stepped her short black boots farther apart and wiggled Sophia's head a few times, getting her in there more tightly.

"You know where you are, precious baby girl, and you know what you'd be doing if I'd unwrap you. You'd be such a pleasant little girl for me now. Your pretty face would be so eager to please me if you were ever somehow free of this."

With a deep sigh, Widow released Sophia, sat, and arranged two leather loops connected to thick ropes around her own ankles. She held a remote switch, pressed the button, and it started to raise her ankles up too.

She laughed softly as she lay back, letting the device whine and first straighten her legs to point up, then begin lifting her too.

As it was hoisting her up, she looked toward Sophia and said, "We'll be so cozy together soon, my sweetest little girl. You were always meant to be my delicious lover girl."

Chapter 33 – Then, We Kill My Father

"Stop," yelled one of the two guards as Risk approached with K Kat.

Risk didn't stop. Neither did the lion.

"Alright, fine," the man said and started to raise his spear.

Two lions raced toward him and his partner, giving them time only for the beginning notes of desperate screams.

Risk shifted back and stood over his killed guard, then picked up his spear.

K Kat took a bite of her kill's leg, wrestling a chunk loose and making a mess.

Risk watched, then said, "Kenzie. You're an animal."

The mountain lion ignored him and enjoyed her raw feast.

The door swung in, and five guards, one in front with his hands empty and up, moved very slowly toward them.

"There's no reason to kill any more of us. Just—"

"You'll give me a reason."

He stopped and stayed quiet, and Risk and K Kat watched him move only enough to breathe.

"Archie wants to see you."

"Who?"

The guard looked down at the feeding lion, grimaced, then looked back up at Risk.

"He has a nickname around this town. You can guess it if you want to, but I'm not saying it. Nope. Not me."

A nearby explosion timed itself well with a blazing fireball sent up on a looping path, traveling high enough to briefly light up the craggy, jagged ceiling of the giant cavern below the bay.

Risk waited for the man to again look his way.

"The madman?" Risk said.

"Aye. Don't tell him that I told you that, though, alright?"

Risk grumbled and looked each way on the street, then down at a mountain lion eating her fill, splattering her snout and whiskers with blood.

"We'll see."

"He'd like you to come inside."

"The madman."

The guard winced and looked each way, then up, then back at Risk.

"Do you mind? It'd be easier for me if you just killed me outright."

"I might."

"You have no sense of humor. Will you please step inside?"

Risk squinted at the man, not answering.

"Alright, fine. Sure, you can bring your lion too. But keep her on a leash, dammit."

Risk grinned and said, "No one leashes Kenzie."

He looked down at the bloody lion and said, "That's her name?"

"No. K Kat."

He sighed and rubbed his hands together, then bowed and said, "Please. Join us."

Then, he turned, shooed his fellow troops to move, then followed them inside a large courtyard.

Risk leaned in to look and so did a lion with a bloody face.

The lead guard stopped and turned his head toward them.

"Come on, then. Don't be shy."

He continued his walk, while Risk grumbled and K Kat was too busy licking her chops clean to say anything.

* * *

"Let's go, lion."

They took a few steps inside, then stopped.

All around the square courtyard, small groups of humans stood watching them, many holding spears or bows or long knives. Between the groups, irregularly spaced, torches burned with enough fury to light the space.

K Kat was the first to look up, and Risk followed her lead. A flat layering of mismatched wooden planks was laid across the space, some showing loops of wires and ropes, and poles from the ground supported other parts of it in key locations. Between the boards, through the cracks, there was only black.

Risk patted the lion's head, and they walked warily toward a man waving to them, smiling, inviting them through a doorway.

The lioness stopped when Risk stopped, and they both looked around again, both noticing that the entrance door to the compound had been closed quietly behind them.

"And you don't need that spear."

Risk tossed it aside and said, "No. I don't."

"Archie's in here," said the waving man, smiling and nodding. "Come on. It's okay."

Risk looked down at K Kat and said, "It's never okay here."

The lion bumped her head into him a few times, and Risk scoffed at seeing that K Kat had left some of the dead guard's blood on his jeans.

They closed the distance and followed the man into a much smaller room. No decorations of any kind interrupted the cracked plaster walls, and a single torch in each corner flickered enough to make shadows dance. A square table in the middle had two chairs on each of its sides, and only two were still available.

But the backs of those chairs were facing the door.

"We'll stand," Risk said, and he and K Kat entered the room and stood off to one side.

At the far side of the table, a man with a short gray beard and intense black eyes watched them closely. A gray ponytail dropped down below a faded black fedora, one without feathers or any other embellishments.

Despite his obvious age, the short sleeves of his casual shirt were stretched around full biceps, and a few buttons had resisted any attempt at spanning across his broad chest.

Risk gave him a short study, no longer than anyone or anything else in the room. K Kat, though, had decided to focus on that man exclusively.

The one who'd invited them into the room said, "That's Archie," and pointed at him.

Archie never moved and rarely blinked.

"What?" Risk said, staring into the man's eyes.

A few quiet moments passed before he spoke.

"You're looking for someone."

"We are."

Archie smiled, looked down and met K Kat's steady gaze, then looked back up and lost his smile.

"At least it's a female."

Risk scoffed and said, "More than you know."

"Maybe I do know. What will you do if you find him?"

"Stop him."

"You might have to kill him."

Risk only shrugged, and the mountain lion swiped her long tongue over her snout, once for each side.

"I . . . am that man."

Risk paused, studying Archie, who remained entirely calm. The men around the table fidgeted and tried to stop their reactions, but they couldn't hide them completely. And Risk saw more than one slip a hand from on the table to under the table.

"Then, I kill you."

Archie smiled and looked at his soldiers, then held both hands out, calming them.

He again held Risk's steady gaze.

"And if I'm your father?"

Risk's eyes narrowed into a squint, and he reached a hand out for K Kat. He touched her gently, fiddling with her ears.

"Sex doesn't make anyone a father."

Quiet seconds passed.

"Yet, I had sex, and here you are. Now, what?"

"Then . . . *we* kill my father."

* * *

Archie stared, showing no expression for a few seconds, then he tipped his head back and laughed at the ceiling.

"Or,"—he paused to snort out another laugh—"you could join me. You and that dangerous cat of yours."

Risk looked the man over, noticing his ageless features despite the gray hair. He gave K Kat one good pat, then looked again into Archie's eyes.

"Why that plan?"

"Humans deserve to run this world without all the fucking freaks fucking everything up."

"Some humans are freaks."

"Not like those goddamn zombeings, for instance. You know what they do, don't you? If they catch a human? They're looking to make some kind of zombie king or queen."

"I heard that. That's crazy."

"Oh, is it? They really are cyborgs, you know. Obsessed with sex when their brain chips are cranking and only wanting to chew on brains when they aren't. There's no living with freaks like that."

"How do they make a king or queen?"

"First of all, son, remember—"

Risk took a step toward him, growling and close to shifting, flexing hands at his sides that could wield sharp claws in less than a heartbeat.

"Don't call me that."

Archie laughed, unimpressed with Risk's display, and said, "Wish I didn't have to. I didn't know your mother was a goddamn shifter freak. What a scary bitch."

Risk laughed, the first time since entering that room, and said, "And you couldn't kill her."

"Didn't want to, at first. Oh, no. She turned herself into something so—hey, sure you want to hear this? There's no one else that can give you the gory details. It's kind of your legacy."

"Go ahead."

"Alright, that's the spirit. Oh, she was a seductress. I don't even know what that was she changed herself into, but let's just say she was soft and warm and squishy all over, and she offered way more than the usual, um, avenues of pleasure."

Risk stared, still flexing his fists.

"Took a while to tap them all."

Even K Kat let out a low grumble.

Archie laughed and said, "A man could go blind trying to fill her everywhere."

He lost his smile and said, "I wasn't gray before that."

Risk scoffed and kept staring.

"Then, I did want to kill her. Just to tie up loose ends. But I couldn't. I just couldn't."

"You loved her?"

"Oh, come on. That's just stupid. No, Asterisk. She—"

"It's Risk."

"Eh. Close enough. You're lucky I figured a better name for you."

"You started calling me Risk?"

"Yeah. You owe me."

"Huh."

Archie continued, saying, "No, I couldn't kill her because she shifted into something so god-awful and fucking scary and dangerous that probably no one could. She had claws as long as my arms, a jaw full of razor fangs that could chomp down on a stampeding boar, a—"

Risk was laughing.

"No," he said to Archie. "No, she didn't."

"She didn't?"

"No. You loved her."

"Dammit. You don't know anything. Forget about her. Where were we?"

"We were at why."

"Right. Okay, it isn't just those damn zombeings. Do you know how many fucking mutants are lurking in all the dark, fucked up little corners out there? Horrible things, Risk."

"Yeah."

"Maybe some of them are my fault. I mean, I've never even tried to figure out that sick radiation at the reactor. We get those fools shoveling dirt just to keep them busy. Their mutating bodies probably give most of the insulation we want anyway. Lost a lot of good people to that shit."

"My navigator."

"What?"

"My navigator is part hawk."

"Kill him. Do it now while—"

"I'm not killing him."

"Alright. Well, maybe he's one of the nice ones. But there are others. Damn, there are others. Used to be good people too. Like this short little guy, really friendly. Smart too. Fucker grew another head. You heard that right. He escaped but not before someone killed head number two."

Risk shrugged and said, "A few freaks."

"Oh, there's more. We had this hot babe that was good with machinery and chemistry and all kinds of shit. I mean, she was a whiz. She could automate anything. Then, a really sick pulse of radiation waved out, catching her while she was close."

"And?"

"Well, fuck, maybe there was some kind of predatory insect in range, with her, because she got strange quick."

"Ugly?"

"No, not at all. She looked even hotter. But you could see it in her eyes. Something was all hideous and wrong with her. I almost killed her, then I sent her packing."

"You spared her?"

"No, I fucked her. Had to tie her down, though, the savage thing. Just too goddamn strong. Gagged that bitch too. I've never heard such a hypnotic, nympho bitch like that before, and I think the worst of her mutations hadn't even hit yet."

"Then, what?"

"Then, I sent her packing. Still fucking gagged and hands tied so she couldn't talk until she was way the fuck away from me. Fuck if I know, but she's probably burrowed in out there in that damn city somewhere too."

"Where? The Maze?"

"Probably somewhere close. Sure. Last we heard, she had contact with some freak from Topside named Bentley."

"Bentley. You're sure?"

"Eh. Pretty sure. Some British fucker."

"If you found her, you'd—"

"I'd fuck her again. Damn right. No. Fuck, no. I'm just talking shit. Nobody with half a brain or even a brain chip should get close to that thing. Even when her mutations were just kicking in, which was when I tapped into that."

"It's not your decision."

"To kill them all? Fuck if it isn't."

Risk took another step closer and placed both hands on the table, staring at Archie.

"Don't, Risk. You know I'm right."

"I have to stop you."

"Your birthright doesn't require you to be a goddamn saint."

He grumbled and said, "Not a saint."

"You know what I mean. Just quit trying so hard. Join the team. That's your best option."

Risk straightened up and looked around the room. All eyes were on him, and most hands were on knife handles at belts, or hidden under the table.

"I'll kill you," he said to Archie.

"I should have killed *you* long ago."

Risk waited, taking slow, steady breaths. So did K Kat by his side.

Archie grinned and said, "But . . . now's good too," and jumped up out of his seat.

Knives and fists and sharp spear tips were racing at Risk and his mountain lion, but his shifting needed no thought or particular focus.

And K Kat had no need to shift at all.

Risk felt the pull of the beast by his side, her lean, muscular body pressed up against him, and he had no time to consider a different plan: he was a lion.

A big one, with the bristling mane high on his back almost grazing the ceiling. His sharp cat eyes had just enough time to see Archie fleeing the room.

And in the next instant, he swiped his claws at the nearest attacker, ripping the head until it hung only by shreds of skin. A man next to him, frozen in fear, made an easy target for his snapping jaws to take and shake, spraying blood everywhere as he crashed him into the brick wall.

K Kat, still beside him, used her natural skills to offset her lesser size. And her roaring was almost a match for his.

Together, they ripped and gouged and dismembered everyone left in that room.

One tried to sit up, and K Kat chomped into his neck and shook him. He didn't try again.

Risk saw something twitch, and he pounced without thinking. And he found that the blood from deeper inside his prey was hotter. So much better.

He and the other lion locked eyes at the sound of sirens screaming in the night.

Risk would have laughed, even as a lion, when he let the lady flee first.

And they both ran out of the building and into the courtyard, where the bigger of the two lions roared and rammed into the main door, splintering it off of its hinges and sending it spinning across the street.

They both saw Bentley at the same time, peeking around a building not far away. And they galloped toward him with cursing, angry voices following close behind.

One gradually became a man, one whose own powers were frighteningly close to those of the beast he had become.

And the other remained a lion.

Not a girl named Kenzie.

Chapter 34 – Get It Nice and Sticky

Marilyn held the cell bars with one hand and looked back at Janie, who had laid herself behind her. She'd snuggled in close, keeping her bared breasts tight against Marilyn's back.

"Wait. What is—"

A cold hand found her top thigh and pulled it up, lifting it too.

"Yeah," Blaine said with a laugh, "just like that. Show me that fine pussy."

"Oh, I don't—"

Blaine, all souped up again, found his target and drove it deep into Marilyn, who gasped and tipped her head back.

"Oh, yeah. A hard cock for you, just like that," Janie said, then reached around her with both hands to fondle her breasts. "So much more for you on that cock. Special delivery of that stuff you love, and it's getting slammed so deep inside your pussy."

Neither of them bothered to look, but the zombies gathered around outside the cage only stared, nodded, and groped themselves and anyone else close enough.

Marilyn's mouth was still open, and she opened her eyes again, too, and saw a pair of zombie hands rubbing and stroking a bulge behind his zipper. He sometimes stopped and bumped himself into the bars, pushing that bulge between them and toward her face.

"Oh, hey," said Janie, "before you get too busy sucking cock, look."

Marilyn craned her neck to look down at her belly and saw the red lines spreading farther and crowding together more. The collection on her thighs was nearing her knees and on her abdomen, they'd passed her navel and seemed intent on finding her breasts, which Janie was squeezing playfully.

"Isn't that skin beautiful now?"

"It's, um—"

"You're hungrier now, aren't you?"

"Hungrier than ever. Yes."

"And horny? Horny and hungry?"

"Mm, yes. Like I can't even believe."

Janie reached back with one hand, and someone handed her the bowl. Marilyn watched as she took a drink of it, then held her gaze while she swished it all around. But she didn't swallow any of it.

While she was tipping Marilyn's face toward her, she licked all over her lips, coating them. She nodded as their lips almost touched.

Marilyn sighed and didn't try to evade the kiss, which Janie made long and deep and very wet. She moved around enough that she was offering every part of her lips to Marilyn, who groaned while licking and sucking the stuff off of her.

Janie backed away only enough that their wet, slimy tongues could play together while Marilyn moaned softly and her stomach growled more.

"That's good," Janie said, then leaned her head to one side to study Marilyn's cheeks and said, "Oh, yeah, you're even more fuckable now."

"The lines make me fuckable?"

"Hell, yeah. You want zombies crazy to fuck you, don't you?"

"Oh, yes. Oh, I sure do."

"And you're hungry for more, aren't you?"

Marilyn nodded and said, "Oh, I sure am," then turned to look at the zipper of the zombie man who had pressed himself right up against the bars.

"Go on," said Janie. "It's special and big and just for you."

Marilyn groaned and pulled down the zipper, then she hesitated.

"It's in there. Take it out. See if you like it, you hungry, horny girl."

Marilyn wiggled two fingers in and fished around, then tugged and pulled until she had a very large, very hard zombie part in her hand.

"Oh my goodness," she said, giggling softly.

"So? What did you find, horny girl?"

"Um, I . . ."

"Say it."

Marilyn giggled and said, "I found a cock."

"Yeah, you sure did find a cock. Here," said Janie, and Marilyn turned her head, never letting go of the zombie, to see her holding up a deep bowl of the same stuff.

"You can't be serious," Marilyn said.

"You know I am. Drown that hard cock in there."

Marilyn let out a sigh that was part whimper, then angled the stiff shaft down toward the bowl in Janie's hand, submerging the end of it completely.

"Stir that cock around. Go on. Get it nice and sticky with all that."

Marilyn swirled it around and dove it in deeper, then slowly and carefully backed it out and left it to point straight toward her. A thick coating clung all around the shaft, and small blobs of the gooey stuff waited on the end.

Her stomach growled.

"Just for you," said Janie "We all want you to be even lovelier. You know you want more of that sweet taste. It's right there on that cock."

She looked up at the grinning zombie and waited, until Janie said, "Uh-uh, gorgeous. Your turn."

"Um, I—"

Janie pinched both of Marilyn's nipples, hard, making her groan to match the sounds from her stomach.

In her ear, she said, "It's time for you to take what you want. You do want to suck that sloppy zombie cock, don't you? Show everyone how bad you want that zombie cock. That fucking sloppy zombie cock!"

Marilyn moved her mouth close, opened it, and turned her eyes up to the zombie whose rod was coated with slop and needed only a slight nudge to get planted inside the warm, wet mouth of a Kildare Killer who was slowly losing herself to life as a zombie.

"You're getting so fuckable," said Janie. "Suck that zombie cock!"

* * *

Risk and K Kat rounded a blind corner and saw no obstacles ahead, so they kept running.

Until Risk heard the lion yip and skidded himself to a stop and looked back at her.

"Dammit."

K Kat was lying on her side, snapping and chewing on the slender wood shaft of an arrow lodged in her back leg. She paused her attempts to remove it, panting at him as he approached but only for a second. Then, she groaned and attacked it again.

"Shh, girl. It'll be okay."

Risk stooped down, held her head with one hand, and touched gently where the sharp metal had entered her leg, which she couldn't stop from twitching.

They both looked up when they heard a man say, "There you are, you fuckers."

Archie's soldier was by himself, the other guards hadn't caught up, and he was fumbling around, trying to nock his next arrow while keeping the shifter and the lion in his sights.

Risk stood, made no move to leave his lion, and faced the man who had loaded his weapon and was raising it to aim.

Then, Bentley the vampire walked casually out from a shadowy corner near the man with the bow.

The soldier snarled and began turning the point to face Bentley instead, as he was much closer.

Bentley kept walking, calm and smiling, and said, "Oh, dammit. Just look at me. Look closely."

The man leaned forward a little and squinted.

"Look me in the eye, you cretin."

When he'd managed to focus on Bentley's eyes, his snarl faded and his arms lost their reasons for pointing an arrow at anyone.

"Yes," said Bentley. "I've been told I'm captivating."

Bentley stopped and held an arm across his face, eyeing the man over it.

"Come to me," he said in his best vampire voice.

The man let his gear tumble from his hands, and he started a slow stumble toward the British fellow wearing only shorts and sneakers.

Never breaking eye contact with the man, Bentley said over his shoulder, "Run. Or limp. Oh, that poor lion."

The man kept walking toward him, a silly grin on his face.

"Bentley, you'll die."

"Ha! I wish. No, Risk. No one escapes me."

Risk stooped down again and put a hand on the lion's side.

He scoffed loudly and said, "I would."

"We can try," said Bentley. "Could be the bloody end of all your fun romps down here in this nightmarish place."

"No. You would die badly."

They heard the clatter of a crowd stomping around the corner, getting louder.

"No time," Risk said, then he shifted back to his oversized lion form and lunged for the dazed vampire victim.

He leaped when he was close enough and came down with both massive front paws on the man's shoulders, folding his spine several different ways. His claws were in deep, so he roared and threw the man to the side, leaving him dead and staring up at the featureless night.

With a quick turn of his head, he bumped a laughing Bentley into the air and sent him several steps closer toward the fallen lion. And he didn't shift back on the way while running with Bentley.

When he could, he closed his mouth on the scruff of K Kat's neck, easily lifted her high above the street surface, and he and Bentley ran to evade their pursuers.

Chapter 35 – Mm, I Do Love You

The hoist whined softly in an otherwise completely silent room. The soft leather loops stayed tight around the ankles of smooth, strong legs wearing short black boots with pointy heels, lifting those heels toward the ceiling until they were beside the equally pointy heels of a captive Kildare Killer.

Widow's long black hair hung straight down toward the floor, while Sophia's was lost and bound away under layers of webbing, so much of it that her entire head was covered. There were no longer any recognizable features—no way to be sure that there was even a face encased by all of it.

And the poisons that Widow had forced into her had stopped almost every normal function except for the overpowering orgasm that never lessened and only spiked with any slightest touch from her captor.

Sophia no longer had any ability to even breathe, and she also wore multiple loops of the material around her ankles, around her waist to further immobilize arms that were already fastened together from the wrists up, and around the smooth, soft skin of her thighs near her knees.

Everywhere else, Widow had left her perfect, unblemished skin visible and available to touch and enjoy.

Widow gave Sophia a light spin, enough that they could face each other, then reached around to place a hand on each of her ass cheeks, which were entirely bare. She squeezed for a moment, then patted lovingly.

"Absolutely scrumptious," she said, holding Sophia against her and lightly sneaking her fingers up and down deep between her cheeks.

Sophia remained motionless, not squirming or trying to evade the woman's touch in the slightest way.

Widow devoted a few moments to kissing where she knew Sophia's lips were hidden by her webs, then tipped her head back and smiled at her captive.

"We should have just a sweet little kiss before we settle in for our very long, special time alone together. Would you like a sweet kiss, my dearest baby?"

Sophia's web-covered head nodded slowly but only once.

"Such a wonderful, cooperative little girl."

Widow reached up toward Sophia's face and slid the back of one of her hands, then the other, across the hardening material covering her lips. It began to soften then separate from the rest of it, and she peeled away pieces of it and let them fall quietly to the floor.

She'd uncovered a pair of full lips that were still forced together from the windings wedged in deep and tight between them.

But they were still soft and not the least bit dry.

"Oh, such a pout from such a pretty girl. Just adorable."

Sophia still had five bands of the webbing pulled deep inside her mouth, but her stretched lips remained somewhat wet, and they stayed completely still.

"Well, this little girl might need her naughty little tongue too."

She touched the backs of her fingers to the backs of her hands, then slid those down between Sophia's lips and dragged them gingerly across the embedded webbing.

After a second or two, those webs began to weaken and dissolve, and Widow reached in to pick out all of the pieces, which she left on the floor beneath them with the others.

Before she'd taken out the last of it, she chuckled softly at the sight of Sophia's lips parting and her mouth staying open.

She turned and leaned an ear close to Sophia's open mouth, waited a moment, then smiled.

"Hmm, my poor little baby is mostly ruined on the inside, and nothing's working anymore. Nothing but what she needs to still be delicious for me and feel that sweet orgasm that comes with my poisons. So sweet. Such a very good and quiet girl for me now. Just a delightful little girl that wants to be touched all over."

She reached back up to hold Sophia's ass cheeks again, then began wedging all of her fingertips between them, pulling and sliding, getting them in deeper.

"Oh, there's that very special, secret place of yours. Such soft little secrets you think you can keep from me."

She wiggled just one of her hands in farther.

"Ooh, such a snug little secret too. You don't want that to stop me, sweet little baby. Silly girl, you have so many ways to tease me."

Two fingers went in just a little farther.

"Aw, there we go. Every littlest touch, even like this, sends sweet orgasm ripples all through you, little girl."

She kissed her on the lips.

"And you love your little tingles so much more now. You don't care at all about anything else."

She kissed her while working those fingers in a bit more.

"Oh, so much better. Hmm, I'll still want to hold you like this, even after we're all done. And when I kiss you, after we're finished, your kisses for me will be even sweeter, even though you'll be far beyond ever knowing it. Will you like it if I keep what you leave behind so I can still enjoy your sweet kisses?"

Sophia's head nodded once, slowly, and Widow smiled at the sight.

"Oh, you're so precious," she told her while using her other hand to pat her ass softly. "I tend to talk a lot at a time like this—before we begin our special, secret time together. You don't mind, do you?"

She didn't wait for any response, just pressed her lips into Sophia's for a few seconds.

"You're already orgasming more than you ever thought possible, but this, our special time before we hide away together, is like foreplay for me. We're so close, and I feel my own orgasm approaching. You, my sweet little thing, will help with that."

She moaned softly and gave Sophia's lips another wet kiss.

"My poisons are filling you up so nicely, and they'll keep you soft and fresh for me too. You'll stay just a sweet, gorgeous doll for me to play with. I'll dress you up real pretty, probably in a flowery little-girl dress like you wore special just to meet me. I'll sit you on my lap, touching you just like this. I'll get my fingers deep into that delightful, hidden part of you so I can hold you very still. Wouldn't you love to stay just a sexy toy girl for me to play with?"

Sophia didn't move at all, not even her lips, and all of the material covering her face had almost set into a single, very tough piece.

"Mm, there we go. So sweet. I'll get a friend named Mortimer or one of his friends to give you some of their fun drug or a microchip, and maybe you'll still be able to obey my orders. Would you like that, baby girl? You'll be a very good and obedient little girl doll for me?"

Sophia remained still, and Widow gave her a quick kiss.

"Yes, you will. I'll get comfortable in my favorite chair, peel my tight skirt out of your way, and put your pretty face in just the right place between my thighs. Then, I might even use a soft blanket to cover you up, make you my very secret little girl. And I'll order my sweet little doll girl to lick. Oh, my doll baby will lick me so sweetly, with no desire to ever stop."

She paused to look at Sophia's lips, which were still pouty and still soft and moist.

"I do love kissing my sweet little girl."

She began a more serious kiss, and Sophia didn't resist in any way. Widow rubbed her lips all over Sophia's, pausing only to lick them outside and inside and moaning softly the entire time.

"Mm, such a tasty little thing. I love little baby girls that want only to please me."

She held her tongue straight out, the tip of it just past Sophia's lips, lips which slowly closed on it and held it. Widow grinned but didn't remove it. She only leaned away, then toward her again, slipping her tongue in and out between Sophia's wet lips, which squeezed her tongue weakly the entire time.

"Mm," she said to the silent mass of webbing that had been sucking her tongue, "that's like a sweet, sexy little fucking before we hide ourselves away together, someplace dark and forgotten where we'll never be disturbed. Does my baby girl like being helpless and getting fucked like this?"

Right away, Sophia barely offered a weak nod and Widow, smiling at the quick response, added, "Oh, my! Do you like to hear me say 'fucking?'"

Sophia nodded weakly again, and her lips were still parted and wet.

"Oh, yes. Everything is magnified for you, you sweet little girl. Okay. Let's have some fun."

Widow wiggled her fingers deeper between Sophia's ass cheeks and said, "Does Baby like to be so helpless that she can't stop her pretty lips from getting fucked?"

Sophia nodded more weakly than before, her lips wet and open.

"Oh, good girl for being so still and quiet. There's so much of my wonderful poisons in you now, sweet baby. You might already be past the point of no return. Even fucking your sweet lips gives you more of my poison. And you want to hear it again, don't you?"

Widow moaned softly and drove her tongue in repeatedly, sometimes licking Sophia's lips, saying, "Mm, fucking your lips. Fucking my helpless baby's lips."

She backed away and smiled at the parted lips still waiting for her.

"Baby girl is helpless and getting fucked," she said, then plunged her tongue in again. "So many sweet little fuckings for my baby girl."

Sophia's lips never stopped squeezing her tongue, bringing her even more of Widow's poisons.

Widow backed her tongue away just enough to say, "My sweet, tasty little girl. All you can manage now is to be sexy for me. Letting me fuck your lips is only the beginning for us. Suck more delightful poisons from my tongue."

She gave Sophia's lips a few more wet intrusions, moaning with each tender thrust, then said, "But you must know, sweet baby, that giving me your dearest juices is now the sexiest thing you can do. Isn't it?"

She waited, and Sophia remained still.

"Answer me, my tasty girl."

Sophia was frozen inside her webs and bindings, her lips still soft and parted slightly, as tempting as they ever were.

"Oh, that's beautiful. It took us both trying patiently together to get you to this point. You've never been more beautiful than right at this moment—just a gorgeous little-girl sponge filled up so nicely with my poisons. So much of it has settled in all over inside you. Don't you just love that you've soaked up as much as possible and you have no hope of ever being free of it? You love that all of your juicy insides have welcomed all of that poison?"

Sophia had no reaction.

"Aw, there we go. All of that wonderful poison won't even let you nod anymore. Nothing inside your tasty body will ever work again. But my every little touch, every caress, only adds to your orgasm. My precious little girl is completely ready to hide away with me now. We'll be alone together for a long, long time. Pressed so close together like two lovers."

She gave Sophia's lips a long, wet kiss, and even her lips didn't move.

"Mm, I do love you, my precious little baby."

She gave Sophia another longer, deeper, more passionate kiss.

"And I know that you love me. More than you've ever loved anyone else. Or ever will."

She turned her head and called out, "Igor!"

* * *

"You're kind of scaring the shit out of me," Bentley said as he tipped his head back to look up at Risk's lion head.

In his mouth, he still held K Kat, who still had an arrow in her back leg. He looked behind them, saw no pursuers, then gently laid the wounded lion on the ground.

His sigh was more of a roar, then he shifted back to himself, first lion's eyes then man's eyes staying focused on Bentley's.

"Better?"

"Much. I had my cold heart set on that convenient little snack back there. You didn't have to kill it."

"More were coming."

"Guess what: I've killed lots of them already."

"All at once?"

"Hmm. Alright. You've raised a valid point."

He looked down at K Kat and said, "What about your girlfriend who's sometimes a lion? Or is it the other way around?"

"Just a friend."

"Whichever she is, that looks kind of nasty. You can't carry her forever. Or maybe you can. Either way, she needs help."

Risk grumbled and looked and listened, but none of the soldiers had yet come their way.

A red flash flew into the sky above the building rooftops, followed by a quick bang. All eyes turned up to watch it. And they saw more than just the target practice launches.

"What in bloody hell is that?"

Risk smiled and said, "A hawk. Sort of."

"Big and round like that?"

"A hawk in a balloon."

"Whatever it is, which you certainly haven't described very clearly, it seems to be coming toward us. I hope that's good."

"It is."

A clamor broke the silence of a descending balloon against a fiery red glare in a black sky. A gang of Archie's troops was fast approaching around a corner.

Bentley sneered in the direction of the soldiers, then looked up at Hawken.

"He could display a sense of urgency, you know. It's the decent thing to do."

Hawken had steered his craft close enough that they could see his gloved hand waving. Bentley waved back, but Risk stooped down and picked K Kat up into his arms, then stood again.

"Hawken," he called up, causing a brief spattering of squawking before the hawk boy navigator answered.

"Risk! I'm not staying long!"

"Neither are we."

The basket scraped across the pavement as the wrinkly balloon drifted along the street, between the buildings. Bentley laughed, grabbed the top rail, and stopped his laughter at losing his footing and getting dragged along.

"Hey, use the brakes!"

"No brakes!" said Hawken, chattering. "Hurry!"

With a one-handed lift and toss from Risk, Bentley tumbled inside and quickly stood. Risk passed the hurt mountain lion over the rail to him, but the weight of her wasted no time in sprawling him out with a big groaning cat atop him.

"She needs a doctor or something," Bentley said as K Kat's tail slapped his face and her body kept him pinned down.

Risk held the rail and jumped over, landing his worn black boots near Bentley and the lion.

"Hawken was a medic."

Bentley looked up and saw, for the first time, the intense, staring red eyes of a hawk, his sharp, hooked beak, and his face coated with feathers.

He stared for a second, then looked back at Risk with his eyes wide.

"When he was Ken."

To the sound of a hawk's mirthful but panicky squawking, flames danced above the craft's iron pot, the balloon stretched and expanded with a deep, hot inhale, and they all fled into the dark sky.

Chapter 36 – The Sweetest, Sickest Orgasms

Marilyn whimpered softly and licked her lips before parting them and watching the zombie bring the head closer to her waiting mouth.

"Just let that cock into your mouth," said Janie, "then suck everything off of it. Suck it and lick it. You'll see that sucking that cock will help with that nasty hunger screaming in your belly."

Marilyn looked up at the zombie as she lay there with her mouth opened upward. He took a step, getting the end of it directly above her mouth, and she gazed up at it without blinking, seeing just how much slime he'd attached to it.

"Oh, look at that," said Janie. "Mm, such a juicy cock for you!"

Her instinct was to close her mouth when she saw a thick drop hanging, ready to fall, but she didn't. Janie's hands held her head in place.

"Uh-uh. Oh, no. Keep that mouth open for that tasty drop. Special delivery: from hard zombie cock to your mouth. Right onto your tongue. Take it."

Marilyn whimpered softly, watching the thick, heavy glob of gooey stuff dangling right above her open mouth.

Janie whispered in her ear, "It's a nice little cock treat for you. Oh, here it goes now."

Marilyn whimpered but kept her mouth open.

"Keep it open! Here it comes!"

The zombie laughed and tapped the side of his shaft, shaking not just that drop loose. It was heavy enough that it carried down with it a long string of slimy goo, with no end in sight.

"Just like that," Janie said, still holding Marilyn's open mouth under the slop as it dribbled off of the hard zombie pole. "Yum. All in your mouth."

The heavy drop landed softly on Marilyn's outstretched tongue, and she moaned while it began to spread out into a thick puddle. Her breaths sped up, and she stayed as still as she could as that drop pulled the sticky cord behind it, all of it slowly falling and coagulating into a gooey mound on her tongue.

"Don't stop," Janie said in her ear. "You love the taste of that, don't you? Fresh off a stiff zombie cock?"

"Uh-huh," she said as the stringy goop continued to feed into her open mouth.

She didn't close her mouth, just moaned softly as it all continued to drip and finally, it stopped, but the end of his rod still waited close to her mouth. Marilyn turned her head to face it, but she looked up at Janie.

While caressing Marilyn's cheeks, Janie said, "Swallow that shit. Go on, get it all into your stomach. You know you want it."

Marilyn swallowed hard, winced, then swallowed again, causing Janie to laugh.

"Mm, yeah, so thick. So thick and gooey. Get it inside!"

With a final hard swallow, Marilyn got it all down.

"Oh, your cheeks look better already," said Janie, touching Lin's soft, creamy white cheeks that had picked up even more thin red lines.

And those lines were all wiggling down lower, starting to settle in on the smooth skin of her neck. From Janie's touch, Marilyn's cheeks also had a few streaks of oil, making her more like them and everything else around her.

"Alright," said Janie, "every tasty little bit dripped off of that damn zombie cock into your pretty mouth. Now, let's get that cock in there."

"But, um, it doesn't have any of that, uh, you know. Stuff on it anymore."

She kissed her ear and said, "No, not *on* it."

"Oh, but then, you must mean—"

"Yes, that cock still has stuff. It has its own more special cock stuff for you. It'll make your skin even lovelier. Wouldn't you want to be even more beautiful?"

Marilyn groaned at getting more hard pinches and twists to her nipples, and she turned her eyes down to focus on the large, stiff zombie part waiting for her.

"You want to suck it."

Marilyn whimpered softly.

"You want so bad to suck a stiff zombie cock. Imagine that cock in your mouth. It's such a bad thing to do that you can't resist it."

Her stomach growled, and Janie was stretching her nipples straight out when Marilyn opened her mouth, so close that she could touch it with her tongue.

"Almost there," she said, roughly pulling her nipples straight out. "Think of that special surprise it has just for you. You know exactly what to do to get that surprise too. To make it squirt in your mouth."

Marilyn moaned and leaned her open mouth toward it, her blue eyes fixed on it.

Janie gave one of Marilyn's nipples a harsh pinch and dug in her nails, causing her to gasp and open her mouth wider.

The zombie grinned and stepped forward just enough to jab the head past Marilyn's wet lips and into her mouth.

"Oh, yeah, there we go."

Marilyn's gasp returned to a soft moaning, even though Janie hadn't released her and her sharp nails were still tormenting her nipple.

Janie reached up with her other hand, giving quick taps to Marilyn's chin until she closed her lips on it, bringing out a deep sigh.

"Good," said Janie. "That cock feels so good in there for you. Beautiful. Do you even know how beautiful you look with a stiff zombie cock in your mouth?"

Marilyn whimpered and nodded.

"Yeah, you do. It's a damn good look for you."

Marilyn moaned and held it tight with her lips.

"What's your hunger telling you to do now?"

Marilyn groaned but didn't let it go.

"Your hunger's telling you to suck. You want so bad to suck that zombie cock. Here, I'll help."

She lightly pushed Marilyn's head forward, driving the hard zombie shaft deeper into her mouth.

"Oh, just like that. Get that fucking thing in there."

Then, she allowed her to back away before pushing her again. She repeated it several times, then gently pulled her hands away, and Marilyn continued to bob her head all on her own, hungrily sucking one zombie while getting fucked by another one, all while captive in a prison cell and surrounded by many more.

"Hmm, we're making some serious progress here," Janie said with a short, sharp laugh. "Girl's in a prison cell, lost underground, getting fucked by one zombie and sucking off another."

She brushed back some of Marilyn's blond mane, giving herself a clearer sight of the thick shaft piercing Marilyn's eager lips.

"You won't be able to stop until you can swallow his cold zombie cum. You feel like you're dying for it. And you are. And you're probably feeling a new, crazy kind of orgasm. You are, aren't you?"

Marilyn, her mouth full, only said, "Mm-hmm."

"So many more lines on your skin now," Janie said while caressing Marilyn's cheeks. "That's good. So lovely and so zombie fuckable. Sucking that cock sure helps."

Marilyn held it at its base and looked, and she saw that the steady fucking from Blaine, plus her hungry sucking of the other zombie, had gotten all of the thin red lines to almost meet somewhere around her ribs.

"Yes, here they go," Janie said. "Fucking and sucking. That's what you can't get enough of."

She and Janie watched as the first pair connected, and Marilyn giggled once when her stomach growled. Another pair linked, and her stomach growled again. She gave up watching because they were all connecting, all the way around her body, and her stomach was in a constant uproar.

With a satisfied shrug, she turned back to the zombie poking through her cage bars, clamped her lips tight around him, and resumed bobbing her head and stroking with her lips.

Janie grabbed Marilyn's wrists and guided her hands up to hold the base of the hard shaft, then whispered, "You know his cum will change you way more than the sick juices you were lapping up. You know, and you can't stop."

Marilyn whimpered and began to stroke it with both hands, pumping it and barely hearing Janie laughing softly and biting her ear lobe while roughly squeezing both of her nipples.

"Yes, pump that cock, you starving girl. Just like that."

Janie began a steady chant in her ear, and the longer it went on, the louder Marilyn's moaning got.

"There's a hard zombie cock in your mouth. Suck that dead cock. Your lips are warm and wet, and that cock is so cold and dead. But you love it. You love sucking zombie cock."

She barely heard Janie end with laughter as she brutally twisted her nipples.

She backed it out of her mouth long enough to say, "Oh my goodness, I'm, I'm about to—"

Janie squeezed her breasts hard and whispered in her ear, "It's the only way you'll ever want to cum again. Mm-hmm. The best possible orgasm, you starving, sexy pervert."

She pushed Marilyn's head forward, burying the thick shaft even deeper in her mouth. Then, she bounced her head over it a few times quickly.

"Good. You're almost one of us, and you'll always crave only the sweetest, sickest orgasms after this."

She gave her head a good shove and held it there, smiling at Marilyn's gagging sounds and how she made no effort to back away.

Not even a little.

She only sped up when Janie said, close to her ear, "That dead zombie cock is so close to cumming in your mouth. Mm, a mouthful of cold dead cum for you!"

Chapter 37 – Their Insatiable Lovemaking

Igor, with his back perpetually cramped and twisted and a cloth sack covering his extra head, opened the stout metal door and entered, walking close enough that Widow could see him.

"It's time," she said to him in a normal voice. "Be sure those shutters are bolted. Pick up those discarded pieces of webbing. And blow out the candles."

"Yes, Mistress."

Widow watched him get started, then turned back to her bound captive and gave her a soft kiss, still speaking normally.

"It's our time, my juicy little baby. Let's hide ourselves in the dark together."

She released Sophia's cheeks and touched her hips lightly, letting all of her fingertips caress the soft, bare skin and spinning her around to face the other way.

"Just me and you," she said, close to Sophia's covered ear. "Oh, we'll stay so, so close together, and neither one of us will be able to stop."

She pinched the waistband of her tiny black panties, then wiggled her hips and tugged them until she had her own tight, thin black strap wrapped around her thighs. She reached both hands around Sophia's hips, then pulled them together as close as she could, trapping Sophia's still unbound hands between them at just the right place.

Widow shifted her own hips a few times, gently arching her back and positioning herself against Sophia.

"Yes, now, you understand why. My baby girl doesn't need fingernails. She wouldn't want them. Just nice, soft fingertips."

Widow kissed the side of Sophia's neck, then whispered near her ear, "The more pleasure you give me, the stronger will be the poisons I'm filling you with. Already, you're almost completely mine. Your sweet, juicy insides have soaked up so much of it that they're good only for me, and they'll never work again. Mm, you'll love what stronger doses will do to you. You do want to hurry my poisons to ruin you inside even more, don't you, my baby girl?"

Sophia didn't move.

"And you know that at some point, after we've been loving each other in the dark, that orgasm that consumes you will stop? And there won't be anything left of you except a sweet little doll for me to play with?"

Sophia's head stayed still.

"Of course, you know, and you can't imagine wanting anything else. Don't be shy with those lovely fingers, my pretty girl. Mm-hmm. Touch my pussy. Slowly now, my tender baby girl."

Widow gasped softly.

"Oh, mm, just like that. Oh, my, that's so nice. You seem to know exactly how I want my pussy touched."

She reached around to hold Sophia's breasts, squeezing them gently and closing her eyes as Sophia softly stroked and rubbed with her fingers between Widow's thighs.

"I know that your lovely breasts have become insanely sensitive too. More than you ever could have imagined. If you could speak, you'd be begging me to do anything I want to them, even cruelty. Maybe especially cruelty. Mm, but I'll touch them nice for you. Just gentle for my baby girl."

With her eyes closed, Widow moaned as she playfully squeezed Sophia's large, soft breasts.

"Yes. Slowly, with those lovely, soft fingertips. You feel almost like you're kissing me there, don't you, sweet girl?"

Sophia didn't respond.

"Oh, those soft, wet fingertips. Such a sweet baby girl for me."

Widow touched Sophia's very stiff nipples gently, bending them then pinching and pulling.

"Oh, you're such an excited little girl for me. You adore kissing me with those soft fingertips, making my poisons even stronger for you. And you love everything that's happening to you. You even love that you're powerless to stop any of it."

She pulled Sophia's nipples straight out and held them there.

"Slowly, now, baby girl, while I give you sweet little pinches. So very slow for me. Yes, touch my pussy so softly. Just like that. Mm."

She closed her eyes and let Sophia continue for several minutes, still stretching away from them the unmistakable signs of Sophia's ecstasy.

Widow sighed then opened her eyes, kissed Sophia's neck and said, "Let's begin our long, long, quiet time together."

She turned her head to say to Igor, "Start the machinery, then go to the roof and make sure the generator doesn't quit until the cycle is done. Then, I give you permission to jump from the roof."

"Jump, Widow? You don't mind? I've wanted to die for so long."

"Yes, I want you to jump. There will be no chance for you to slip up and tell anyone where we are, and no one even knows the place exists. My sweet baby and I both want to be locked in up there, impossible to get free until I'm hugging and touching just a beautiful, empty doll."

"I can finally die."

"Yes, you can. You were about to kill yourself when I found you, weren't you? Haven't you enjoyed those times I let you touch me?"

"Yes, Widow. You know I have."

"Then, you've already gotten more out of life than most. Do as I command."

"Yes, Widow."

He turned to leave but stopped when she said, "And Igor, weld that door shut before you go up to the roof. I want to take my time, and this tasty baby doesn't want anyone to stop me. My delicious baby girl wants to give me all of herself."

"Yes, Widow."

Igor nodded, used a tall ladder to attach the sticky ends of six wide web tapes to their ankles, then hit a button to start the automated process.

Widow kept her bare legs pressed against Sophia's smooth bare legs, the fronts of her thighs squeezed warm and tight against the backs of Sophia's thighs, their pointy heels all mixed together high above them.

And the two of them, suspended from the ceiling, began to rotate.

Six canisters of webbing, each with a long coil of strap about the width of a hand, played out from around them and began to wrap near their ankles where Igor had stuck them. Four pointy heels were crowded together and angled toward the ceiling and as they spun, six bands of material began traveling downward to cover more of their legs in overlapping layers.

Before any of the gummy layers of it got as far as their hips, Widow placed her palms flat on the smooth skin below Sophia's navel, then slid her fingers to just the right place.

"See, little girl? I'll touch you so softly too."

Only a second later, Widow said, "Oh, you really are the sweetest thing. Yes, baby girl, you can still feel this and respond to it. Oh, you're offering such a sweet pussy to me. Such a precious, very juicy little girl."

She kissed Sophia's neck where her lips were almost touching it already.

"Just let the feelings take you away. Alone with me, the two of us so close in our cozy nest, is where you've always belonged. It feels that way, doesn't it, baby girl?"

Sophia had no response.

"Slowly, little baby girl. Oh, yes, just like that. Nice and slow with those soft kisses for me. Mine are soft too. See?"

Sophia's webbed head tipped back, her mouth open slightly, as Widow began to rub her gently. Then, the constant web winding covered their hips, too, locking in both pairs of hands, soft fingers between each other's thighs.

"Mm, we'll just have to keep touching each other. Slowly, now, baby girl. Mm, that's so nice. Soft and slow for me."

The motor whined reliably, and Widow and Sophia together spun slowly, and the gathering coating of webbing traveled beyond their waists. The first layer higher squeezed both of Sophia's breasts, compressing them and exaggerating her pointy nipples. The next band traveled past just above her nipples, leaving only the two of them pointing out from the accumulating webs.

The next winding band tightly covered them altogether, hiding away any hint of their size and shape and level of Sophia's sexual excitement.

Before it got all the way up to their heads, Widow sighed and said, "It's just you and me, now, my sweet baby girl, and I feel so greedy. Do you mind if I take every last drop from this beautiful body?"

Sophia's webbed head didn't move.

"Such a sweet, lovable girl. No one's going to interrupt our intimate time together. I'm so glad you want to give me all of it. Be a good girl while I give your pretty neck a bigger, deeper kiss, okay?"

Sophia was only quiet and still.

"Oh, such a sweet girl. Yes, it'll be a very nice, final kiss for you. I'll try not to drain your wonderful juices too fast, but Baby, when a body is upside down, you must know how exciting and urgent that makes it for me. And you, my pretty little girl, while I'm loving you, just enjoy that orgasm as it carries you far away."

She touched her nose softly against the skin of Sophia's neck, rubbed it a few times, then said, "Just what we both have always wanted. And to think that you wanted to hurt me just a few moments ago. You can't even imagine that now. No, not anymore, my sweet, precious, juicy little girl."

She gently kissed Sophia's neck, in an area that was unmarked by all of the biting and sucking Widow had already done.

"You were always mine, Baby. And our private cocoon won't ever let me stop sucking out all of your precious juices until I have every tasty drop. Ours is the truest love you'll ever know."

She sank her sharp teeth as deeply as possible into Sophia's neck and began to feed, rocking her head gently to find the best angle, and they both kept spinning, which forced the webbing to cover their heads and bind them together, neither of them able to stop any of it.

The winding process continued back up to the top, fed by all of the large cannisters which had begun to play out much thicker bands of material. It covered along their necks, tightly around their heads, some even wrapping brutally deep between the glistening lips of Sophia's silent, gasping mouth, then traveled at a leisurely pace back to the top of the cocoon.

The motor kept whining, Widow and Sophia kept spinning together, and the layering continued from top to bottom and back again many times, like the spools might never be depleted, until the couple was encased in a single, swollen mass of webbing, hanging from sturdy ropes in a dark room. The hardening material covered even both pairs of heels entirely but left Widow's long black hair still hanging down.

Finally, after spinning for an endless time, the strands of webs reached their ends on the spools, and the incessant turning of the cocoon drew the last of it from all of the cannisters. The canisters got pulled off of their tables and spun with the cocoon until each strand had reached its end. That forced the containers to break free, and they fell to the floor, each rolling in a different direction.

The motor for spinning the cocoon slowed, then clicked when it stopped.

And the hidden couple spun silently several more times, gradually slowed, then stopped. They became as still and silent as any piece of furniture in that dark room, but all of the layers were busy fusing together to form a tough shell, so durable that few tools would ever be able to damage it in the slightest.

Widow's automated system began to lift them higher, up through the opening and past the thick opened hatch lifted from an equally thick concrete floor. Above that floor, their cocoon would be welcomed by a long-forgotten three-story attic that had been boarded up long before to have no other openings than the hatchway through the floor.

The motor whined softly and steadily lifted them through the floor opening, then through three stories of darkness, then up among the wood trusses until they could be no closer to the roof. When they'd reached their planned destination, the mechanisms locked the cocoon there, too high above the attic floor for anyone to reach.

And with all of the sheets and stuffed sacks and clutter that Widow had Igor hang up there, crowded everywhere between all of the trusses, their cocoon looked only like more useless abandoned stuff. There was nothing about it to warrant any attention at all, even if there was light.

Anyone that looked at it would never suspect that Widow was in there with Sophia, sucking everything out of her while their hands were immobilized where all they could do was touch each other.

The process, nearly complete, continued by lowering the hatch door with a soft thump, which made the absence of any light in the abandoned attic absolute. Powerful motors on opposite sides of the closed hatch door turned screws which scraped heavy pallets of bricks over it. The gears then locked themselves in place, and small charges detonated to disconnect it all from the power supply.

Widow had secluded herself away with Sophia, her captive Kildare Killer, in a place without light and without access . . . a cozy, selfish hideaway where they were just beginning to share a fatal intimacy and give each other constant ecstasy.

Neither nearly naked woman, immobile under layers of hardening cocoon, could speak.

One because her fangs were deep into soft flesh as she patiently sucked, hungry for the hot juices.

The other because she'd welcomed so many poisons with the purpose of halting everything inside her, ruining it all except for what she needed to feel, and give, an endless orgasm.

But they both heard the machinery finish its work, scraping pallets of bricks over their haven's only entrance.

And they both listened with relief and satisfaction as the small charges popped, rendering the machinery powerless to ever be used to interrupt them.

And they both wished to never be discovered or have their quiet love affair stopped.

They desired only to continue their insatiable lovemaking in unbroken silence and darkness, in a forgotten attic in an unknown building, lost among countless other abandoned buildings somewhere deep below San Francisco Bay.

* * *

"Higher," said Risk. "Above the arrows."

"Okay, Risk," Hawken said as he flapped open the vessel's pot from his perch high above the basket.

Flames snaked up inside the balloon, expanding it, making it stretch and groan. All of the ropes and cables tightened, and they quickly cleared the lower structures through which they'd been chased and hunted.

Risk pointed toward the groupings of taller buildings ahead. All of the windows were covered with planks and sheets of corrugated metal, and some with tarps that hung motionless in the still air.

No light escaped any of the windows.

"Over those too," Risk said.

"Alright. Let's go up."

Hawken stoked the fires and let out modest blasts from the spout, sending their craft higher and toward the tall buildings.

"Something's there," Hawken said, pointing down toward the rooftop that they'd just crested and were still rising above.

Bentley looked over the edge and said, "Oh, that's—um . . ."

"What? Speak."

"Or else, what?" the vampire said with a sneer.

"Or try to fly."

He scoffed and looked down as they floated quietly and unseen a balloon's height above a small, twisted man sitting near a shadowy area that hid something emitting a low humming.

"I know that vile, tasteless little—I mean, I know of him. Heard of him, is what I'm saying."

"Who is he?"

"I've, uh, heard that his name is Igor."

Risk watched Bentley closely, noticing that his breathing had become strained and his eyes were intently staring down at the man below them.

"Hold it here," he said up to Hawken.

"Yeah, Risk."

The slowing jets from the teapot's spout made hardly any sound, but they were enough to bring the basket to rest above the scene on the rooftop.

Risk focused again on Bentley.

"What aren't you saying?"

"Hmm. I usually say just exactly what I want. If there was anything—"

Risk had closed the distance, just a few steps, and didn't shift into anything. He did take the gasping vampire and easily lifted him up high enough to hold him out over the gravel surface of the roof below them.

"Quietly," said Risk. "Talk."

Bentley grimaced, looked down, then back at Risk.

"Okay!" he whispered. "Bring me back first. I can't fly!"

"No. You can't."

He let go with one hand, and Bentley gasped quietly while he teetered from one hand holding his upper arm.

He stared back at Risk, his chest heaving, and saw Risk only holding one finger to his lips. He nodded his understanding.

"He works for someone I, uh, heard of."

"Who?"

"Someone quite hideous."

"A name."

Bentley looked down, got shaken lightly, then looked again at Risk.

"Alright! Something that calls itself Widow."

"Something?"

"Dammit, aren't you getting tired yet? You should really—"

"Let you fly. Yeah."

"No! Bring me back!"

"Keep talking."

"Okay, she's not completely a something. She's a deadly gorgeous monster, is what she is."

Risk tipped his head and studied Bentley for a second.

"I, um, heard that her body is just unbelievable. From her diet, people say."

"You know more. Last chance."

He started lifting and lowering the vampire, who tried to hold Risk's arm with both of his hands.

"Yeah, you're right," he said after seconds of silence from Bentley. "I am kind of tired."

"Wait! Okay, already! It was Widow that hit me on the head and took Sophia. I couldn't stop her!"

"Why didn't you say so then?"

"And have that bitch coming after me? Oh, no. Uh-uh. I'd be dead almost as quick as if I tried to fly."

Risk leaned enough to look down, watched Igor for a few quiet seconds, then looked up.

"Down, Hawken. Quiet."

He pulled Bentley back inside and set him down, and Bentley promptly collapsed as if wounded like the lion.

"Oh, dear me," he said as he fanned himself.

Hawken pulled a rope, opening a hatch near the top of the balloon, and the basket began to descend, right over Igor as he monitored Widow's generator.

Chapter 38 – A Single Mane of Black Hair

Hawken's excellent navigation skills, performed accurately and quietly, got the basket to touch down without a sound. He kept it in place with gentle, silent toots of the spout, correcting every motion of the basket.

Risk gestured for Hawken and Bentley to stay there, and he ended by pointing at K Kat. He waited for Hawken to show that he understood.

The face of a hawk nodded.

Risk swung one leg over the rim, then the other, and landed with only a soft crunch on the flat roof's coating of gravel. Without enough sound to be heard over the humming machinery, he tied a single rope to an air vent, anchoring their craft, then gave Hawken a thumbs up sign.

He watched for only a second to see that Hawken was climbing down to tend to K Kat, then his eyes never left the mutant slave of someone or something that called herself Widow.

He took one quiet step, watching Igor sitting motionless, facing away toward a generator that clicked once, then went silent. Risk froze in place.

The small man tending the machinery didn't make any effort to get it running again. Instead, he stood and began a slow walk toward the nearest parapet, beyond which, far below, waited the unyielding pavement of the street.

But his first step never touched before he was lifted off of his feet by Risk's hold on the back of his ragged jacket.

"Hey! What the—"

Risk slapped toward his head but with Igor struggling to free himself, the blow struck the wrong head. The cloth sack fell to the roof, and two dead eyes sunk deep into a shriveled head stared backwards at Risk.

"What the fuck?"

He turned the freak around, changing to his other hand and holding a bunch of the soiled jacket under Igor's chin.

"Who are you? What do you want?"

"Besides killing you?"

He cackled and said, "I'm already dead!"

He looked down at his feet kicking high above the roof.

"If you'd put me down, that is."

"Widow," said Risk.

"What's a widow?"

Risk snapped him around like a rag and said, "You'll eat your other head."

Igor swallowed noticeably, then shook his functioning head.

"If you vomit, you'll eat that too."

"Oh, that's sick. What's wrong with you?"

"Widow," he said, reaching for a deflated bag of a head, slumped over with its useless mouth open.

"Okay, okay! She's inside."

"Alone?"

He grinned and chuckled.

"There's so little left by now that you could say she's alone. Sure."

Risk ripped the defective head off the man's back with one strong yank.

"Oh, shit! Oh, that hurt. Dammit."

He pressed it into Igor's face, causing him to try to turn his head and fight for his next breath. From being forced into him, gooey garbage, stuff that had never really been completely alive, began splotching out through the rip hole.

Risk pulled it away for a second, long enough for Igor to say, "Alright! Yes, she has someone. Her baby. Another soft little girl, like she prefers. Now, will you please throw me off the damn building?"

"Not you."

He threw the spare head, underhanded, over the parapet, and two seconds later, they heard a sound like a rotten pumpkin launched into a brick wall.

"Not you, not yet. Show me."

Igor pointed at a doorway, back in some dark shadows, and Risk began a walk toward it, carrying a headless man whose other head knew enough to stay quiet.

*   *   *

Through the doorway, Risk ran and carried Igor with him into a stairwell with only minimal illumination. He paused to look down and saw two shorter flights of stairs between each floor, switching back and providing only a modest landing area between them.

"Where?"

"Down. There's no other way to go."

"You fucker. You'll still eat that head."

Risk ran to the first landing, his gouged black work boots pounding every other serrated steel tread. With his free hand, he touched the wall for just a second, then ran down the next set to the floor below.

There were no doors to exit the stairwell, so he ran down to the next level. Again, no doors leading anywhere.

After running down more stairs, he finally found a door and jerked it open, swinging it into Igor's head.

"Hey, dammit."

"Shut up. Where?"

"That way. Down the hall."

Risk followed his pointing finger and soon stood beside a heavy metal door with only a half-hearted weld line near its handle.

"Here?"

"In there. Yeah."

"If you're lying . . ."

"It's all I know! I swear!"

Risk grumbled and took hold of the handle, still holding the short mutant above the floor with his other hand.

"Don't you ever get tired?"

"Shut up."

He did shut up when he saw fur growing on every area of exposed skin. Already generous muscles swelled further, to the point of stretching his black leather vest into what could have been a coat of paint.

With a loud growl, like a wolf angry at still being part human, he put a boot against the wall and jerked the entire door loose. Hinge pins and door handle parts rattled across the concrete floor.

"Holy shit," Igor said, shaking his head.

"Shut up."

He shifted back quickly, then took them both into the room.

*   *   *

Only shy traces of light from the hallway filtered into the spacious room, and Risk waited, Igor still in the air, for his eyes to adjust.

While waiting, he said, "They were here?"

"Yeah. In this room. Last time I saw them."

"You saw her?"

"Widow?"

"No, fucker."

"Her sweet little girl, as she likes to call them?"

"Yeah."

"Yeah, I saw her. Touched her too. Really nice tits."

"Shut up."

"I would have sucked the hell out of them, too, if I'd had more—"

Risk slammed him into the floor like a bag of dirty laundry, then held him high again.

"Fuck, that's not fun. Why don't you just kill me?"

"Wait for it."

Risk blinked a few times and studied the room. There were only some cushions and blankets on the floor, nice but dusty furniture all around, including simple vases lying scattered around in random locations.

But there was no Widow and no Sophia.

"Dammit. Fuck."

He closed his eyes and began deep breaths, but Igor interrupted that.

"If you're done with me, I could—"

"Shut up."

He lowered the broken mutant quickly to the floor but didn't slam him.

"Remember the floor?"

"Yeah. Like you said. I'll shut up."

He lifted him back up.

Risk closed his eyes again, breathed deeply a few times, then looked up. He looked at every big square that comprised the ceiling, all identical and none with a working light.

He sighed and looked down, then he spun himself to face the entry door.

"Four flights. One fucking door."

He looked up again.

"Fuck."

He walked toward the door, with Igor above him saying, "You can let me go, right? I helped?"

Again standing in the hallway, near the stairwell, Risk grunted and said, "Lying fucker. You wanted to die?"

"Yeah, I—"

With a human roar, he slammed Igor hard enough to leave a pattern of red spokes from where he'd hit, and Widow's mutant slave got his final wish.

He tossed what was left of him down the stairs and ran up to the next level. Only a brief touch was given to the concrete wall before Risk backed away enough to kick at it.

It cracked, he roared, kicked, and it cracked some more. So, he kicked it some more. He kept kicking it.

When he'd cleared enough of it to get through, he first stuck a dusty, nearly destroyed boot through the opening, then leaned himself in and stood.

"Dammit."

He saw nothing but black in every direction except for down near his boots, where light from the stairwell was venturing in.

"Give it a second," he said to himself, and he left his eyes open.

"No, wait," he said, almost laughing and ending with a quick snort.

His eyes became those of an owl, and he didn't try to constrain the shift, letting a few feathers and a sharp beak take over too.

He looked through the dark, to the left, the right, every direction, and saw dusty pallets covered with machine parts, crates and dead equipment, even a couple of pallets of bricks in the middle.

Looking up, he whistled softly and said to himself, "Oh, fuck," when he saw the trusses high above him and small areas of roof beyond them.

Blocking some trusses and packed between all of them waited garbage of every kind: bloated bags of trash, old quilted blankets in bundles, and tarps stapled and hanging everywhere to hide whatever else was up there.

He looked down and said, "Dammit."

But he snapped his head back up and forced his owl eyes to focus at one precise location among the trash and waste packed up against the roof.

At a single mane of black hair hanging from an odd white sack.

"Sophia."

Still staring, he said, "Below the Bay? You suck."

* * *

The eyes of the owl scanned the room again and saw nothing tall enough to get Risk up there. He closed those eyes and took a deep breath.

"Never been a bird," he said, then laughed once.

"Oh, well. First time for—"

Quick thumping on the stairs made him turn just in time to see K Kat bound through the hole that he'd kicked in the wall. Her bandaged leg slowed her some but not much.

She jumped up into his arms, and he held her, belly up, as she licked at his face.

"Kenzie?" he said, laughing. "It doesn't matter. Look. Fia."

He pointed up, toward the black hair, and lion eyes looked too. He watched the mountain lion as she scanned all around that general area. Then, her eyes locked onto the hair and stayed locked as she snorted once.

"Good girl. Can you climb?"

Then, he looked across the room, toward rough wooden columns built into the walls and extending partway out into the room.

K Kat didn't wait to answer him. She squirmed out of his arms and ran to the nearest one.

She paused at the bottom, looking up, then leaped high and dug in her claws. But she yipped softly and fell, and she lay panting on her side while Risk rushed to her.

"K Kat," he said as he rubbed around her ears. "It's okay. I'll—"

She pushed his hand away with her snout, snarling, then got back up on her paws. Risk took a step back, and the mountain lion leaped again. She held on and waited there for a few seconds, but she made no sound and only took a few deep breaths.

With short, quick moves, like a lumberjack on a tree trunk, the lioness clawed her way to the top, then scrambled up onto the nearest truss. She carefully stepped from truss to truss, sometimes growling softly and sending odd items falling to the floor.

After more maneuvering, the lion reached the cocoon, and she stood, her paws against it, to study the ropes feeding up out of it to a motor near the roof's peak.

Risk stepped around, trying to find where to stand directly beneath Sophia. He thought he had it, and he waved to the lion.

"Okay. I'm ready."

He heard her growling and ripping and snapping and saw the cocoon spinning slowly, twitching itself lower as each lion bite severed a rope strand.

She looked down before finishing her work.

"Now. Cut it."

She cut it, and when it hit his arms, it buckled his strong legs, sending him down on one knee. But he'd protected the cargo and never let it hit.

He shifted it around and stood, looking up at the lion, who looked back and whined.

He gently laid the cocoon off to the side and said to the lion, "Trust me."

She did, and she jumped. He caught her more easily than he'd caught the cocoon, and he held her while she lapped at his face a few times.

"Thank you. Good girl."

And he kissed her too.

Chapter 39 – The Pretty Girl's Skull

"Ah, yeah, that's nice. Gag yourself on that cock. You want so bad to get that cock's cold cum into that angry stomach!"

Janie twisted both of Marilyn's nipples, causing her to gasp, and the zombie man just outside her cage laughed and gagged her even more.

While the crowd remained hushed and busy with their hands, some reached through and fluffed around her hair and rubbed her and pinched her where they could.

Marilyn kept sucking, her lips wet and dripping down her chin.

In her ear, Janie said, "Don't panic. He'll be right back. He's just juicing his cock up again for you."

Blaine backed out his thick zombie rod and a few seconds later, Janie grabbed her ass cheek, the one highest above the bed, and stretched it back like she was trying to pry her open.

"He wants to go deeper. You want his cock to go deeper. Do you want that cock deeper in your pussy? Huh?"

"Yes, I do. Deeper in my pussy!"

"For that crazy hunger?"

"I'm so hungry!"

He drove deep inside her again, easily, all lubed up with slop, and Marilyn's stomach growled as soon as he started stirring around the fresh muck.

Janie left one of her nipples alone, kept twisting the other, and gave her ass cheek a hard slap.

To Blaine, she said, "She needs more. Fucking more of that, Blaine," and she handed him the bowl.

"Easy enough," he said. "I'm filling her goddamn pussy with it."

He slipped himself out halfway, held the bowl over what he could see of his rigid tool, then tipped the bowl to get another thick, sloppy rope of it to slowly snake its way down.

After it had coiled around and formed a small glob on his hard shaft, he drove himself in. Marilyn moaned, her stomach growled, and she stroked more quickly the one in her mouth.

"Keep going," said Janie. "Juice all of it into her pussy. She wants it."

Blaine backed out again, let the still-falling gooey strand wind back and forth over his shaft, then he drove it back in.

"Just like that!" Janie yelled and spanked Marilyn again.

She leaned over to kiss Marilyn's red-streaked cheek while Blaine kept delivering the goods.

"Feel that? How wild it is to be so hungry and horny at the same time?"

"Mm-hmm."

Janie bit her ear, enough to make it bleed, then turned to look at Blaine.

"Uh-oh, I know that look. He's about to cum right in your pussy. Oh, man, it's just what your pussy needs. Shit like zombie cum in your pussy will really change you. You want it?"

"Mm-hmm."

"No, really, do you want that cold cum sprayed way, way inside your pussy?"

Marilyn paused her sucking just long enough to say, "Oh, hell, yes. Yes! I'm starving!"

Janie gave Blaine the thumbs-up sign, then focused again on Marilyn's nipples, torturing them.

She whispered in her ear, "Any second now, his cock is exploding with cum. So deep inside your starving pussy."

Marilyn started moaning and kept sucking, and Janie got to chanting again.

"A dead cock in your pussy. Your pussy's starving. A dead cock cumming inside your pussy."

Marilyn began whimpering.

Janie laughed and said, "He was going to cum in you whether you wanted it or not. It might be better if you don't want it. Say you don't want it."

Marilyn just kept whimpering.

Janie slapped her ass and said, "Say no, you don't want it. You don't want that zombie to fuck you!"

Marilyn backed the cock out of her mouth and said, "Don't cum in me, Blaine. Don't! I don't want zombie cum in me!"

Janie twisted her nipples and yelled, "He's about to cum in you! Cold zombie cum rammed so fucking deep in your pussy!"

Marilyn paused her sucking just long enough to say, "Oh, no, anything but that! Please don't cum in me, you damn zombie!"

She went back to sucking, getting her nipples brutalized, and Blaine screamed when he delivered something vile and cold into Marilyn's softest, warmest place.

And Janie laughed almost immediately.

"Oh, fuck, look at that!"

Janie kept laughing and pointed, so Marilyn looked, too, and they watched the red lines closest to Blaine's pounding expand to triple their thickness, and that increase continued to propagate away from there, down her still-smooth thighs and up over her soft belly.

"Just lovely. You're making real progress with all your sucking and fucking."

Marilyn stared, almost in shock, at so much of her skin being matted with thick red lines. She felt Janie touch her cheeks, smearing more traces of crude oil on her, then she said, "Hey, you should meet those sexy lines halfway. Get some zombie cum in that pretty mouth."

"Oh my goodness, yes."

Marilyn turned back to work, moaning and pumping, and Janie kept repeating in her ear, "Suck that dead cock. That cock is so dead. Make that dead cock squirt in your mouth. Dead cum from a dead cock, all in your pretty mouth."

Marilyn's eyes were rolling up, and she kept stroking the dead man's post, listening to Janie chanting about dead guys and their dead parts.

"Pull that cock. Wring that cold cum out of it. Suck it!"

Then, with Marilyn's next long, slimy stroke, she got the first cold squirt to zip out and coat her tongue.

Her stomach growled, and Janie said, "Good. Yeah, get all that dead cum."

Marilyn moaned while pumping it, and she felt squirt after cold squirt shooting inside her mouth and sticking everywhere.

"Swallow, now. Don't you want to eat dead cum? Haven't you always wanted to swallow a dead man's cum?"

Marilyn groaned and swallowed, and only some of it made it, leaving her gagging but laughing too.

"Keep swallowing! Get that shit into your pissed-off stomach!"

She swallowed a few more times, finally getting all of the cold goo into her stomach as if it were one long, thin glob of it, and her stomach thanked her with loud rumbling.

Janie laughed and said, "Yuck, that's sick! But you did a good job. Look!"

She looked down, with Janie, at her still mostly white breasts, but the lines there were thickening like the others. It was happening quickly, and her beautiful breasts were more red than white, and Janie's rough fondling had left oily streaks all over them too.

Together, they watched as the first thick lines met and joined just below her breasts, and she snapped her head back as her stomach convulsed and roared.

More thick lines found matches and locked together, and every joining made her squirm from her insides flipping around.

"Oh, I'm so hungry!"

"And you're more beautiful all the time, you horny little zombie lover. Oh, look!"

Marilyn turned her head and saw that a fresh zombie had replaced the last guy, and he was ready, zipper down and pointed right at her. She looked up and saw who it was.

"Mortimer? Really?"

"Oh, I'm sorry, but I get so fucking horny too. Yes, Marilyn, suck my cock. Suck the goddamn zombie cock!"

"But don't bite it!" Janie said, laughing. "Even though you want to. Just suck it. Mm-hmm. Suck another zombie cock."

Marilyn groaned and wrapped her lips around it, doing as she was told.

"Hey," she heard Janie say, "let's really get you going."

Marilyn didn't stop, but she felt Blaine and Janie dragging the bed closer to the bars. They'd positioned it so that it was near a corner, with her ass end near one set of bars and her mouth near another.

Hands tugged at her thighs, pressing them up against her abdomen, and the crowd was silent, but most had frantic hands in their pants. Many of them were reaching through the bars, some rubbing their oily hands all over her breasts, others spanking her and leaving streaks of oil.

Before Marilyn could even ask what was going on, she found out. Mortimer jammed his very hard zombie rod back into her mouth, and another, who she couldn't see, pushed into her pussy. Both got busy with quick, hard thrusts as hands from the crowd rubbed her and pinched her and slapped her, leaving oil streaks everywhere.

The one in her pussy couldn't last, and she felt the cold squirts inside, then dripping out of her and onto the bed. The one in her mouth exploded, and she swallowed like a dog drinking from a fire hose.

Mortimer said, "Sorry, but not sorry! Just be glad things are still buzzing!"

He left his trousers open and walked back into the crowd.

"More," Janie yelled to the crowd. "Line your asses up! Girl loves her dead cocks!"

She got filled again, both ends, and they both made quick work of it. Two more stepped up, then laughed while they were finishing, leaving it all inside her somewhere.

Then, another two. And more.

Janie didn't stop them until Marilyn had satisfied at least ten at each end of her.

"Ready for the next step, zombie lover?"

Marilyn didn't hesitate, just nodded, licking the last of the mess off of her lips. The one that she'd just finished sucking dry moved back into the crowd, and two from the zombie mob slumped a body against the cage, the dead girl's head resting between two bars.

The pretty girl's skull was cracked just enough that a pencil, or maybe a tongue could slip in to touch the girl's brains, which were still warm.

The crowd got even quieter, and Janie said in Marilyn's ear, "Just a taste, gorgeous zombie lover girl. Aren't you hungry still?"

"Mm-hmm. Oh, I'm so hungry."

"Just a taste with that tongue. Go on. You'll love how warm and juicy it is."

Marilyn whimpered as she extended her already sloppy tongue out all the way and leaned toward the cracked skull with her insides jerking around and screaming for more.

Chapter 40 – A Double Dose of Female Flesh

"Dammit," Risk said to K Kat with two more steps to go before reaching the small landing that led to the roof. "Sophia's heavy."

He shifted the weighty bundle onto his other shoulder and paused for a few deep breaths.

"Almost there."

The lioness waited with him, on the same step, until he was ready to continue.

He took another step, and so did she. They both took the next one, the final step, together, and he kicked the rusted metal door out into the night.

They heard the screeching before the frantic calling of a hawk.

One bat flew past the door, a flash of black against the night behind it.

"Dammit."

K Kat crouched low, looking up and around, and leaped at the next one, her mighty jaws snapping closed on a wing in flight. The creature howled, and the lion shook it around even before her paws again fell onto the gravel rooftop.

She quickly lunged at its throat, wrestled it every possible way until its neck snapped, then looked up at Risk.

"Good girl."

Hawken yelled, "More are coming! We have to go! I already untied her!"

Risk groaned under the burden on his shoulder but held it with just one hand, patting the lioness once with his other.

"Sophia's so heavy. Come on."

They hurried across the roof toward the basket, which Hawken was able to keep fairly stationary with careful jets from the teapot. K Kat hesitated before jumping, and Risk gave her bandaged leg a glance.

"It'll get better, girl."

She didn't wait any longer and jumped up and over the rim, then quickly stood, with her paws holding on, and watched Risk.

"I do wish you'd make a better effort," Bentley said with a sneer. "We'll all be bat food if you keep dawdling."

Risk grumbled and raised the bundle up, letting it rest on the rail.

"That's, um, that's your friend inside that thing?"

"Sophia. Yeah."

"You should leave it," said the vampire. "Just leave it here on the roof. She's probably dead by now anyway."

"No."

"It's too heavy for this amateur balloon thing that—"

"No. Shut up."

Risk started shifting it, getting it ready to be lowered onto the basket floor.

A diving bat gave notice with its screaming.

Risk said, "Hold this."

"What? I'm not touching—"

"Hold it!"

Bentley held it with both hands, balancing the heavy load on the narrow rim circling around the wall of the basket.

Risk had just enough time to let it go, then face the bat. He didn't shift. He didn't make a sound. He leaped into it directly, missing the mark with his hands, which were aimed for the thing's throat.

He settled for a solid hold high up on the spindly appendages that supported its wings, but it could still fly.

Or at least flap its wings, which it did, keeping them both in the air a good jump above the roof surface.

Risk let out a roar that caused even K Kat to shrink back, and he snapped what he held, leaving the wings hanging and useless as they both fell to the gravel.

Before the thing could bite Risk, Risk bit the thing.

And he ripped out its throat, leaving the head loose and facing down in the growing puddle of its murky blood.

"We don't have time!" said Bentley. "Your hawk is right—more are coming!"

Risk wiped an arm across his face, cleaning some of his skin and smearing the blood into his whiskers, and hurried back to the basket.

"This garbage might be toxic," Bentley said. "Everything in these buildings is toxic. We have to leave it."

"No."

"She's already dead, and you're going to kill us too!"

"Sophia's not dead. Move."

Bentley held Risk's uncompromising gaze for just a second, then backed himself to the other side. Risk balanced the cocoon while he jumped himself into the basket, then he rolled it and tipped it and lowered it to the floor.

"It's too heavy," said Bentley. "Throw it back out!"

"The freak by the machine," said Risk. "You see him anymore?"

Bentley swallowed hard and crossed his arms.

"Well, no. I suppose I'm next, is that it?"

Risk looked over the side, then back at Bentley.

"We're too heavy?"

Bentley glanced at the swarm of bats approaching, and Hawken didn't wait for orders—the balloon craft began to rise into the dark sky from the flames he was teasing up from the iron pot.

"Uh, no," said Bentley. "We're okay. Um, we're quite dandy, actually."

"Good."

*　*　*

From high above, Risk and Bentley watched as legions of giant bats descended on the roof, a few of them ripping apart and choking down wet slices of the one that Risk had slaughtered.

Looking up, Risk said, "Hawken. Good work."

The sharp eyes of a hawk focused on the man below, and the feathery head tipped each way, then held still.

"Helping is good."

Risk nodded, and Hawken didn't break his gaze.

Behind him, Bentley said, "Those savage bats are—"

But Risk's waving hand stopped him. He leaned a little to better see the feathered face of his navigator.

"It's all I have left, Risk."

Risk sighed, then said, "This place has taken much from you."

The hawk dragged the back of a gloved hand across his face and kept looking down.

"You're worth more than you know, Hawken. Thank you."

He looked up high into the balloon and shivered before looking back down at Risk.

"I never helped anyone before. Not before I died."

Risk looked each way out of the basket, at the black sky above a dangerous black city, at sprawling fires with circling bats, and at the sea of flames before he again looked up.

He nodded while saying, "This place has some value."

Hawken's eyes blinked more quickly than normal, then he flipped his hood up, retreating into its shadows.

Risk scoffed, then smiled.

"It's appreciated."

The navigator nodded, then looked ahead, tending the flames and charting their course. Risk continued to watch him in silence until Bentley spoke again.

"Well," said Bentley, causing Risk to turn toward him, "you watch for bats, and I'll help out this enterprise by unmasking, uh, Sophia? That was her name?"

"That *is* her name."

"Right. Yeah."

The vampire, still wearing only shorts and shoes, began to pick at the end of a wrapping somewhere near the middle of the cocoon.

"This stuff is disgusting," he muttered to himself. "Bloody disgusting."

Still trying to pry up the end of a band, he looked over at Risk.

"It's going to take a while. There's no need to supervise every little task around here."

Risk grumbled and scanned all around for attackers.

Bentley groaned out a low sigh and kept working at the binding, sometimes glancing at Risk and not making any progress.

A minute passed, then Risk turned back around and said, "No. Her head first."

"Oh," said Bentley, speaking slowly. "Of course. Alright. That makes sense. I'll start there instead."

He only stared at Risk, then shrugged. Risk grumbled and resumed his guard duty.

Bentley poked around until he found an end of a strip that hadn't completely fused to the layer below it, and he began to work at it with a fingernail.

Risk didn't wait another minute before again checking on his progress, saw that there wasn't any, then scoffed and walked across the basket.

"It's impossible," said Bentley. "This mucky web stuff, I mean. It's not too late to throw this mess over."

"No."

He shoved Bentley to the side, causing him to stumble and fall against pillows and burlap blankets. He stayed there, watching and squinting.

Risk held up the black mane, then reached a set of short sharp claws to an area of the cocoon near it. He grimaced as he pushed in the points, then began to pry some of it loose.

He'd managed to peel back a few of the outer layers, and that only revealed more layers beneath them.

"Dammit."

He cleared a bigger area, leaving shreds of sticky, gauzy material torn away to each side, then he dug at the inner layers.

"Careful," said Bentley. "I mean, those claws are . . . ghastly."

Risk ignored him and kept working at the cocoon until he'd sliced away enough to see the back of a head with thick black hair.

Focusing in one direction, he tore loose enough to see a cheek, and he kept going, working like a surgeon, one that used savage claws instead of a scalpel.

He bent back a section of the stuff and said, "Fuck."

He'd found a ball of the same messy stuff hardening around something, all of it encased within the outer cocoon shell.

"It's not too late," said Bentley. "I'll help. Right over the side."

"Shut up."

Risk gave his attention to that inner object, something wrapped separately, and was able to start tearing a large section of it away.

"Oh, fuck!"

He'd found the back and side of Sophia's head, and the other cheek, the one that he'd found first, was pressed tightly into the back of it.

"Throw it out now! I'm telling you!"

He paid no attention to Bentley and hurried to remove all of the webbing from around both heads. Sophia's long braid was still coiled and held against her head, and Widow's long hair stayed hanging outside of the cocoon.

"What the fuck?"

Risk stared at Bentley only long enough to see his weak smile and shrug.

He spun the cocoon around slowly and stopped at the sight of cold black eyes staring back at him from a beauty of a woman.

A woman whose wet, red lips were fastened tightly against Sophia's neck.

He leaned in closer and saw the woman blink her eyes slowly, and there was a soft wet sheen to them.

"What the fuck is this?"

He reached out with both hands, one for each head, and Bentley yelled, "Don't touch them! Just don't!"

With a hand on each head, Risk turned to Bentley and said, "Why not?"

Bentley pointed and scrunched up his face.

"She, um, she—"

"That's Widow?"

"Oh . . . yeah. Yep. I mean, from what I've heard about her. Yeah."

"You did this," Risk said, glaring at Bentley.

"No! I told you, someone hit me on the head, and maybe it was Widow, or maybe it was that puny freak slave of hers, or maybe—"

"I'm killing you."

"Don't! Let me live, and I'll tell you something that'll help."

"Talk."

"Alright! I, uh, kind of know where the zombies hang out."

"With Marilyn?"

Bentley scoffed and said, "Well, what's left of her. By now, she—"

"Stop. Tell Hawken."

Bentley looked up and said, "That old building called Bay Tower. You know of it?"

Hawken said, "Used to have a bunker under it. Yeah."

"Still does. That's the fucking zombie nest."

"Take us," said Risk.

Hawken nodded and changed course.

Risk looked again at what he'd uncovered in the cocoon.

"That's Widow alright," said Bentley. "You'll hurt Sophia really bad if you pull them apart. I mean, if she isn't already dead."

"She's not dead."

"Maybe, uh, worse than dead."

Risk rotated the cocoon some more where it sat leaning up against the basket wall. Widow's eyes continued to blink slowly, and they never left his.

When he could see Sophia's face, he let go of both of them and rubbed his own face before looking again.

Sophia was pale and lifeless, her mouth hanging open. And after he'd rotated the cocoon more, he could see two thin blood tracks, already dried and continuing somewhere down inside the tough outer shell.

Risk reached for Widow's forehead, and she peeled back her lips and hissed, which revealed that she had a pair of long fangs deep in Sophia's neck.

He studied Widow's eyes for a moment, enough time for her to blink a few lazy times. Her black pupils seemed unable to hold steady as they kept floating to one side or the other.

"What's wrong with her?"

"Which one?" said Bentley.

"Widow."

"She, uh . . . how can I put this? I'll just say it: she's in a nonstop orgasm."

"Huh. Looks like it. How?"

"Uh, partly, um, from that bite. She loves to bite."

"What about Sophia?"

"She's the one being bit. Duh. Oh, and she, well, she . . ."

Risk scoffed and said, "Orgasm too?"

"Yep. Yeah. You got it. Oh, and almost dead too. That's an important detail."

Risk reached for the back of Widow's neck, but he didn't squeeze it. She still gazed into his eyes, showing no sign of alarm.

"Uh," said Bentley, "I wouldn't do that. You hurt her and you'll kill Sophia for sure."

"How?"

"Poison. She'll blast it all right into your little distressed damsel there."

Risk pulled his hand back, and Widow showed no reaction.

"How, then?"

"You have to make a swap," said the vampire.

"Explain."

"She's having an orgasm like we can't imagine. You can't just bring that to a cold stop."

"What, then?"

"Like I said: a swap. Give her a different one."

"You mean—"

"That's exactly what I mean."

"How do you know?"

"What's the saying? Oh. Fangs of a feather flock to—never mind. You get the picture."

Risk grumbled.

"Of course, more of that vile cocoon will need to be—"

"You do it."

"Do *her*, you mean?"

"Yeah."

Bentley laughed up at the underside of the balloon high above them.

"Oh, uh, that would be a most emphatic 'no.' Really, I couldn't even fake it. No, it's up to you. Did I say, 'up?' Yes, I believe I did."

Grumbling, Risk used his claws to rip apart more of the cocoon, working down along the outside shell and baring Widow's back and freeing Sophia's breasts.

He stopped to lean out, then squint at the sight of Sophia's nipples.

"Don't stop to admire the view," said Bentley. "Clock's ticking. Like I said, your little tart is orgasming her brains out."

Risk scoffed and tore it apart down to their waists, making obvious what both were doing with their fingertips for each other.

"Well, that's a sight," said Bentley. "Told you: orgasms. Big orgasms. I believe it's an appropriate time to call them monster orgasms. Until one's dead and the other has sucked out every last—"

"Shut up."

Risk shook his head and tore away more of the cocoon until he'd almost reached their knees. He could see the smooth white bands binding Sophia's thighs and Widow's panties twisted like a thin black cord around her thighs.

He spent a long moment looking over Widow's shapely ass and legs. He leaned to see Sophia's equally attractive legs pressed into Widow's. He couldn't see Sophia's hands, but he leaned around and shook his head at the sight of Widow's fingers slowly, skillfully, keeping her prey in a constant state of ecstasy while she sucked the life out of her.

"You're wasting time," said Bentley.

"We're there," Hawken called. "I'll land on the roof."

"No. Stay high."

"Right."

Risk looked over the rail at the wrecked building and said, "Marilyn."

"Yeah, she's probably in real trouble," said Bentley. "So is the sassy brunette, though. Quite the dilemma you face, hero."

Risk pried his eyes away from the sight of a double dose of female flesh, all of their fingers busy and orgasms flooding both of them.

He scowled at Bentley and said, "Do you care about anybody?"

Bentley scoffed and didn't hesitate a second longer.

"No."

"Easier that way?"

"What do you think?"

Chapter 41 – Bite the Goddamn Brain

"Mm, yeah. There you go, zombie girl. Stick out that greedy, slimy tongue."

Marilyn whimpered softly and leaned toward the cracked skull that zombies outside her cage were holding in place just for her. The skull still wore patches of scalp and pretty blond hair, and it was still attached to a young woman that no one had even taken the time to undress.

"Some new arrivals just don't last too fucking long," Janie said with a giggle.

The girl's dead eyes stared past Marilyn, and thin trickles of blood and other juices leaked out from the crack and broke into smaller trails on her cheek before steadily dripping onto her blouse.

The crack in her head was about the width of a pencil.

The tip of Marilyn's tongue was about the width of a pencil too.

And she and Janie stared into the crevice at spongy gray and pink brain matter with a wet sheen.

With her cheek against Marilyn's, all eyes on the brain, Janie said, "Just a sweet little taste. It's so warm and fresh for you. Think how that'll feel on your tongue."

With her tongue close to the split open skull, the brain moist and waiting at the bottom of a thin crack, Marilyn whimpered and hesitated.

"Mm, so tasty. So warm and tasty on your tongue. It'll help with that horrible hunger you have. You're starving so bad, aren't you?"

"Mm-hmm. It hurts so bad!"

"Taste it. Just a tiny little taste."

Marilyn whimpered and kept her eyes on it.

"You liked licking zombie nipples and zombie cocks, didn't you?"

"Mm-hmm."

"This is the same. It's the sexiest thing ever. You can't help yourself. Lick it and feel the sickest orgasm you can ever imagine."

Marilyn moaned as she poked her tongue very slowly into the split, then touched just the tip of it to the brain.

She groaned and grabbed at her belly, and Janie grinned at seeing the lines closest to Marilyn's lips start to turn black.

"That's so good! Yeah, it's what you need the most. Lick it. Lick it, you dirty zombie girl. Your belly is telling you to lick it, isn't it?"

"Oh my goodness, yes. Mm-hmm."

"How about that sloppy pussy? Is it telling you to lick it too?"

"It sure is! Yes!"

"Sick orgasm. Mm-hmm. Lick the fresh brain. Lick it!"

Marilyn held her tongue just outside the skull, then moaned loudly when she poked it back in and swept it up from the lowest point to the highest inside the crack, licking the dead girl's brain the entire way.

She moaned softly and rubbed her belly, just caressed it lightly, and the nearly constant growling from it lessened.

And Janie moved her hand down to Marilyn's pussy, rubbed it all over, then poked a couple of fingers inside.

"Yeah, just like that. That helps that nasty hunger, doesn't it?"

Marilyn nodded with her tongue still buried in the crack.

"Oh, but you're still such a hungry, dirty little thing. And your pussy wants it so bad. Lick it again."

Marilyn whimpered as she licked it twice, breathing heavily as she pushed her tongue as far inside the skull as she could.

"More," said Janie as she began steady, short thrusts, rubbing her roughly. "Really, it's the only thing that helps. And it'll give you such a sweet, sick orgasm. Mm."

She whimpered and moaned as she licked it continuously from bottom to top, never slowing the licking or the moaning.

Janie held her blond mane out of the way for her, getting more oil in it, and said, "That's it. Yeah, that's really good. All you want is to keep the taste of that on your tongue. Keep licking while I enjoy your very nice zombie girl pussy."

The blackness of the lines on Marilyn's chin and cheeks spread slowly down to her neck. The thick black lines all tangled together, and she kept moaning and licking.

Janie leaned past her to watch as the red lines on Marilyn's large, soft breasts began to change to black. She released Marilyn's hair and gave up on her pussy, pinched both of her nipples, and pulled them cruelly as far forward as possible.

Even Marilyn paused her mad licking to look down at the sight.

"So lovely now," said Janie. "Don't you think?"

Marilyn, breathing deep and fast, looked into Janie's eyes and said, "Oh, yes. Mm-hmm."

Their lips met for a short, ravenous kiss, then Janie said, "You want those permanent, though, right? Don't you want to be lovely like that forever?"

"Mm-hmm. Yes, I want to be lovely and starving like this forever."

"Good. I knew it."

Janie tipped her head back toward the cracked skull that Marilyn had been furiously licking, and they both watched as strong zombie hands reached into the crack, then splintered the skull open with a sickening snap.

There was no longer anything in the way, and the dead girl's brain was sitting there like a plump ball of pudding in a bleeding bowl.

Janie pinched Marilyn's nipples hard, making her squeal, then pulled on them, lifting them and forcing her up onto her hands and knees.

"Maybe you need some more of that really special stuff inside you. You liked that, didn't you?"

Marilyn nodded.

"Just in a different place. Yeah, a different place this time."

She gave her nipples a hard twist, then said, "You have a very nice *other* place for that cold zombie cock. You know what I mean. Imagine that."

Marilyn groaned and arched her back, angling her bare ass higher and presenting a fresh opening for a fresh zombie.

Marilyn didn't turn when she heard Mortimer chuckling, then a key turning in a lock, then an old jail cell door swinging open.

"Meet Dane," Janie said, laughing. "Dane! That's funny. Guess what the fuck he has for you. Yeah, that's right."

The new zombie guy stepped closer, his long member dripping with bloody goo, and rubbed the head of it all around her tight hole.

Janie said, "Think about that hard zombie cock spreading that all around in there. Just imagine that. You want it, don't you?"

Marilyn moaned and nodded her head, and Dane planted just the head insider her, then slapped her ass a few times, leaving more splashes of crude mixed in with all of the jagged red lines on her creamy skin.

Janie leaned closer, where she could hear Marilyn's soft whimpering and whispered in her ear.

"You want it deep, don't you?"

Marilyn nodded, still staring at the exposed brain.

"I mean, all the way. You need that stuff way, way in there, right?"

She whimpered louder and nodded more vigorously.

Janie grinned and looked back at the newest zombie stud, Dane.

"All the way. You bottom out that fucking zombie cock."

He did, all at once, and Marilyn's mouth opened in a silent scream.

Janie gave Marilyn's nipples a brutal twist and hard stretch outward.

"Now, you're ready. Oh, you are so ready. Just a small bite. Imagine your teeth sinking into that, all warm and tasty for you. Think how it'll feel when you dig your sharp teeth into it, then rip loose a piece."

Marilyn gasped, staring at the exposed brain, and the steady pounding into her ass kept driving her face closer to the split open skull.

"Mm, yum. You won't even want to chew it. No, you want to swallow a nice, juicy chunk, get it inside you as quick as you can."

Marilyn's breaths got heavier, some of them snorted out, and she never looked away from the brain. She opened her mouth and bared her teeth, and Janie clamped down even harder on her nipples, using her fingernails.

"Bite the goddamn brain. Swallow a nice, warm, juicy chunk of it. You want that brain inside you. It'll be the sickest orgasm you ever had. It's the sweetest goddamn sex ever."

Marilyn groaned as she leaned her open mouth and sharp teeth toward the waiting brain, and Dane kept plowing his cold hard post all the way into her ass, bottoming out with every merciless thrust.

Chapter 42 – While She's So Helpless

"Get up," Risk said to the vampire reclining on pillows up against the basket's wall.

"Yeah, man," he said while getting up. "You might as well get comfortable, make a thing of it."

"Not a thing. Just—"

"Saving the hot brunette. Yeah. Sure."

He fluffed up the pillows, laid them out like a bed, and covered it all with a blanket.

"No time to buy her dinner, I suppose. Oh, wait. She's already—"

"Shut up. Help me move them."

"Oh, you do need help with that. Wouldn't want to rip those fangs loose. There's that nasty shot of poison, too, which would be bad. Like, instantly bad."

Together, Risk and Bentley waddled the cocoon, which still kept the girls wrapped in a thick layer to just above their knees, over to the makeshift bed. Then, they carefully tipped the entire thing until the two were lying on their sides, with Sophia facing the basket wall.

Bentley stood over the two, who were still embracing and fingering each other, one with fangs in the other's neck. He leaned closer.

"You can even hear the sucking sounds. Gosh, I hope I'm not that uncultured about it."

"Step aside."

"Right," he said as he backed away. "Time to do some hard labor. Get deep into that hero role of yours. Drive home the—"

"I'll feed you to the zombies."

"Huh. Okay. Got it."

Risk looked down at black eyes almost lost in rapture that stared back at him, calmly watching his every move.

Widow's cheeks tightened at regular intervals, like clockwork every twenty seconds, as she drew Sophia's juices up from the deepest reaches inside her and out through the punctures in her neck.

He saw that he'd cleaned away all of the cocoon material, freeing Widow's hands. But her fingers still moved slowly and gently where she held them high between Sophia's thighs.

Sophia's appearance was mostly that of a dying woman, or one that might already be dead. But some high level of ecstasy was keeping her nipples long and stiff and pointing straight out from her breasts.

Even her lips looked soft and wet, as if she'd licked them often inside the cocoon.

But Risk's eyes were drawn to Widow's tight, firm ass, so round and soft. Delicate and tempting, unlike the brutality of her existence.

His breathing picked up its pace while he was lying down behind her, already forgetting his vampire audience. Probably the hawk too.

With only a slight distance between them, he reached out, still locked on her steady gaze, and brushed her black mane to one side, revealing the soft skin of her neck. No bite marks were there, unlike Sophia's neck, which he'd seen had been littered with them.

The hair was out of the way enough, but he brushed at it again, letting his fingers touch that soft skin that she'd kept hidden. It felt as smooth as it looked, and he caressed it again.

And still, her black eyes, blinking so slowly and showing that her calm appearance belied the storming orgasm she felt, gazed at him, tracking his every move.

He leaned forward and kissed her neck and backed away quickly, licking his lips.

"Careful, there," said the vampire. "Best not to have any more contact than you need."

Risk ignored the advice. He leaned forward again, nosed around in her hair, inhaling deeply, then kissed her neck again. More than once.

Many times.

When he leaned away from her, he held her gaze while he loosened his buckle, then his zipper.

The look in her eyes never changed.

Her cheeks showed that she was still sucking on Sophia, drawing every juicy drop out of her.

And she'd never moved her hands away from the orgasm she was so generously providing to her prey.

And her prey, though appearing more dead than alive, gave her the same pleasure with soft fingertips, all with nails clipped down to nothing.

Risk grabbed at the silky black rope wound tightly around Widow's strong thighs. He wedged one hand under her hips so that he could hold it with both.

And he twisted it around, never moving it, but letting his hands and fingers feel just how soft and warm were those thighs. Still touching her without intentionally touching her, he went for her neck again.

Only one kiss, a quick one, turned into licking. Licking all over her neck. Wide strokes, everywhere he could reach, even curling himself to reach his tongue lower, tasting the soft skin of her shoulders and back.

He didn't stop or even slow when the vampire said, "Oh, boy. Awful idea."

Risk licked all around, turning himself enough that he was kissing her cheeks, then the very edge of her lips, so close to Sophia's neck that he could have kissed her too.

Still tasting Widow's wet lips, he let go of her rolled-up panties and grabbed at her ass instead, nudging, pulling, opening her up.

And he found just the right spot.

So warm. So juicy.

Juicy enough for two.

He held her by her hips and drove himself into her, and her only reaction was a quickening of her breaths.

He tightened his hold, pulling her hips into him with each bold thrust, slapping skin against skin.

But she still hadn't taken back her fangs. She was still sucking on Sophia at the same steady pace.

"Sophia," he said, groaning it out.

He let go of Widow's hips, reached farther, and found Sophia's waist. And Widow's arms were there.

Touching her arms gently, he traveled his hands lower and lower, until he felt the woman's fingers moving so slowly, so gently, so expertly.

And he held her hands, following her lead, pushing here, relaxing there, matching her every move so that the two of them, together, were keeping Sophia in a state of dying rapture.

He attacked Widow's neck again, kissing and licking and sometimes biting, all while his hands were moving again.

Up to Sophia's breasts.

He took one in each hand, still drilling into Widow from behind, and squeezed them and palmed them flat against her body.

Widow moaned, so softly that he almost missed it, and he moaned with her. And without planning it, he found Sophia's nipples, two stiff little points, undeniably alive on what might already be a woman's dead body.

He caressed them and pinched them, tugging them all around while he licked and bit at Widow's neck and pounded his hips into her, driving his hard shaft as far as he could.

The basket shook from their sexual delirium, the three lovers in an odd, tragic embrace.

Risk felt Widow's chest expanding with a deep breath, and it quickly rushed out.

Then, she repeated it, while none of them slowed, each giving another something.

Like she'd reached a peak that she couldn't prevent herself from falling from, Widow took a deep breath, backed her bloody fangs out of Sophia, and opened her mouth to scream.

But she didn't scream, she only tipped her head back, her mouth open wide and showing Sophia's blood wet all over her teeth, fangs, and lips.

With her mouth still open, and still rubbing Sophia so softly and being just as softly rubbed by her, she turned her head toward Risk.

He caught a quick glimpse of her grisly fangs, the only outward sign of horror on the body of a goddess. She licked the blood all around quickly, starving for it, then she lunged her lips toward his.

He was ready, and they kissed and licked each other's lips.

The taste of Sophia's blood made him thrust even harder into her, and the violence of it made her squeal like a little girl, then she cackled and laughed up at the balloon and a hawk staring down at them.

She quit her constant pleasuring between Sophia's thighs and pushed the spent body away, then broke her kissing with Risk. With a grunt, she uncoupled them, spun around quickly, and mounted him after she'd coaxed him onto his back.

He lay flat on the burlap while she sat on his lap, all the way down, keeping him as deep as possible inside her. She sat straight up, began bouncing slowly on him, sometimes just shifting her hips around, and her eyes never left his.

When she reached for her breasts, his eyes followed, and he watched as she squeezed them and bounced them, then tugged at her nipples.

She kept that up when he looked back into her eyes, which had never stopped showing the ecstasy that consumed her.

The vampire said, "Risk, uh . . ."

He reached for her hips and held her lightly, not interfering, letting her set her own tempo to get just what she wanted from him.

She groaned and let go of her breasts, then rubbed up against her nipples with both hands several times quickly, bending them up each time, playing them like strings on a deadly musical instrument while she hissed softly and licked her lips.

Then, she placed her palms on his chest, still staring into his eyes.

"Uh, hey," said Bentley. "Risk. Really. Um . . ."

She began leaning toward him, tipping her head and gazing into his eyes, grinning and showing her fangs.

But she closed her lips and rested them against his, and they kissed, playful tongues touching everything.

"Uh, really," said Bentley, "You, uh . . ."

Widow giggled softly, then whispered in his ear, "Such a handsome baby boy for me. Mm, you're just adorable."

She kissed his ear, then all around it, then whispered again.

"Ooh, such a good fucking you're giving me. Oh, you feel so good in my pussy. Don't stop, you delicious, powerful beast. Mm, I'm so soft and helpless and can't stop you."

He didn't stop or even slow. With every contraction of his rock-hard abdomen, he was lifting her, pounding himself into her.

"Risk, really," said the vampire. "You should, I mean . . ."

She kissed her way down from his ear, her lips soft and so wet, saying, "Such a very good boy for me. Mm, such a precious, tasty little boy."

Bentley's kick sent her head back, and she left it tipped back to hiss up at him, her fangs out and hideous.

"Risk! Now, if your damn brain still works!"

Risk shook his head and struck the side of Widow's head, sending her tumbling across the basket. She jumped up into a low crouch and hissed at both of them.

"Dammit," he said, "What the . . ."

Risk rushed to her, easily overpowered her, and picked her up by her waist.

Her arms were flailing, her legs were kicking, and bloody spit was frothing out with every hiss.

He began to reach her out over the railing, until he heard Sophia behind him say, softly, "No! Don't!"

He held her out, ready to give her to the dark and dangerous city far below, and turned his head.

Sophia was still encased in cocoon, still bound tightly around her waist and thighs, and still unable to keep her big blue eyes open for long.

"Why the fuck not?" he said.

She forced her eyes to stay open, offered him a weak smile, and said, "Because I . . . love her."

He scowled at Sophia, who was looking not at him but at the monster in his hands. He turned to look up at the woman he was close to dropping over the side.

And she wasn't looking at him either. She was smiling at Sophia and licking her lips.

He jerked his head around to see Sophia again.

Slumped over, bound, weak, and nearly dead, she was still blowing kisses to the woman who had been orgasming her while sucking out of her every last drop of her life.

"Fuck."

He dragged the spider back into the basket and tossed her roughly to the floor. She reached out and started rubbing his leg, and he kicked it loose.

Looking up toward Hawken, he said, "Set it down."

Then, he looked at Bentley and said, "Watch them both."

He patted the lion's head and said, "You too, K Kat."

The basket scraped along the tar roof, and Hawken got it to stay still.

Risk jumped out, then held the rail, then turned back toward Bentley when he said, "Hey."

"What?"

"If those two dolls are just making love, should I let them go? I mean, if there are no horrific teeth stabbing soft flesh, and it's just two naked, sexy, long-haired, willing and sort of still tied-up, horny babes who can't stop themselves from—"

"Dammit.

Risk shook his head at the grinning vampire. A second later, he had to fight his own grin.

"I have to find Marilyn."

He snarled at Bentley then left to find Marilyn in the lair of the zombeings.

*　*　*

Bentley kept grinning as he watched Risk tread across the black tar roof of the building which he'd told him housed the zombie colony. Across the basket, standing just enough to watch, too, Widow glared and monitored his progress.

Risk pulled open a heavy, rusty metal door with a squeal, stepped into its shadows, and left it open.

"He is a heartless man," Widow said in a quite ordinary voice, like they were having coffee together at a diner, causing Bentley to turn himself around.

He reached out each way to hold the basket wall's top rail and said, "Oh, I don't know. He acts rather crude, at times, but he seems like a pretty fair chap."

She looked at K Kat and said, "And what of this unwanted cat?"

Widow bared her fangs and hissed, and said, "Go help him! He'll need your help!"

The mountain lion's only reaction was to bare her own fangs and snarl.

Widow took a step closer and reached a finger out toward the cat's nose. K Kat sniffed it, hid her fangs, and shrank back from her.

Then, she jumped up, resting her paws on the edge rail for less than a second and jumped to the roof. They watched her run toward the building after Risk.

Widow tipped her head down just once toward the unconscious Kildare Killer only steps away from her short black boots.

"He left her tied up so tightly. Imagine her discomfort."

Bentley studied Sophia as she lay on her back on a burlap blanket over an array of pillows. Her arms were still completely bound beneath her, top to bottom and tied around her waist. She still wore a solid band of webbing material around her thighs, just above her knees. And her ankles were held close together by more of the same stuff, all of it hardening and becoming more solid every second.

From her arms being jammed underneath her, her back was arched and her breasts were lifted up, moving with her easy breaths.

Her head had rolled to one side, and her mouth hung open.

And Bentley noticed that, despite the look of imminent death, her lips carried a wet sheen and her nipples hinted that Widow's orgasm hadn't lessened, whether from her poisons, or her gentle touch between her thighs while in their cocoon, or both.

"At least, she's still alive," the vampire said.

"Yes. Able to speak too. Curious. But bound so tightly."

"She's alright," Bentley said with a smirk. "Risk will be back soon."

"Perhaps not. The zombies seek a king, don't they?"

"Uh, yeah. I heard that. So?"

"Perhaps he'll stay with them. Perhaps he'll want to be a king."

"Uh, I kind of doubt that. Nobody's that daft."

"If he finds the girl, Marilyn, she might—"

"Sophia's sister. Yeah. Her twin."

Widow tipped her head and gave him a smile.

"Oh, how delightful. Mm, a darling twin little girl. I'd so like to meet her, if she's not already their queen. But until then, this one,"—she tipped her head toward prone Sophia again—"should be unbound."

She began to lean over, and Bentley said, "Uh, no. Not you. Move away from her."

"Ooh, so forceful. Very well."

She took a couple of steps away along the curved wicker wall, and Bentley approached Sophia. Kneeling beside her, he tried peeling back the tight wrappings around her waist, and he couldn't find any end to get it started.

Widow only nodded at his failing, and he looked up at her.

"What is this shit? It doesn't come apart."

"I'm able to remove the bindings. Will you refrain from biting me if I free the girl?"

Bentley sneered and said, "Oh, fine. No sudden moves, though, alright?"

"Nothing sudden, no. I'll move very slowly so you can watch everything in great detail."

Holding his gaze with serious black eyes contrasting with a modest grin, Widow stooped down, then eased herself onto her knees. She leaned forward to crawl, and she waited, still watching Bentley. And she smiled at seeing his eyes studying her bare ass, the backs of her strong thighs, and sometimes the thin black rope of her panties still tight around her thighs.

She focused on Sophia, whose head was the closest part to her, and crawled the short distance. With her face directly over Sophia's, she brushed her own black mane over the far side, and some of it hung low enough to rest on Sophia's cheek.

Widow looked back at Bentley, and she saw his eyes snap back from leering at her ass to hold her gaze.

And she let her voice ooze out of her like a hot mixture of honey and blood.

"Don't blame me for loving her. She's a beautiful little girl, isn't she?"

Bentley looked all along Sophia, all the way to her pointy black heels, then back to her face, with Widow's right above it.

"Uh, yeah. I suppose she is."

"Even more beautiful because she's so completely helpless? Little baby girls are so adorable when they're helpless, aren't they?"

"Um, I don't know."

"Hmm."

Widow leaned down enough to kiss Sophia's upturned cheek, then stayed close and gazed up at Bentley again.

Bentley stared at Sophia's chest rising even higher with a deep breath, and she let out a slow sigh. Then, she turned her head to face up at Widow.

Widow, still watching Bentley, said while mixing more streaks of hot blood in with the honey of her voice, "And don't blame this beautiful little girl for loving me too. We'd both love just a kiss before I unbind her. We both love to kiss while she's so helpless. Risk wouldn't mind."

"I, um . . ."

"He'd want to watch us."

Widow sighed and tipped down enough to touch her lips to Sophia's, and she stayed there, kissing her, letting more of her poisons seep into her.

Bentley leaned and watched their tongues softly touching each other's the few times when Widow backed away and smiled at the nearly-dead girl beneath her.

Widow rose up, and Sophia weakly sought her with her lips, trying to pick up her head high enough to keep kissing her.

"I'll start with freeing her thighs," Widow said. "That soft skin has suffered enough with such harsh bindings."

She walked herself forward only a very small amount, just far enough to position her breasts over Sophia's lips, which were still blindly seeking Widow's lips.

"She loves me more than she ever has anyone," Widow said to Bentley. "Mm, I'll just get started on those nasty straps around her thighs. Very slowly. You can watch closely."

She reached for the straps with one hand while lowering herself, and they both heard Sophia sigh when her lips found one of Widow's nipples.

"Oh, I'm so awkward sometimes," she said. "But the sweet little baby does love to suck. Isn't she beautiful now, just helpless and sucking on the one she loves?"

Bentley only stared.

"It's okay if the little girl sucks for just a second, isn't it? She so loves to suck, especially when she's bound up so tightly."

Bentley groaned but didn't speak.

Widow made no effort to unwrap anything, only watched Bentley's face as he watched Sophia, still completely bound and unconscious, suckling Widow's nipple like a baby.

"You, um . . . you should probably, uh, stop . . . that."

"Oh, I know I should. It's just so difficult for two lovers to not touch in intimate ways. I'll just free those ankles for this sweet baby. She's such a precious little baby girl."

Widow lifted her breasts away, and Sophia's lips reached up for them. Her tongue came out, wet and curling around, seeking another taste.

But Widow had risen up to kneel, and she tugged at her panties until she'd slipped them down her thighs, then over her calves, and finally, around and off of her short black boots.

"You, um, you didn't need to—you could have just pulled . . . them . . ."

Widow dropped back onto her hands and moved herself forward, her knees sometimes dragging on the coarse burlap blanket. She'd gone far enough to place her knees near Sophia's narrow waist, and she squeezed them in close.

Then, she turned back to watch Bentley.

And she held his gaze with a soft smile and slowly blinking eyes as she leaned her hips back and down, toward Sophia's tongue that was seeking any part of Widow to suck.

Chapter 43 – A Tasty, Horny Zombie Girl

"Keep pounding her ass," Janie said, laughing. "Horny girl likes it deep."

"Like this?" Dane said, grinning as he thrust his hips forward, driving himself deeper into Marilyn.

"That's all you got? Give her that hard cock, dammit. Pound it in her ass!"

Dane laughed and said, "What a dirty fucking zombie girl. Oh, yeah, I'll pound it. With my hard zombie cock!"

He kept ramming it, sometimes slapping her ass, which had a dense web of jagged lines and streaks and splatters of crude oil.

Marilyn was leaning toward the pried open skull just beyond the bars. She kept her lips peeled back as far she could, and she was lightly chattering together her exposed teeth.

Janie was up close behind her, one hand on each of her cheeks, which were smeared with crude oil and red lines that had changed to black from licking the fresh brain.

"Bite that fucking brain! It's warm and so juicy! Bite it!"

Marilyn pushed her face in, the corners of her mouth dragging across shattered bone and bloody, torn tissue.

"More! You love Dane's hard zombie cock in your ass, now get those teeth the fuck in there!"

Marilyn wiggled her mouth in even farther, and Janie leaned over to watch. She saw Marilyn's jaws closing as she moaned wildly, uncontrollably.

"You're having a fucking orgasm, you hot zombie girl. I told you that would happen. Take a fucking bite and explode that sick zombie orgasm!"

Marilyn shook her head slightly, squishing things around, and her teeth were still embedded in the dead girl's brains.

"Bite the damn thing, and your fucking orgasm will explode. Bite it now while that zombie cock is ramming your ass!"

Marilyn was groaning but still hadn't bitten a chunk for herself.

"I know what you need, you filthy fucking zombie girl."

Janie gathered up Marilyn's blond mane above her head, then handed it to a few of the zombies outside the cage, and they kept her head in place. Then, Janie grabbed Marilyn's shirt from beside her on the bed.

"Let's give that damn zombie orgasm of yours a hot boost, alright? Fuck, yeah."

She whipped the shirt around, fashioning it into a rope, while outside the cage, zombies, who seemed to know what Janie wanted next, slowly raised the dead girl's open skull higher. Cold zombie hands snagged and tugged upward on Marilyn's hair, and she followed, keeping her teeth in the brain. They positioned her so that she was kneeling completely upright and holding the bars with both hands.

The grabbing hands still twisted and ripped at her hair, and other cold and leathery hands squeezed her breasts, leaving streaks of oil from pulling and pinching her nipples.

"Get your damn cock out of her ass, you idiot! The dirty zombie girl needs her pussy attacked. She wants it to hurt!"

"But I like fucking her ass!"

Outside the cage, another zombie girl screamed, "Fuck my ass! Do my ass, Dane!"

She dropped her pants quickly and backed her ass into the bars, right next to Marilyn.

"You heard her," said Janie. "Fuck that zombie whore's ass instead!"

"Fuck, I sure will! Damn, what a whore!"

He did.

"Finally!" Janie said, cackling out an insane laugh.

Then, she fed the thick shirt rope between Marilyn's thighs, rubbing it on her pussy way more than was necessary, then held one end of it up along Marilyn's back and the other end just under her breasts.

"You'll love this," she said. "You'll love it so much you'll lose your mind, and you'll choke down all of that fucking brain."

She started slow, tugging both ends straight up, and Marilyn's breasts began to bounce along with every jerk upward.

"Does that hurt?"

Marilyn nodded.

"Enough to bite into that brain? It's the only thing that will stop this pain."

Janie jerked the rope up, twisting and wedging it in as deep as it could go before letting it relax.

"Eat that brain. It's the only way. The pain will become just another orgasm, you horny zombie girl."

Janie applied more force until she was snapping the rope up violently, almost lifting Marilyn up each time and bouncing her breasts all around. Faces with grimy, snarling lips were pressed between the bars, trying to taste any part of her breasts they could reach.

Marilyn moaned loudly, and Janie said, "That's a monster orgasm you're having. Literally! You hot, horny, dirty zombie girl!"

After ten more hard strikes with the tight cloth rope, Marilyn began to spread her knees wider, and Janie popped her eyebrows up at the sight. The zombies outside Marilyn's cage were lowering the dead girl and relaxing Marilyn's bunched-up hair, letting her settle with more of the softness between her legs exposed.

"Oh, my kind of zombie girl. Alright, you asked for it. You want so much pain that you'll have to bite off a chunk. You're such a nasty, horny zombie girl!"

Janie snapped her fingers at Blaine, who was sitting close by, smoking a cigarette. He started to unbuckle his belt.

"Uh-uh. Come here. All this brain eating is getting me hotter and hornier too."

"Oh, yeah. Me too!"

He stepped up onto the bed and walked close to Janie. She unzipped his jeans and pulled out a thick pole that had already reclaimed every rock bit of hardness it had earlier.

"Mm, this is how to take a zombie's belt."

She leaned forward and wrapped her lips around it, sucking it like crazy while slipping his belt out through the loops.

With the belt in her hands, she started biting him until he screamed and fled across the cell.

"Good times!" she said, then she turned back to Marilyn, who was moaning with her teeth deep in a dead girl's brain.

"This'll be good. You think you're cumming now? Let's treat that pussy of yours the way you want it now. And how you always fucking will."

She fed the wide leather belt between Marilyn's thighs and let it sag in the middle while she held it near her hips front and back.

"Such a nice, soft pussy. Oh, so sensitive! Well, this is exactly what the fuck it needs."

She snapped the ends of the heavy belt straight out front and back, flapping the coarse leather into her. Marilyn groaned but still didn't bite loose a chunk.

Janie snapped it up again, striking Marilyn at her most sensitive place with a sharp slapping sound.

"Zombie girls like it rough," she explained to Marilyn. "They love their soft pussies getting brutalized."

She lowered it until it touched the bed, then jerked the ends out quickly, making a louder slapping sound.

"And your pussy is so sweet and soft, isn't it?"

Marilyn tried to nod and not let go of the brain.

"And you want even more brutality for that baby soft pussy, don't you?"

Marilyn only snorted out a loud groan.

"Of course, you do. I'll brutalize it for you. Oh yeah, Honey, I'll brutalize your sweet pussy."

She lowered it and snapped it up again. Over and over, she snapped the hard leather into Marilyn's pussy, which shook around her big soft breasts every time, causing a chorus of groans and whimpers from all of the zombie lips chasing her nipples around.

While zombies cheered, Marilyn moaned loudly, and her teeth stayed deep inside the warm brains of a girl the zombie hoard had slaughtered just for her, a girl whose dead eyes were unmoving and staring somewhere at the zombie mob that had killer her.

And Janie kept laughing and snapping that belt just as hard as she could into Marilyn's soft, exposed pussy.

"Bite the fucking brain! Swallow some of that juicy, goddamn brain! You fucking, dirty zombie girl!"

*　*　*

"Mm," Widow moaned, her thick honey voice oozing. "My precious little baby girl."

Sophia's low, soft moaning got silenced when Widow sat herself down. She shifted her hips around, finding the tightest possible fit.

"Oh, mm, just like that."

"Hey. You, uh . . . you might be, um, suffocating her."

"Mm-hmm, and my baby girl loves it. She's showing me with every soft little lick. My dear baby knows to lick me just right."

She lifted her hips enough that Bentley could see Sophia's face, and he watched as she raised her lips and tongue up to meet Widow again. When she did touch her again with her tongue, and stayed there, Widow eased her hips back down again, pinning Sophia to the blanket.

Then, she shifted her hips around gently again to wedge Sophia in as deeply as she could.

"Mm," she said to Bentley. "See how much she loves me? Such a sweet little baby girl."

"You," he said staring at Widow's thighs and ass leaving not much of Sophia's face to be seen, "you should just untie her. You shouldn't be, um, you—"

"But she loves me. I'm all my precious baby wants now."

"No, she'll be fine, if you would just—"

"Oh, no," she said, chuckling. "She's already mostly just a beautiful little doll baby, all emptied out. This is all she'll be able to do until we're done. Don't deny the sweet baby girl these last bits of pleasure."

"She's not, I mean, she—"

"Dead? Hmm. Almost. Except for the sweetest of all possible orgasms, one she wants more than life itself."

"Still, you shouldn't—"

"Come here," she said, fixing her black stare on him.

"Me?"

"Yes. I smell your difference. You know I won't bite your kind."

"You can tell?"

Widow nodded, grinning, and licked her lips.

"I won't bite."

She pursed her lips, which were puffy and wet, and blew him a kiss.

He stared, his mouth moving silently.

"But I will suck. Mm, I love to suck."

He took a step closer and stopped. They both listened to Sophia moaning, her face between Widow's thighs as she lay there, still bound and totally helpless.

"Oh, I do love to suck. Especially when I'm being licked so sweetly."

He took another step closer.

"See my lips? So soft and wet. Imagine that. Just imagine how they feel."

Bentley stood close, and Widow tipped herself upright and placed her hands on Sophia's breasts, where she gently squeezed them and played with her nipples.

"I do so love to suck. With lips so soft and wet."

Bentley unbuttoned his shorts and reached for the zipper.

"But I, um, girls aren't really my—"

"That's okay. But my little doll is licking me so sweetly, and I just want something for my lips and tongue too. You don't mind, do you?"

"I, um, well . . ."

"No, you don't mind."

She finished unzipping for him, reached in, and found what she wanted.

"It's, uh, it's just kind of—"

"Shh, now, scary vampire man. Shh . . ."

She took him lightly between her lips and squeezed while looking up at him. Her hands were still enjoying Sophia's large, soft breasts, and Sophia was moaning weakly where she was trapped between Widow's thighs, left with only one way to show her adoration.

Bentley tipped his head back and gasped, ignoring Hawken's stare and shaking head high above him. Then, he looked down and touched Widow's hair.

"Oh my God," he said.

She backed her lips away, it stayed where she'd left it, and she held his gaze, smiling up at him.

"I know of a vampire man that trades victims for blood. Blood that's not mutant blood."

"Oh," he said, grimacing and staring down at his erection, then back into her eyes. "That would be, um, a good deal for whoever—"

"You're not that vampire, are you?"

"Who, me? Why, no, I'd never—"

She hissed, showing him the ghastly length of her fangs.

"Yet you, also a vampire, are nearby when my secret nest is found?"

"What secret nest? I don't know what you're—"

She cackled softly, still showing her fangs, and said, "Then, you have nothing to worry about, do you? Let me suck more. Put that hard vampire weapon back in my warm, wet mouth."

He stared down at her wet teeth and said, "I, um, maybe that's—"

"Mm, I do love to suck. I'll be very careful for you."

He watched her lips ease down into a smile, showing not even the points of her fangs.

"There. Just a warm, wet hole for you."

He groaned and moved it closer to her mouth, and she waited, looking up at him.

"No danger, vampire man. Just a mouth that's offering to suck you."

He moaned and pushed himself in past her lips. She took it far inside her mouth and began bouncing her head forward and back, her lips getting him wetter each time.

"Mm," she moaned, keeping a steady pace.

Then, Bentley said, "Ow! Hey!"

"Oh, I'm so sorry. I'm trying to just be warm and wet for you. Don't you just love warm and wet?"

"Oh, fuck yeah."

"Then, shh . . ."

She resumed her steady sucking of the surprised and thrilled vampire, and she began pinching and tugging on Sophia's nipples.

The still captured Kildare Killer licked and sucked, hungry for her lover, and took inside herself yet more of her poisons. Every littlest touch of her tongue wrecked her insides even more and hastened her toward being nothing but a doll of a beautiful little girl, empty and lifeless.

Chapter 44 – A Soft, Smooth Little Doll

After running down more flights of metal stairs than he could count, Risk jumped the last five steps, planting his worn boots on a filthy and cluttered concrete floor. The dim hallway could take him to the left or to the right.

But the screaming and laughing were coming from the right.

He ran past one weak wall light after another in the wide passage, stopping when he arrived at closed double doors, beyond which it sounded like a frantic mob at a sporting event.

He pulled open one door enough to look inside.

Near the door were the first of the crowd, all with their backs to him. But their hands were waving around high above them, and they were all yelling and laughing.

He stuck his head in and tried to see what had them so agitated and above a sea of them, against the far wall of the large room, he saw the iron bars of a cage where they were embedded in the ceiling.

"Dammit."

He slipped himself back into the hallway and began to ease the door shut quietly, saying to himself, "Goddamn freaks."

Then, he heard someone in the crowd, near the door, say, "It's really her! It's Marilyn!"

"Fuck."

He jerked the door open, slamming it into the wall, and strode into the room. No one had even heard him, and none turned to see him.

Pushing them aside enough to clear himself a path, he noticed their pale skin and ragged clothing. Most had streaks of black crude on their exposed skin, and a few had clumps of it hanging in their hair.

He bumped aside an otherwise attractive young woman, who looked at him and said, "Oh, you want a better view? Smart!"

Continuing through the swarm, a man said, "Well, easy, there, big fella. Go on and get yourself a look."

Another said, "Oh, pardon me. Sorry to be in your way."

He grumbled and pushed more aside, his eyes mostly on the cage.

Halfway there, he rose up on his toes, holding shoulders near him for balance.

And at just the right time, the shuffling and jostling spectators parted enough to open a path toward the woman in the cage.

And what she was doing.

And having done to her.

Only then did he understand the loud snapping sounds that he'd heard while hiking toward the cage.

"Fuck."

He tossed the nearest spectators aside roughly, yet they were still all very polite and asking his forgiveness for hindering him.

Finally near the cell, he threw one laughing man to the right and a hooting woman to the left.

People close behind him said, "She's almost there!" and "Oh, that's just beautiful!"

Risk stared at Marilyn's face between cell bars and nearly outside the cage, with her mouth deep inside the open skull of a cute dead girl held for her by two laughing zombies.

Close enough to almost touch her, he watched her crazed eyes focus on his.

"Mare?"

She winced and snarled at him like she had no idea who he was.

Janie saw him, too, and frowned at him before snapping the belt sharply up between Marilyn's thighs.

Risk noticed Marilyn's breasts bouncing from the impact, her nipples big and stiff, and she had thick, jagged black lines all over the creamy white skin of her face, down all over her neck, and spreading, even as he watched, to coat her breasts and claw their way down toward her belly.

She didn't try to evade any next strike that would catch her.

No, she kept her thighs spread to give the laughing zombie girl all the room she needed.

And Janie, grinning and nodding at Risk, jerked her hands out, sending the rough, heavy leather up again to smack hard against Marilyn, who still stared at him as blood and gore got squeezed out from the skull, dripping down over the dead girl's face.

Still holding Risk's frozen stare, Janie yelled, "Eat the brain! Eat that goddamn juicy chunk of brain!"

She snapped the belt again and even over the cheering and hollering, Risk heard Marilyn moan.

"Dammit!"

Risk hurried the last steps and stood close, then he reached into the cage and held Marilyn's head, his hands against her oil-streaked blond mane.

She looked up at him, snorting through her nose, and she moaned again just after Janie had given the thick leather strap a brutal snap, shaking every part of her except for her mouth, where she kept her teeth deep inside the young girl's brain.

"Fuck!"

Risk backed his hands away and swiped through the bars at Janie, who laughed and leaned away from his grasp.

"She loves it!" Janie yelled. "Oh, her pussy's so sweet and soft!"

She cracked the belt into it.

"She has such a sensitive zombie pussy, and I'm giving her just what the fuck she wants!"

She drove the hard leather into it again.

Risk swiped at her, and she easily evaded him, safe behind the stout steel bars.

Janie smiled at him and said, "After she eats, we'll all make that soft pussy of hers feel better. Oh, yes, we all will!"

She gave Marilyn another brutal hit.

Risk gave up on Janie and looked back at Marilyn just in time to see her shaking her mouth around inside the skull, like a shark in a frenzy, and she ripped loose a chunk too big to fit into her mouth—almost the entire brain.

And he had only a second to watch the slop quickly run down her chin, then onto her chest, then a thick slimy drop hanging from a nipple, too thick to let it go.

He reached for her and her meal, but she'd already begun a retreat inside the cage, out of his reach, but still keeping her legs spread for Janie and her heavy leather belt.

Marilyn watched him, a dripping mess in her mouth, as Janie snapped the belt into her again and said, "Swallow that shit! Suck down that juicy fucking brain, you hot, horny, filthy zombie girl!"

She cackled and snapped the belt again, shaking Marilyn's blood-covered breasts, blood which had coated over some of the thick black lines embedded almost everywhere on her skin.

And Marilyn snarled as she stared out of her cage at Risk and reached up both hands to smear the drips and bloody globs all around on her breasts.

*   *   *

Widow grinned with Bentley still in her mouth, and she never slowed her playful pinching and tugging of Sophia's nipples. Beneath her, so completely smothered between her strong thighs, Sophia licked her lover and welcomed the generous, juicy release of her poisons.

She let Bentley stand at attention, his fleshy flagpole jutting straight out while she looked down, and she flicked Sophia's nipples a few times, then looked back up at Bentley.

"Mm, so sweet. My little baby girl is almost done. Those ruined insides of her aren't even too juicy anymore. Mm, but still, such tempting, teasing big-girl nipples."

She gave him a few vigorous sucks, causing him to groan, then backed away again.

"Doesn't that sound so sweet? Just a precious, empty little doll of a girl?"

She put her lips back around him right away, and he said, "Uh, yeah. Sure. That's, I mean . . ."

"Mm-hmm."

She popped him out for just a second.

"You know that feeling all too well. The exquisite, luxurious pleasure of sucking out every sweet little drop. Oh, we can't stop till we're done, you and I."

She took him inside her mouth again.

While looking up at him, using her lips and tongue expertly, she dared to give him a just barely noticeable nick with a fang.

She noted his immediate twitch, but he didn't step away. And he didn't leave the warmth and wetness of her mouth.

Widow grinned while still sucking, and he reached down to hold her head with both hands.

And she gave him another very tiny little nick.

And just a bit of poisons.

Then, another, slightly deeper nibble and a quick dose of her poisons.

The same poisons that she was still feeding, lick by slow and affectionate lick, to the bound and helpless, almost-empty doll girl smothering quietly beneath her.

*　*　*

Risk looked up at the sooty ceiling and yelled, "Fuck!"

And that scream turned into an angry scream.

And that angry scream evolved into a dangerous, predatory growl as he shifted into a lion, growing thick brown fur everywhere, gaining muscle for his feline legs, and sprouting a bushy mane along his spine.

He swiped his claws through the bars, snagging the belt from one of Janie's hands but not the other. She stared back in shock and let the belt hang from that hand.

Marilyn's chest was still heaving with her deep, rapid breaths, and she kept rubbing slime all over her breasts.

Risk roared outside the cage, then calmed himself completely.

The lion stood silent before a room of hushed zombies, and he took one deep breath.

As he let that breath trickle back out with a low, constant growl, his brown lion fur began changing to black. His lion mane shrunk away and merged with a back as wide as the cell's bed. Legs, lion legs, became arms and legs, thick with impossibly large muscles and wrapped in dense, coarse black fur.

The giant gorilla stood upright from where he'd been down on his leathery palms, and his head almost touched the ceiling.

He didn't look behind him. They were quiet. Not one ventured to even speak to him and certainly not to touch him.

With a mad roar and a few quick pounds to his chest, the gorilla grabbed the two closest bars, screamed like thunder, and pulled them apart.

The oily, rusted steel bent as his powerful arms and back forced an opening into the cage.

But it wasn't happening quickly enough, so the gorilla wailed and began ripping at the bars, breaking them and yanking them up and out of the concrete floor.

He spun around quickly, a bar in his hand, and sliced it through the crowd, ripping open torsos and sending heads flying.

With another bar in his other tight grasp, he whipped through the zombie horde in the other direction, splattering dead body parts everywhere, leaving gore and gristle dripping from the ceiling.

The silent crowd kept back, and the murderous, shifted Risk snarled at them before turning back toward the cell.

Snorting, but staring calmly, the giant ape reached through toward Marilyn, who still took deep breaths and still had a brain in her jaws. But her slime-coated hands had stopped fondling her own breasts and only held them instead.

She remained as shocked as the rest, and Risk reached out one massive hand. With two thick black fingers, he pinched the brain still ripe and dripping, gave it a soft tug, and pulled it away from Marilyn's mouth.

She left her bloody mouth open, teeth bared still, and she was covered all over with blood and bits of brain and black, crooked lines.

He let the slop drop to the floor behind him and looked into Marilyn's crazed eyes. She snarled and bit at him, then hissed, showing teeth in a mouth wet with blood.

The gorilla grunted softly and punched the side of her head.

It was enough to briefly turn her toward Janie, who was still frozen, staring, and with the brutal belt hanging from one hand. But Marilyn faced him again, snarling worse, hissing so hard that bloody droplets sprayed out, and she showed teeth, sharp teeth that she—

Risk roared and swung his heavy ape hand from the other side, toppling her off of the bed where she lay unconscious.

"No!" said Janie. "Goddamn gorilla!"

She threw the belt at Risk, missing him, and covered Marilyn, shielding her and hissing up at the mad gorilla.

A gorilla mad enough to grab the top of her head in one gigantic hand, give it a quick snap upward with a satisfied grunt, and sever it from her twitching body.

He looked at Janie's dead face, then set it down on the bed to reach for Marilyn. A hearty roar in the direction of Blaine and Dane, both huddled in the corner, convinced them to flee the cell.

With both hands near Marilyn's armpits, he lifted her up off of the jail cell floor.

And the buzzing stopped.

Janie's head opened its eyes and hissed.

The gorilla spun around and saw the docile, fun-loving crowd revert to their vicious, hungry zombie state, all outside the cell.

While he held Marilyn in his arms, inside the cell.

*　*　*

"Hey," said Bentley, "not like it hurts or anything because—"

She let it rest straight out long enough to say, "Because you're a vicious vampire."

"Yeah, that. But, uh, careful with those teeth, alright?"

"I'm doing this very, very carefully."

She slipped her lips back around him and said, "Mm," as she bobbed her head steadily.

"As long as they're not those, um, fangs. No fangs."

She shook her head, never losing him, and said, "Mm-mm."

A second later, he winced from another tiny bite, just one more to join all the rest of the small punctures she'd been leaving all around his hard shaft.

She used one hand to hold him away, still brushing it against her lips, and said, "I have a delicious idea for you."

"More than this? What, may I ask?"

She kept holding him and released Sophia's breast, then leaned forward, still smothering her, and hooked the bindings around her ankles.

While lifting Sophia's legs, Widow looked up at Bentley and kept going until she held the bound legs straight up.

She rubbed all over the backs of Sophia's thighs and said, "Mm, so soft. Such a soft, smooth little doll for us."

Bentley, his eyes kind of wild, looked at every part of Sophia and every part of Widow, whose own breasts were swaying gently as she wiggled herself down more tightly onto Sophia.

"You should lie down," she told him. "Make yourself comfortable. Our little baby girl has such a nice place for,"—she sucked him in, moaned, then let him back out—"you."

She resumed her steady sucking of him, looking up at him while he considered it. A few seconds later, she let him go.

"She's so soft and juicy there. But only there now. Just a juicy, spongy little baby girl. She wants to help you with those tiny little accidental bites."

"That, uh, that would help?"

"Mm-hmm. It would help you so much."

"And I, um, would just—"

"Mm-hmm. Ram yourself into the helpless little girl. Push your violent vampire tool deep inside her, where she's so nice and tight. She's still so warm, but she might not be for long."

Bentley hesitated, watching Widow caressing up and down the backs of Sophia's long legs, sometimes pulling them close to kiss and lick what she could reach.

She held them pressed against her cheek, sharp black heels pointed straight up, and looked into Bentley's eyes.

"Or maybe after she's . . . gone?"

She saw Bentley swallow roughly, his eyes scanning Sophia's breasts, across her trim belly, then slowly up along her smooth legs.

He ended by gazing into Widow's black eyes with a faint grin.

"Oh, good choice," she said, smiling. "After, then."

A low growling got Widow to look up at K Kat looking down at her over the basket's rim, her snout bordered by her massive paws.

"What, foolish cat?"

The mountain lion glanced at Sophia, then bared her fangs and stared again at Widow.

Widow scoffed and spat toward the lion, and some of it struck her face and got in her eyes, causing her to blink first, then yip. She dropped down and out of their sight.

Widow yelled, "Go find your owner! Bad cat!"

She calmed herself and smiled again at Bentley.

"Pesky, useless beast," she said.

She wiggled her hips to tighten herself down even more on Sophia's face, then held her bound legs close with one hand and licked them while her other hand gently patted Sophia's ass.

"Soon," she said, "she'll be just a very quiet little doll. Mm, yeah. Quiet little doll babies are just the sweetest."

She smiled up at the vampire, whose eyes were locked on the hand gently rubbing all over the bound, nearly-dead Kildare Killer's bare ass.

The British vampire began groaning, even before she'd finished saying, "Mm, they're so eager to please. Silent little doll girls would never dream of saying no."

* * *

Mindless zombies were biting and snapping and trying to get at the gorilla in the cage. Marilyn, unconscious and limp over his shoulder, dripped blood and gore from her mouth, dribbling it down into the thick black fur on his back.

Risk kicked and punched at them, keeping them at bay and trying to clear enough room to escape, when he had to stop.

He had a quick, violent convulsion.

And he was Risk again.

"Dammit. Too long. Fuck!"

He'd just started fighting the mob again, when he heard a savage roar from the back of the crowd, near the door. Some of his attackers turned to look but most didn't, and he had to keep trying to repel them and see what was causing the commotion at the same time.

At the back of the herd of crazed zombies, Risk saw blood spurting up, arms shaking around then falling as separate pieces, and more than one head tumbling around in the air before spinning out of sight into the mob.

A path was being cleared and when enough zombies had been ripped apart and mutilated, K Kat appeared in the open. She hadn't had time to look his way yet, and she ripped an arm off of one, took a bite into the belly of another, uncoiling entrails to be stomped, then leaped to snap her jaws shut on another's head, which she shook like a toy until it broke loose, oozing slop everywhere.

She let the head fall, then stood still and looked at Risk.

"Good girl!" he said, and she panted for only a second before she dismembered and disemboweled the two that were closest to breaching the jail cell's mutilated bars.

She roared at the ceiling and turned to face the rest of the zombies, and all of them were advancing toward them, snarling and snapping their jaws, stepping on and kicking aside body parts. Fearless with unpowered brain chips. One slipped in a puddle of muck and got stepped on, too, flattening its throat and causing one of its eyes to hang out on a wet cord.

"Go!" Risk yelled to the lioness. "Go now!"

She led the way, ripping and tearing with claws and fangs. And Risk followed closely, delivering lethal punches through heads and kicks that shattered bones. Both left a messy, slimy, lumpy trail behind them.

At the door, K Kat was first into the hallway, and she ran for the stairs with Risk and Marilyn close behind her. The zombie hoard spilled out of their meeting room and followed, even the ones with many missing parts, if they had enough remaining appendages that they could still move.

K Kat raced up the stairs, not hindered by her bandaged leg. And Risk turned to kick a zombie's face. Then . . .

The buzzing flickered and became steady.

Risk delayed his kick.

The zombie whose face was about to be crushed smiled up at him.

"Oh," he said while pulling up his zipper. "Leaving so soon? I'm Mortimer. We haven't even been properly acquainted!"

Risk scowled at the friendly old zombie, then felt K Kat nuzzling her snout against his jeans, so he began rubbing around her ears.

"Below the Bay," he said to the older zombie gentleman's confused stare.

He looked down at K Kat, and she up at him, panting.

"It really sucks."

Chapter 45 – Such Hungry Little Babies

Before walking out onto the roof, Risk leaned enough to look around past the door that he'd left open. The roof was empty except for a stationary basket and its balloon swollen above it, barely discernible against the blackness of the sky.

Beyond the edges of the rooftop, black night dominated but couldn't snuff out distant fires or the burning sea. Thin spindles of smoke twisted silently toward the jagged ceiling that supported a vast bay above it.

In the basket, no one was looking his way. No one was looking in any direction.

He glanced down at K Kat and held a finger to his lips.

She panted up at him.

He whispered, "Good girl," and they started walking toward the vessel.

As they drew near, Risk tipped his head a few times, and K Kat's ears twitched around at the sound of voices out of sight inside the basket.

He again prompted the lioness to wait and stay quiet, then he turned so that Marilyn, still draped over a shoulder, was away from the wicker, then he looked over the edge.

What he saw was Sophia, still completely bound, on her back on the makeshift bed.

Sitting on her face, smothering her, was Widow, and he couldn't help lingering at the sight of the smooth skin of her strong legs and the tempting curves of her bare ass.

He noticed that she used one hand to play with her captive's breasts while she bounced up and down on her gently, keeping her own breasts jiggling softly.

He almost scoffed at the sight until he saw that Bentley, charged with keeping some level of peace and harmony in his absence to rescue Marilyn, was lying near Sophia's bound legs, which Widow was holding straight up with her other hand and licking.

After dwelling on the sight of Sophia's pointy black heels above all of it, he noticed that Bentley's shorts were down around his knees.

And the leering, wincing vampire was about to strike with another vampire part, something much larger and longer than any fang.

Risk stood all the way up and yelled, "Hey! What the hell?"

Widow never looked and never slowed her soft grinding on Sophia's face. She kept licking her long legs, which were bound and held close.

She stopped only enough to say to Bentley, "Hurry! Get it in there, even just once!"

The vampire was almost hyperventilating as he stared at Sophia's sweet prize, tucked tight between the smooth skin of the backs of her thighs.

He shifted closer and made contact.

"Dammit!" said Risk. "Don't!"

Risk set down Marilyn near the lion, then pointed at her. She seemed to know to stay and guard her. Then, he hopped over the railing.

Just as Bentley drove himself all the way into Sophia.

Widow cackled and said, in a normal voice, "Ah, there we go. Oh, that's so nice."

But Risk was there with a strong grip on the vampire's throat. He pulled him away from Sophia, disengaging them, and threw him roughly across the basket's floor.

He lay there grinning, his pants down and his anatomy enraged and on display.

Before Risk could even cuss at him or strike at Widow, Bentley lost his grin and started to scowl. His breaths slowed and he slumped back against the wall with his eyes rolled back.

Risk said to Widow, "Get off her."

"She doesn't want me to. You heard her: she loves me."

He grabbed her arm and slammed her straight to the hard wooden floor beside Sophia.

Widow only laughed and crawled toward Bentley, while Risk leaned close to Sophia, listening near her lips.

"Good," he said and stood.

He looked up at Hawken, and the navigator only shrugged, holding his gloved hands out.

Risk grumbled and said, "Afraid?"

He nodded and said, "What could I do?"

Risk looked again at Bentley. His eyes had recovered and were blinking slowly. He tumbled himself onto Widow's lap, facing up, and she held Risk's gaze.

"I have him now too. He tasted my poisons in such a sweet way. My dearest little doll baby helped."

Bentley was shifting himself around, and she cradled his head as he found one of her nipples and began to suckle it.

Risk sneered at them, grumbling, then looked at Sophia, bound tightly and unconscious but alive, then at the wall of the basket beyond which Marilyn lay, bloody, streaked with black lines, and with a mouth coated with brain residue.

"Below the Fucking Bay."

He looked up at Hawken and said, "How's the fire?"

"Ready."

The rooftop door squealed and got banged by a train of friendly zombies filing out, talking jovially amongst themselves.

He heard Widow saying softly, "Yes, more is good. Suck out some more. Such a good boy," but Risk didn't look.

He checked Sophia one more time, then left the basket to lift up Marilyn. K Kat jumped inside, and Risk handed her over, lowering her gently, and the lioness helped as well as she could.

Then, he turned to face the zombies, who had formed a small audience near the basket.

"It was nice of you to visit," said Mortimer. "We do apologize if things got, um, inconvenient."

A young woman to his right said, "And don't for a minute think that we're angry at some of our group being, uh, injured. Things like that just happen."

"Fucking zombies."

Mortimer grinned and shook a finger at Risk.

"Uh, uh, uh! Zombeings, please."

Risk grumbled.

From farther back in the group, someone said, "It was nice meeting Marilyn!"

Another one, a woman, called out, "We really do love Marilyn!"

"I still want to bite her!" yelled someone from farther back.

Risk hopped over the railing and yelled up to Hawken.

"Go. Up in the fucking air."

* * *

"Yes, Risk. Up," said Hawken, then he popped up the lid of the big pot, sending flames reaching into the balloon.

The fabric stretched with groans and crackles, the ropes and cables supporting the basket tightened, and they rose up from the building's roof.

At the sound of more voices, Risk looked over the side to see the crowd of zombeings waving goodbye.

He turned around and watched Widow gazing back at him, her black eyes unreadable as she played with Bentley's hair while he was suckling at her breast.

He looked down at Marilyn, smeared with crude oil and blood and brain slop, and her soft white skin riddled with thick, jagged black lines everywhere.

After letting out a deep breath, he focused on Sophia, who was still trying to raise up her head and touch something with her tongue.

"Fuck."

He went to her first and spent a few minutes fighting with her bindings, sometimes using claws, sometimes biting with teeth that likely no real animal ever had.

With all of it in pieces scattered around them, he touched her cheek. She opened her eyes and blinked them slowly, then her head tipped again. He watched her take a few comfortable breaths, then covered her with the blanket.

He looked over the side and saw that they were high, but they were still over the building. So, he scoffed and threw all of Widow's binding webs over.

Kneeling beside Marilyn next, he tapped her cheeks lightly.

"Mare. Mare, wake up."

She sighed and licked her lips, which looked like they were trying to form words.

He leaned closer, his ear near her lips, and felt her breathing.

And he smelled the death all over her, which caused him to scowl and straighten back up. But he spent a moment smoothing back her oily hair, then wiping some slimy bits off of her face.

Widow giggled softly, as if trying to stay quiet, and Risk spun around to look.

"Dammit."

Sophia had crawled over and turned to lay her head on Widow's lap. And Widow held her up so that she could suckle at her breast, while Bentley was still busy with the other one.

Widow held his gaze, her black eyes unreadable, and shrugged.

"They love me," she said. "Such hungry little babies for me."

Risk shook his head and stared.

"Perhaps you'd like a little taste? You can't imagine the sweet, heavenly feeling of it. You'll never want to stop enjoying all of my juices. Mm, from every part of me."

She stretched her legs out and apart, then tipped her short black boots a few times, rolling her bare legs.

"Every part. Some are juicier than you can imagine."

Risk stomped toward her and grabbed Sophia's shoulders. But he pulled her gently, and he and Widow both watched as her soft, wet lips held the nipple as long as possible, until it finally popped out, causing Widow's full, round breast to bounce as thin trickles of something dribbled down and dripped to her lap.

He laid Sophia back on the bed and covered her again with the blanket.

He glanced at Marilyn, saw that she was still lying in the same place, then he gave Sophia another look. She'd stayed under the blanket.

So, he strode over to Widow and Bentley, grabbed the vampire by one arm and lifted him straight up, taking a wet nipple for part of the ride.

Risk immediately held him out over whatever was far below them, looked at Widow, and said, "You're next."

Widow said, "Oh, just like a killer. Nothing but a killer of a man."

Risk scoffed and stared at Bentley, numb and not caring in the least.

"And you need me if my baby girl is ever to recover."

"Why?"

With a meager smile, Widow said, "After such ecstasy with me, the grief alone would kill her if she couldn't at least see me."

He grumbled and looked up to Hawken.

"Can you spare a rope?"

Hawken looked around himself at the tangle of ropes and cords and cables, then tapped one of them, then went back to navigating.

Risk kept Bentley out, ready to drop, and untied the rope, which he looped and retied around the vampire's ankles.

Then, he let him drop and hang some distance below them.

He checked Sophia with a quick look and saw that she was still okay.

A glance at Marilyn showed that she was doing as well as could be expected.

But he caught his breath when he looked again at Widow.

She'd picked up her knees, resting her high-heeled black boots on the floor of the basket. She'd spread her legs wide, keeping her knees far apart. And she gently rubbed her fingertips up and down on her thighs, just touching along the edges what she knew would draw Risk's eyes.

"You've already had a sample. You'd like more. So much more. Mm, try with your tongue this time."

He scoffed but didn't look away.

"Yes, you see how warm and wet I am. Imagine your tongue, softly at first then lapping like a hungry beast. How long before you have to impale me?"

He stared without speaking as she raised one leg straight up, then the other, and held them there without using her hands. But her hands were still rubbing around on her thighs, teasing all around her temptation.

"It would be so easy to impale me. No one would stop you."

He took a step closer.

"And I promise not to bite."

He took another step and froze, staring at her gentle touching.

"Dammit."

Chapter 46 – To The Crypt Building

Risk turned his eyes away from the sight of Widow's raised legs and the hands that were rubbing her thighs and more, inviting not just his eyes to enjoy her.

"No thanks."

Her voice oozed out from between her lips like liquid sugar.

She laughed softly and said, "You're afraid you'll want me to bite. Oh, you'd love how that feels."

Risk scoffed, looking up into the balloon, and said, "Shut up."

"Hmm. Later, then."

But he glared at her again when she said, "Hmm, the little blond baby girl is waking up. I wish to meet her."

She was looking past him at Marilyn, nodding, when he said, "Leave her alone."

He hurried the few steps to stoop down between Marilyn and Widow, blocking the sight of her, and tapped her cheek a few times. Her blinking eyes began to focus, and she took a couple of quick breaths.

Her blank eyes fixed on his for only a moment, then she sat herself up against the basket wall, and Risk brushed filthy strands of her hair to each side, getting it off of her face.

"Mare. Mare, are you okay?"

"I, um . . ."

She fixed her blue eyes on Sophia, mostly just a body slumped under a blanket.

"Is she dead?"

Risk looked quickly, then said, "No. She's your sister."

"Oh."

Marilyn nodded and kept looking at the body.

"Okay. Is she dead?"

"She's not dead."

She started breathing more deeply, and her eyes scanned all around the basket several times.

"Who *is* dead? Show me."

"No. No one's dead."

She sighed and glanced around the basket's interior, then K Kat came near and sniffed her all over. When the furry snout traced paths along her legs, she looked down and gasped at seeing blood and jagged black lines and globs of pinkish mushy stuff.

"Oh my goodness," she said, then snapped her big eyes up to look at Risk. "I remember it all."

"It's over," he said. "You're safe."

She bit her lip and shook her head, her blue eyes squinting at him.

"What?" he said.

"I'm still . . . so hungry."

"We'll find food."

"I—oh, food. Okay. Thanks."

"Other than hungry, how are you?"

"I'm okay. Oh, itchy too."

She giggled and added, "But I always am anyway. Thanks for saving me. I'd kiss you, but—"

"Later," he said, then used a finger to flick off of her chin one of the squishy bits of muck.

She giggled softly and looked down for a few seconds, shaking her head at seeing how filthy she'd become, then nodded.

He rummaged around to one side and pulled something out, holding it up for her.

She laughed at the shirt missing a right sleeve, but nodded and smiled at him, her eyes brightening.

"Okay. Thank you."

He nodded and left her with the lion.

"Fia," he said, shaking her lightly.

She rolled back enough to see him and opened her eyes, which were also regaining their bright blue, much like Marilyn's.

"Risk," she said, her voice raspy. "I'm so goddamn thirsty."

He reached around for a water jug, and he tipped it back to let her drink. She drank a lot, then he capped it and set it aside.

"Sheesh. What I've been through."

He nodded, then tipped his head back toward Marilyn.

"You and Mare, how could—"

She smiled weakly and said, "Say my name?"

He nodded and said, "Fia."

She sighed and nodded too.

"It's because we're not from here. You must have known."

"I suspected."

"We're . . . different. Even our blood."

"Not just burning hands."

"No."

"Good. That saved you both."

She grinned and yawned at the same time, then she shook her head gently and looked up at him.

"Say my name again?"

He smiled and brushed back a few wisps of her hair that weren't in the gummy, tied-up braid that her sister had given her before so much had happened.

"Fia. And you're a mess."

"Me?" she said. "Look at Sis."

They both looked, and Marilyn only frowned back at them both, then she relaxed in a weak grin.

"Mare," he said, not waiting to be asked. "Mare."

They all turned toward Widow when she said, "Fia. That's a pretty name. For a pretty baby."

"Stop," said Risk.

Sophia threw aside her rough blanket and naked, except for her high heels, she began crawling toward her.

Risk laughed and picked her up with one arm around her waist, then set her back on the bed and covered her.

"Stay," he said.

"Hmm, can't stay away, huh? He told you to stay, Sissy."

"He can be funny, too, Sis."

Sophia kept staring at her sister.

"He saved us."

Marilyn nodded, and they both looked up at him, but he was standing near Widow, facing her.

"When you go over at the end of a rope, it won't be your ankles."

She scowled and glared up at him, then he leaned over and picked up her panties.

He threw them down at her and said, "At least, put these on."

Widow scoffed and said, "Oh, but they're all sticky with my delightful web. I'll wait."

Risk grumbled until he heard Bentley from over the side.

"I can help!"

Risk leaned over and said, "Help how?"

The hanging vampire snickered and tried to curl to look up at him.

"Their clothes are dirty. *They* are dirty. Hell, we're all dirty. Even you."

Risk looked down at traces of web hanging onto him and streaks and splatterings of blood and goo.

"He's not wrong," Sophia said.

Marilyn only shook her head, sniffed at herself, and wrinkled her nose.

"What, then?"

"I know where to go. I can tell you."

"For what?"

"To clean up."

"Tell me."

He looked down at a grim cityscape slipping by silently, far below them.

"Um, I'd rather be in the basket."

Risk took a minute to look first at Marilyn, who was mostly naked except for a shirt missing one sleeve, her high white heels, and crooked, tangled black lines littering her skin. Streaks of blood and bloody little chunks clung to her everywhere, all mixed in with her hair too.

He studied Sophia, noting the patches of webbing stuck in her thick knotted braid and knowing that her skin, under the blanket, was plastered with many bits and pieces too.

And she was only looking at Widow, so he snapped his fingers.

Sophia coughed, fought to hide a grin, then turned her head to share a smile with her sister.

Widow countered Risk's scowl at her with a sly smile and said, "Help the poor vampire boy. Then, we can all go and get nice and bubbly and clean together."

Risk shook his head and scoffed at her, then reached for the rope to bring up the grinning vampire who'd been smitten by spider poison lust.

He didn't stop or turn to see when Marilyn said, "Sissy? A vampire?"

Sophia sighed loudly, then said, "It's a long story. Yeah, Sis."

*　*　*

Risk had pulled up enough rope that he could grab Bentley's ankles, and he began to drag him roughly over the wicker basket's rim.

"Hey," he said, "easy, alright? I'm not even wearing a shirt!"

Risk grumbled and dropped him heavily onto the wood floor, where the vampire sat up and tried brushing off of himself dirt and slivers of wood and wicker.

"Talk."

"I'd really like to untie my ankles first, if you don't mind."

Risk leaned enough to look over the edge, then up at Hawken. "No lower."

"Alright," said the hawk boy navigator.

He focused again on Bentley.

"Oh. Never mind. Let's just leave that rope there for now."

"Talk."

"You're certainly not much for pleasantries, are you?"

He got a less than lethal kick from a worn black work boot.

"Okay! Fine!"

He looked up at Hawken, whose red eyes were bearing down on him from high up in the ropes and cables of their craft.

"There's a place with the last working hot water in this vile dump. It's a place called The Spa. You know of it?"

The navigator said, "No. I know buildings."

"Oh, of course. Because you're always floating around up here. Which is better than slinking around down there, trying to—"

He got a harder kick.

"Ow! Hey, come on, already!"

He looked back up at the hawk boy.

"It's known as The Crypt Building. You've heard of it?"

Before Hawken could answer, Risk said, "Crypt? Burial?"

Bentley laughed and said, "No, it's not real. That's all fake reputation. The few that know about it want to keep their little oasis secret. Can't blame them."

"No buried bodies?" said Marilyn.

Risk kept his eyes on Bentley when he smirked, causing the vampire to say, "That one surely needs a bath."

They both looked up when Hawken spoke.

"I know it. It's close. Risk?"

Risk pointed out from the basket blindly, then lowered his arm. Above them, Hawken gave a few sideways blasts, rocking the basket at first, then aiming their craft to float to The Crypt Building.

* * *

Risk stood between Widow, who'd stopped her self-gratification and had put back on her panties, and Bentley, who still had a thick rope coiled and knotted around his ankles. He looked at them, then at Sophia under the blanket, then ended with a study of Marilyn, a filthy, bloody mess and wearing another of Ham's shirts.

She giggled and said, "Can't be done."

He looked into her eyes and said, "What?"

"Make all of this nonsense turn out okay."

He grumbled and turned to Sophia when she spoke from under her blanket.

"He has to try, Sis. He wants to be—"

"Good. Yes, I know, Sissy."

"How far?" Risk called up to his navigator.

"Right there," he said, pointing toward a shorter, more squat building wedged in among taller, thinner ones, all of them looking bombed out and deserted.

"Roof."

"Alright, Risk."

He kept watching all of the craft's passengers as Hawken let some air out of the balloon, dropping their altitude, and used side blasts to move them toward the destination.

Over the wide roof, which was bounded by a high parapet and hosting scattered garbage and old equipment everywhere, the navigator let out more air with a sharp whistle.

"Uh-oh!" said the hawk as the basket descended quickly. "Hold on!"

Risk grumbled and looked around. Everyone appeared ready for impact.

The basket hit hard, shaking him where he stood but not toppling him. K Kat remained low, looking up at Risk.

"Okay, now," he told her, and she stood up all the way.

Hawken kept busy up on his narrow plank platform, feeding more hot air to the balloon and jetting to the sides, maneuvering the scraping basket closer to a rusty, wrecked block of building mechanical equipment.

"I'll tie it," Risk said and hopped out.

The basket dragged and slid around, but he got a thick rope looped around part of the metal support frame, and Hawken made the final adjustments to their position.

When Risk looked back into the basket, Bentley said, "I can't believe I still don't have a shirt. You just had to give it to that girl, didn't you?"

Marilyn looked around, then up at Risk.

"Her?" she said, pointing at Widow. "You gave his shirt to her?"

"No, not her."

He pointed at K Kat.

Sophia had been watching and listening, covered entirely except for her face.

"You gave the lion a shirt? Why?"

"She wasn't a lion."

"No, that can't be," Marilyn said to herself.

"She, um," said Sophia, "she—"

"Was Kenzie," said Risk.

"How?"

"Later," he said, and he looked up when Hawken spoke to them all.

"This building," he said, pointing down at the roof, "used to have a storage floor. Military stuff."

"What kind?"

"Uniforms, Risk. It's probably looted long ago."

"Yeah."

"Sis needs clothes," said Sophia. "Me too."

"That one too," Bentley said as he pointed at Widow. "That all needs to be covered up."

She grinned up at him, then lost her smile when she saw the scorn for her on Risk's face.

Holding his gaze, her black eyes intense and unreadable, she shrugged.

"I did not ask for this. You know that."

Risk grumbled and shook his head.

Everyone watched her quietly, and only the stretching and relaxing of the balloon and its cables and rope, and an occasional scraping of wicker on gravel broke the silence.

Risk nodded to her after a moment, getting a faint smile from her, then looked around until he saw the entrance.

Pointing that way, he said, "All of us. Inside."

He looked up and said, "Hawken?"

"I'm okay out here. Food would be good."

"Alright."

K Kat stretched, arching her back, then jumped out to stand beside Risk. He helped Sophia next, keeping the burlap wrapped around her. Marilyn winced when she stood and held the rail.

"Sore?"

"Uh, yeah. You would be too."

He grumbled and helped her out, and she found that the blanket was big enough for her and Sophia if they stayed close enough together.

Bentley freed his ankles, hopped over the edge, and started walking toward the door.

Widow stood and walked to the railing and waited.

"Uh, better not touch her," Sophia said. "Or you might—"

"Fall in love?" Marilyn said with a giggle.

"Sis, it's just that—"

"Sissy, I'm just teasing. Whatever your story is, mine is so much worse."

"Never mind, then," said Widow, and she crawled over in such an effortless way, her arms and legs all working together with such grace and unerring precision, her limbs placing her hands and short boots at a steady, never varying speed, that the others only stood and watched.

Chapter 47 – A Proud DNA-Hole

Risk grabbed hold of the rusty door handle, but he only sighed and left it shut. Still holding it, he turned enough to study each of his companions one at a time, and they all waited and watched him back.

Bentley laughed and said, "There's no good answer, Risk. None. I'd say, send the spider first, then—"

Widow cackled and said, her voice normal, "Oh, no. I'm a woman. I'm very much a woman. All of you can attest to that."

She focused on Marilyn and added, "Hmm, except for this delightful blond-haired baby girl."

Sophia said, "She called you a baby girl, Sis."

"Hmm, that means you're already her black-haired baby girl, aren't you, Sissy?"

"Well, Sis, it's just that—"

"Bentley's right," said Risk, then he looked at Widow, who was studying both of the twins. "You first."

"Fine."

She strutted past all of them, digging the heels of her short black boots into the rooftop's gravel and giving each step enough of an impact to bounce her uncovered breasts.

Sophia cleared her throat softly when Widow passed her, and that got Marilyn to watch as her sister's eyes scanned up and down on the woman strutting toward the entryway. As soon as she'd passed, Marilyn turned to look, too, and shook her head at the sway of her hips and her perfect ass covered with only tiny, thin black panties.

"Oh, my," she said, so softly that no one, not even Sophia, could hear her.

Even more softly, she said, "And Sissy was her baby girl. Hmm."

But Risk heard her, and he said, "Hold it."

Widow stopped just outside the doorway, and she didn't turn around.

"Here."

She brushed back her hair, then turned and saw him taking of his black leather vest.

"Put it on."

Widow didn't try to hide her eyes scanning him all over. She began with his shoulders and arms, lingered on his wide chest, then grinned as she leaned forward to see how far past his belt his rows of abdominal muscles might extend.

"You're quite the gentleman," she said, tipping her head and looking into his eyes.

She took it from his hand, slipped her arms through, then flopped her mane over the back. His vest was large enough that it covered her breasts, but it left a tempting trail of smooth skin from her chin, between the soft curves of her breasts, then down across her firm abdomen, ending at the thin elastic band of her panties.

Marilyn took a quick look at her sister and saw that her blue eyes were watching closely every little move that Widow made.

"When you want it back," she said, then turned and took a step and stopped, putting her past the door and almost taken by shadows, "you'll have to take it from me. It's the nature of this place that we must take what we want."

She turned just enough to hold Bentley's gaze but only for a second. Then, she resumed her trek into the depths of the building, and they all listened to her sharp heels striking the metal stair treads.

"K Kat," said Risk, "watch her."

The mountain lion grazed his leg as she trotted past all of them and into the small stairwell structure, and no one heard her soft paws as she followed after Widow.

"I'll bring up the rear," Bentley said, then snickered while leaning to look at two Kildare Killer asses hidden under burlap.

Risk scoffed, then extended a hand toward the doorway while looking at the girls.

"Come on, Sis."

Holding Marilyn under the blanket, Sophia led them both through the doorway, and Risk, after glaring at the vampire for a second, followed them.

Before entering, Bentley called back to Hawken, "Save my seat!"

Risk stepped back out enough to look up at Hawken.

He shook his head, and the navigator nodded and gave a thumbs-up sign with a very small hand in a leather glove. Bentley had turned his head quickly enough between the two to witness it all.

"Aw, come on," he said, but Risk had already turned and began thumping his boots down the stairs.

"Dammit," said the vampire. "That's just bloody inconsiderate. Hey, Risk!"

Risk leaned his head out of the small stairwell building's shadows and said, "What?"

"You didn't mean that, right? A return trip would be a decent thing for you and that hawkish fellow to offer me."

"Return to where?"

"Uh, good point. Um, wherever you're going, I suppose. The British Isles, ideally, if I could somehow eke some kindness out of your cold heart."

Risk shook his head and said, "Remember where we are," and grumbled as he turned back toward the stairway.

"I have some value," Bentley said, drawing another pause and a stern look from Risk. "I truly do."

"Like what?"

"Uh," he said, looking around, "Oh! If you were to land on a building that harbored a pack of those zombeing things, you'd want to know, wouldn't you?"

"We won't."

He turned again and said over his shoulder, "They're too far ahead. Let's go."

"Hold it again! That foul cat beast has them in her sights. They're fine. Oh, wait—you might need a translator!"

"I don't."

"I'm good at writing things up. I used to be an English professor, you know. Oh, yeah. Guess where."

"We don't have—"

"That's right. In England. Kind of makes sense. Teaching English in England. There's a certain—hey!"

Risk had grumbled and began the long walk down the flights of stairs, with his boots striking much harder than necessary.

"Hey, wait for me!"

Bentley laughed to himself and followed Risk into the depths of The Crypt Building.

*　*　*

Widow had led the way down many flights of stairs, and she and the twins had tried every door leading off of the stairwell, finding all of them locked.

At the next door, which looked like all the rest to the girls, Widow said in a normal tone, "This is the one."

"How would you know that?" said Marilyn.

She pointed at a line of large and small pipes running along the ceiling and through the wall.

"Probably water lines. At one time. This is it."

She tried the knob, found that it was unlocked, and left it closed. She leaned her back into it and looked from one Kildare Killer to the other, both of whom took a step back.

And K Kat sat in front of them, watching Widow.

"Fia, is it?"

Sophia nodded and said, "To some, sure."

"To me, then, too. Your hair."

Sophia turned her eyes up to see, and her sister took a better look at it too.

"Oh, Sissy, it's still all pinned up. Let me—"

"I'd like to help," Widow said with a relaxed smile. "I need to be of some use, too, don't I?"

"Uh, sure," said Marilyn. "Um, but all it needs is—"

"Turn around."

They both stared at her, and Sophia started to say, "Uh, I could even—"

Widow smiled and let the words flow out slow and easy, honey warmed in a soft, almost naked woman's body.

"Turn around, pretty twin girls."

Marilyn giggled once and said, "We are twins, Sissy," and they turned around, still holding each other around the waist and covered with their burlap blanket.

"Yes, twins. Mm-hmm, just like that."

She cut off the honey just long enough to say, "Cat?"

K Kat only stared, then Widow reached a hand toward the lion's face with her index finger extended, almost touching her nose.

The lion sniffed it, then yipped softly and hurried to one side, leaving room for Widow to walk up close behind them.

She reached up for Sophia's hair, spoke with a syrupy tongue again, and said, "Such a very nice braid."

Marilyn said, "I braided that for her."

"And you did a very pretty job of it."

She removed a couple of small fasteners, with Marilyn watching and with Sophia holding her breath and staring straight ahead.

Widow bounced her thick black braid around, then laid it down the center of her back.

"Very pretty."

She saw Marilyn watching and said, "I could do yours, if you'd like."

"Um, I don't know."

"You're both very tired and weak from your ordeals. I can tell. You're both barely holding on. Let me help."

"Um, if I really need a—"

"Oh, you might need a braid. Two gorgeous twin girls flying all around in a balloon? With some shady characters and a lion too? Oh no, I insist."

"Well, um, okay."

Widow touched the side of Sophia's neck lightly with her fingertips while she was moving herself to stand directly behind Marilyn. Only then did she remove them and reach both hands for Marilyn's hair.

"Such pretty blond hair you have. It's delightful."

"Oh, thanks."

She began fluffing it all back, sometimes touching the skin of Marilyn's neck, which still had streaks of oil and jagged black lines marring her skin everywhere.

Marilyn stood completely still while Widow fussed with her hair, and she let Marilyn's hair go to hold her shoulders.

"Oh, you'll have to stand very still for me."

"But I was already—"

"Shh, now."

She leaned in close, letting her hips contact Marilyn and stay there.

She kept the two of them pressed together, then said, "Mm, yeah. Very still for me. Yes, just like that."

Sophia's breaths had quickened, and she squeezed her sister's hand, hidden under the blanket.

"Let's just get this all gathered up," said Widow, and her fingertips bumped and rubbed on Marilyn's skin, both sides of her neck, with every motion of her hands.

She kept gathering and touching while saying, "Oh, I might have missed just a few. Here, let me . . ."

She reached around and touched her cheek, seeking imaginary hair. And when Marilyn didn't move or complain or question her, she slid her fingertips lightly across her cheek.

"Still a few more . . ."

Marilyn held still for her, and Widow caressed her cheeks several more times.

"Good girl," she said. "Stay very still for me, and we'll fix up this pretty hair. Yes, just like that."

She reached far enough to just touch the edge of Marilyn's lips.

"Oh, there are just a few more. I'll find them. Just stay very still for me."

Marilyn only breathed and stayed very quiet.

"Almost there."

She barely touched Marilyn's lips again, and she didn't move at all.

"Mm, almost there."

She touched Marilyn's lips near their middle, with just one fingertip, then she spread them apart just a little, just enough to slide her finger between them as she pulled her finger back to rub softly across her cheek again.

"That's very good. Just like that."

Without looking, Widow reached her other hand around Sophia, touched her cheek lightly, then wiggled two of her fingers between her lips.

Sophia didn't protest, but she did whimper softly just once, and Widow let her fingers explore deeper, smiling at the feeling of Sophia's soft lips closing around them.

"Oh, just a few more loose pretty blond hairs. Stay very still for me."

She slipped two fingers, almost their entire lengths, into Marilyn's mouth, and she nodded at Marilyn still not moving at all.

"Aw, there we go," she said as Marilyn moaned softly and closed her lips too. "Such a good little girl. So very quiet for me now."

When both of them started sucking lightly on her fingers, Widow sighed and said, "Mm, such precious little twin girls."

They both looked straight ahead, squeezing each other's hand under their blanket and breathing deeply.

"Such soft, tender little baby girls for me. I just love little twin baby girls."

She tipped her head up at the sound of Risk and Bentley traveling down the stairs, still many flights up.

Widow drove her fingers deeper into each of their mouths, till they could go in no farther, then leaned in close between them.

"Suck for me, pretty little girls."

Sophia whimpered again, and Marilyn moaned softly. Both used their lips more, squeezing Widow's fingers tightly.

"Oh, yes, just like that. Suck for me, my soft, sweet little babies."

Two pairs of Kildare Killer lips hugged and hungrily sucked on Widow's wet fingers, but the footsteps above them were heavy and drawing closer.

"Quickly, my little girls. Suck more."

She wiggled her hands to extend four fingers deep into each mouth, resting her palms on their chins, then shifted them around, rubbing them across their wet lips.

Then, she leaned between them to watch their throats as they swallowed every few seconds.

"Mm, yes. You've both sucked so much already. Such good little girls for me."

She leaned into Marilyn's hair first, inhaled, then did the same at the side of Sophia's punctured neck before giving her wounds a kiss.

"It's our little secret, sweet baby girls. Just for the three of us. Remember how this feels. Mm, it feels so good to be my babies."

Risk was only several landings above them.

"We'll hide away, all three of us. My twin babies and I will be bound together for such a long time."

She slipped her fingers out from between their wet lips, and she lowered her hands enough to take a breast of each and fondle them gently through the cloth covering them.

She leaned enough to kiss Marilyn's neck, then she whispered in her ear, "You'll love having your face hidden away under so many layers."

She found Marilyn's nipple and began giving it soft pinches.

"Your pretty face will stay in a silent scream where no one will ever see it, but you'll still be so soft and juicy all over for me."

She gave Marilyn a harder pinch, causing a soft gasp.

"Your precious little sister too. I'll have such fun with those lovely, sucking mouths of yours. You'll be such pretty little girls for me. So pretty and quiet."

From two landings above, Bentley called out, "Are you there? Where are you all? We must be getting close!"

"Hmm, maybe I'll bind you two with your soft lips together. Yes, that would be so sweet: two pretty little twin baby girls kissing till their very end."

Widow heard Risk, not far above them, grumble his response.

Widow kissed each quickly and said, "When you give yourselves to me, your sweetest ecstasy will be knowing that I'll do whatever I want with you. The more helpless you become to anything I desire from you, the more pleasure you'll feel."

Risk and Bentley were about to make their final turn.

"And what I desire from you both will be quite cruel. Mm, yes. So exquisitely cruel. You may find that you love being cruel to each other to please me."

She gave each held breast a hard squeeze, causing them both to open their mouths in silent gasps.

"You'll love realizing that your softness and helplessness is begging for cruelty."

She timed it well and stepped back from them just as Risk turned on the next landing up and stomped down the last flight to join them.

* * *

Risk took one step away from the stairs, then stopped.

He squinted at Marilyn and Sophia, both still close together under a shared blanket and facing away.

K Kat, a few steps down the hallway, looked at him silently.

"What's going on?"

Widow smiled and said, "We were waiting for you."

"Oh. Alright. Mare? Fia?"

He watched them both take deep breaths, then they shuffled themselves around to face him.

"We're just tired, Sissy and I."

"Yeah. Sis is right."

"Uh, yeah. You should be."

"Looks like the last chance," Bentley said.

Risk held up on knocking to look at Bentley.

"Last chance?"

He pointed at the door and said, "Yeah. Well, we're running out of chances anyway. Uh, for that spa. If the stories are true."

"You don't know?"

"Uh. No, I'm sure. Go ahead. Knock."

"It's open," said Widow.

"Oh," said Bentley. "Okay."

"Still, it's good to be polite," she said.

Risk grumbled and was about to strike the door when Marilyn giggled and said, "I almost had a braid too. Just like Sissy."

He lowered his hand and studied them. Marilyn gave her unbraided mane a quick shake, but Sophia only looked at the floor.

"Uh, good. That's good."

He raised his hand again, and Sophia said, "Widow offered."

He turned to her and said, "She offered what?"

"She . . . she, um, offered to give Sis a braid."

He looked from one twin to another, then at Widow, who only shrugged.

"We didn't have time," Widow said, quite normally. "You boys didn't dawdle long enough up there on the roof."

Risk was about to knock again, until Widow said, "She really does have gorgeous hair too."

He turned to her.

"Like her sister," said Bentley. "Both of them. The two of them together. They have really nice hair."

"Enough," he said and pounded on the door.

They waited. Bentley exaggerated a sigh.

Risk pounded again, and the door opened inward with a soft squeal.

"Oh my goodness," Marilyn said only loud enough for her sister to hear.

"Sheesh," Sophia said, barely breathing out the word.

Before them stood an average looking older man, wearing a tattered black tuxedo. His bow tie was mostly shredded and the bellhop hat on his head leaned to one side.

"I'm the manager. What do you want?"

Before anyone could answer, he dragged an oily cloth all along under his nose, snorting softly into it and not trying to hide what he was depositing on the cloth to gum up those oil stains.

Bentley said, "Um . . ."

"We, uh . . ." Risk said, then leaned his head, staring.

The man's nose encroached halfway across each of his cheeks. A wide, flat thing that tapered down from between his eyes like a ski jump slope.

And beneath it, all pointing toward the floor, was an evenly spaced line of six nostrils.

"Hey," said Bentley, doing his best to contain a laugh, "you're another one of those—"

He pointed at Bentley's face.

"Don't you dare call me a freak."

"But you, um, something happened to—"

"Well? Something happened to your shirt, and you don't hear me trying to belittle you about it. I'm not a freak. I'm not. I'm a restart. That's the preferred term."

Risk grumbled and shook his head. Widow smirked. The twins stared, their eyes kind of glazed over.

Bentley laughed and said, "I've heard an even better term for when, uh, stuff like that,"—he traced a circle with his pointing finger toward the man's face—"happens. Want to hear it?"

"No. I sure don't."

"Me neither," said Risk. "Let's get—"

"I'm telling you anyway. You, you handsome devil, might be classified by some in this hellish, burning pit as a . . . DNA-Hole."

Everyone only stared at him.

"What? Don't you get it? I mean, DNA and all, right?"

Widow smiled at the man, leaning to look under his chin, and said, "He didn't mean anything by—"

"No, wait. I kind of like it. Do you think I ever get to laugh about this bullshit? Huh? Ever? No. That shirtless young man has just gained you all entrance to The Spa. So says the manager of the place, me, a proud DNA-Hole."

Chapter 48 – Squeezed Into Just One Tub

While standing aside and holding the door open, the manager of the place said, "I'm Dan. I've been running this place for . . ."

He stopped and squinted at Bentley, smirking as he walked past him and into the large, luxurious room.

"I really have," he said to him. "I was appointed manager of this place—"

"No. Not that."

"What, then?"

Bentley grinned at everyone staring at him. Even Widow seemed curious.

"The letters," he said.

"Mail stopped long ago, young fellow. All the pigeons got eaten too. Ever see one of those goddamn bats snag one right out—"

Bentley let out a good laugh and shook his head.

"No. Oh, I'm sorry, maybe I shouldn't. Okay, I will. The letters of your name are the same as for DNA."

"I get it," said Risk. "Funny."

"Well, then, why aren't you laughing?"

"I don't think he ever laughs," said Widow, then she looked at the twins. "Girls? Twin girls? Any opinion?"

"There's not too much funny here," Marilyn said as she shook her head.

"Sis is right. So, he should laugh about whatever he—"

"Not just him," Widow said, smiling at each of them. "We should all find what pleasure we can wherever we can. Isn't that right, girls? I mean, twin girls?"

They looked only at her and nodded silently, then she looked back at Risk, who was squinting at her.

He looked at Dan and said, "We need to clean up."

Dan looked them over, especially Marilyn and Sophia, nodding his head the entire time.

"I'll say. What the hell you all been into?"

Bentley chuckled and said, "Where to begin?"

"With a hot bath?" said Widow. "These two, especially, could use some cleaning up."

"Yeah," said Dan, "I see that. That one,"—he pointed at Marilyn—"got herself messed up with those—"

"Zombeings," said Marilyn. "They prefer that."

"I'll give them that. Sure. They didn't get blasted with radiation bullshit and get their DNA scrambled. No, they—say, I'll fill you in later. I'm a bit of an historian, too, around here."

"We're all very tired," said Bentley, "even though we're laughing a lot."

He glanced at Risk, then continued.

"Some of us, I mean. I'm actually kind of slap-happy. Maybe from almost learning to fly just a minute ago."

Dan wiped across his many nostrils both ways, then jammed the rag up into one, then another, twisting it around.

"Sheesh," Sophia whispered to her sister.

"Uh-huh. Very true, Sissy."

"You can all just take a seat," he said, sweeping his arm around the room, which housed several distinct seating areas with plush upholstered furnishings. "Or whichever of you needs it the most can take a truly hot bath. Except for what's getting boiled by goddamn fires out there. But you don't want that. No, no one would want that."

"Sis really needs a bath the most," Sophia said, tipping her head toward Marilyn.

"Well," said Marilyn, "Sissy still has gummy stuff in her hair and stuck, for some reason, all over her. She needs it more."

Dan laughed and said, "Hell, it's a big jacuzzi. The jets are shot to hell, but the heaters are good. Room enough for both of you."

Widow hurried to say, "Did you notice that they're twins? Twin girls? They probably do almost everything together. If there's that much room, they can both get squeezed into just one . . . tub."

They turned toward each other, and Marilyn said, "It's okay by me, Sissy."

Sophia shrugged and said, "Sure. Why not?"

*   *   *

"Right through here," Dan said after he'd twisted a polished doorknob and pushed the door into a clean, dimly-lit hallway.

He led the girls in, and Widow waited near the open door, watching him lead the twins along a hall with doors on both sides. She took note of which door he opened, one farther along on the left, then she let the door close as she remained in the big room with Risk and Bentley.

"This one here," Dan said, opening the door to the bath, "is the one you want."

He stepped to one side so they could look into the room.

Against the far wall, beneath a window blocking out only night and shielded by several layers of chain link fence, waited a pink jacuzzi tub barely big enough only for two.

The large, nearly square room was decorated in solid colors, mostly soft pinks and light blues. Large tiles, separated by clean white grout, gave way to undamaged plaster walls and a textured ceiling with recessed light fixtures. Along one wall, a wide vanity with an even wider mirror waited with a single upholstered chair.

Off to the right, there was a closed door.

"That one leads to the suite, which is quite nice. But what you need most is the bath."

"I, um, thought you said the tub was big," said Sophia.

"Well, I, um, it was the honeymoon suite. It's meant for romance and—"

"Ooh," said Marilyn. "That's funny, Sissy."

"—and it's bigger than most. And really, it's the only hot bath you'll find."

He shooed the two girls inside, saying, "Everything either of you could need is there. There's shampoo, sort of, soap, sort of, and—"

Marilyn giggled and said, "It's fine. It's all very nice. Thank you."

"You're very welcome," he said before snorting a thick liquid out of three of his nostrils.

He rubbed it into the floor with his shoe.

"Carry on!"

"Wait," said Marilyn. "What about everyone else?"

"Why, when you're done, I suppose. If they don't want to wait, I'll just run some hot water into buckets and give them some rags and soap."

The twins stared at him.

"A sponge? Maybe?"

Sophia cleared her throat and said, "Uh, we'll try to be quick."

"There are heaters in the tub to keep the water however hot you fancy it. Take your time. Ladies," he said, then gave them a quick salute.

He closed the door with a soft thump, leaving Marilyn and Sophia alone in the room.

"Sheesh."

"Yes. Uh-uh. You're going to need that word a lot until we get home again."

"If ever, Sis."

"Sissy, no, don't talk like that. Risk will take us home."

Sophia sighed and said, "Alright. He probably will."

They walked together to the tub. Marilyn turned the knobs to get a good temperature, and the clean interior started to fill.

She squeezed her sister's waist and said, "It'll feel so good to be clean again."

"You're a mess. What happened to you?"

"Oh, Sissy, I'd rather not say. Not yet. I can tell you that I've never been so itchy in my life, though."

"Huh. I know the feeling."

"You do?"

"Yeah, Sis. Widow, she, uh, she can—"

"Sissy, I have a confession."

"Sure. What is it?"

"Just now, outside, I was so itchy that I even, um, I—"

"You can tell me, Sis. Just say it."

"I felt like I was having some kind of orgasm when I was, uh, I was sucking on Widow. Her fingers, I mean."

Sophia turned to face her, so close that they could rub noses.

"Sis. I was doing the same at the same time."

"That's funny—we were both sucking her fingers at the same time and—"

"—and we were both having orgasms. But trust me, she doesn't mean for it to be funny."

Marilyn held her sister's gaze, blue eyes staring into blue eyes, and said, "No. I guess it wasn't exactly funny. It was just insanely good."

"Sis, you don't know the half of it."

"Mm, I think I'd like to. Not just half of it."

"Yeah, you would. You got just a tiny hint of what that woman can do. If she had you all, um . . ."

"All what?"

"Nothing. I just mean that she's kind of unbelievable with that."

"Mm, I want more, Sissy. I even liked how she was talking to us."

"Which part?"

"Sissy, we were her sweet little baby girls! She said she loved little twin baby girls too."

"Oh my God. I liked her talking like that too. She, uh, she did so much of that. Just the sound of her voice sometimes. It felt like she was touching me with it. Especially when I was, um . . ."

Marilyn nodded, then waited for more.

"But Sis, we can't. We just can't. Let's focus on getting cleaned up, then we have to find a way to get the hell out of this place."

Marilyn rubbed her nose on her sister's and said, "Okay, Sissy. But I'm so itchy I can't stand it. I'd take my chances to feel more of that."

Sophia sighed and stared up at the ceiling.

"I know we shouldn't. But I, uh, maybe we can figure that out later."

* * *

Dan gathered up the wet rags and slopped them into one of the hot water buckets.

"Better?" he said.

Risk, Widow, and Bentley were still drying themselves off with clean towels after sponging off what they could of whatever filth each had picked up.

Bentley handed the towel back and said, "Much better. Not exactly a hot shower, but we are in Hell, after all."

Risk grumbled and shook his head and didn't comment. But he did watch as Widow leaned over and rubbed the damp towel all over her legs, leaving them damp and glistening.

She stopped, still leaning, and turned her eyes up toward him and smiled.

He grumbled and looked away, and she stood straight up and gave the towel to Dan.

"Thank you. Clean is good."

"Yeah, uh-huh."

He set all of it off to the side, then stood with his hands on his hips.

"While those delightful girls are getting spiffied up," Dan said as he led Risk, Bentley, and Widow toward a seating area, "we have some time for you weary travelers to rest."

Three overstuffed upholstered chairs and three couches, all of them with their own matching ottomans, sat in a nearly perfect circle and faced each other. Three ornate tables with softly glowing lamps served between each chair and couch pair, and a large round table rested on a clean area rug in the middle.

A full bottle of something waited there, surrounded by spotless glass tumblers. Dan didn't ask, just poured four of them full and handed them around.

"Cheers," he said and took a sip.

"Crude wine?" said Bentley.

"Uh-uh. Crude whiskey. Strong. It'll burn the hair off your ass."

"Lovely. Just what anyone would want," he said and tried it. "Huh. Not bad."

He nodded at the sight of Risk trying it, too, but Widow wouldn't touch hers.

"We should have come here long ago," Bentley said as he plopped down in one of the chairs. "I might never leave."

"You will if those confounded bats ever get inside," Dan said while pointing toward the iron bars stacked closely across the window areas, which held no glass. "Those bars do the trick, and I shutter them up tight when I'm not in here watching."

He scrubbed around his nostrils and watched Risk when he said, "We've been through a lot. Thanks."

Widow said, "What happened with the blond twin? She had the markings of becoming a zombie."

"She was close," Risk said.

"Zombeings," Dan said while shaking his head but never letting his oily rag get too far away. "They like that better. And they should. It's a much more accurate term."

"Do we even care?" said Bentley. "Those bloody freaks are,"— he saw Dan, the rag still, staring at him—"I mean, those *people* are—"

Dan laughed once at the ceiling, then said, "People? Oh, come on. I'm not that sensitive about my, um, modifications."

"Explain," said Risk. "For Widow and him."

"I have a right proper name, you know."

Risk grumbled and ignored him.

"Alright," said Dan, "I will. Happy to. You see, before any of their kind were here, they were there."

He pointed up but didn't look. None of them did.

"Scientists. Those are the true freaks, if you ask me. They created a computerized brain kind of thing and got the foul thing to work. Quite well. It could carry on intelligent conversations, had instant access to all the info shoveled into it, and was just an overall pleasant sort of thing to have around."

"Charming," Bentley said with a scoff.

Dan leveled a squinting stare at him, then pointed and grinned.

"You're a vampire, aren't you, young fellow?"

Bentley nodded.

"Never bit into a microchip anything, have you?"

"There are better things to bite," Widow said as she fussed with Risk's vest, which was close to opening up and exposing her breasts.

That drew Dan's eyes, and he said, "Uh, yep."

He looked into her eyes and said, "Much better things to, uh, to . . ."

He shook his head and addressed all three of them.

"So, the damn microchip bastards needed bodies. It's what scientists do: they just keep pushing things. Ever hear of clones? Course you have. They ordered up a herd of them. All different ages, male, female . . . they took anything they could get. Kept them on ice for a while, then planted the computer brain people things inside the cloned people body things."

"Then, they ended up here?"

"Nope," he said to Bentley. "Not just yet. Ever heard of upgrades? Course you have. Some hotshot programmer coded up some bullshit to give them all libidos. You know what that is, right?"

He waited, and they kept watching and listening.

"Huh. Course you do. Anyway, they loaded up their chips with that shit, then someone, probably the goddamn CEO, flipped the goddamn switch. My Lord, they all instantly spasmed and seized up with orgasms like you wouldn't believe."

Widow didn't wait. She said, "I know what orgasms are," then she looked at Risk.

He only grumbled and looked back at Dan.

"What's wrong with that?" said Bentley. "Jolly good for those, um, oh, shit, come on. They're freaks. But good for them anyway."

"Yeah. Oh, yeah, they're freaks, but that wasn't good for them. You remember the rest of this cautionary little tale? Hmm? Cloned bodies. Bodies that were never alive. Those reprogrammed brains went nuts with monster orgasms inside—"

"Dead bodies."

Dan pointed at Risk and nodded.

"One way ticket to Hell. Which is here. Which you already know."

"It's not Hell," Bentley said, shaking his head at Dan. "It's just hot like it."

"Right," said Dan. "Sure. So, you've all heard the buzzing?"

They all nodded.

"Know exactly what that is?"

Widow and Bentley shook their heads, but Risk scoffed and waited.

"It's a wireless power something-or-other that keeps all of those high-tech brains firing. Stop the buzzing, stop the power, stop the—"

"Brains?" said Bentley. "Good grief, that explains it. Then, they just—"

"Go insane. Yeah. Another fun little bit of programming bullshit. Bet none of you knew this. When some hotshot computer whiz punk gave them their sex-freak upgrade, he gave them all what he understood of the typical zombie mindset. Which is?"

He looked around and waited. Finally, Bentley spoke.

"Brains? They want—"

"Yes, young man. You get the top prize. Those fools actually think they're actual zombies."

"But they're not?"

"Nope. Just insane, fucked up computer things in dead clone bodies."

Risk said, "Wait. They almost turned Mare into one."

"The blond girl?" said Dan. "Huh. They almost turned her into something, that's true. I can't even tell you what kind of bizarre hellish crude drugs they use."

"She wouldn't have been a zombie?" said Risk.

"Nope. Oh, no. Something worse probably."

"Lovely," said Widow.

"And when the buzzing is working?" said Widow. "What then?"

"Then? They're very polite, still quite nice to share a conversation with, but just beneath the surface, they're absolutely crazy for sex. The more bizarre and violent the better."

"Nice," said Bentley. "I knew there was a good reason to avoid them."

"Oh," said Dan. "One other thing."

He left them waiting with a dramatic pause.

"Those fools sure like to talk dirty too. My guess is that that programmer sneaked something into their code. A trigger. Oh, they love their dirty talk. So dirty it'll make you blush."

"Doubtful," Widow said.

Risk grumbled and tried some more of the crude whiskey.

*　*　*

"We can think about that later, Sissy. Come on. Let's get in the bubbles."

"You really are a mess, Sis."

"Mm-hmm."

They still held hands under the scratchy blanket as they walked the few steps back to the tub. Both let go of it, and Marilyn quickly lost Ham's oversized shirt too.

"Just the heels, Sis."

She held Marilyn's shoulder and reached down to unbuckle both black straps and let them fall to the side. Marilyn did the same with her high white heels.

"Hot water, Sissy! And bubbles!"

She giggled as she got in and leaned her back against one end, then she splashed the water, looking up at Sophia.

"Come on, Sissy. Don't be a dirty girl forever."

"That's funny, Sis."

"True too."

Sophia moaned as she sank into the steaming water at the other end, and they each picked a side and extended their legs.

"Oh, this feels so good," said Marilyn. "Except, I still feel kind of funny."

"Yeah. Me too. It hasn't stopped since that wine at Ham's house."

"Oh, you're right. But I think it's more from, um, Widow, when we—"

"When we sucked Widow."

Marilyn stared a few seconds before smiling.

"Um, yes. We did. I'm still tingling from that. It just made me even itchier."

"Me too, Sis. She's . . . incredible. Maybe if we get cleaned up, it'll help. You've got a lot of muck on you."

"I hope these lines can somehow wash away too."

"They probably will. What are those anyway?"

"Oh my goodness, Sissy. That was the weirdest time I ever had."

"How so?"

"I think I almost became a zombie. No, I'm sure of it—I was real close."

"How could you let that happen to you, Sis?"

"Hmm, because it felt good. I was so hungry and itchy at the same time. It started with—"

"With you getting swarmed by that mob of them. They took you away."

"Yes, they did. We went through all kinds of dark scary places underground, then into a big room where they put me in a cage."

"Huh. Sis in a cage. That's already kind of hot."

"It wasn't. It was scary. But they were all very polite, and they had a huge crush on that other Marilyn. They watched her recorded movies all the time. They thought I was her!"

"You're better than she ever was."

"Aw, thanks, Sissy. That's what I told them, and they said if I proved I was better, they might let me go."

"So, you did?"

"I showed them my boobies."

Sophia grinned and said, "Come on, Sis. Act it out."

Marilyn raised her breasts above the water line and swayed them back and forth, and Sophia stared without smiling.

After a few seconds, Marilyn splashed at her sister and said, "Sissy, there's more story."

Sophia looked up quickly, then said, "Oh, uh, yeah. I'm just, um, kind of exhausted and feel kind of funny. Go on. What else?"

"That silly buzzing noise stopped, and they turned into zombies. My clothes got ripped off and dragged away, and I hid under blankets on the bed."

"At least they gave you a bed."

"Yes. Quite nice of them. Then, they sent in this really hot young couple to bring me clothes and food. Sissy, they were so fit it was unbelievable."

"But they were zombies, too, right?"

"Well, yes, they were. And they all seemed quite content about it."

"Go on. Keep going."

"That cute girl, Janie, seduced me in front of the entire crowd. I don't know why I was so itchy. I was out of control. We kissed, and she even got me to suck on her nipples, which were stunning."

"My God, Sis, that's hot. What else?"

"Janie was feeding me this, I don't know, some kind of stuff. It made me even hungrier and itchier. Her guy friend, Blaine was his name, even started screwing me—right in that cage!"

"*Your* cage, Sis."

"Yes, *my* cage. Oh my gosh, then I gave blow jobs and—"

"Plural, Sis? Really?"

"Oh my goodness, yes. I don't know how long I was giving blow jobs and getting screwed at the same time."

"All zombies, Sis?"

"Mm-hmm. Sissy, they were like rock. Ooh, cold, though."

"Yeah, I bet. Go on."

"So, it went on and on, and I just got hungrier and itchier every time."

Marilyn smiled as she looked at the water, feeling her sister rubbing her legs.

"Just to, uh, help you clean up, Sis."

"Mm-hmm. You too, Sissy," she said and started rubbing Sophia's legs.

"I won't even tell you what they wanted me to do, Sissy, but that hot girl, Janie, was whipping me with—"

"Across your back? Whipping you?"

"Uh-uh. Oh no, Sissy. I was kneeling and holding the bars, and I kept my knees far enough apart. She used a thick, hard leather belt, and she kept snapping it up at—"

"Your pussy, Sis? No way."

"Yes, Sissy. She was abusing my pussy, and it felt so good. It hurt, but it still made me even crazier. Oh, wow, what an orgasm."

"That's unbelievable."

Sophia reached farther along her sister's legs under the sudsy water.

"Your poor pussy. I can't reach it, Sis."

"Sissy, you're funny."

"At least, those lines are fading. Your skin is more normal already."

"Really?" She looked at her arms, then her breasts and said, "Huh. Good. I don't like them anymore."

"Huh? You liked them before?"

Marilyn only shrugged, then said, "Then, Risk came in and rescued me, and that was a scary thing too. I'll tell you about that later. What happened to you?"

"Oh, that. I, um, I was—"

"Alone with Widow? Sissy, she's something unbelievable too. I'm still tingling from—"

"Sucking her. We were—"

"I kind of even like the sound of that. Say it again."

Sophia grinned and held her sister's gaze.

"We were both sucking Widow."

"Mm-hmm. Yes, we were. Only her fingers, Sissy."

She giggled and added, "That time anyway!"

"Sis, you're funny. Um, somehow, she captured me, and she kept me tied up. She—"

"How? Details, Sissy."

Sophia smiled, and they kept rubbing each other's legs.

"When I woke up, my arms were tied behind me and when I tried to burn my way out, Widow told me to—"

"Did she call you her little baby?"

"Oh, a lot. Yeah. She—"

"Aw, you were all alone with her, and you were her little baby girl."

"Yeah, and she was biting me a lot. See?"

Sophia lifted her chin and showed Marilyn all of her little punctures.

"That's so sweet. I'm sure you're very tasty."

"Uh, sure, but Sis, she was sucking out my blood, and she was putting some kind of poisons into me."

Marilyn shivered in the hot water and said, "That's got some kind of romantic feel to it, Sissy."

Sophia grinned and said, "Uh, yeah. And all of that gave me a constant orgasm. Sis, it was really constant. It never stopped."

"Not even a little?"

"Nope. Every time she touched me anywhere, it spiked that orgasm too. Everything she did, even cruel things, just made that orgasm even sweeter."

"Oh, yes, Sissy. I think I felt that when—"

"When we were sucking her."

She grinned at Marilyn's eyes almost closing at what she'd said, so she continued.

"When you and I were sucking her, and we were her sweet little baby girls, Sis."

"Sissy," Marilyn said, her chest starting to heave gently with her deeper breaths, "I'm getting so itchy I can't stand it."

She noticed that her sister was again looking down at her breasts when she said, "Uh, me too, Sis. God, I'm so itchy."

Marilyn reached out of the water and held the rim of the tub on each side, and she began to slide herself closer to Sophia.

"Meet me halfway, Sissy."

Sophia nodded, even though it wasn't a question, and began shifting herself closer too. They met in the middle, their legs apart and overlapping so that they could get close, almost close enough to touch under the sudsy water, and looked into each other's bright blue eyes.

Marilyn leaned enough to close the distance, their lips almost touching.

"I'm just so itchy, Sissy. Just a tiny little kiss would help."

"Mm, sure," Sophia said as she pressed her lips into Marilyn's.

It lasted only a second, and Marilyn backed away with a soft, forced giggle. But Sophia was still gazing into her eyes, so Marilyn's attempt at laughter faded and stopped.

They tipped their heads at the same time, for a better match, and began a serious kiss, and each used one hand to hold the other's head in place.

The kiss went on for thirty seconds, sometimes with them tipping their heads the other way, then resuming it with more urgency.

But almost at the same time, they let each other go and leaned away just enough to speak.

"Oh my goodness, Sissy. It's this place, isn't it?"

Sophia waited a few seconds, then said, "Uh, no, Sis. It's Widow. I think she gave us some of that orgasm poison of hers."

"Mm, yes. I believe you're right. I want more of it. I want a constant orgasm, Sissy."

"She wants to do that to both of us."

Marilyn was nodding, so Sophia added, "At the same time."

Marilyn stopped nodding and said softly, "Because we're her soft little twin baby girls."

"She does love soft and tender, Sis. Juicy too. She loved that I was so juicy for her."

"Mm, I can do that. I could be very soft and tender and juicy for her."

She began leaning toward Sophia again, looking down at her lips, and Sophia yelled, "Risk! Come here!"

Chapter 49 – When We Have Time

Risk had his glass tipped back, and he'd finished most of his crude whiskey.

"Hey," said Bentley. "Easy on the sauce. I take it you're not much of a drinker, are you?"

"No."

He let the last few drops fall into his open mouth and kept the glass up when they all heard Sophia yell for him.

"Water got cold or something?" said Dan. "Lights are still on. Should be holding the heat."

Widow held Bentley's gaze for a second, long enough for him to give the slightest of nods, then looked away.

Risk started to rise and said, "I'll—"

Bentley laughed and pushed him back into his seat.

"They're fine. Probably just so many bubbles they lost the bar of soap."

Risk stared at him.

"Or something like that. Nothing to worry about."

"Still," said Widow. "Someone should take a look. I'll go."

She got up and Risk stayed seated, watching her hips swaying and her solid ass teasing its curves above and below the tiniest of thin black panties. She seemed to be striking her heels into the clean wood floor more than necessary to walk across the expansive room.

"Bubble baths," said Bentley, and Risk didn't look at him. "Although, I could use some of that too. Eh. Buckets of hot water are just so primitive."

Risk watched Widow brush her hair back with both hands, and her thick black mane swayed easily across the back of his black leather vest.

"Huh. Cold water would be worse, though."

She'd reached the door and had a hand on the knob.

"What do you think, Risk? A hot bath. That's the life, even here. People—hey, are you listening?"

Risk belched softly and turned toward Bentley.

"People think vampires like cold and damp places. Well, we don't."

Bentley glanced quickly at Widow and saw her opening the door to the hallway, stepping through, then closing it again.

"At least, this fucking vampire doesn't. Oh, no. This spa, right here, is fine by me. Just settle into those comfy cushions, and I'll explain to you with my best lecture hall oration just exactly why."

* * *

Marilyn giggled softly after Sophia had screamed for Risk.

"Oh, Sissy. We're just playing because we're itchy. We don't need to bother him. I promise I won't bite you."

They turned only their faces, and they were cheek to cheek when Widow opened the door and stepped into the spa room. She smiled at the twins in the tub and leaned her back into the door, closing it quietly.

"Widow," said Sophia.

"Fia. I love that name for you. It's very pretty."

The twins stayed close and looked up at the woman who, from their lower position, seemed to be mostly long, smooth, and strong legs up on pointy black heels.

"Oh, I think I might have interrupted . . . a kiss?"

"Um," said Marilyn, "we, uh, were just—"

"Two pretty girls should kiss whenever they can. And you two are very pretty little girls. Little twin girls."

"Um . . ."

"Marilyn, is it? Do you have a special name too?"

"I, uh, yes. It's Mare."

"Oh, that's so nice. Girls, I want you to listen closely."

They both nodded, so close that their cheeks were still touching. Widow's voice began to flow like a slow, warm stream, caressing its way comfortably into their ears.

"First, I'm so sorry I disturbed you two little girls in your hot bath together. And it's so precious how close together you are. Look at each other for me."

They turned their heads to face each other, and they looked into each other's eyes.

"Now," said Widow, "each of you look at your sister's lips."

They turned their eyes lower.

"Aren't they beautiful?"

They both nodded.

Widow began a soft chant.

"So plump and soft. Lips that are so sweet for kissing. A sweet little baby sister with such sweet lips. Mm, you should never feel that you can't kiss each other."

She gave them a few seconds to study more closely the other's lips. And her voice got warmer, more syrupy.

"Touch your lips together. Just enough to feel how soft they are. It's okay."

They leaned enough that their lips were pressed together.

"Oh, that's nice. Such very soft lips. Lips that should be kissed," Widow said, her voice as warm as their bathwater. "Really kissed. Little girls should give very good kisses to such soft lips like those."

They still hesitated, and Widow chanted more.

"Mare, your little sister is so wet and warm with you in all those bubbles. She has such soft lips for you to kiss. She's just a baby. A baby with such very, very soft lips."

Marilyn groaned and pushed harder into Sophia's lips, and Sophia returned it. They'd begun a very deep, passionate kiss, their mouths opening at times so that just their tongues could play.

"Don't stop, sweet little girls. Don't stop that kiss that you both love from each other. Mare, reach between your baby sister's legs. She's already so close to you."

Marilyn backed away from the kiss only enough to stammer.

"Um, and then, uh—"

"Yes, of course. Oh, you want to hear the words. Touch the baby girl's pussy, little baby Mare. Go on. She's a very soft little baby."

Marilyn lowered a hand below the water and when she found her sister, Sophia gasped softly.

"Yes, good girl. Fia? Your pretty sister has a sweet pussy too. Be a good little girl and show her how much you love it. You do want to be a good girl, don't you?"

Sophia nodded, her big blue eyes focused on Widow as she got her hand under the water.

"Say it, then, pretty little girl."

Sophia kept watching Widow and said, "I do want—"

"Oh, no, not to me. Tell her."

Sophia turned toward her sister, who was already trembling from the soft touching between her thighs.

"Sis, I—"

"Whisper in her ear, baby girl Fia. Very close in the baby's ear."

Sophia leaned closer, until her lips were brushing against her sister's ear, then she whispered, "I want to be your very good girl."

Marilyn didn't wait to be told.

"Sissy," she whispered in Sophia's ear, "Be a good little girl for me."

"Aw," said Widow, "that's so sweet. Now, look at me, both of my precious little babies."

They did, cheek to cheek, each with a hand under the water.

"Keep your eyes on me," Widow said as she opened the vest. "Think about your lips here, on my nipples, while each of you gives your sister just a finger or two. Oh, better make it two. Be good little girls and wiggle them right into each other. Mm, it's so warm in there for you."

Sophia blinked hard at feeling Marilyn's fingers probing her, and Marilyn gasped when she felt her sister's fingers.

"Remember how it feels," Widow said, "to be my sweet little girls. My baby girls have no reason to ever stop touching each other. Mm, such delightful little girls."

*　*　*

"Enough," Risk said as he stood up, but he staggered a little step and reached back for the arm of his chair.

"Easy there, big guy," said Bentley. "Too much crude whiskey, I think. You should probably just sit for another minute or two."

He reached a hand out for Risk's hip and gave him a shove back into his seat. His hand found the bottle, and he poured more into Risk's glass, then held it over his lap.

"This'll help. Just a bit more. Come on."

Risk grumbled but accepted the glass, then tipped it back for only a small amount. As soon as he'd lowered it, Bentley poured more.

"Dan," Bentley said to Risk, "was telling us all about those zombie characters. Remember them? I want to hear more about those zany scientists. I mean, Risk, who were these people? What did they think they were doing?"

Risk set his glass on the table and stood and when Bentley tried to make him sit again, he brushed his hand aside.

"Stop. Save my seat."

He began a slow walk toward the spa room, and Bentley leaned closer to Dan and said, "That was actually kind of funny."

"Hey, Risk!" Bentley called out, and Risk stopped to look.

The vampire held up Risk's glass and said, "You'd better take this. Old Dan, here, might drink it for himself."

Dan laughed and said, "Yeah. Yeah, I might."

Risk was still watching when Bentley fought to contain his laughter said, "Don't make me say it. Just don't."

"Say it," said Dan. "Go ahead!"

He pointed at Dan, looked at Risk, and said, "He might inhale it!" Risk grumbled and began the walk back for his drink.

* * *

Widow heard Bentley's loud voice from down the hall outside the spa room and quietly pried the door open enough to look. She waited, peeking through a narrow slit at the closed door to the main recreation room. After thirty seconds, not seeing anyone approaching, she laughed to herself and quietly closed the door.

She leaned away from it and saw that it had a weak locking mechanism, so she engaged it, then turned back to the twins. Their cheeks were still pressed together, and both of them were panting softly.

Widow took a step closer to where she could see the water, and she saw the ripples and waves from two arms moving just enough.

"Such good little girls. So sweet to touch each other for me."

She walked right up to the side of the tub and knelt, then reached a hand out for each. She touched her fingertips to the wet skin on their necks, rubbing both of them softly.

"Mare," she said, and Marilyn raised her eyebrows a bit.

"Dearest little Fia loved doing this for me. She was such a darling little girl for me. Watch."

Widow leaned toward Sophia and extended her tongue. Marilyn watched her sister whimper softly, then part her lips and close her eyes, and Widow slipped her tongue between Sophia's lips.

Sophia squeezed it with her lips, which got Widow to moan softly and wiggle it in and out between Sophia's wet lips.

After ten seconds of that, Widow backed away, and Sophia kept her eyes closed, licked her lips, and swallowed repeatedly.

"Mm," she said, then kissed Sophia's forehead, leaving a wet spot. "Such a tight little hole you made for me."

She rested her cheek against Sophia and smiled at Marilyn.

"She loved it. She loved what I called it too. Would you like to know what we called that, sweet little Mare?"

Marilyn nodded.

Widow leaned close enough to touch noses with Marilyn.

"We called that our sweet little fucking. Little baby Fia loved having her lips fucked like that. You would, too, wouldn't you?"

Marilyn nodded, then held still when her lips could reach Widow's tongue. And she, like her sister had, eagerly sucked Widow's poisons just as long as she could.

Widow backed away and said, "Mm, such sweet little fuckings for such sweet little baby girls. Wouldn't you both love that so much more if you were helpless? Wouldn't you love to be sweet, helpless little baby girls for me?"

Marilyn groaned and nodded, and she kept busy between her sister's thighs.

"Sucking my tongue is such a good thing for you to do. You've both gotten a very good taste of me already. Soon, I'll give you both so much more. We'll have so much time and privacy for all sorts of delicious things."

She looked into each pair of blue eyes for a moment.

"Cruel things too. Little girls like you would love some very cruel things when you're helpless for me. You won't ever want any of it to stop."

She kept rubbing around their necks and eased them to face each other.

"I have so much more to give to my precious twin babies. You'll eagerly taste me in so many ways."

She gently moved them closer to each other and smiled at their lips joining as they locked themselves into a very deep kiss.

"So precious. Such tasty little girls, kissing and touching each other in a hot bubble bath."

She reached in, under the water, and felt what Sophia's hand was doing with her sister.

"Oh, that's so nice. Yes, Fia. Touch her so softly. Very slowly for little baby Mare."

She shifted her hand over to between Sophia's thighs, felt around, then said, "Oh, Mare. Three fingers. Such a daring baby girl. You'd surely want to bite the baby girl if I told you to."

She brought her hand out of the water, then fussed with their hair as they waited, cheek to cheek as she knelt beside the tub.

"Yes, I'm sure you would, little Mare."

She nudged Sophia to tip her head back, then moved Marilyn so that her lips were at her sister's neck.

"Kiss her. Kiss where she's already been bitten so many times."

Widow rubbed her fingertips up and down the bare, wet skin of their backs as Marilyn gently kissed Sophia's neck.

"Good, little Mare. She tastes so good. Open your mouth, sweet little girl. Touch your sharp teeth to her."

Marilyn groaned and opened wide, her teeth about to chew into Sophia's throat.

"Yes, just like that. Oh, such a cruel thing. But you both see how good it would feel."

She tipped their heads apart and said, "Soon, little Mare. Oh, girls, when he have our special time together."

She kissed each of their cheeks, then stood, looking down on them as they kissed and pleasured each other, each having taken in a large dose of her poisons.

"When we have time, we'll have a cruel little blond baby girl and a dark-haired little girl that loves to be the victim more than anything. And we'll all be lost in such a deep orgasm that'll never end."

Widow took two steps backwards, back toward the door, then turned and walked the rest of the way, being sure that her heels could be heard by the twins in the tub.

* * *

With his drink in his hand, Risk again walked toward the spa room.

Bentley called to him again.

"Hey, Risk! How about a refill?"

He didn't turn around, and he didn't walk back to them. He kept going until he got his hand firmly on the doorknob and swung in the door.

He grumbled at seeing a hallway with many doors spaced evenly along each side, and he turned to look back at Dan.

"Hey," he said.

Dan looked up, saw Risk's confused expression, and said, "Bubble bath? Third door on the left."

* * *

Widow shook water off of her arm, then quietly unlocked the door.

A second later, the knob turned, the door swung in, and Risk towered over her, scowling.

"What are you doing?"

She answered in a voice without honey or anything else flowing.

"Me? What have you been doing? Those darling twins called for you, and you just kept drinking?"

She shook her head and walked out, past Risk as he glared at her and grumbled.

Then, he looked toward the girls, both wet and soapy and turned to see who had come into the room.

But they were sitting quite close together in their hot, soapy bath.

And they didn't look like talking was on their minds at all.

Chapter 50 – Where the Hell Am I Now?

"So. You two are alright?"

Sophia sighed deeply, staring at him without answering. He squinted at her for a few seconds, then focused on Marilyn's eyes.

She blinked slowly, then closed her eyes with a smile.

"Uh, you called me."

Sophia smirked weakly and said, "Um, Widow helped. Didn't she, Sis?"

"Mm-hmm. Oh, yes, she did."

"With?"

"Uh," Sophia said as she looked around lazily, "with . . . the bubble bath stuff."

He looked past them at a small plastic bottle sitting nearby on a ledge.

"You can reach it?"

"I'm reaching it," Marilyn said, with her hand busy between Sophia's thighs.

"She means that we can reach it now."

"I'm so close to . . . reaching things," Marilyn said with a soft giggle.

Risk looked from one to the other and reached up to scratch his head.

"Well, good. She helped."

"Oh, yes," said Marilyn. "Mm-hmm."

Risk looked back at the open door, then again at the twins.

"You two feel alright?"

"I'm just tired. It's been a lot."

"Sissy's right. Me too. Long day."

"The bath helps?"

Marilyn giggled softly and said, "It feels very good to get clean. Very good. Doesn't it, Sissy?"

"Uh . . . yep. I, uh . . . yep."

"I'll go, then."

"No, you can stay," Sophia said.

"Yes, stay," said Marilyn.

"Uh, alright. I thought—"

"We're not shy because you're here," Marilyn said, then shrugged her shoulders after he'd stared at her for a second.

"Not shy. We're just . . . oh, yep."

"Alright," he said, then he turned around, halfway between them and the door, and sat with his back to them.

"Nice of you to give Widow your vest," said Sophia.

"Mm-hmm," said Marilyn. "You have a strong back."

"Nice hair too."

"Uh, thanks."

"You could take back your vest, though," said Sophia. "Widow doesn't mind being all, um, topless and—"

"She has very nice breasts, Sissy. Very nice."

Risk puffed up his cheeks with a deep breath, then let it seep out.

"Doesn't she?"

"Um . . . yeah, Mare."

Sophia moaned softly, quickly turned it into a laugh, and said, "And her legs and her—"

"Hey! I, um, I'll tell you about my parents," said Risk.

"Oh, we kind of met your mom," said Marilyn.

"Not your father, though."

"No, Fia. But I just did."

"Oh, that's wonderful. Do you look like him? Is he nice?"

"No, Mare. Not nice."

"Well," said Sophia, "this place is kind of rough on everyone."

"Not us, Sissy. We're very soft and smooth."

"Oh. Oh, you're right. Yeah, we really are. Soapy too."

"Mm-hmm."

Risk coughed and kept his eyes on the door.

"We're after that madman. Remember?"

"I remember. It's not fun."

"No, Fia. I found him."

"Wow," Marilyn said slowly. "You found the madman and your father all while I was busy with zombeings and Sissy was doing all kinds of romantic things with Widow?"

"Romantic? Huh. I didn't tell you half of those things, Sis."

"Well, I didn't tell you all about my times in the zombie kingdom."

"That's what you're calling their place?"

Marilyn shrugged, then caused some splashing.

"Shh, Sissy. Don't worry about that right now."

Sophia tipped back her head and closed her eyes.

Smiling, she said, "Alright. No, I sure won't."

Marilyn gave her sister another quick touch, splashing more, then said, "You found both of them, Risk?"

"Yeah, Mare. They're the same."

Sophia laughed softly, shook her head at the splashing water, and said, "Same as what? Same as how you remembered them or something?"

Risk said, "I've never met either. They're the same man."

* * *

Widow sat on the chair next to Dan's couch, with Bentley using a chair on the other side of him. Both had watched her slow strut back from the spa room, Dan with an intense stare and Bentley with a goofy, dazed one.

"How are they?"

"They're doing well, Bentley. It was good that I had a few moments to, um, speak with them."

457

"What about?" said Dan. "Oh, hey, did the water get warm enough for their bath?"

"Yes," said Widow. "They're having a delightful time together in their hot, soapy bath."

She watched him squirming in his seat.

"They, uh, they're both, um—"

"Yes, Dan. And you must know that the tub isn't very large, so those two gorgeous twin girls have to sit so close together."

He swallowed hard.

"In the hot water."

His head started to shake slowly.

"And they're all bubbly too. So much smooth skin all wet and bubbly."

His breaths were snorting weakly out of all six of his nostrils.

She smiled, looking into his eyes, and said, "You don't get too many pretty girls here, do you?"

"Uh-uh. No. Not like before. But that was—"

"A long, long time ago?"

He nodded quickly and said, "Yeah. Oh, God. Long time."

She got up, took a few steps, letting her heels strike the floor, and sat next to him. His hand was fidgeting on the cushion next to him, so she reached down and covered it with hers.

She let her voice pour out like molasses spiked with a love potion.

"There, there," she said. "Poor little spa manager man."

"Yeah. Uh-huh. That's me."

She rubbed her fingertips all over his hand for a few seconds, took a quick look to see Bentley smiling at the sight of it, then reached up for Dan's cheek.

She began rubbing his skin all over with her soft fingertips. He shook for a second, then tipped his head to kiss her hand.

She saw what he was doing and let him find her fingers instead. He let them into his mouth and immediately started sucking them.

"Mm, that's nice. It's so good to suck, isn't it?"

He nodded, kept sucking, and looked into her eyes.

"It feels so good. Don't even think of stopping."

Around the fingers in his mouth, he grunted, "Uh-uh."

She reached out with her other hand for his cheek, and she rubbed and caressed what she could with a very wide nose in the way.

"Good, Dan," she said as she leaned in closer.

His breaths were fast and getting frantic.

"I like to suck too. Did you know that about me? That I like to suck?"

He shook his head and grunted.

She leaned in toward his neck, holding his gaze the entire way.

"I do so love to suck. I'd love to suck for you. Can I suck for you, Dan?"

"Uh-huh," he grunted past the fingers in his mouth, and his eyes scanned all around her face, dwelling on her lips.

Then, he looked lower at where Risk's leather vest had opened wide. Widow's breasts were swaying softly as she wiggled herself closer to him, and his eyes never left her prominent nipples until . . .

Until she'd leaned close enough to sink her fangs into the old, leathery skin of his neck.

He twitched once, stopped moving altogether, then resumed his sucking on her fingers with even more urgency.

Widow, at his neck, withdrew her fangs only for a moment to shift her bite over and leave more room on the old mutant's neck. Then, she drove them back in, sucking out his blood and flooding him with her poisons.

And on the other side of his neck, Bentley had also settled in, sharp vampire fangs easily piercing deep into the man's neck.

Widow reached over, searched until she'd found what she wanted between Bentley's legs, and began to give him something with a slow, steady motion that made him even crazier for the man's blood.

All while she was furtively feeding him more poisons, too, and cementing his fate as her replacement for Igor.

* * *

At hearing the serious tone of Risk's revelation about his father, the girls stopped their fun playing underwater, and both reached up to hold the tub's rim.

"Risk," said Sophia. "That's horrible. Are you alright?"

"I never knew him. But now, I know something."

"What's that?"

"Why I try so hard, Mare."

"With what?"

"To be a good man, Fia."

"Huh? What do you mean?" said Marilyn.

"I met my father today."

He paused, and the twins looked at each other, then back at Risk.

"And I knew what he's always been."

"Uh, what's that?"

They watched him sigh out a deep breath.

"Fallen."

Sophia squinted at her sister, and Marilyn only shrugged.

"He turned his back on being good."

"I suppose so," said Sophia. "Raped your mom."

"And now, he's a madman too."

"Yeah, Mare."

"Oh," said Sophia. "I get it. You kind of inherited that from him so, you're kind of half—"

"Yeah. Something else."

"Mom was human. Is human," said Marilyn.

She smirked at her sister, then added, "Mostly. But your dad isn't so, you're half—"

"Yeah. No wonder I have to be good."

"We want to be good too," Marilyn said, then leaned closer to whisper in her sister's ear, "Good little girls."

Sophia was already close, so she whispered right back, "For Widow. Yeah, good little—"

"Baby girls, Sissy," she whispered, "and she likes us to kiss," then she rubbed her cheek along her sister's until their lips met.

Sometimes looking toward Risk, seeing that he was still facing away, and probably brooding, they continued a very soft, quiet kiss. The seconds dragged on, and they were very careful to not make a sound.

They backed away from each other when Risk said, "I don't know how to be good, though."

"Uh, that's not easy," said Marilyn.

Sophia leaned closer and whispered in Marilyn's ear, "Sure, it is. Just give yourself to Widow."

Marilyn whispered softly, "Easy for us, Sissy. We just need to be her little baby girls."

"Twin baby girls."

"Oh, soft too."

"Mm," whispered Sophia as she felt along the inside of one of Marilyn's thighs, "very soft."

Marilyn was getting closer along between Sophia's thighs too.

"Mm-hmm. Two very soft little twin baby girls."

"Mm. For Widow."

They met in an easy, quiet kiss just as their hands found where they'd been before, and they picked up where they'd left off.

"What's with the whispering?"

They ended their kiss. But only their kiss.

"Oh, just, um, wondering if the water's still warm enough."

"Yes, like Sissy said. Hey, Risk? Maybe it's just impossible to be good,"—she smiled at her sister—"for most people in a horrible place like this."

"You might be right. Yeah."

K Kat nosed the door open farther and padded her way toward Risk, and Marilyn and Sophia stopped everything.

Everything except what they were still feeling inside from Widow's poisons.

They watched with barely concealed smiles as the big mountain lion lay beside Risk and rested her head on his lap.

* * *

"Well, I think we're pretty well cleaned up."

"Glad you had a bath, Fia."

"Sis is still kind of funny, though, with all those silly lines all over her. Sis, you'll have to tell me exactly how those got there."

"Oh, uh, I don't think so, Sissy. Not all of it. Risk?"

"Yeah, Mare?"

"Promise you won't tell? Not my proudest moment."

"Well, shit, now I really want to hear."

"Sorry, Fia. Have to respect Mare's wishes."

"Huh. Fine. I'll probably still tell her everything I've been through."

"Why?"

"Oh, uh, I don't know. Maybe it'll, I don't know, help me recover?"

"Good one, Sissy. I'm sure it will. Probably more like reminiscing, though."

Sophia watched Risk rubbing around K Kat's ears for half a minute. Marilyn joined her.

"Sis, it doesn't look like Kenzie will ever recover."

"No. Not looking good."

Without looking at them, Risk handed something toward them.

Marilyn stood, dripping onto the floor, and Sophia patted her ass quietly, getting a surprised yip from her.

"Oh, it's a bottle of something," Marilyn said. "What is this, Risk?"

"'Joose."

"What kind of juice? Oh, wait—Zoojoose?"

"Yeah. I tried it before. It didn't work so well."

"What happened?"

He coughed.

"Uh, it, um, didn't last."

"Let's try it, Sissy. Maybe Kenzie can come back, even for a while?"

"Yeah, Sis. We should try."

She leaned close to Marilyn and whispered in her ear, "Would Widow like her too?"

Marilyn whispered back, "She's not a twin like we are. She might like her, but I think she loves us."

"She does love us, Sis. We're special. Still, though, it could be fun, right?"

"Okay. Yes. Let's do it."

"Risk," Marilyn said after clearing her throat, "we're going to try with K Kat."

"Now?"

"Uh-huh. Don't peek."

"That's funny, Sis."

Sophia stood, too, and dripped first in the tub, then on the floor when she and Marilyn approached the lion lying near Risk.

They each took a side and stooped down, sometimes giggling and glancing at Risk, who still sat facing the door.

"Give her a few drops, Sissy. Too much might not be good either."

"Right. Okay."

Sophia coaxed the lioness onto her back, like they were playing, and uncapped the bottle.

"Sis, scratch her belly or something. Keep her distracted."

"Okay," Marilyn said, then she started first under the lion's chin, then worked her way down.

"Such a good lion," she said. "Such a good girl."

Sophia froze and stared at her.

"Uh, maybe say something different, Sis."

"Oh. I think I understand. Okay. Good lion. Such a good she-lion. How's that, Sissy?"

"Better. Alright, K Kat, open up."

She poked around the lion's snout and got her to open and close her mouth. Timing it just right, Sophia got a quick stream of the stuff into her mouth, and she swallowed it all, then licked her chops.

"Alright," Sophia said, petting the lion's head and rubbing around her ears. "Do your thing."

They watched and waited, but K Kat only turned her eyes, looking at each of them.

"Remind her," said Risk.

"Huh?"

"Mare, remind Kenzie. Tell her."

"Oh, I get it. Okay."

She laid herself beside the lion, then Sophia took the other side. They hugged her like a plush pillow and began talking with their mouths up close near her ears.

"We met you at the Prism, Kenzie. Remember that?"

"Sissy liked you right from the start," Marilyn said with a giggle. "Okay, me too. You were too hot for that bar."

"Then, we took you to Dayzee's mansion. You had me pinned down upstairs, and we—"

"Somehow took off all of your clothes. Uh-huh," said Marilyn. "Oh. Except for your high heels."

"Yours were red," Sophia said, her smile fading. "Those were hot."

Marilyn stopped smiling, too, and said, "We were all naked together so many times. Like when we all tried on those sexy little babydolls."

Sophia was leaning closer, like she was about to kiss the lion.

Marilyn said, "We all wore just lingerie and heels. I'll never forget that. Do you remember?"

Sophia was close, and the lion shook and shivered and went blurry for a second.

When the blurriness cleared, Marilyn and Sophia were lying next to Kenzie, who wore only Bentley's polo shirt.

Sophia closed the distance and kissed her cheek.

"Mm, me too," Marilyn said, then kissed her other cheek.

"Oh my God," Kenzie said, already starting to breathe more heavily. "Where the hell am I now?"

Sophia backed away a little and said, "Between two naked Kildare Killers."

"No high heels, though, Sissy. Oh, and maybe we're the Kool Killer Kuties again. Kenzie, can you stay with us? Or do you—"

"Have to be a lion some more?" Sophia finished for her.

Kenzie gave Marilyn a quick kiss on her lips, then turned toward Sophia. Their lips met, and it wasn't a quick kiss.

Marilyn let go enough to clap her hands silently, with a renewed smile.

Kenzie ended the kiss and said, "I don't want to be a lion anymore! I want to go home!"

She started to shake as her eyes darted all around the room.

"How is this happening to me? It's been crazy since that fire in Dayzee's house. I was screaming, the lions were screaming, and I don't know what happened next! Where are we?"

Her shaking turned into a seizure, and Risk finally turned to look.

"Hey, take her shirt."

"Oh, Risk," Marilyn said with a stern shake of her head. "Shame on you. It already barely covers all of her goodies."

"Really, Risk," said Sophia, "she's already kind of—"

"No. Get it quick. It's Bentley's."

"Huh? Well, sure," said Sophia, and she and Marilyn raised Kenzie's arms and pulled the shirt up and off of her.

"Oh my goodness," Marilyn said. "She's a very good girl."

Sophia, her eyes on Kenzie's breasts, said, "Sis, maybe we need to try harder. Know what I mean?"

"Oh, I think. To keep her Kenzie, you mean?"

"Yeah. No time to argue."

They both leaned their faces toward Kenzie's breasts, which were rising and falling from her heaving chest. The seizures were getting more violent.

"It's for Kenzie, Sissy."

"Uh, sure, Sis. Yep."

They leaned in for a kiss and more, but each got short brown cat hairs stuck to their lips.

"Yuck!" Marilyn said and spit them off to one side.

Sophia backed away from the cat, laughing, and sat back on her heels.

"Oh, well. K Kat is nice too."

She tossed Bentley's shirt toward Risk. He caught it and smiled at them.

"She's still a good girl."

Sophia shrugged and drew in a slow breath as she stared at her sister.

Marilyn nodded and whispered, "Soon, Sissy. You're a very good little girl too."

"We're twins, Sis," Sophia whispered. "Little twin baby girls."

"What?" said Risk.

They turned to him just as K Kat rolled over and up onto her paws.

"Oh, nothing."

Chapter 51 – We're Hiking to the Reactor

Widow slid her fangs out of Dan's neck and leaned back enough to look at him. She'd finished with her speaking like dripping honey.

"Hmm. He didn't have much to begin with. I like soft and tender so much better."

Still, she bit into him again in a fresh spot. Dan only stared across the room, a weak hint of a smile on his face.

Bentley hardly removed his fangs and mostly spoke around them.

"I'm getting a lot of it. Is that wrong?"

Widow laughed softly as she backed away again to watch the vampire working on the spa manager's neck.

"It's good that you ask. You have my permission to drain it all."

Bentley groaned and leaned in harder, making sucking sounds and pushing the man back deeper into the couch cushions.

She watched him for a moment, still rubbing him with her hand through his open zipper.

"It feels good, doesn't it?"

Bentley nodded and didn't stop.

"You're different. I'm able to give you a lot of my sweet poisons quickly, not like those two delicate, precious little girls. You already have so much in you that I can tell you, and you still won't stop."

He didn't stop.

"Another second or two, and you'll be my slave forever. My last one was a nuisance and got himself killed before he could kill himself like I commanded. Can you follow orders?"

He nodded and kept sucking Dan's blood.

"Will you devote your miserable existence to me?"

He moaned and sucked harder. And she got more vigorous with her hand.

"Good. So very good. Move aside."

She nudged him off of Dan's neck, then sat on the old mutant's lap, straddling him.

"Watch," she told Bentley as she opened Risk's black leather vest and slipped it halfway down her arms and back. "See how wonderful? When you serve me well, you'll be rewarded with some quiet time of sucking more sweet poisons from me. Would you like that?"

"Oh, hell yeah. Yeah."

"You know it'll taste so much better after I've bound you up completely, don't you?"

"Mm-hmm. Oh, yeah. I need to be tied up."

"Yes. Suck, then, my faithful slave. Just a taste for now."

Bentley moaned and took a nipple between his lips and sucked so hard that his cheeks were drawing in.

"Mm, such good poisons for you. It's your first time with a steady, constant orgasm. No more sudden, explosive orgasms which don't last nearly long enough, you unworthy slave man."

He looked up at her, then focused on her other nipple, but she stopped him after only a few seconds.

"Good boy. But you need much more of my very tasty poisons. Rise up. Give me your throat."

Bentley got up on his knees by her side and tipped his head to give her plenty of room to bite.

She leaned forward until her breasts were squeezed against Dan's face, the outer two nostrils on each.

"You couldn't run now if you wanted to," she said to Bentley, sometimes laughing. "So, I'll tell you just for my own amusement: I've known all along that you are the vampire that's been providing my meals and picking up the clean blood. You ratted me out and spoiled my long feast with my tender baby lover girl. Now, you're just my slave. And I'll be sure you die a horrible death. When I'm done with you."

Then, she bit into Bentley's neck, sucking his vampire blood and giving him much more poison at once than she ever could have given to either of the Kildare Killers.

*   *   *

Risk held the door, ready to open it, and didn't watch Sophia wrap the old blanket over herself or Marilyn slipping back on Ham's dress shirt with a missing right sleeve.

"We're ready," Sophia said.

Risk turned and was about to speak, then Marilyn said, "Oh, just a second. Our heels, Sissy."

"Oh, yeah. Alright."

They leaned on each other for balance and got them on and tied around their ankles.

"Now?" Risk said, grinning.

They swayed their hips and clicked their heels as they strutted toward him and the open door.

The mountain lion watched their long legs as they approached Risk, then she followed after them.

Risk, smiling, leaned out to watch the three of them traveling the hallway toward Widow, Bentley, and Dan.

*   *   *

Sophia was the first to strut into the main room, and she let her heels announce her arrival. But she stopped immediately, causing Marilyn to bump her from behind, then the lion collided with Marilyn.

"What?" Risk said from farther behind.

"Uh, you'd better get out here."

He gently but forcefully moved all of them aside and saw what had frozen Sophia in her tracks.

Widow was seated on Dan's lap with Risk's black leather vest halfway down her back. They had a side view from the spa room, and they watched her rubbing her breasts across the pale mutant's face.

He only looked up with a weak grin and eyes about to shut.

Kneeling just past her was Bentley, and Widow's black mane shifted slowly as she sucked at the vampire's throat.

"Dammit."

Risk stomped toward them, with K Kat close enough to stay in contact with his leg, but Marilyn and Sophia stayed back, just outside the doorway leading to the spa.

Marilyn dragged in a deep breath and said softly. "Sissy, look at Widow."

"I'm looking, Sis. Damn. From the side, she, uh . . ."

"You wish you were that old mutant, don't you?"

"Uh, maybe not the dead part. Or the mutant part. Wait. Is he dead?"

"Close, at least. I wonder if he—"

"Yeah, Sis. I'm sure of it. He's probably feeling the best orgasm he ever had."

"I want the best orgasm," Marilyn said with a pout.

"Even if you don't survive?"

"Um . . . ask me when I'm having it, Sissy."

Sophia laughed and said, "The answer then would be no. A big no."

"How can you be so sure?"

"Been there. I didn't want it to stop, no matter what."

"Oh, my."

Risk had reached the tight group involved with biting and killing, and he hesitated, reaching for one, then the other, then leaving his hands on his hips.

"Fuck."

"Sissy, what if we could somehow just have sex with her, then she—"

"I'm not even sure she's a she, Sis. Not completely."

"Oh. That's kind of scary. Kind of exciting, too, though. Maybe."

"You'd know for sure if you were all tied up, hanging upside down with her."

"Oh, Sissy, that's how it was? Tell me more."

"Later. Or maybe you'll see for yourself."

Marilyn clapped silently and whispered, "She said she'd tie us together, kissing. Sissy, she wants all three of us together in a—"

"Neverending orgasm. Yeah, Sis."

Risk scoffed and grabbed both of Widow's arms, then paused again. He let go with one, then grabbed her mane and pulled it back. She turned enough to bare her bloody fangs and hiss at him.

"Oh, fuck," he said and tossed her roughly to the floor, where she scurried to sit up against the nearest chair and glared at him.

He pointed at her, eliciting another hiss, then pushed Bentley to the side, and he tumbled clumsily off of the couch and lay on the floor.

Risk leaned each way, looking into the heavy eyes of Dan as blood trickled from all of the holes in his neck. He slapped him a few times, and Dan shook his head and looked up at him.

"Shit," he said. "I think I'm about dead."

"Maybe not," said Risk.

Behind him, Widow laughed, then said, "I took a lot from him."

Risk turned enough to scowl at her.

Marilyn whispered, "What did she take from you, Sissy?"

"Blood. It was more about what she gave me."

"Mm-hmm. Yes."

"And all the things she did to me."

"More than just hanging you up with her? Was that like a trapeze?"

"Oh, Sis, we couldn't have been any closer, and she trimmed my nails, and that was so that I could—"

They looked toward the commotion when Bentley found some energy and stood, still wobbly, and staggered himself to stand between Risk and Widow.

Risk stood and faced them both, and Dan slumped back deeper into his couch.

Risk said to the vampire, "You killed him."

"Pesky nuisance to try to live without enough blood. Poor chap."

Risk had a view of Widow when she stretched her arms out and arched her back. His eyes got pulled down to watch her breasts, and he didn't look up at the black eyes that he knew were focused on him.

She relaxed and said, "It's more what I gave him. This one,"—she tipped her head toward her slave—"got a lot too."

"What?"

"Uh, nothing. Nothing at all. Just my intoxicating beauty."

Sophia whispered, "Her poisons, Sis. That's what she meant."

"Oh, Sissy, we sucked some of that from her."

"Uh-huh. We sucked at the same time."

Marilyn sighed and whispered, "It's kind of fun to be someone's sweet little baby girl."

"Uh, yep. That and that orgasm. Damn."

They looked up and saw that Risk had been watching them, scratching at his chin.

"I should kill both of you," Risk said to Widow and Bentley, and they both only scoffed.

"No, don't!" said Sophia.

Risk turned her way with a scowl.

"She meant, um, it's just not good to kill, that's all."

He squinted at them for a second, then focused again on the vampire blocking him from Widow.

"I won't let you," Bentley said and held his arms wide to shield Widow.

"You're the hero now?"

"Just for her. Sure. Now, I can, uh . . . oh dear."

He held his head with both hands and staggered without taking a step.

Risk grumbled and looked toward the twins. They looked up from Widow to meet his gaze.

"Clothes," he said, letting his eyes scan them down then up again.

He turned to Dan, who had lost consciousness again, and slapped him a couple of times.

"Dan."

His eyes creaked open, and he said, "Huh?"

"Clothes. Where?"

He pointed toward the entry doorway from the hall, then his arm fell.

Risk slapped him again.

"Which floor?"

"Basement."

"Thanks," Risk said, then he watched Dan's head turn slowly toward Widow.

Barely able to speak, Dan managed to say, "More . . . bites."

Widow ignored Risk's confused look and said to the man, "You've had enough. It's your time. Just die."

Risk again looked toward the twins for a second, and they both shrugged.

He looked down at the polo shirt that he'd dropped nearby when he'd first grabbed Widow. Leaning, he picked it up, then tossed it toward Bentley.

The vampire moved too slowly to do anything but let it cover his head.

"Ooh," said Sophia.

"Mm, I know what you're thinking. Widow told me she'd cover my head too. Just like she did to you, Sissy. Did she cover it real good?"

"Yeah, Sis. She was kind of cruel about some of it too. Oh, she sure loved wrapping me up tight."

"She said that too. She said she might make us be cruel to each other. Would you? Would you be cruel to me if Widow made you?"

"Uh, maybe. I don't know. I'm more—"

Marilyn giggled softly and said, "She said you like being just a sweet little victim. Is that true?"

"I, um, I—"

"Aw, I'd be cruel to you, Sissy. Oh, yes," Marilyn said with a giggle. "I'd bite you too. I almost bit you in the tub."

They looked away from the vampire peeling a polo shirt off of his head.

"I'm so sure I'd bite you, Sissy."

"Because you'd get a bigger orgasm?"

"Mm-hmm. And I'd be giving yours a boost too," Marilyn said and clapped her hands quietly.

Then, Risk said to Widow and the vampire, "We're leaving. Not you two."

Widow, still seated, squirmed out of Risk's leather vest and handed it up to him.

He took it, still glaring at her, and she said, "Unless you plan to touch these breasts for me, I'll need clothing too."

"No touching."

She smiled up at him and said, "Hmm. Lips, then? A tongue?"

He took the hand that she'd extended up to him and lifted her up onto her high heels, saying, "None of that."

She looked toward the twins and took a deep breath for them to watch. Then, she rubbed her hands down over her ass, covered only in tiny, very thin black panties, and felt all around her thighs.

"Then, let's get some clothes."

She looked at Bentley and said, "You can stay."

He nodded, then bowed and stayed down.

"Risk. He can dispose of the mutant corpse while we shop."

Risk grumbled as he looked around the room at all of them, including the dead one. He was still shaking his head when Widow turned and strutted toward the twins, who were still huddled close together near the door.

She stopped a few steps from them, spent a lot of time looking at their legs, then into their eyes. After returning their smiles, she spun around again, then shook back her mane.

"The three of us will shop. You can help the vampire with the body."

Risk squinted at her, a look of disbelief on his face.

"I'll pick out some very nice things for them. Something suitable for two very pretty little twin girls. Matching outfits."

She turned just enough to see their chests rising with their deeper breaths, then she faced Risk again.

"They'll need help getting dressed too. I'll even make it fun for them."

"No. You'll—"

"Ask them," she said, grinning at him. "You're not their boss, are you?"

"No, I'm not."

He scowled at Widow then looked past her. He didn't get an answer right away.

Marilyn leaned toward her sister and said, "He really isn't our boss, Sissy."

"I'd rather have Widow's orgasms bossing me around."

"And me being cruel. Don't forget that."

"I can't forget that, Sis. Yep. We'll get our chance."

"Yes, Sissy. To be her sweet little babies."

"Sweet little *twin* babies, Sis. Yep."

"We might need your help, Risk," Sophia said in a louder voice. "You know, moving heavy things around. Stuff like that."

"Okay, Mare, Fia. Let's go."

*　*　*

They'd walked quietly down many more flights of metal stairs and reached the bottom, where a rusted double door looked like it had been quietly rotting, undisturbed, for many years.

"Go," Risk said and gave Widow's back a push.

She put her hands on her hips and said over her shoulder, "I have led the way, four of us and an unruly cat. No, you go. I'm not entering first."

"Why not?"

"You're the big, strong hero. It's your job."

Risk turned to look at the twins, and they were grinning, then they shrugged. Even K Kat seemed to shrug.

He turned back around, nudged Widow to one side, and grumbled as he swung the door open with a pained squeal. The door opened to nothing but blackness, and Risk fumbled around inside until he'd found a light switch, which he tipped up. A room that spanned the width and length of the entire building lit up with dim ceiling lights.

Mismatched tables were placed all around in no particular order, each covered in boxes and bags. Along the walls, shelves held more. He took a step inside, looked around, then chose a direction and took two more steps.

Widow grinned and closed the door as far as possible without rattling any of its mechanisms, then she turned to the twins.

"I know you two are special," she said. "You, Fia, should be dead by now. But you've healed already."

Sophia nodded and said, "Fine, you figured it out. We're not from Earth."

"Huh. That explains it. So, my poisons don't have such dire results with you. Which means,"—she looked into each pair of blue eyes—"you can—"

"You tried to kill me," Sophia said without a trace of a smile.

Widow glared at her, then she let it soften into a modest grin.

"I didn't ask to be this way. Should I just lie down and die?"

Sophia sighed and looked at the floor.

Marilyn said, "You were just surviving. Sissy and I understand that."

Sophia didn't look up, but she said, "I suppose you're okay with those zombies, then, huh, Sis?"

"Oh," Marilyn said, then looked down too. "Maybe it really is this world, Sissy. It's just bad."

"Yes, Mare," said Widow. "You can't blame me, I hope. The point is, we can have all the fun without the lasting effects. How about that?"

Sophia looked up quickly.

"Yes," said Widow, "you remember how it felt."

She blended a little stream of fine, warm honey into her voice.

"No matter how bad it was, baby Fia, you liked how it felt."

"You mean, Sis and I could—"

"Recall how it felt when I'd caused everything inside you to stop. Oh, you were wrapped up so nice and tight. You know that you've never been more beautiful than right then."

Sophia took two deep breaths, quickly, then said, "And I—"

The honey flowed, warmer and stickier, as she gazed into Sophia's big blue eyes.

"You were bound into a silent scream. And I touched you and bit you as I pleased."

"And, and I was just—"

"You were all mine, for any cruel, self-serving thing I wished."

"I was so helpless."

"Yes. And you would both feel the same unbelievable—"

The door swung out enough to bump her into taking a few steps.

"Let's go," Risk said while leaning out.

"We just wished that you would be sure it's safe first," Widow said with her voice normal again.

"It's safe."

He moved to one side, held the door open, and the twins and Widow and K Kat entered the storeroom. They all stopped to study everything.

"Bet there's no babydolls, Sissy."

"Nope. Just garbage soldier clothes, probably."

"We're hiking to the reactor," said Risk. "Dress for it."

Widow held up a camouflage tank top and said, "There are plenty of these. What do you think?"

Marilyn sighed and said, "I suppose. It's better than Ham's old shirt."

"Sexier," said her sister. "How about skirts? Are there any—"

"Pants," Risk said. "Over there."

They looked and saw a table stacked with camo trousers of every size.

"Boots," he said, pointing in another direction.

All three women looked that way, then down at their own footwear, which was high-heeled white shoes for Marilyn, black ones for Sophia, and short black boots with high pointy heels for Widow.

"You can't be serious," Sophia said with a scoff. "Sis and I never wear anything but heels."

"Sissy's right. Our fans expect us to—"

Risk grinned and said, "Look around."

"Oh. He's right, Sissy. We don't have any fans here."

"Alright, boots, then," said Sophia. "But we're bringing along my heels."

Risk took a few steps over to another table, rummaged around, then held up a small backpack.

Marilyn sighed and said, "Camouflage for everybody, I guess. Boots too."

"Not Kenzie, though."

"No, Sissy. Her claws would just rip things up anyway."

"Over there," Risk said to Widow, pointing to an area on one side of the room.

"You two," he said to the twins, then pointed the opposite way.

They complied and got dressed. All three put on camo pants, camo tank tops, and dark green boots.

Risk tossed a dark green cap to each of them, too, then placed one on his own head.

* * *

"Sissy, you're still stunning, even in those old army pants."

Marilyn was following close behind Sophia, the two of them leading the party out of the storeroom.

"Thanks, Sis. I hate to admit it, but these boots are kind of comfortable."

Marilyn sighed and said, "Yes. I suppose that's true."

Risk followed them into the hallway with K Kat close by his side. Widow was the last, and she pushed the door shut.

They walked in silence up the steps until they reached ground level.

"You," Risk said, pointing at Widow, "go wherever."

He looked at the twins and said, "We're going to the reactor."

"Oh, right," said Sophia. "To stop that madman."

"I could be of some help," Widow said. "There's nothing here for me anyway. Even that slave isn't worth much."

"And you already killed the mutant."

Risk pointed toward the doors to the lobby, and said, "Back out on the streets, then."

Widow said, "No. I'll go back up there. Maybe take a hot bath."

"It sure was hot enough," Sophia said.

"Bubbly too."

Widow said, "Good. We'll walk up together. You're going to the roof? For that demented balloon ride vehicle?"

"Oh, Risk," said Sophia. "Why don't we just go outside and call that hawk guy down? That's a lot of steps."

"Sissy's right. Even in these unfashionable boots."

"We can do that. Alright."

He looked at Widow and pointed again at the stairs.

Widow sighed, climbed four of them, then turned around again.

She looked at Sophia and said, "I hope to see you again sometime."

Sophia sighed and looked at her boots, but she didn't respond.

Widow focused on Marilyn and said, "I didn't really get a chance to, um, *meet* you."

Marilyn giggled softly and looked down too.

Widow continued, saying, "Not yet, anyway."

She turned and resumed her journey higher up, and they all watched her swaying her hips, her figure still obvious even in the unflattering clothing, until she was out of sight.

"Let's go," Risk said and patted K Kat when she fell in near his leg.

He and the lion led the way through the doorway into the lobby, and they all began walking toward the glass doors to the sidewalk, which looked like they'd been painted black.

"Nice," Sophia said as she scanned around the room. "Every building in this horrible place has a bar."

"I could use a drink," said Marilyn, and Risk and the lion ignored her and kept walking.

"We might need it," she said, watching them walking away.

Risk stopped and turned, then resumed fussing with the big cat's ears.

"We might."

Marilyn clapped while Sophia headed for the bar, carefully looked before stepping behind it, then looked through the bottles.

She held one out, blew dust off of it, then held it out again.

"Is whiskey alright?"

"Good for me, Sissy."

"Good," said Risk, and Sophia hurried to catch up with them.

She stowed the bottle in the lightweight backpack Risk wore, then gasped.

"Oh my God. We never gave Widow back her boots."

"She's got boots."

"No, Risk, not gross army boots. Her sexy black boots."

"They were quite sexy," said Marilyn.

"Too bad," he said as he turned and resumed their walk.

He swung open one of the glass doors, he and K Kat walked through, and Risk held it open for the twins.

"Why, thanks. I think."

Marilyn looked all around and said, "Sissy, I forgot how scary this place is."

"Scary enough inside, too, Sis."

Risk walked farther out and looked up toward the top of the building.

He grumbled while the twins looked up too.

"Uh, where's the balloon?"

"I don't know, Fia."

"Your hawk friend left us here?"

"Seems so, Mare."

He looked one way along the dark street, then the other.

Then, he grumbled and said, "We walk."

He didn't wait for anyone to agree, just picked a direction and started out. The twins walked behind him, a few steps back.

"Sis," Sophia said after they'd walked half a block, "did those zombies say anything to you about any kind of drug?"

"Huh? No, I don't think so. Unless it was in whatever they were feeding me."

"What were they feeding you?"

"I don't know, and they wouldn't say. Just some gooey, slimy stuff."

"Sounds gross," said Sophia. "How'd they get you to eat it?"

"Oh, let's just say that Janie was very persuasive. Why, Sissy, did Widow say something?"

"Yeah, she did. Something called Key S. I don't know if I believe her or—"

Risk stopped abruptly and turned to face them.

"You said Key S?"

"Yeah. Widow mentioned that. Why? You've heard of it?"

"Yeah. Dammit."

He shook his head, then grumbled while turning to resume their trek.

* * *

While walking, watching in every direction for threats, they all heard so many wings flapping that it could have been an explosion, but it didn't fade.

"Run!" Marilyn yelled, but Risk held his hand up.

"No. Wait."

He pointed over the buildings which hid whatever was causing the noise.

They all watched as a cloud of bats rose up, all beating their wings like mad and each holding onto its own cable. They kept themselves apart enough to not get tangled up, but they stayed together, a tight mob of them.

"Oh my goodness," said Marilyn. "What now?"

"That," Risk said.

As the flock gained altitude, a giant dark ball appeared, suspended from all of those individual ropes and cables held by countless bats.

"No way," said Sophia. "That can't be the—"

"Huh. What else could it be, Fia?"

"Oh, it's that madman moon thing? That's what that is?"

No one answered as they watched the frenzied bats lifting it higher into the dark sky.

"Yeah, Mare. They'll tie it up there."

"The moon," said Sophia. "It's their fucking moon?"

"For the nearwolves," said Risk.

"That doesn't sound good," Marilyn said as she looked all around. "Um, where are they, Risk?"

"Everywhere."

"Uh," said Sophia, "that's not good. You mean like—"

Risk held Sophia's gaze as he pointed one way, then another way, then yet another way.

"You can't even count them."

"How could that be?" said Marilyn. "Why are there so many here?"

"I told you before," said Risk. "They don't just kill up there."

He pointed straight up, but he kept looking from one pair of blue eyes to the other.

"They're already killing. Easy enough for them to rape too."

"Oh my," said Marilyn. "They raped and killed all those women up there, then they—"

"Not just women, Mare."

Risk shook his head and turned, leading them through a dark city that would soon be lit by the fake light of a fake moon.

Chapter 52 – I'm Killing Them All, Son

They heard the explosion, a low booming somewhere far in the direction of the burning ocean.

Risk scoffed and said, "Damn storms."

He turned to the girls and said, "Time to hide."

"That's funny, though," Marilyn said. "Where Sissy and I came from, we—"

"Beverly Hills. I remember."

"Yes, under Dayzee's house. But all of us used to say 'damn this' and 'damn that' for all kinds of things. Right, Sissy?"

"Yeah, Sis. It started with 'damn lions,' I think."

They all looked down at K Kat, who was taking turns looking up at each of them.

"Oh, um, not you, though."

Risk said, "That helps, Mare. Still, let's go there."

He pointed toward a narrow alley between two buildings, took both by their arms, and started that way.

"Uh, it's kind of dark in there."

"Yeah, Fia. I'll go in first."

He did, and the lion then the girls followed him just as the first gust hit. Those smaller winds were brief, and they quickly ramped up into howling waves of air that smelled of oil. Some of it slivered off and raced around them and deeper into the alley.

The girls backed in farther toward Risk, so close that the lion yipped and stood up to not get stepped on. They all huddled together until the winds died down, then stopped altogether.

"I kind of hate this place," Marilyn said with a pout. "Damn storms."

Sophia turned enough to face Risk, up close, and said, "See? Like that. That's why we were surprised when you said 'damn reactor' kind of when we first met you. I mean, when we—"

"Sissy, we sure met him already by that time."

"Yeah. Oh, yeah."

"Alright," he said. "We have to move."

"Before the next storm?"

"No, Mare. Before the moon."

"Oh. That's right. Then, the werewolves."

"No, Sis. 'Nearwolves.'"

"Oh. That's even more right. Okay."

They all filed out of the alley, checked each way, then got back to their hike toward the reactor.

"What's that up ahead, Risk?"

The dim streetlights came to an end and beyond the last one, the ground and street gave way to a flat, smooth, black expanse.

"Oil."

"No wonder the place stinks of it."

"Yeah, Fia. There's lot of it."

"So, you just, what? Scoop it up and burn it?"

"Sure. But the reactor's for electric."

"When it's working?"

"Yeah, Fia. Like now."

"Risk? Just what the hell is this place?" said Marilyn. "Mutants and monsters and God knows what else. And a nuclear reactor too?"

"Sis has a point. We haven't been bugging you, but we have time. Really, what the hell?"

He took a few steps before answering.

"No one here knows. People and other things just end up here. You know how."

"Not you, though, right?"

"No, Mare. I was born here. We think it was military a long time ago. Abandoned. We don't know why. Maybe something else long before that."

"God," Sophia said, looking around. "You've been here all your life?"

"Most. Yeah."

"Not all?"

"No, Mare. I got up top sometimes. But I'm used to it here."

"And what do you do all day? Hunt bats?"

"Hunt bats that hunt humans Topside."

"That's disgusting," said Marilyn, frowning. "Oh, does that mean there's a door up there somewhere?"

"We think so. No bat will talk."

Sophia snickered and said, "Try torturing them."

He stopped, they continued a step, then stopped, too, and faced him.

He said, "We're running out of ways."

The girls looked at each other. Marilyn shook her head, but Sophia only shrugged before they turned and continued their hike.

* * *

"Careful," he said. "That could be deep."

Sophia looked at her boots resting in a shallow puddle of oil.

"Sheesh. How deep?"

"Enough to keep you. Let's walk around it."

"Are we close?"

"Yeah, Mare. Look," he said, pointing across the field of oil.

A compact collection of dingy buildings huddled together just beyond a torn chain-link fence. A few lights mounted high on the structures cast a dim glow over most of it.

"Shouldn't there be, I don't know, like towers and things?" said Marilyn. "California has some of those reactor places."

"Most of it is underground."

"People work there?"

"Mutants. Some straight humans. They—"

"He said 'straight humans,' Sissy. That's kind of funny."

"Uh, no, Sis. Not really."

"Oh. Okay."

Risk continued, saying, "Anyone that works there becomes a mutant, some worse than others."

"Ham?"

"Yeah, Ham. It could have been worse for him. The straight humans stay in a shielded control room. The others? They're doomed from day one."

"Why do they stay, then?"

"Food, Mare. What's left of it is stockpiled under them."

"Uh," said Sophia, still careful to avoid swimming in oil, "should I ask what we ate at Ham's?"

Risk grumbled, and they kept walking.

A few seconds later, she said, "Sheesh," softly.

"I was waiting for that, Sissy."

"Hold up," he said, stopping them in a shadowy area. "I need to watch. They have guards."

"Mutant guards, I bet."

"Yep."

While watching the reactor buildings for any movement, Risk said, "What did you hear about Key S?"

Sophia coughed, then said, "Widow mentioned it. She said that it, um, kind of—"

"Made you honest? Brought out stuff hidden in you?"

"Uh, yeah. She said that."

Marilyn giggled and said, "What did it bring out of you, Sissy?"

"Oh, uh, I don't know. Nothing. She's insane. She was just talking."

"Where did you get the drugs?" Marilyn said, looking at her sister.

"Well, that's the thing, Sis. I didn't. I never—"

"Crude wine," Risk said, then grumbled.

"Huh? Oh, you mean—"

"Pauline. If you did get some, that's where."

"Why would she drug me?"

He almost growled, then said, "I'll find out. But that's only a rumor about Key S. Few believe it can do that."

"Wait," said Sophia. "That drug, even if I had it in my wine, doesn't do that? It doesn't reveal secrets and stuff?"

"Some say it's only hallucinogenic. I don't know."

He looked at Marilyn and said, "If it was in the wine, you got it too."

"Oh, that might explain why—"

Sophia waited a second, then said, "What, Sis? Explain what."

"Um, just that I felt funny after that. That's all. Sissy, it was probably just wine anyway."

Sophia looked at the ground and kicked her boots into it.

"Yeah, Sis. That, uh . . . yeah."

"Let's go," he said and took their hands, leading them mostly in the shadows toward the reactor.

He pried up a flap of fence that had already been cut and let first the lion through, then the twins. After stepping through himself, he let it fall and mostly close up again.

He'd just caught up with them and was walking between them when they all stopped at a dog's barking alternating with someone yelling, "Hold it!"

They turned and saw only a dog. A big one. Coming quickly toward them and mostly in the shadows along the building.

Risk stepped in front of the girls and raised his arms, and K Kat stood with him. Then, the beast barked while it was in the shadows, then stopped when it was in the light.

And its human face said, "Stop right there!"

"Oh my goodness, Sissy!"

"Uh, Risk? What the hell?"

He was already lowering himself toward the ground when K Kat roared and tore a path straight toward the mutant beast.

"No, girl! No!"

She didn't come back and instead, pounced on the dog-thing, and they tumbled around in and out of the shadows, a tangle of fangs and claws, growling and barking, and a human voice saying "Stop! Ow!"

Risk started to chase after the lioness, but more barking and human voices were coming from behind them. He turned to face the threat from that direction and again kept the twins behind him.

The girls watched two of the mutant things racing toward them and kept their hands on Risk's back.

Until they felt him shifting, growing muscle that stretched his leather vest. They watched his outstretched hands grow sickening claws. And they heard a low growl that made them take a step backwards.

With hands around each other's waist, Sophia held up her red-hot hand toward K Kat and her battle. And Marilyn held hers up toward Risk and his attackers.

Sophia said, under her breath, "Good girl, Kenzie," when she saw K Kat shaking the dying dog-person by its neck.

But Marilyn squeezed her sister's waist more tightly when one of Risk's adversaries got past him.

"Oh, Sissy, hang on!"

She let go of her sister and quickly heated up her other hand, and Sophia held onto her from behind and watched over her shoulder.

Marilyn had just enough time to say, "Come to momma!" and the dog leaped, sending its snarling human face toward her.

She clapped her hands on each side of its head, and the instant frying didn't give the thing time to even yip. Its body fell to the ground and lay there smoldering from a stump that used to have a head.

"Oh, Sis. Good one!"

"We're killers, Sissy. We shouldn't forget that."

"Nope. Never."

Sophia kept holding her sister from behind as they both watched Risk finish off his foe. But they recoiled at the sight of whatever he'd become gnawing into the dead body, ripping pieces loose, and spitting them aside.

"Sheesh, Sis."

Marilyn turned just her head and said, "Very much, Sissy. So, you weren't much of a killer with Widow, were you?"

"Oh, uh, no. I, um, couldn't. Not without burning everything down and killing myself too."

"Mm. Uh-huh."

"Oh, you don't believe me? You think I—"

"Would you even think of burning her if that all happened again? The exact same way?"

Sophia sighed and kicked at the ground.

"If she invited you in for a cup of tea, then explained to you exactly what she wanted to do to you. Would you scream and run from her? Or would you stay and be her baby girl?"

Marilyn waited a few seconds, but there was no answer from Sophia, so she giggled softly, then patted the hands still holding her waist.

"Oh, Sissy, I don't think I would either. She's so hot. And those orgasms. Mm."

"Uh, well, I don't know, Sis. How about you and Janie and all those zombies? What exactly happened there, Ms. Kildare Killer?"

"Oh. Um, they're a very persuasive sort. I, uh, didn't do a lot of burning. Um, not much."

"But you could have, right? I thought about it. I threatened to burn too."

"Well, Sissy, the important thing is what if, I don't know, Widow captured us both? And she wanted us to really be her sweet little twin baby girls? Huh? What if we were having spectacular orgasms together?"

She waited, and seconds passed before Sophia sighed and said, "Yeah. Spectacular."

She smiled and kept her hands over her sister's.

The shifted Risk creature was finishing up when they all heard a woman scream inside the building.

Risk became himself almost instantly and said, "Inside!"

*　*　*

Risk, still just himself, jerked open a metal door so hard that it was left hanging on just its top hinge. He ran inside first, then waited for the twins and K Kat to join him.

He tipped his head around, listening and looking along the hallways that led to each side and straight ahead.

The woman cried out again from somewhere along the hallway in front of them, and Risk led the way, stomping his heavy boots and looking quickly to each side through windows and doorways.

He finally froze for just a second, looking to his right, then kicked in a door that was made to open out.

The girls stood behind him, looking around him, and K Kat stayed behind them all, watching both ways.

Ten steps into the room, a woman was bent over the edge of a table. Her dirty work pants were pulled down around her knees, and she had one cheek flat on the surface.

A man was holding, in one hand, both of her wrists behind her back while he raped her at a steady, deliberate pace.

In his other hand, raised high over the woman, he held an axe.

He never slowed, but he turned with a smile toward the intruders.

And they saw who it was: Archie.

The madman.

And Risk's father.

"Hey!" said Sophia. "Let her go!"

"Stop that!" yelled Marilyn. "You, stop that!"

Risk held them back and shook his head as his father looked back at him with a grin.

"Father."

"Yeah, Son. I'm getting the hell out of here. You know why."

"Don't do it."

"I'm so close. I can't stop now."

"Sheesh," Sophia said under her breath.

"Very true, Sissy. Yes."

"Call off the plan."

Archie laughed, still thrusting, and said, "Oh, I don't think so. It's too late anyway. If you had any sense, you'd fuck one of those bimbos and get your own sorry ass out of this place."

"Hey," said Marilyn. "We're not bimbos."

"You tell him, Sis. That really put him in his place."

Marilyn pouted and didn't argue.

Risk said, "Don't kill her. Stop the goddamn plan."

"Uh," said Archie with a big grin, "I'm killing her. And I'm not stopping the goddamn plan. I'll visit this dump again after it's all cleaned up."

"You're slaughtering them. You're a butcher."

"You just killed three of my best men out there. They were—"

"They were dogs too," said Sophia. "Uh, sort of."

Archie nodded and said, "Yeah. Both at the same time. My guards are kind of cool, huh? Their time was coming to an end anyway."

He grinned and looked at the woman on the table, then said, "Hey, me too."

Risk shook his head at his father but didn't speak soon enough.

"I'm killing them all, Son. All the goddamn freaks and mutants, then the goddamn nearwolves too. All gone!"

"Risk!" said Marilyn. "Stop him before he kills her!"

"Uh, Sis, I think it might be—"

"Too late," said Risk. "Yeah."

Archie's eyes blinked hard a few times, and his face twisted into a satisfied grin that was kind of a grimace too.

And Risk and the Killers watched the axe fall.

And they saw the exact moment when it hit the woman's neck and Archie fell back and vanished into a wet pool that was really a solid floor.

* * *

"Oh, my," said Marilyn. "That's what we did, too, Sissy."

"Uh, yeah. Except for the raping, then killing."

"True. Risk, is she dead?"

"With an axe in her neck? Yeah. I think so."

He led the way to the table, then checked for a pulse in her neck. With a short grumble, he wiggled the blade out of her and sent it clattering across the room.

"Uh, Risk? I thought only you could do that. That sex and death thing."

"Not just me, Mare. He's . . . like me. Or I'm like him."

"Not following," Sophia said as she watched her sister giving the dead woman's head a close investigation.

Risk took a step back and fixed his hands on his hips.

"I told you. My father is . . ."

He raked both sets of fingers back through his wavy black hair.

"A fallen one."

"Well, yeah," said Sophia. "Not exactly a nice—"

"Not a fallen . . . man."

"Oh," said Marilyn. "Um . . . oh my. You mean, he was, um, not just—"

"Not just a man. No, Mare."

Both twins stared at him as he looked from one to the other. Seconds passed.

"So, you," said Sophia, pointing at him, "you're kind of, uh, you—"

He nodded and said, "Not just a man. Yeah."

He studied their staring eyes for a few seconds, then turned his gaze upon the corpse, and they all watched as it slid off and slumped awkwardly onto the floor.

"That necklace," Sophia said, pointing at the jewelry around the dead woman's neck.

"What about it?"

"I don't know, Sis, I just . . ."

She leaned over and held it, turning it to get a better look.

"I know this design. It's from a place on Sunset, in West Hollywood."

"Okay, she had good taste in jewelry. So?"

"Sis, it's our only clue. Maybe they had a thing, and he went there? Could that be?"

They both looked at Risk and waited.

He scoffed and said, "It's all we got. If we survive."

Chapter 53 – Fake Moon Phosphorous Ball

"There could be more guards. Stay close. Watch out."

Risk left them together, and he and the mountain lion began a search of the room.

"Sissy, this is a scary place. I want to go home."

"Me too, Sis. And that damn moon isn't even lit up yet."

"Damn moon."

"That's a first," said Sophia. "I like that."

"Thanks. Hey, what do you think about the Key S drug?"

"Um, it's probably like Risk said—makes you hallucinate."

Marilyn said, "Did you feel like you were hallucinating when you were with Widow?"

"Uh, no. It all seemed normal. Well, except for what was happening."

"Okay, Sissy, so maybe it's not some kind of hallucinating stuff. Maybe it really does bring out something in people? Could that be?"

"Uh, I don't know. Hey, what's Risk looking for?"

"Sissy, this is serious. I probably got that stuff too. I mean, if you did. So, I'm curious: what did it bring out about you?"

"I must have been drugged," said Sophia, "because when Widow told me what it brought out about me, I—"

"You didn't say that before. Widow told you? What did she say?"

"Don't laugh, Sis. And remember that it's just some crazy drug, alright?"

"I promise. What did she say?"

"And remember that I was lost in the best orgasm ever."

"I won't forget that. Uh-uh."

"Alright, Sis. She said my fantasy is to be a helpless little baby girl."

"Well, you did put on those frilly panties, remember?"

"It's all Pauline had, Sis, alright?"

"Sure. But you really liked looking like a baby girl. You liked acting like one too."

"I, uh, I remember. Yeah. I kind of did."

"The dress, too, Sissy. You liked your lacy little-girl dress, didn't you?"

"Uh, sure. Yeah."

"Okay. What else?"

"She said I want to be helpless for a woman. She actually said 'not for a man.' She said my thing is to be a helpless baby girl for another woman."

"You can't be serious. Not for a man? You're sure?"

"That's what she said. Yep."

"Helpless, how?"

"In every way possible. For anything she wanted."

Marilyn turned her sister to face her and held both of her arms.

"Sissy, isn't that exactly what happened to you?"

"Uh, kind of. Yeah. She even asked me if that's what I wanted. Can you imagine?"

"How did she know to even ask that?"

"Sis, she said it was obvious. She said she knew just by looking at me."

"Okay. That's weird. But what did you answer?"

Sophia looked down at the floor and kicked her army boot a couple of times.

Not looking up, she said, "I said 'yes.'"

"Oh, Sissy. You said yes?"

"Uh, three times, Sis. Yep."

"Oh my. Did you mean it?"

Sophia looked back up into her sister's eyes.

"Yeah, Sis. I meant it. I just don't know if it was the drugs at the time, or maybe—"

"Hmm, I bet it was the orgasm. I'd say or do just about anything with a good orgasm going on."

"You think? Yeah, that could be it."

"Maybe it came from Widow, Sissy. That idea. Maybe that's part of her thing. Like hypnotizing and stuff."

Marilyn looked around to make sure that Risk and K Kat weren't close enough to hear.

"I only sucked on her fingers, and I think, um . . ."

"Yeah, Sis?"

"I think I'd love to be a helpless baby girl for her too. And I'm not even having an orgasm right now."

Sophia laughed and said, "But you're always close, Sis."

"Mm-hmm. Oh, yeah. Okay, I might be having a very tiny one right now. Hey, if we ever see her again, I think we have her figured out. I think we could just take the monster orgasms, and she can't really hurt us."

"You think?"

"We're killers, Sissy. Yes, I think so."

"She's gone, though, Sis. We left her at that crypt place."

"Oh. Yes, that's true."

She sighed and added, "Too bad. We've never been helpless sweet little twin baby girls for someone before."

"Uh, kind of. At the bottom of the stairs. Remember that?"

"Mm-hmm. I do. Oh, in the hot bubble bath too. Sissy, she made us so itchy that we did all kinds of things."

"We did kind of go a little crazy. You think she'd make us like that again? God, Sis, how much would she make us do?"

"Hmm. I can only imagine. And I imagine we'd have to do whatever she wanted us to do."

"Yeah, Sis. Like in our cozy bath. Well, it's too late anyway. I mean, since she's probably dead and gone by now."

"Who said she was dead?"

"Alright, just gone."

Marilyn shrugged and said, "Guess we'll never know. Oh, here comes Risk."

He hurried back to them and said, "There's a bomb. It's counting down, and I can't stop it."

"We have to get out of here, then."

"Yeah, Mare, but that's not enough."

"Why not? Too big of a boom?"

"Real big, Fia. If the reactor goes, it might blow out the ceiling. The sky."

"But there's a lot of water up there, right?"

He nodded to Marilyn, then turned toward Sophia.

"Ham's mountain, then?" she said. "In case this nasty place gets flooded?"

"Good idea. Yeah. Let's go."

* * *

Risked leaned out of the same doorway that they'd used to enter the building and looked both ways.

"It's good. Let's go."

He led them out on a brisk walk across the open area, but they stopped halfway to the fence, and he said, "We need a ride."

"Oh. The hawk," said Marilyn. "In a balloon."

"He's not actually in the balloon, Sis."

Risk was scanning the black sky, so the girls joined him. He grumbled as he pointed in one direction, and they looked too.

"Oh, boy," said Marilyn. "Here we go."

The fake moon phosphorous ball was stationary high above them. The bats had connected all of their cables or at least enough to hold it in place. There was no sound from them, but tiny black clouds were moving around up there.

"Say it, Sis."

"I'll say it," said Risk. "Damn moon."

"Where the hell is the balloon, Risk?"

"I don't know, Fia. He doesn't like bats."

"Maybe they were tormenting him up on that crypt building."

"Yeah, Mare. Could be."

"Oh, no," said Sophia, and she pointed lower, just over the buildings in the distance.

From among them, a red fireball was climbing into the sky on a path that would slam it into the fake moon.

"Just wonderful," Marilyn said. "As Dayzee would say."

"She did say that a lot."

They watched in silence as the flaming projectile neared the black ball hanging from the ceiling.

It struck, and the moon burned bright white, adding light around the reactor buildings and everywhere else.

They heard the first howling somewhere far in the distance.

"Dammit."

"This isn't good."

"No, Sissy. Uh-uh. Not without that balloon boy thing."

K Kat yipped, and they looked down at her where she sat up against Risk's leg. Her ears were circling, then she leaned and looked into the darkness beyond the fence.

She growled and began a sprint toward whatever she'd seen.

"No!" Risk yelled and ran after her.

He called back over his shoulder, "Stay together. I'll get the lion."

They watched him merge with the shadows and growling and howling in the night, all under a full moon.

"Sissy, we're as good as dead."

"Maybe. Or maybe we already are. I don't know."

"This is Hell? No, Sissy. Uh-uh. No way."

"Well if it is, how many times can we get killed?"

Marilyn looked down around their boots and said, "Well, how many more 'belows' are below Below the Bay?"

Sophia shook her head and said, "I just can't let myself laugh right now. Good one, though, Sis."

Marilyn shrugged and said, "Oh, I don't even know what I'm saying anymore. I'm just starving still."

Sophia snickered and said, "Yeah, Sis. For brains?"

After a few seconds without a response, Sophia looked over at her sister, then waved a hand in front of her face.

"Sis?"

"Sissy, I almost ate a brain. Risk stopped me. I was crazy, and I would have been a real zombie after that."

"Oh my God, Sis. You wanted it?"

"I wanted that dead lady's brain, too, Sis. The one with the axe in her back."

"Uh, yeah. But it didn't open her skull or anything."

"Oh. No, it didn't. But I would have just bit right into it."

"Sheesh."

"Yes. You wouldn't believe how good it felt to be so hungry and so itchy, all at the same time. Yes. I wanted it."

"Huh. Alright. Well, I, um, wanted everything Widow did to me too. I think she almost killed me."

"But she can't. She said so, right? Because we're different."

"Uh, yeah. But I didn't know that. God, the things she did to me."

"Aw, and you liked it because you like being a helpless little baby girl for—"

"A woman. She said for a woman."

"Yes, Widow said that. But what do you say, Sissy?"

They heard Risk's boots and saw him running back toward them with K Kat. The lioness had blood all over her snout, and Risk had some splattered across his cheeks and in his whiskers.

"Good," he said, "you're still—"

He looked past them and above them and pointed.

They turned and saw for themselves a giant balloon, lit by fake moonlight, sailing their way over the reactor buildings.

"About goddamn time," Risk said.

* * *

"Hawken! Over here!"

The hawk boy navigator could barely be heard from high above, saying, "I see you!"

Beyond the fence, the howling of nearwolves was gaining strength.

The girls looked that way, then back at the balloon craft.

"Uh, hurry would be nice," said Sophia.

"It's not one of Dayzee's sports cars, Sissy."

"Huh. Yeah. Maybe more of a limo. Carries people around."

They heard the hot air leaking out of the open flap above the balloon as it sank toward the ground near them. But the basket was still out of reach when they ran toward it and stood under it.

And behind them, nearwolves had breached the fence and were howling and racing toward them.

"Sissy, I don't want to get ripped apart!"

Sophia didn't snicker when she said, "Says the girl that eats brains."

"I didn't eat any!"

"Huh. Would have, I bet."

"Hurry!" said Risk.

They got to where Risk could jump and touch the bottom of the basket, and Hawken kept up its descent. It dropped the remaining distance quickly and scraped along as the balloon continued to drift

"Catch it," said Risk. "Hurry!"

He let the lion and the girls get ahead of him and snorted out a laugh at K Kat easily jumping into the moving basket. He held Marilyn's waist, lifted her, and shifted her over the edge. Sophia was next, and he set her inside quickly.

Holding the rim as it slid and scraped across the field, Risk turned to see a pack of nearwolves that would be on him in mere seconds.

"Fuck."

He jumped inside and yelled up to Hawken, "Go! Get us higher!"

The flames danced and roared as the hawk boy flung wide open the lid on the big pot, and they heard the balloon fabric groaning as it stretched back out. All of the cables began snapping tight, and Marilyn tried to stand to look over the edge at their pursuers.

"No," Risk said and pushed her down, just as big furry hands with long claws appeared on the rim.

"Dammit."

He was about to reach for those paws, when the girls nudged him aside, each with a burning hand.

The nearwolf howled like there were dozens of fake moons enticing it into madness. They both looked over, and Marilyn had time to send it a cute wave before they all heard the body thump.

Then, the pack attacked their fallen comrade, and grunting replaced howling, but none of them in the basket watched. Risk sat with his back against the basket wall, and the twins took seats beside him. K Kat lounged between his outstretched legs, her head up on one and her eyes watching his.

"Good girl," he said, then patted her head.

He looked one way, then the other.

"Both of you too."

He looked up and said to Hawken, "Ham's. As quick as you can."

"Time enough to climb?"

"Yeah. Then, straight line."

"Alright."

"We're going over the city?"

"Yeah, Fia. Straight line to Ham's."

Marilyn said, "Do those nearwolf things have guns? Or arrows?"

"No. Just claws. Teeth. When they're wolves, that's all they know."

"Alright," Sophia said as she stood and stretched. "I'm going to watch, then."

Risk nodded, and Sophia walked to the far side of the basket and grabbed the rail, looking out and down at the approaching city.

"Will this place really flood?"

"Probably not, Mare. Still, it's safer at Ham's."

"Okay. Until, when? Forever?"

Below them, everywhere along the way, they heard the howling of the wolves, driven mad by a moon none thought they'd ever see again. And along with their howling, there was the screaming of every mutant getting slaughtered and eaten.

Risk sighed and shook his head.

"The plan is to leave the moon burning. Let them all go insane."

"Then, what? They eat each other?"

"That's the plan, Mare."

"Oh my goodness. I might never leave Ham's house."

Risk laughed once, and she looked enough to see him smiling.

But Sophia was waving her hand behind herself while she was still watching their flight, and that caught Marilyn's attention. Risk looked too.

She said, "Hey, uh, Risk? Come here, alright?"

He stood, then noticed Marilyn holding up a hand. He took it and easily lifted her up onto her combat boots.

"Why, thank you."

"You're welcome."

They both walked over and took places at the rail, Risk in the middle and Sophia to his left.

"What? We're high enough."

He looked over the edge and shook his head. Neither of the twins looked, but they all heard the mad slaughter everywhere.

"Yeah," she said. "I hope so. But look."

She pointed almost straight ahead, just a little off to the right.

"There," she said. "See that?"

"The Crypt Building. Yeah."

"On top," she said, still pointing. "Look. Look!"

Risk squinted to try peering through the darkness grudgingly fleeing from the artificial moon, and he laughed and shook his head.

"I see her."

"Who?" said Marilyn. "Who's there?"

Softly, Sophia said, "Widow. Widow's on the roof."

"Not for long," Risk said, and he pointed lower.

They watched crazed nearwolves scaling the sides of the building, as if they could smell the only truly living thing left there.

"Risk, those things are going after her?"

"Yeah, Mare. They'll kill everything."

"We have to save her."

"No, Fia."

"Risk, we have to."

"No."

She turned to him, and he met her gaze.

"I haven't asked for anything, have I?"

He squinted at her for a second, then looked away.

"No. Nothing."

"Just this, then. Let's land just long enough to pick her up."

He snapped his head toward her and said, "Why?"

She coughed a few times and tried not to smile at the sight of her sister clapping her hands silently, where Risk couldn't see it.

"Because, um, killing isn't good, right?"

He shook his head and said, "I'm not killing her."

He pointed toward the nearwolves climbing up toward her and said, "They are."

"I know. But, um, we kind of are, too, if we can save her and we don't."

Risk grumbled and turned to look at Marilyn, who'd just barely managed to quit clapping in time.

"Sissy does have a point."

Risk looked at Widow on the roof, much closer than when she'd first been seen by Sophia.

All of them noticed that she didn't appear alarmed at all. She stood with her hands on her hips, wrapped in camouflage military dress, a glorious black mane puffing out from under a drab green cap, and staring up at them calmly.

"Dammit."

Risk looked up and said, "Hawken. One more."

Chapter 54 – Like an Army Is Coming

"Not so close," Risk said as Hawken piloted their craft toward The Crypt Building and the moon-mad attackers hanging on the sides and howling at the approaching vehicle.

"Alright."

The navigator nodded, then spouted a few sideways blasts, slowing their motion, then sent flames up into the balloon to take them higher to clear the building's parapet.

Marilyn looked over the side, down along the building, at scores of nearwolves climbing window ledges and using vents and flagpoles and whatever else was still planted on the building's side.

"Why don't they just go inside?"

"They are, Mare. Inside too," Risk said while watching closely the path Hawken was steering.

The basket cleared the low wall along the building's perimeter, and they saw Widow near the doorway that led into the heart of the building.

"Shouldn't she be running and screaming, Sissy? She knows what's coming to get her."

"Huh. Not her style, Sis."

"Take it in close," Risk said up to the small fellow with the face of a hawk. "Easy."

"Here is the best. Too many hazards."

"Alright. Set it down."

All three stood along the basket's rim as it descended from a height Hawken had maintained to keep the wolves, if any were there, from jumping up for the basket.

But he let hot air out of the balloon's top flap, and they scraped along the gravel before he was able to hold it steady.

He called up to Hawken, "Stay ready."

"Alright."

Risk waved and called out to Widow, "Come on."

She stood near the door, still wearing camouflage pants and a tank top, plus green boots and a cap, and she kept her hands on her hips as she looked in each direction, then back at the basket.

"Now?" said Risk.

"Sissy, what's she doing?"

"I don't know, Sis. Maybe she—"

Widow called to Risk in a steady voice, "Risk. Do you want me to join you?"

"Get in the basket. They're coming up the sides."

She didn't move, just said, "Do you wish for my company?"

"Sissy, she's crazy! I'd be running!"

"Me too. She's waiting for an invitation?"

The twins heard Risk grumble, then say, softly, "Fuck. Fucking games."

He put his hands up to amplify his voice and said, "I want your company. Come now."

She still didn't move.

"And you adorable twin girls? Do you wish me to join you?"

"Dammit," Risk said to himself, just loud enough for the girls to hear.

Sophia didn't hesitate.

"Yes, Widow! Join us!"

Marilyn yelled, "Before the nearwolves get you!"

"Dear little blond baby sister, do you wish for me to join you?"

"What the hell, Sis?"

"She's a control freak, Sissy. You should know that by now."

"Oh, in ways you can't even imagine, Sis."

Hawken squawked high above on his perch, then pointed back toward the edge of the building. All heads turned, and they saw the first nearwolf breach the top and creep over, snarling and looking everywhere.

More quickly followed, and they all saw the balloon, the food inside, and more food standing near a door.

A few of them loitered for a quick howl at the fake moon, then they joined the rest that were already sprinting on all fours toward their next kills.

Marilyn called out, "We all wish for you to join us. Hurry!"

She didn't hurry. In what seemed to be a deliberate strut, she walked toward the basket and all the staring eyes. And Risk's shaking head.

"They're coming!" said Marilyn. "Please, hurry!"

"Uh, Sis. I think we're dead. Soon anyway."

Standing near the basket, she extended a hand up toward Risk.

He grumbled, then leaned out with both hands, held her under her arms, and effortlessly lifted her up and onto the craft's wooden floor.

Risk looked up and said, "Up, Hawken! Now!"

"Alright! Finally! Fuck!"

The flames crackled and shivered upward, sending clouds of oily hot air to stretch the balloon, pull all of its ropes and cables tight, then lift them up as straight as Hawken could manage.

"High enough?"

Risk glanced over and saw the beasts swarming right below them, some leaping and almost reaching a claw high enough to hook the wicker.

"More. More altitude."

"Alright. Up."

* * *

"No. Stay there," Risk said, pointing at Widow alone on one side of the basket.

She sat with her back to the wall and her knees pulled up close.

Risk and the twins and K Kat were as far from her as possible.

Sophia whispered to her sister, "She can't claim that she won't bite, Sis."

"Oh my, no. Not her."

"What was that down there?" Risk said, glaring at Widow.

"Nothing," she said, then looked away, over the edge. "An odd form of panic, perhaps."

Risk grumbled and began checking cables and scouting the landscape ahead.

Marilyn leaned close and whispered to Sophia, "Sissy, maybe even she wants to feel needed?"

Sophia kept watching Widow and nodded.

"Yeah, Sis," she whispered. "I never thought of her being lonely."

"Oh. Maybe she is. Sissy?"

"Yeah, Sis?"

"Maybe Risk too?"

"Oh. Wow."

"Has he ever been in love?"

"God," she said and kept her eyes on him.

Marilyn waited for more of an answer, but all she got from her sister was a deep raspy sigh, and she felt the shrug.

"Where are we going?" Widow said, causing Risk to stop and study her again.

He grumbled and went back to scanning the landscape ahead of them.

"Ham's mountain."

"Good. Safer than that building."

He turned enough to study her from between the girls.

"You know of it?"

"Oh, no. It's just that you said 'mountain.' That sounds safer."

"What of the vampire?"

"Bentley?" she said, then she scoffed. "He's become an experiment."

"A what?"

Widow smiled and said, "I gave him a plan: convert one of those beasts, then command it against the next. There's a slim chance he can create an army and survive."

"Sheesh," said Sophia. "What would they be? Some kind of triple mutants?"

Marilyn was counting on her fingers.

"People. Wolves. And vampires. Wow."

Risk scoffed and said, "No chance."

He grumbled and turned his back to her, then he and the twins looked down as Hawken got them traveling over the building tops and the streets between them.

Everywhere they looked, nearwolves, some alone and many in packs, were either chasing their prey or feeding on what they'd killed. Their howls mixed with their growling and grunting, and the screams of their victims lasted only seconds before new screams replaced them in different locations.

"That's a lot of wolf people," Marilyn said, shaking her head at the carnage.

Risk said, "Like I said . . ."

"I remember," she said. "They almost always—"

"Rape," said Sophia, also watching the bloodbath. "They almost always rape while they're killing. They just take what they want."

Risk and Marilyn, to his right, turned enough to study Sophia, who continued.

"That's a real victim," she said, almost to herself. "To be raped and killed, all of it by some kind of beast."

She pulled in a deep breath, then let it seep back out.

"That's, um . . . just dreadful."

Risk turned to Marilyn and squinted for a second, but Marilyn only shrugged in response, then offered a weak smile. Then, she looked down at a street that they'd just begun to pass over.

"Oh, Risk. Look. Zombies."

"Huh. Yeah."

He tipped his head each way, then said, "Listen."

"I hear it. Buzzing."

"Yeah, Mare. Keeping them calm."

"They don't have a chance, then," said Sophia. "They'll get ripped apart like everyone else."

"Not fair," Marilyn said with a quick stomp of a boot. "They're nice enough when they're buzzing. They're just, um, sex freaks. Kind of."

"Tell us about it, Sis."

"Oh, I think I've said enough. Oh, one more thing: they sure talk dirty. I almost blushed."

"Huh," said her sister. "That's not something you do often. And I like how you said 'almost.'"

They watched as a pack of the beasts rounded the corner. And though they couldn't hear it, it appeared that the zombies were attempting to engage them in conversation.

"Huh," said Risk. "Talking. That never works."

"Didn't help me either," said Marilyn. "Sissy?"

Sophia turned enough to give a quick glance at Widow, then turned herself right back around and whispered to Marilyn.

"Uh, maybe. She liked when I complained and threatened."

"Hmm. Like a helpless little baby. Oh, then you gave her the right answers too."

Sophia sighed and managed a smile, then said, "I, uh, yeah. I did."

"Ham's mountain," said Hawken, and they all looked up from the butchery in the city streets and on its rooftops and the occasional jumper trying to escape through a high window.

They were coasting toward the side of a steep mountain, still near the bottom of it, and no amount of squinting or straining would reveal the higher regions that were swallowed in the night.

Marilyn pointed toward the bottom and said, "Uh-oh. Here too."

"Dammit."

Large groups of nearwolves, each with a shadow from a phosphorous moon, were beginning a tortuous climb toward Ham's house. Though quick and agile, their journey was over and around jagged stones that denied them any easy path.

But they still took enough time to scream their passion and madness toward a moon that had been calculated to burn long enough for all of them to eat each other.

*   *   *

"Set her down," Risk said while monitoring the craft's position.

He leaned over to watch the very bottom of the basket just clear the sharp points of Ham's tall iron fence.

Hawken said, "Alright," and gave them all a soft landing in the usual spot, next to Ham's vehicle.

"Ziggy," Hawken said, waving to the navigator high up in the workings of the other balloon craft.

A raspy laugh and a burst of flames was Ziggy's response.

Risk hopped out, followed by K Kat, and she stayed close to him as he looped and tied two ropes to the heavy hooks embedded in the stone floor.

"Okay," he said to the navigator, then he reached a hand out toward the twins.

"We're going inside. They'll be up here soon."

Marilyn took his hand and swung a leg over the edge, then hopped into his arms.

"What about Hawken?" she said.

"He'll fly. Stay up."

"Oh, he's probably afraid too."

"No. It's more about the balloon. They're smart enough to rip it up."

Sophia had been listening and said, "Hey, how come the bats don't?"

"Because they're not smart enough. They just go for food."

"Damn bats," said Marilyn. "Oh, and damn wolves too."

He reached for Sophia and while he was helping her onto the patio, she said, "What about the other one, Ziggy?"

Risk laughed and said, "No one messes with Ziggy."

Sophia joined her sister near the entrance to Ham's house, and they watched as Risk lifted Widow up and over the basket's edge, then took a step back from her.

"You too," he said. "Inside."

"Thank you," she said, her voice normal. "Before we go in, just remember that a war like this can make people crazy. Don't always believe what they say."

"Huh?"

"Nothing. I'm just nervous about the nearwolves. I'm not making any sense."

Risk squinted at her for a second, taking note of her lack of urgency to get inside and her calm, steady breathing.

"Alright. Wait there."

He pointed toward the twins, then loosened the anchor ropes, coiled them, and tossed them back into the basket.

"Wait," he yelled up to the hawk.

He reached over the side and snagged the small bag containing two pairs of high-heeled shoes and one pair of high-heeled boots plus a bottle of whiskey.

Then, he gave Hawken a thumbs-up and said, "Go. Stay close if you can."

"Alright. See you."

Risk stayed near the basket, watching his navigator work. He stoked the flames up from the iron pot, and he and Hawken both smiled at the sight and sound of the balloon stretching out and the ropes and cables tightening up.

After the balloon had carried the basket higher than Risk could have reached with his best jump, he turned toward the three women and a lion close together near the door, all watching him.

"Not much time," he said, pointing to Ham's house.

"All of us. Inside."

* * *

Risk held out an arm to keep all of them back and behind him as he pounded several times on the door.

They waited, and no one came.

"Huh."

He tried the door and found that it wasn't barricaded.

"Maybe they saw us coming?"

"Maybe, Fia. But they'd still come to the door."

He opened the door slowly and only to look around inside, then back at the high fence bordering the patio area.

"Risk," Marilyn whispered, "you think there are already some of those wolf things in there?"

He turned back to her just long enough to say, "No, not them. Could be any kind of nightmare."

Risk turned back to the interior of the house, and Marilyn stared at her sister with her eyebrows popped up high.

Sophia smirked and said, "Sis, he's right. This entire place is a nightmare."

He waved for them to follow and seconds later, they all stood near the closed door and all stared at the same thing.

Pauline. On her back on the floor near the couch. Naked.

With the handle of a knife rising up from her chest.

"Oh my goodness!"

"Sheesh, Sis."

Beside her lay Ham, holding another knife in one hand and the other trying, and failing, to keep blood from flowing out of a stab wound in his gut.

Risk hurried over, but the rest of them stayed back.

"Ham," Risk said while holding the dying man. "You knew it couldn't work."

Ham grimaced and said, "Worth a fucking try. I'm ready to die, but not to get chewed up by fucking freak wolves."

"They're coming up the mountain."

"I know. Didn't know if you'd make it back either."

"You killed Pauline."

Ham scoffed and said, "Bitch didn't have the decency to die quick. Oh, no. She had just enough fucking time to kill me too."

Risk brushed some of his hair off of his face.

Ham's voice had weakened considerably when he said, "When you hunt those fucking bats, Risk."

He wheezed in a few breaths.

"Yeah, Ham?"

"Remember . . . that I'm with you."

His head tipped and his breaths become too shallow to notice. His lips fumbled for a second, then his eyes closed.

"In the sky," he said.

Risk touched his neck, then turned toward the women. He shook his head.

"So, the woman is dead too?"

Risk squinted at Widow and said, "Yeah. She's dead. Her name was Pauline."

"I remember," said Widow. "I mean, you, uh, just said that."

He stood and walked toward them.

"We'll need to barricade all the—"

"Risk?"

"Yeah, Mare."

"Ham was trying that sex and death thing?"

"Yeah."

"You said that he already knew it wouldn't work, though. Why wouldn't it work? Isn't that what got them here?"

He nodded and said, "Yeah. They died to get here. There's no going back from that."

"Oh."

Widow leaned toward Sophia and said, "Sex and death?"

"Oh, uh, yeah. Risk can do it. He can get us out of here. Looks like no one else can."

"Why can't anyone else do it?" Marilyn said.

"I told you. I'm different. Because of my father."

"Oh, that's right. You're both some kind of—"

"We have to move. Secure this place like an army is coming for us."

He paused to look at every pair of eyes staring into his.

He scoffed and said, "Because one is."

* * *

Satisfied that they'd improved the strength of their fortifications, Risk said, "I'll check," and walked toward the front door.

"Check what?"

"How close they are, Mare."

"Can I come out too? Will it be safe?"

He said, "Yeah, come on," then scoffed and added, "Safe for now."

Sophia said, "I'm coming too. I'll bring the lion."

"That's funny, Sissy. Like a lion needs you to lead her around."

They followed Risk through the front entryway, closed it after themselves, then approached the tall fence quietly. Below them, but spanning side to side like a wave, there were hundreds of nearwolves climbing, stopping to howl at the burning ball of phosphorous, then climbing more.

Some looked up and saw them looking down, which got them agitated and more ambitious in their attempts to scramble up the side of Ham's mountain.

"How long before they get us?"

"They won't, Mare."

Sophia scoffed and said, "I don't know how you can say that. There's thousands of them."

"There's not that many, Sissy. A lot, though. That's true."

"So, let's get that balloon back," said Sophia. "Why can't we just stay up in that?"

Risk shook his head and said, "We could. But he's gone. I thought Ham and Pauline were alive, and that would have been too many."

"Oh," said Marilyn. "Yes, that would have been quite the crowd."

They watched the approaching beasts in silence for a few moments. K Kat stood with them, on Risk's right between him and Marilyn. Sophia stood to his left.

He sighed, then leaned enough to grab a thin burlap blanket, which he held around all of them.

"This is like when we first got here," Marilyn said with a soft giggle that she cut short.

She swallowed hard and added, "Except now, there's moonlight."

She looked toward Risk, and all she saw was him shaking his head and looking out at a city full of screams and flickering lights and fires.

"I'm a failure," he said.

"What?" said Sophia. "No, you're not. You got us here."

"Yes," said Marilyn, "away from those things. Sort of. You can only do so much, Risk."

"No. Not that. Just . . . everything. I'm trying to be a good man."

"You are a good man," said Marilyn. "You are."

"You really are," said Sophia. "You've helped us so—"

"Thanks. Both of you. But I've killed . . . so much."

Before the girls could answer his claim, he said, "And soon, I'll have to kill more."

* * *

Widow watched the front door close as Risk pulled it shut. She waited only a few seconds, watching it, then reached for the bag Risk had remembered to grab from the basket before Hawken had sailed away.

She reached in and held up her short black boots with spiky heels and tight lacing all the way up in front.

"These will help," she said to herself. "I know tasty little Fia likes them."

She grinned and walked straight toward the door to Pauline's room, ignoring the others. Inside, she went directly to the dresser and slid open the second drawer from the bottom.

"Hmm. Baby Mare will like any of this too."

She held up a thin black button-up blouse.

"She'll love the way I look in this. Pauline always did."

She took everything in her arms, the blouse and the boots, left Pauline's room, and walked straight to a heavy wooden door. It took some effort just to swing it open, but she managed and walked down the few stairs, flipping a switch along the way.

A large room carved out of the mountain lit up, and she stopped after she'd reached the floor. A glance at the bed brought a smile, as did the sight of several large pottery cannisters on the bed's nightstands and against the far wall, stored away in a line.

"This could work. This has to fucking work."

While walking toward one of the canisters near the bed, she grinned at the ropes hanging from an electric hoist mounted up between the floor joists high above the bed.

She set down her blouse and boots, then reached for the cannister. A quick pinch and a short pull brought out a length of sticky webbing.

"Hmm, not the usual this time. Not with what I'll have to do to those women that I'll treat like juicy baby girls."

She replaced both bedside cannisters with others from the storage. From one of them, she pulled out a short length and nodded at the much thicker, much stickier material.

"Oh yeah, this is a time to use it. It'll set like concrete really quick. Mm, they'll be such helpless little girls. Nearly useless."

She worked it back in and turned the cannister, leaving it at the best angle for access.

"Sweet little Fia will like being even more helpless for me. And her baby sister probably isn't much different. Oh, that's what I'll do with the blonde: I'll get her to accept her fate willingly. Hmm, that'll be such a sweet little victory."

With her hands on her hips, she nodded at the cannister of her stickiest, most dangerous webbing.

"They'll be just two soft, tender little broken doll babies."

She wiped her sticky fingers together, then tugged on the ropes above the bed.

She laughed softly and said, "And they think they're safe from me. Hmm."

She leaned and looked toward the stairs back up into the house and listened.

Then, she sat on the bed, leaning against the pillows, and reached down to unfasten her camouflage pants. With a deep sigh, she inserted a hand, shifting her hips to get her fingertips in just the right place.

"Mm. This always works. My sweet poisons will be so much stronger. Too strong even for those precious little girls not from Earth."

She laid her head back, closed her eyes, and the only motion in the dim basement room was Widow's hand as she gently touched herself.

Chapter 55 – So Much Stronger Now

"Risk," said Marilyn, still under the blanket with him and her sister and the mountain lion, "you didn't want to kill. You had to."

He scoffed quietly and looked down again at the approaching nearwolves. From them and the rampage in the city beyond them, it was a moonlit night of howling and screaming and slaughter.

"I'm no better than them."

"That's just not true," said Sophia. "They're just monsters, killing for the thrill of it."

He scoffed and shook his head.

"They're people too. They didn't ask to be wolves."

"Oh. Yeah, that's true. Anyway, I'm probably worse."

He turned enough to look into her blue eyes.

"How?"

"Because I wanted everything Widow did to me. Well, not at first, but her poisons put me in a place where it was just this constant ecstasy. I knew what she was doing to me, and I didn't care. I wanted all of it."

"Sissy, that had to be from her poisons, right?"

"Uh, yeah. Probably. She's got some crazy kind of poisons she was filling me up with."

"But they aren't strong enough to hurt us for long, Sissy. She said so. You would have been dead by now."

"True. Yeah. Good thing we're, um, different."

"So, none of that was your fault, Sissy. Blame it all on Widow."

"Alright. Sure. What about you, though?"

"Oh, good point. I'm worse than both of you. Since we're all going to get ripped to pieces soon, I might as well just say it: I bit into a brain, and I would have swallowed it if Risk hadn't saved me."

Risk turned to Marilyn with a grin and a single nod.

"Anytime. Not again, though."

"Uh, Sis? You actually bit into a brain?"

"Mm-hmm. Yes, I did. I ripped out a big, juicy chunk. Oh, wow, it was so juicy, and I—"

"How did you get to the point where you wanted that?"

"Oh, Sissy, I think maybe it was from what they were feeding me."

"Which was?"

"Um, I think it was some kind of brain juice. Not the actual brain, though."

"Oh, well, I guess that's okay, then. Sure. Just brain slop."

"Funny, Sissy. But it's still kind of my fault because I never should have tasted any of that at all. I got, um, tempted into it. By a really hot zombie girl."

"How?"

"She, um, put some on her nipples, and I was already so itchy for her that I didn't care what it was. Oh my, it all went downhill from there. Quickly!"

"She was hot? Can't blame you."

"Sissy, she was cold. She was a zombie!"

Risk finally spoke, after turning his head many times.

"Zombeing. She was a zombeing."

"I'm not sure that makes it any better," said Marilyn.

"Both of you," said Risk. "Don't forget the Key S."

"Oh yeah, we were going to ask Pauline about that."

"Yeah, Fia. Not anymore."

"No," said Marilyn. "But are you sure what Sissy and I felt was just from that drug?"

Risk shrugged and focused on the nearwolves making steady, howling progress toward Ham's house.

"I don't know. I don't even take Zoojoose."

"You don't have to. You already can do some wild stuff."

"Yeah, Fia. Thanks to my mom."

"Oh, I forgot about her!" said Marilyn. "Should we, I don't know, do something with her?"

"No. Nothing except stop the nearwolves."

He looked toward Ham's balloon craft, then said, "Hang on. One last check on Ziggy."

He put the blanket back around their shoulders, then took the couple dozen steps to get to the basket of Ham's craft.

"Sis? Um, I think that Key S stuff would have worn off by now."

"It hasn't?"

"Uh-uh. I know it doesn't make any sense, but I still want to be Widow's helpless baby girl."

"You liked her calling you that. Yes."

"Not just that. It was all the sexy bondage stuff too. I don't get it, but it was so sweet to be that helpless for her."

"Mm. I think I'd like it, too, and I didn't even get the full treatment. Sissy, if it won't kill us, and if there's ever a chance with all the nearwolves and things, maybe we—"

"Could volunteer?"

She smiled at Marilyn nodding.

"You're in, Sis? We could let her do whatever, and it won't kill us anyway."

Marilyn clapped her hands silently.

"Twins, Sissy. We'll be her helpless twin baby girls."

Sophia looked down, and they both paused to listen to the howling on the mountainside.

"Uh, we'll be dead soon. Anyway, it's fun to think about. Oh, here comes Risk."

A few steps later, he was back near them but not inside the blanket.

"Is Ziggy going to be okay?"

"Yeah, Mare. He's fine."

"Does he ever, uh, run out of fire or whatever he does?"

Risk shrugged and said, "Probably not. I think he eats oil."

"Sheesh."

*   *   *

"Mm," Widow said softly as she kept rubbing between her thighs, "just like that."

She reached her free hand up under her camo tank top and started fondling her breasts.

"Oh, so close now."

She began to buck her hips up, getting into a steady rhythm while still rubbing and fondling.

"Oh," she said, and it turned into a laugh that she tried to stifle. "Oh, yeah, just like that. So soft. So slow. Mm . . ."

She withdrew her hand from her pants, but the other one wasn't quite done yet. But her eyes had opened, and she stayed lying back against a stack of pillows while she smiled up at the ropes and hoist.

"Mm. Not as nice as when a precious, helpless baby does that for me. Still, damn good, though."

She left her breasts alone, then said, "Oh, I can feel it. It's all so much stronger now."

She began sucking the fingers that she'd just slipped back out from between her thighs.

"Mm, oh my, that's strong. Those juicy little babies could die from even my first little bite."

She sucked her fingers more, then laughed softly.

"Right from the beginning, they'd be just sweet, empty little doll babies. Still so juicy and eager to please. Mm, and Risk will never even know."

She zipped up her pants and swung her legs off of the side of the bed.

Looking toward the stairs, she tipped her head a few times, listening.

"Hmm. Still outside? Silly."

She began the hike up the steps then stopped halfway to listen again.

She finished the climb and looked out into the house. After seeing no one and the front door ajar, she walked quietly to a different room, not Pauline's, and laid herself across the bed.

* * *

"Hey, Risk," said Marilyn. "I think we left that 'joose stuff by the bathtub. I wish we still had it."

"It's dangerous, Mare."

"Not for me. For Kenzie."

"K Kat, Sis. Unless we had that stuff."

Risk took it out of his pants pocket.

"I picked it up."

"Oh, good. I want to change her back. Can we try?"

"Mare, it gave her seizures."

"And I want to ask her what she thinks of this place," said Sophia.

"Yes, Sissy. I bet she has some stories to tell. Oh, like when you and I were in so much, um, trouble."

"Yeah. Hey, Risk, did anything exciting happen? With K Kat, I mean?"

"Uh, not really. No."

"Can we have the 'joose?" said Marilyn. "It's probably our last chance ever to make her Kenzie again."

"I'm with Sis on this one. Let's do it."

Risk grimaced while looking down on the advancing wolf beasts. He finally scoffed and handed it to Marilyn.

She said, "Are you sure there's time?"

He shrugged and said, "Worth a try. It might really be the last chance."

"Yes. Sadly, that's true."

He shook his head and said, "You might have to try harder this time."

"Like how?"

"Like luring her back, Mare. Maybe not just friendship."

"Sex," Sophia said, nodding her head and grinning at her sister.

"Oh, Sissy, I don't know. Not with a lion."

"Sis, no. Me neither. I mean, we can tempt her with all the things we'll do for her."

"You mean 'to her' Sissy. Yes. That'll bring her back if anything will."

"We have to keep her at least long enough to talk to us."

"Yes, we will. And who knows? Maybe she'll stay back forever."

Risk was shaking his head, scowling without the girls seeing it.

He sighed and said, "Yeah, that should work. One more thing."

"What?" said Marilyn.

"Show her."

Sophia grinned and pointed at him.

"Yep. Oh, yeah. Sis and I are getting naked."

"Well, Sissy, it's only appropriate. Kenzie will already be naked too."

Chapter 56 – Waiting In the Dark

"I'll let you know when to run," Risk said and faced Ham's tall fence, leaning enough to watch the approaching monsters. "It's a rough climb."

Marilyn handed her sister a small blanket and said, "Sissy, get out of those silly army clothes."

"Well, you too, Sis. Need some help?"

Marilyn laughed and said, "Mm, helping yourself is what you mean."

"Yep."

"I'll manage. This is about Kenzie, remember?"

"Oh, yeah. Alright."

The lion had been watching them undress, twitching her ears at their giggling, then laid herself down to keep watching them.

"Kenzie's ready, Sissy."

"Still K Kat, though. We'll fix that."

The twins laid themselves down along the sides of the mountain lion. Marilyn rubbed around her ears and looked into her eyes.

"Do you remember me? I'm Marilyn. I remember you. You're Kenzie."

"Sis, it's like you're in kindergarten or something."

Marilyn pouted, then smiled about it.

Sophia turned the lion's head toward her and held it with both hands.

"You and I were up in that bed in Dayzee's mansion. Remember that? You didn't want me calling anyone up there to bother us, then you got me undressed."

"Sissy, I think you probably got her undressed too."

The lion glanced at Marilyn, then focused again on Sophia.

"You had me pinned down. Wow, the things we were going to do up there. Hey, do you remember your name for me?"

"I do," said Marilyn.

"I know you do, Sis. Let her talk."

"That's funny, Sissy. That is the point, though, too."

A human voice screamed out from somewhere down the mountainside.

"Risk, what was that?"

"A human. Or a mutant. Hiding."

"What happened?"

"They're done hiding, Mare. Better hurry."

Sophia shook the lion's head lightly and said, "Kenzie, you have to listen to us. We know you're in there."

"No," said Risk. "Remember: it might be impossible to be good in this place. So, don't try. Not with the lion."

"Oh," said Marilyn, "like make stuff up? Crazy stuff?"

"We can do that," said Sophia. "That's what you mean?"

"Not just crazy. Sex."

*　　*　　*

Widow had rolled herself facedown on the bed, and she was raising and lowering her ass in a measured rhythm, using both hands between her thighs.

"Mm, even stronger. Such strong, sweet poisons for those two."

She heard a human scream from somewhere outside.

"Already? Those wolves aren't that fast."

She jumped up, still wearing camouflage and boots, and walked toward the door, still fingering herself and fondling her breasts.

Leaning her head around the door just enough to see what was happening, she scoffed at the sight of the twins lying on the patio with the lion between them, both looking like they might be naked under their small blankets.

And she saw that they'd put back on their high heels.

"Good," she said, smiling. "I like my helpless baby girls to be sexy for me."

She left the door partway open and walked briskly toward the door to the basement hideaway room. After starting down the stairs, she pulled it closed, turned out the light, and carefully felt her way around until she could lie on the bed.

Just waiting in the dark.

* * *

"I'll start, Sis."

Sophia leaned in closer, until her nose was almost touching the lion's nose.

"I'll let you tie me up. Even better, I'll pretend I don't want you to. You can start by tying my wrists together behind my back. That'll get me helpless for you real quick."

"What else, Sissy?"

"Don't stop there, Kenzie. Tie all the way up my arms too. Make it so I can't possibly get them free. I won't be able to stop you when you unbutton my blouse and slip that over my shoulders. Just leave it there. Same with the bra. Just unclasp that and open it wide. You remember my breasts. I won't be able to stop anything you want to do with them."

Marilyn giggled and grabbed at the small blanket covering her naked sister. She tossed it aside and looked at her breasts.

"She could even be cruel, Sissy. Cruel is good. Or so I've heard."

"Mm-hmm, Kenzie. You might have to go ahead and wiggle my panties off of me before you bind my legs together."

"I'd help you with both of those, Kenzie. Did you know that Sissy and I undress each other all the time?"

Sophia tossed aside Marilyn's blanket, leaving her lying close to the lion wearing nothing but her heels.

"Oh, now I'm naked too. I'd tie Sissy's legs really tight for you."

"You'd want to tie something around my waist, too, just to be sure. Oh, you'd need somewhere to sit for that, wouldn't you?"

Marilyn whispered in the lion's ear, "Sit on Sissy's face, Kenzie. Such a pretty place to sit. She won't be able to stop you or get away. Oh, no, she'll have to do as she's told."

Sophia moaned softly and said, "Mm, I'd have to be such a good little girl."

Marilyn kissed the lion and said in her ear, "She means she'll have to lick you. She promises she'd do a very nice job too."

Sophia glanced back at Risk and saw that he was watching them, not the nearwolves, and his eyes couldn't have gotten any bigger. She grinned and continued with K Kat.

"And I sure won't be complaining. I'll be busy, though, like Sis said. You'll know it. I'll be a very good little girl and never stop licking."

"I'd get behind you," said Marilyn, "and lie really close so as soon as you got up on your knees, I'd be able to kiss Sissy. I bet you'd like to watch that."

Then, she giggled and added, "Hmm, and guess what Sissy's lips would taste like."

The lion started kicking and whimpering softly.

"I might even bite her," Marilyn said with a giggle.

She got serious and added, "I'm sure I'd want to bite her."

"I'd want Sis to bite me. I'd be so helpless to both of you. You could both bite me, and I couldn't stop it."

"I'd bite right into her head," said Marilyn. "Oh, you know I would. And maybe you'd be touching Sissy right then, someplace special. We'd both be having fun with her."

"Sis likes to bite. Oh, she sure does like to bite."

"I like being tied up, too, though. Kenzie, you'd have to tie up both of us. Then, you could invite Widow into the room. We'd be just sweet twin baby girl presents that you could give her. Have you met Widow?"

"Oh, she's hot," said Sophia. "And cruel. Sis and I love being her little baby girls."

Marilyn looked up and held Risk's steady gaze while he was shaking his head at the spectacle.

"Sissy and I are her sweet little twin baby girls. And you know what we like best, Kenzie?"

Sophia whispered in the lion's ear: "Being helpless for her."

"Mm-hmm," Marilyn whispered in the big cat's other ear. "Naked, tied-up, helpless, no choice but to do every little thing she—"

The mountain lion shook a few times, snarled at the black sky, then Kenzie was lying between the twins, completely naked.

"Kenzie!" said Sophia. "You're back!"

She leaned over and kissed her before she could speak.

While they were kissing, Marilyn said, "Aw, that's sweet. But she—hey, Sissy, it's my turn."

Sophia backed away, and Marilyn continued the kiss with Kenzie. Then, she backed away too.

They both watched her smiling, looking from one to the other, and taking deep breaths, causing her bare breasts to rise and fall. The twins rubbed around on her belly and sometimes squeezed her breasts.

"Kenzie," said Sophia, "can you talk?"

"Say something, Kenzie."

With the background growling from hungry nearwolves louder than ever, Risk yelled, "They're here!"

Kenzie shivered, shook, and blinked her eyes rapidly before shifting back into a lion.

The girls didn't jump up. They just kept hugging K Kat, who tolerated it for only a few seconds, then she squirmed herself free and jumped up onto her paws.

"Dammit," said Risk. "Inside."

*   *   *

Marilyn and Sophia both gave the lion a good rubbing around her ears, kissed the sides of her head, then rummaged around for their blankets.

While wrapping in those, they heard Risk growling as one of the nearwolves got its head high enough over the mountain's rocks to look at them, howl at the impostor moon, then stare at them again.

Another joined him on the left. Then, one more on the right.

Risk started backing toward the twins, his arms out as a shield, and K Kat, again a lion, stood by his side. Both uttered low growling.

While hurrying toward the door, Marilyn said, "Sissy, we got to see Kenzie again. She sure is a beautiful girl."

Sophia sighed and said, "Yeah, she really is. Um, maybe we can try again sometime?"

"I'd like to. Let's plan on it. But not right now!"

Marilyn began scurrying along on her high heels, and Sophia ran as well she could on hers. The door was still open, and they rushed inside, then looked back out.

"No, girl," said Risk. "You first."

K Kat grumbled and ran in next.

Risk kept his eyes on the wolves as they began biting at the fence and trying to climb it. And he kept backing himself toward the door.

"Risk, hurry!"

"I am, Mare. Get the post ready to bar the door."

"Uh, we can't pick it up," Sophia said as she tapped the log leaning against the inside wall.

"Alright. Give me room, then."

One of the nearwolves had reached the top and took a few seconds to test the sharpness of the points. It snarled, then howled up at the moon.

And it didn't care that it had ripped itself open climbing over.

Risk rushed inside, and the last any of them saw was the beast sprinting toward them on all fours, dripping a trail of its own blood and looking like nothing but sharp teeth.

"Hurry, Risk!"

Risk groaned when he picked up the heavy piece of timber and dropped it in place, just as the rampaging nearwolf crashed into the door from the outside.

It held, but it shook every time any of them rammed it.

"Back," he said, still watching the door taking a beating. "All of you. Move back."

He noticed something against his leg, so he looked down at a muscular female mountain lion with her fangs bared, staring at the door.

"Good girl. I hope you don't need those beautiful fangs."

Chapter 57 – We're All So Helpless

"Oh, Sissy, this isn't good."

"Not at all, Sis. Could we even burn them? Would we have time?"

"I don't think so. They'd rip us apart, even if we started burning. They're too wild."

The heavy thumps on the door were getting closer together and more violent.

"They're getting mad now," Risk said. "Hungrier."

"Oh," said Marilyn, "maybe the longer that moon is shining."

"Yeah. Probably."

He pointed behind him without looking and said, "Through that door—used to be Pauline's safe room. No one else was allowed. Doesn't matter now. Go in and lock it."

"What about you?" said Marilyn. "Can we help?"

"We're killers, right?" said Sophia. "We can do something."

He turned his head to face them.

"Wait for me. Leave the lion out here. We'll all escape together if we have to."

"Can't we just go do that now?" Marilyn said, near tears.

"I have to try," he said.

"Try what?" said Sophia. "You can't stop this."

"Maybe not. If I can't, then we'll escape. All of us. You remember how."

He paused, looking from one pair of blue eyes to the other.

With a hesitant grin, he pointed at Marilyn, lingered on her, then turned the finger to point at Sophia.

"Your turn," he said, then he faced the door again.

The twins had arms around each other's waist, and they were walking backwards slowly, toward the safe room door and still holding up their useless blankets.

"Maybe . . . don't watch," Risk said.

The pounding on the door increased, and they did watch.

With one violent spasm that forced a raspy scream up at the ceiling, his shift left him as a wolf, too, but with arms almost touching the floor as his head nearly scraped the ceiling.

At the end of each arm, leathery paws grew claws as long as the knife still in Pauline's chest. Or in Ham's hand.

The Risk thing roared at the ceiling, then waited near the door, ready to strike should any of the beasts break through. Even K Kat had backed away from it.

And the battering on the door continued.

"Sis, should we, I don't know, bring those bodies too? So those monsters don't eat them or something?"

Marilyn gave a glance toward them, then leaned closer, studying Pauline.

"Sissy, I didn't notice before. Look."

Sophia, still holding her sister, took her along for a couple of steps toward the body.

"Sheesh," she said as they both saw all of the tiny puncture wounds on Pauline's neck. "Her hair covered all of that."

"Oh, Sissy, there are so many dangerous things here. Something bit her too."

"Yeah, Sis. A lot of times."

The beast that used to be and still was Risk turned and snarled, then waved a long, lethal arm toward their escape room.

"Sissy, he's right. We have to just go."

"Alright. Let's just—"

The door shattered and the log blocking it splintered, then the next ramming sent it to the floor in pieces. The first nearwolf through snarled as it looked around, then froze at the sight of what Risk had become.

Risk didn't freeze. He swung a hairy arm like a punch, but the nails were out, and they sliced neatly through the beast's neck, sending its head bouncing.

"Don't say it, Sis. Just don't."

"I want to."

The second nearwolf came through and rushed at Risk, but Risk punched his claws up into the thing's belly, lifting it off of the floor as its insides spilled out into a sloppy puddle.

Before he could drop the body, the third attacked and raked a claw across his ribs, sending sprays of blood across the room.

Risk howled at the ceiling, then leaned and rammed his shoulder into the beast, backing it into the far wall, where he sent one set of claws into the soft flesh under its chin.

He held it there, twitching and off of the floor for a second, then he snarled and slammed it down.

Turning quickly toward the girls, he said, in a raspy wolf-like voice, "Go! Go now!"

* * *

Before Sophia swung shut the heavy door to the safe room, she called out to Risk, "Just come with us, Risk!"

"No. Lock the door. I'll tell you when I'm done out here."

"Sissy," Marilyn said, tugging on her sister's arm, "he wants us to go. If we don't, he'll have to protect us too!"

"And that could get him killed. Yeah, Sis. Alright."

She closed it with a solid thump while Marilyn searched for and found a light switch. After she'd flipped on the lights, Sophia was able to see the door's lock and engage it.

Still holding their blankets and each other around their waists, they listened to the battle raging just past the heavy, locked door.

"Sis, there are too many. Even for Risk."

Marilyn sighed and squeezed her sister closer.

"I hope not. He's strong and brave. Those nearwolf things will probably run away because he's so scary."

"Sis, listen to yourself. Then, listen to what's going on out there. Those things don't run from anything."

"Oh. And Risk is already hurt."

"And, um, K Kat is the smallest out of all of them. She doesn't have a chance to—"

"No. Sissy, no, she'll be fine, and we'll get Kenzie back. I promise."

They listened for a few more seconds, and it was only getting more intense with mad howling, furniture breaking, and bodies slamming into the hideaway's door.

"Uh-oh, Sissy. I think Widow was taking a nap somewhere. I didn't even remember to chase her in here too."

"Oh, damn, that's right. She'll never survive out there."

"You're going to miss her, aren't you?"

"Uh, yeah. I guess. Kind of. You know, Sis, if I had another chance, I'd play along with all of that. Just for the fun of it."

"Ooh, it would be fun. Yes. And it wouldn't kill us anyway."

"Uh, yeah. That too. Um, Sis? I don't believe Key S did anything to me. I felt fine when Pauline was finding us clothes, and I wanted so bad to wear those frilly panties."

"I know," said Marilyn. "I could tell. It was obvious."

Sophia turned toward her and said, "That's what Widow said."

"What about?"

"She said it was just so obvious that I secretly wanted to be someone's helpless baby girl."

"Really?"

"Uh, there's more. She really did say that I, uh, want to be a baby, a, uh, helpless baby for, um, a woman."

"She wasn't just teasing you?"

"No. She sounded sure of it too. She said it was so obvious about me, everything I did. Especially those baby-girl panties."

"Is that true, Sissy?"

She looked back at the door and let out a deep sigh.

"I, uh, kind of thought that when I put on those panties. It was just a quick thought, though. Not like I was dwelling on it."

"Hmm. That's not so bad. What about the rest of it? All the things she did to you?"

Sophia faced her sister again.

"Sis, we're just about dead anyway. There's no time left. I don't know if it was Key S, but I craved everything she did to me. Some of the time, I was only pretending to not want it."

Marilyn bobbed her eyebrows and said, "Did that make it even more exciting?"

"Oh, yeah. But God, she had such complete control over me."

"How was it when Risk saved you?"

"Oh, that. I was all bound up in that webbing, and we were hanging upside-down together. She'd trimmed my nails, and we got wrapped in a cocoon thing, me in front of her. Sis, my hands were locked in right where all I could do was touch her pussy, and she did the same for me, while she was biting into my neck. We were totally wrapped up in that stuff."

"Oh my goodness. Bet you wanted like hell to get out of that."

"No. I didn't want Risk to find us. I knew what was happening to me. But Sis, it felt so good. She called me her little lover girl, and you know what? She was right."

"Because you were so close and touching each other like that?"

"Sis, it was all of it. Her last words before she bit me for the last time was that we had the truest love ever. Sis, she told me, kind of, that she was the love of my life!"

"Was she?"

"Uh, I kind of thought so. Then, I mean. I don't know."

"Oh, my. Well, my turn to confess, I guess. Sissy, they were making me take more and more brain stuff in me. I already told you I was giving them all blow jobs, and my ass was right up against the bars. Sissy, I didn't see who was screwing me, but a lot of them did.

Oh, I liked that. I felt so cheap and dirty. And I *was* dirty with oil and slime and stuff. But all of those cocks had brains smeared on them, so that all got inside me too."

"My God, Sis. That's like some sick horror movie."

"It wasn't! All I wanted was more. And before Risk came for me, I was kneeling on the bed, and Janie was snapping that belt into my pussy. She was talking so dirty, Sissy, that it was driving me even more crazy. I bit into some girl's brain, someone they'd killed just for me. I had a chunk in my mouth when Risk came for me. And I didn't want to let it go. He had to knock me out!"

"He just punched you? Just like that?"

"No. Oh, no, Sissy, he was a gorilla. A big, mean gorilla."

"Sheesh. What is going on with us, Sis? Could it be the Key S stuff?"

Marilyn shrugged and said, "Maybe it's just this world."

Their eyes nearly popped out when each felt a warm hand softly touch her back. And they heard a familiar woman's voice, sounding rather uninterested and calm, despite the battle raging beyond the door.

"Mare. Fia. I'm so glad you're here with me."

∗　∗　∗

Without turning to look, Marilyn said, "Widow? We thought you were still out there."

"Mm," she said, her voice even and calm. "Lucky for me, I hid down here when things starting getting dangerous."

She rubbed Sophia's back through her blanket. And she began to let her voice drip out, thick and sticky and irresistible like some forbidden honey.

"Little Fia likes dangerous."

She touched Marilyn's hair.

"How about sweet little Mare?"

Neither one answered, but they turned just enough to look at each other. A few seconds passed, then they offered each other the faintest of grins.

"We're surely going to die down here," Widow said. "The question we should ask is how?"

Sophia said, "What do you mean?"

"Fear when facing death might seem inevitable. But aren't pretty girls meant more for pleasure than anything else?"

Sophia drew in a breath and squeezed her sister's hand, and they both turned to face the woman locked with them in safe room while Risk battled nearwolves gone insane from the light of a fake moon.

"Yes, pretty girls are meant for pleasure. Any kind of pleasure."

All three were up on high heels, and the twins had to look up only a slight amount to see Widow's eyes, which were even blacker than they'd remembered. The dim light couldn't hide the red of her lips as she tipped her head and smiled at each of them.

"Am I dressed for battle with wolves?" she said with sugar in her voice. "Or pleasure?"

The twins looked away from Widow's eyes and lips, and they lingered at the sight of her breasts. She'd fastened only the bottom two buttons of her sheer black blouse, and the fabric did little to hide her excitement.

When she pulled down on the shirt with both hands, the girls looked lower and saw that it was short, stopping well above the elastic band of her silky white panties and leaving more skin for them to see.

They'd just started their glance down at her high-heeled black boots, but she brushed her thick black mane back with both hands, causing them to look up again.

"You two little girls had a very nice soapy bath together."

They squeezed each other's hand, hidden under their small blankets, and nodded.

"Such clean little girls now. So much soft, tender skin."

She looked into Marilyn's eyes and said, "Baby Mare, do you remember kissing your little sister in your bubble bath?"

Marilyn did nothing but nod and look into her eyes.

"Baby Fia? Do you remember *touching* your sweet little sister, under the water?"

Sophia sighed quickly, then said, "Yeah. Um, I mean, yes."

"She's very soft, isn't she?"

Sophia trembled once and then nodded.

They looked into Widow's steady black gaze when she said, "Do you both remember being my sweet little baby girls?"

They nodded.

"How did that feel?"

Marilyn nodded and said, "Good. Really good."

"Fia?"

"Good like I can't even believe."

She touched her poisonous fingertips to Marilyn's cheeks, causing her to close her eyes from the immediate effect.

Looking into Sophia's eyes, she said, "I wish to touch you too. I want to touch your soft, baby skin, dear little Fia."

Sophia whimpered once, softly, as she caressed her cheek with her other hand, using her soft fingertips to give Sophia some of what Marilyn had taken in too.

"Mm, so nice. I think we all agree to what's about to happen next."

She held their cheeks with the palms of her hands, moving her hands slowly and keeping her skin rubbing against theirs.

"Hmm. We're all so helpless to stop any of it."

Chapter 58 – Some Time Together

Risk got slammed into the girls' door by two rampaging wolf beasts, then they each grabbed an arm and threw him high near the ceiling and out into the middle of the room. His wolf head shattered a wooden tabletop hard enough that he groaned and couldn't stop himself from shifting back to his natural human form.

The same two began tentative steps toward something that had been a giant, deadly wolf only a second earlier. They snarled and led with claws out, then one of them howled from a mountain lion closing her jaws on the back of its neck. It spun around, trying to shake K Kat loose and whipping the mountain lion around like a toy from Pauline's bed.

"Good girl!" Risk called. "Bite those fuckers while I shift into something more dangerous!"

Still sprawled out near the shattered table, he snorted as he twitched and spasmed and erupted into a meaner, stronger gorilla than when he'd rescued Marilyn from the zombie horde.

While the lion kept her grip, her fangs in deep and causing the thing to howl and try to swipe back with its already bloody claws, Risk slammed his gorilla hands together, crushing the other nearwolf's head like a rotten grape. He didn't look up to see how much of it had squirted high enough to hang on the ceiling.

But he did rush to K Kat's aid. The lion never let go, and Risk reached around the thing's chest and squeezed. Unable to breathe, and with a toothy mountain lion hanging on with her fangs, the thing silently whipped its claws across the gorilla's back. Risk winced from the new deep wounds before he roared and squeezed and every bone inside his grasp cracked and splintered, and he let the body thud to the floor.

Where K Kat promptly ripped out its throat.

They both turned at the sound of Hawken screaming for help outside on the patio.

"Dammit."

The lion waited, watching Risk, still a gorilla, until he said, "Go, girl. I'll be out."

She snarled and pawed at him, then ran out through the front door.

Risk kept watching the front of the house as he pounded on the door to the basement while he was abandoning battle as a gorilla.

"Hawken needs help," he yelled through the closed and locked door. "Don't come out. Wait for me."

He didn't linger there for a reply, just ran out to help K Kat with Hawken, who was still squawking and screaming and sometimes annunciating a very clear, "Fuck!"

*   *   *

"Oh, hear that?" said Widow, smiling at the twins. "He says he'll be back after some nonsense with his balloon and probably that cat too. But until then, we do have some time together."

Marilyn and Sophia were naked except for their high heels and the blankets over their backs, which each of them held closed in front. Both watched Widow as she took her time in scanning down, then up, spending the most time on their legs.

"I have an absolute fascination with legs, you know."

She smiled at Marilyn, then kept the smile as she turned her eyes to Sophia's. She again slipped her fingertips across their cheeks and sometimes near their ears.

"So soft. Such very soft, smooth skin."

She turned her eyes to Marilyn again, who was taking quicker breaths and watching Widow with big eyes.

"And the little blond twin girl too. Hmm, two soft little twin girls."

The twins turned to face each other, and Marilyn turned far enough that she could wink one eye for her sister to see, and she got a very slight smile back from her before they faced Widow again.

She touched their cheeks lightly while saying, "Risk will likely vanquish those fiends soon, then he'll be in here with that pesky cat. So, why not have just a little fun? It'll only be for a few minutes, I'm sure."

Marilyn nodded, and Sophia sighed and said, "Alright. Sure."

"Oh, good."

Widow rubbed their lips with her thumbs, just at the very edge at first, then along the top and bottom, just touching them all over while looking into their eyes.

"Such very soft lips too. Baby girls should have soft lips, shouldn't they?"

The girls both nodded.

"I remember two soft little babies sucking while they enjoyed their hot bubble bath together."

They nodded again.

"Yes. Very soft."

Almost like a chant, Widow added, "Babies . . . sucking so nicely."

She wiggled her thumb between Sophia's lips first, watching her closely, and smiled when those lips held her thumb even as Widow played with her, sometimes going in deeper.

"Oh, good little girl. Yes, just like that."

She turned her eyes to Marilyn and said, "Little Mare? Open up, dear baby girl."

She raised her eyebrows and waited, watching Marilyn's lips until she parted them.

And she waited longer, gazing into Marilyn's blue eyes as she waited with her mouth open, then said, "Such a good little girl."

Still holding her gaze, Widow smiled as she rubbed her thumb into Marilyn's mouth, and her lips closed around it.

"Mm, we're off to a good start. Just two darling little baby girls, sucking thumbs. They're so good to suck, aren't they?"

Both nodded and when Marilyn squeezed her sister's hand, Sophia didn't squeeze back. She tried again and still got no response.

Widow let them play, sending her stronger poisons into them, and the girls, not knowing, thinking they were safe, kept sucking what she'd put into their mouths.

"I think just a little bit more for my sweet girls," she said, and she rubbed her thumbs around inside their lips, sometimes bending them out and getting them wetter.

"Oh, that's so sweet. Such very good babies. But you want to be the best little baby girls for me, don't you?"

Sophia nodded right away, and Marilyn sighed, then nodded too.

Widow leaned first to whisper in Sophia's ear.

"Very good babies are helpless for me, aren't they, little Fia?"

She slipped her thumb out but kept it close to Sophia's lips.

"Uh, yeah. Uh-huh."

Widow kissed her cheek, then whispered to Marilyn, "I'd love to have two little twin baby girls helpless for me. Doesn't that sound good, baby Mare?"

She only pushed her thumb farther into Marilyn's mouth.

"Mm. Mm-hmm."

"Good little girls. Follow me."

She turned and began a slow strut toward the bed, and both of them watched her legs and ass the entire way, even while they whispered to each other.

"Sissy, this is okay. We'll just play along until Risk gets us, okay?"

"Yeah, Sis. I'm in. But I'm more tired than I thought I was. How about you?"

"Oh, I do feel it some just now. Yes."

"Yeah, just now. Because we've been through so much, right?"

"Um, probably," said Marilyn. "Yes."

"Come on. This'll be fun, Sis. I'm really going to play along."

They walked until they were near Widow and the bed, then Sophia dropped her blanket.

"Oh," said Widow, "how sweet! Just a soft little naked girl. For me?"

Sophia gave Widow a second to examine her in front, then turned herself around.

"Mm-hmm," she said. "Soft and naked for you."

Then, she crossed her wrists behind her, keeping her arms straight.

"Hmm, little Fia is so trusting."

Widow stepped close behind her, held her by her hips, and pulled them together.

In her ear, she said, "Trusting little girls should be so careful. Such dreadful things can happen to them."

She released her hips and rubbed her fingertips up and down her arms.

"You still wish to be helpless for me, though, don't you?"

Sophia nodded without turning around.

"Mm, such a good little baby for me."

Widow took a few steps toward the nightstand and pulled out a length of webbing.

She made sure to click the heels of her boots while walking back toward Marilyn, where she handed it to her.

Marilyn hesitated, looking down at it, then at Sophia's wrists.

"Take it. Your little baby sister will love how quickly it sets. Oh, she'll be nice and helpless soon."

Marilyn took it, and Widow walked around to face Sophia.

She leaned in close, with one hand on each of her cheeks.

"You're very good little blond sister will help bind you. Isn't it sweet that your very own sister is making you helpless for me?"

Sophia opened her mouth, and her lips moved for just a second before Widow leaned in and held her in a wet, poison-filled kiss while she was being bound with the special webbing by her sister.

She broke the kiss to look around at the progress and said, "Be sure that it's nice and tight, little Mare."

"Um, okay."

With poisonous hands on Sophia's soft cheeks, she leaned in and resumed the kiss until Marilyn had finished.

Then, Widow backed away and grinned.

"Mm, just a little more helpless. It feels good, doesn't it?"

Sophia was taking deeper breaths, and she nodded.

Widow looked down at Sophia's breasts.

"Mm, such teasing big-girl breasts on just a little baby girl."

She shook her head, smiling at Sophia, then walked over for more webbing. She brought the whole cannister closer for Marilyn.

"Just for fun, Baby Mare, tie her arms all the way up."

"Uh, really?"

"She wants to be helpless. You can ask her."

"Uh, Sissy? You, um, want to be even more helpless?"

"Uh, yeah. Yeah, I do, Sis."

"There. You see?"

Marilyn shrugged and pulled out a length, tore it off, then started near her sister's bound wrists. She wrapped it around, overlapping every piece, with Widow watching closely.

She fed through the last of it, as high up as it could go.

"Smooth it down. Little Fia wants it to set nice and tight."

"Um, okay."

"Good girl, little Mare. Let's lay your sweet sister down on the bed now."

"Um, sure."

Together, they got Sophia to step lightly on her spiky heels, place one knee up on the bed, then the other, then she crawled forward and they helped her to lie facedown on the soft blanket.

Widow got up on the bed, too, and knelt near Sophia's hips, then said, "You too, Mare. Come up."

Marilyn shrugged and took the spot across from Widow, and they faced each other, both on their knees, with Sophia lying between them, naked except for her heels and with arms completely bound from her wrists all the way up.

"How does it feel," Widow said as she reached out for Marilyn's cheek again, "to have someone so helpless and at your mercy?"

"Uh, she is kind of helpless. Um, she—"

Widow slipped her thumb between Marilyn's lips and said, "Shh. Just suck for a moment. Suck like a little baby."

She watched Marilyn's blue eyes looking only into hers, and Marilyn sucked enthusiastically on her thumb.

"Yes, it's so good for you."

Widow tipped her head and smiled at her swallowing every couple of seconds.

"Good. Yes, just like that. More."

Marilyn kept sucking and looking into her eyes.

Widow withdrew her thumb and rubbed her lips a few times with it, and she said, "Oh, how nice," when Marilyn's lips tried to pull it back inside.

She let her suck more, then took one of her hands and placed it on Sophia's bare ass cheek.

"Yes, it's good. It's so good for you to suck. Again, isn't it so wonderful to have your very own little sister helpless like that?"

Marilyn nodded and said, "Uh, yes. It kind of . . . is."

"Would you like it if she was even more helpless?"

"Yes. Oh, yes, I think I would."

"Mm. Yes, you will. Here."

She handed Marilyn another length of the banding.

"Bind the sweet baby's ankles."

"Um . . ."

Widow rubbed Marilyn's hand around on her sister's ass cheek and said, "Mm, feel how soft."

Marilyn watched her hand caressing her sister and said, "Yes, she's very soft."

"She's a soft baby that loves being helpless. Go on. Bind her ankles."

Marilyn patted her sister a few times, then took the webbing from Widow's hand. She lifted Sophia's legs and kept her ankles close together, then wrapped them many times with the sticky material.

Then, she lay her sister's legs back down.

Widow began touching one of Sophia's calves, sliding her fingertips up and down it.

"Touch her. She's a very soft baby girl."

Marilyn did the same as Widow with Sophia's other leg. When Widow moved up to Sophia's thigh, rubbing it gently, touching it all over, Marilyn did too.

Widow leaned close enough to kiss Marilyn and said, "We have a sweet, helpless little baby girl, don't we?"

Marilyn nodded and whimpered softly, and Widow kissed her for half a minute, making it a wet kiss and using her tongue generously, then backed away.

She pinched off another length of the binding strap and handed it to Marilyn.

"Tie her up like a juicy little farm animal. Tie her ankles to her wrists."

Marilyn looked down at her captured sister, whose back was showing the quicker breaths she was taking.

"Go on, little Mare. A soft baby should be tied up nice and tight."

Marilyn sighed, then tied the end first to the straps around Sophia's ankles, then fed the other end through the part of the binding around her sister's wrists.

"Pull it tight for her. Go on."

Marilyn stared down at her naked sister as she pulled the strap tighter, raising her sharp black heels to point straight up.

"More. Tighter."

Marilyn sighed and tightened up the strap, leaving Sophia's heels near her hands.

"A knot. Tie a knot."

"What kind?"

"Oh, a pretty bow would be nice."

Marilyn did it and when Widow started rubbing Sophia's ass cheek, as much as she could reach, Marilyn did the same on her side.

Widow smiled at Marilyn until she looked up at her.

"We have a very helpless little baby girl now. How does that feel?"

Marilyn took a deep breath and let it out quickly.

"Good. It feels good."

"Lie down for just a moment. Let's enjoy this together. Your baby sister will stay nice and quiet for us."

Widow laid herself down so that her face was near Sophia's hips, and Marilyn did the same. They looked at each other across the very soft and smooth skin of tied-up Sophia's bare ass, some of it covered by her tightly bound arms.

Widow shifted forward enough to rest her cheek on Sophia.

She tipped herself enough to graze Sophia with her lips, giving her a light kiss, then said, "You too, little blond one."

Marilyn rested her cheek on Sophia's other side.

"And a kiss," said Widow. "Let's give her soft skin a little kiss together."

Looking into each other's eyes, they tipped their heads enough that each could hold their lips against the bare skin of Sophia's ass.

Widow ended her kiss first, then shifted closer to Marilyn.

With their noses sometimes rubbing, Widow said, "We have a very soft, tied-up little baby girl, don't we?"

Marilyn whimpered softly, then nodded.

And they kissed, both of them resting their cheeks as well as they could on the bare ass of the sister whom Marilyn had just hog-tied.

Widow broke their kiss and giggled softly when Sophia groaned and turned her head to look the other way.

"Well, sweet little baby Mare, we can't have that noise while we kiss, can we?"

Marilyn kissed her quickly, then said, "No. No we cannot."

Chapter 59 – You Really Need to Fight Now

Risk ran past the damaged front door of Ham's house on a mountain and stopped out on the patio.

"Oh, fuck."

Hawken had landed in his usual place, but no one had tied the basket in place. Without a steady hand on the spout to keep it still, the entire craft was drifting around, sometimes colliding with Ham's craft and scraping the basket across the stone.

The two ravenous nearwolves in the basket howled at him and the lion, then started climbing up the ropes and cables to join the other one already up there—the one that would devour Hawken in only seconds.

"Hawken!"

"Sorry!" he screamed as he kicked at the furry arms swiping at him with sharp claws.

"K Kat, in the basket."

He grabbed the top edge and jumped into the basket, but K Kat didn't need to grab anything—she easily leaped in and immediately joined the battle.

Risk, still his human self, grabbed a furry leg and pulled down. Since the beast had been reaching for Hawken, it fell easily but landed hard. Its back crunched backwards when it got folded over the basket's edge.

K Kat growled and ripped at the thing's throat, shaking herself each way until she'd pulled loose shredded chunks of it. She jumped her front paws up onto the rail and spat out the bloody pieces.

Risk glanced down and smiled.

"Good girl."

He reached up for another of the nearwolves, not the one that was almost upon Hawken, who was squawking and kicking and trying to climb higher into the balloon.

Risk's new quarry saw the attack coming and held on while trying to kick him in return.

"Dammit."

He shifted quickly just his right arm, forcing out the longest claws he could, and he raked them across the thing's legs with blinding speed, sending red spray everywhere.

The nearwolf shrieked even as it fell and when it landed, it stopped screaming because its throat was in the snarling jaws of an enraged mountain lion.

"Risk!"

Risk looked up and saw no one on the navigator's perch except for a savage, wolf-like creature. Beyond that beast, Hawken was still climbing the few cords that ran to the balloon's top. The wolf bumped the hot iron pot, and the lid lifted and stayed lifted, stuck in place.

"No!" Risk screamed and started to climb, but another attacker climbed into the basket.

He turned to fight that one and heard the balloon stretching and groaning as it swelled with hot air. All of the cables and ropes snapped into place, every one of them pulled tight.

And they all began to rise.

"Fuck!"

He and K Kat fought the largest of the wolves yet, one that seemed to know not to make dumb mistakes. It swiped when it could and stayed out of Risk's striking range.

The seconds hurried past, and the basket kept rising.

K Kat tried to attack from one side, then the other, and all she met was the thing's claws. She yipped and fell near Risk's boots, and he didn't take the time to look at her.

But he did see, on the edge of his vision, the roof of Ham's house far below them as they all drifted away from the mountain and on a course to take them over a city under siege.

*   *   *

"Oh," said Widow, "your baby sister is a talkative little girl, disturbing our sweet kissing. She doesn't remember something, but I do."

"What?" said Marilyn.

Widow kissed her again, rubbing their lips together and giving her more of her strongest poisons.

"Well, baby Mare, it's just that even a little bit of cruelty can feel so sweet to a bound-up little baby. Don't you agree?"

Marilyn nodded, and they kissed for thirty seconds, their cheeks resting on Sophia's bare ass while she sometimes struggled against her hog-tie bonds.

"Oh, that little baby girl needs to be more quiet for us. I think she's begging for someone to be cruel with her. She likes that so much when she's helpless. Just a soft little baby girl, isn't she?"

Marilyn stayed close enough to kiss Widow and caressed her sister's soft skin.

"Mm," said Marilyn, "she's a very soft little baby girl. Mm-hmm. So helpless too."

Widow rose up enough to lean over and pinch another generous length of sticky strapping.

"Here," she said as she handed it to Marilyn. "Just slip that between the little baby's lips. It'll help her to be a very good and quiet little girl for us."

"Uh, sure. Okay."

Marilyn got up and sat back on her heels, and Widow did the same on the other side of Sophia. Marilyn held the strap with both hands and lowered it in front of her sister's face, then giggled softly as she wiggled it in between her lips.

"Hmm, I'm gagging you, Sissy. You're a naughty, noisy little girl."

Sophia tried to form words, but it was all garbled.

"Like that?" she said to Widow.

"Oh, little Mare, no. It has to be tighter. The baby wants it tighter."

Marilyn gave it a good pull, lifting Sophia's head off of the bed while the tight banding stretched her cheeks back.

"Better?"

"Well, a little, sweet little Mare. Think about how helpless she is. You can really pull that tight, can't you?"

"I could. Yes."

"Whether the helpless baby girl likes it or not?"

"Mm. Yes. That's very true. I kind of hope the baby doesn't like it."

"Yes, that's the best. Let's say she doesn't like it, then. But we do."

Marilyn pulled back hard on the strap, and Sophia groaned as the band stretched her cheeks far back and dug deeper into her mouth.

"Yes, just like that. Now, don't let it get any looser, just tie it back there."

Marilyn held it tight and tied a knot.

Widow leaned to look at Sophia's stretched lips, pulled down at the ends and forming a silent scream.

"Look at your little sister's lips, baby girl. What do you think?"

Marilyn leaned and looked, then smiled.

"Mm, I like it. That's kind of cruel."

"Yes, you're being a very good girl, tying that so tight. Now, loop that around her wrists too."

"Uh, really?"

"Yes, of course. Think of how helpless she'll be. Such a helpless, quiet little baby girl."

She held Marilyn's gaze and leaned close enough to touch lips to lips.

"Then, we can do anything we want with her."

She gave her a wet kiss and backed away.

"Anything at all."

Marilyn whimpered softly.

"We'll have a very precious little doll of a baby girl. Mm, for whatever we want."

Both closed their eyes as they gave each other a longer, wetter kiss.

Then, Marilyn pulled the strap back, lifting her sister's head up and tilting it way back, then looped the end through the strapping around her wrists.

She was about to tie it there when Widow said, "Tighter would be good, baby Mare."

Marilyn sighed and pulled the strap much tighter, then tied her sister in place with her head suspended way back. Widow took the nearest of Marilyn's hands and got her going on rubbing around her sister's bare ass cheek.

"See? How does it feel to have such a trussed-up little girl like that?"

Marilyn stared down at her helpless, struggling sister and said, "I like it. I like it a lot."

"Isn't she so pretty now? Much prettier when she's all tied-up and helpless?"

"Mm-hmm," she said, still rubbing around everywhere she could reach. "She's even prettier now."

"Yes, it's just wonderful. Would you like to watch me give your baby sister a little bite?"

"Uh, yes. I kind of would. On her neck?"

"Well, yes, of course. Lie down like I am."

Widow lay beside Sophia on one side and Marilyn on the other.

"Let's hug our little baby girl, Mare."

They both slipped an arm under Sophia and held themselves close to her, both of their mouths by Sophia's neck while each used her free hand to touch the other everywhere that they could reach.

"Hmm," said Widow, "just a little nibble to start. Baby Mare, you should try just a little nibble too. You want to, don't you?"

Marilyn was breathing deeply and sniffing all around her sister's neck.

"Yes. Yes, I sure do."

"The zombies knew about you, didn't they? That you're always so close to being a cruel, biting little girl?"

"Yes, they must have known."

"And you knew, too, didn't you? Even before the Key S?"

Marilyn groaned softly and said, "Yes."

"Of course, you did. Let's bite our helpless baby together, then."

She sank in her fangs and injected the strongest poisons she'd ever had. Almost immediately, Sophia stopped whimpering and went limp.

Widow felt the rapid effects, then backed away enough to watch Marilyn bare her teeth at her sister's throat, start heavier breathing, then bite into her enough to make blood run down her neck.

"Mm," said Widow, "taste that. Taste your juicy baby sister."

Marilyn moaned and started sucking at it, her teeth still in Sophia's neck.

"Good little girl. Such a good baby girl for sucking up her sweet juices."

Widow reached up high enough to fluff Marilyn's blond mane while she was biting into Sophia's neck.

"And you've always known that biting soft, helpless baby girls is what you want most, haven't you?"

Marilyn moaned, still biting, and managed to say, "Mm-hmm."

"Yes, baby girls are the softest and sweetest. So juicy."

Marilyn backed away, her lips dripping blood, and Widow shifted closer to kiss those lips. And as Sophia faded even further, Marilyn and Widow, both hugging her tight and touching each other all over, kissed and licked her blood from each other's lips and tongue.

Widow backed away a little, licking her lips, and said, "See how she's slowing down so nicely? I gave her some of my sweet poisons just for fun. She's loving it."

"She's okay, though, right? It's just for fun?"

"Yes, of course, and she's having such a nice orgasm. She's almost lost in it, the sweet little girl. Oh, and a few more tight bands through the baby girl's mouth would be fun, don't you think?"

"Oh, yes. Yes. I'll get it."

Marilyn got up enough to grab another long strand of the webbing then knelt near Sophia.

"Here," Widow said, then put two fingers up for Marilyn to suck.

She took them between her lips and sucked, and Widow smiled at the sight of her swallowing repeatedly.

"Good little girl. It's so good for you to suck."

With her fingers still tight between Marilyn's lips, Widow laughed softly and said, "Mm, is there any part of me you wouldn't suck right now?"

Marilyn kept sucking while shaking her head.

"Ah. Such a sweet little thing," she said and let her keep sucking.

Marilyn didn't wait for encouragement before wedging the next strapping between Sophia's lips and pulling it tight.

"Mm, that's so nice. Keep going."

Marilyn looped it around again, keeping it tight, then again, filling her sister's mouth and making her struggle to breathe.

"Aw, the poor little thing," Widow said while Marilyn sucked her fingers and tied the material in place. "Such cruel treatment. But she loves to offer herself as a helpless little girl. Oh, she's so helpless now."

Widow gently tipped Sophia onto her side, and she and Marilyn watched her bare breasts sometimes shaking very slightly from her struggles to breathe.

"Look," Widow said as she pinched one of Sophia's nipples. "The little baby loves it. Why don't you lie down with her, sweet little baby Mare?"

"Okay."

Marilyn lay facing her sister and brushed a few stray black hairs back off of her face. Sophia's bright blue eyes were barely open and blinking slowly.

Widow lay down behind Marilyn and swept her blond mane back off of her neck, then she spoke softly in her ear while slipping fingers between her lips, which Marilyn quickly began to suck.

"Watch her closely, my sweet little girl. Watch the soft, helpless baby girl."

Marilyn nodded and kept looking from her sister's eyes, which were starting to close, to her large breasts, which were becoming motionless.

Sophia's eyes closed and didn't open, and her chest came to a complete stop.

"Aw, see?" said Widow. "Isn't she a very good and quiet little girl now?"

"Mm-hmm. Oh my, yes."

"I knew you'd love that. And you love that we did that to her, with our binding and biting?"

"Mm. Mm-hmm."

She gently nudged Marilyn, tipping her until she was facedown, then she laid herself on top of her.

"Good girl. Mm, just like that. I have a secret for you too."

"What?"

Widow laughed gently, then spoke in Marilyn's ear.

"I've been using poisons that are so much stronger than before. You and your sweet baby sister are in real trouble."

Marilyn tried to get up, but Widow had her in a tight hug which pinned her arms to her sides.

"Hey, no! This was supposed to be—"

"Shh, now, baby girl," Widow said after she'd reached one hand up to cover Marilyn's mouth. "Just be a good girl and listen, okay?"

She waited, and it took a few seconds, but Marilyn nodded.

"Good girl. Listen closely, and you'll understand that what I'm saying is true. This world is brutal and unforgiving. Your life here could end at any time."

She let her hand fall away from Marilyn's mouth, but she still rubbed her skin across her lips, taking her time.

Marilyn only breathed and listened.

"Many die lonely and tragic deaths here, surrounded by only anger and hate. Up above, Topside, isn't all that different. Now, think of the simple beauty of dying in the arms of one who loves you. One who loves you so completely that they adore every part of you. Her love for you is so deep and so perfect that she can't live without consuming everything that you are. And all the while, she's telling you the truth about how she feels: that you're beautiful and adorable, that she loves you as she would a child, an infant, even, and she wants to be as close as possible to you, in every intimate way, until the very end."

Marilyn's deep breaths had calmed, and Widow could feel that she was no longer even close to trying to escape.

She kissed Marilyn's neck softly and said, "Such a love is so rare in such a harsh world. That is the love I feel for you."

She kissed her again, and her lips felt Marilyn trembling softly in her arms.

"Do you wish to feel such absolute love, my dearest baby girl?"

She waited patiently, and Marilyn nodded with a very soft whimper.

"You understand now, don't you? To love is to consume, and to consume is to love?"

Marilyn sighed and nodded in Widow's arms.

"There, there. Good baby girl. And would my sweet baby like to feel a very nice big-girl orgasm, better than she can even imagine right now?"

Marilyn didn't hesitate to nod her head several times.

"Just a little bite. Just a little love bite for my baby. Does she want that?"

Marilyn moaned and nodded again.

Widow kissed her, then whispered, "Such a good baby for me. Your orgasm will be so much more intense if it takes you after you've struggled to save yourself. Because you're going to be bitten. A cruel woman is going to sink her very sharp fangs into your soft neck, and she's going to attach herself there and suck."

Marilyn whimpered but didn't struggle to escape.

"Do you want that stronger orgasm, sweet baby girl?"

Marilyn whimpered and said, "Yes!"

"Okay. Yes, it can be so much better for you."

Widow moaned while kissing her again, then said, "Oh, you really need to fight now, sweet baby. Mm, my poisons are so much stronger now. Fight me!"

Marilyn groaned and fought against Widow's arms, which were too strong and holding her tight. Even the weight of her on Marilyn's back made it impossible for her to roll away from the woman.

As Marilyn's wild blond mane whipped each way, Widow waited, her fangs poised to strike, until the soft, smooth, unprotected skin of Marilyn's neck offered itself to her bite.

"Fight, sweet little one! Fight for your life!"

Marilyn's neck finally gave her that invitation, and Widow moaned as she sank her fangs into Marilyn's neck, and she kept them there as the blond Kildare Killer's fighting weakened. But she didn't prolong the bite and the deep injection of her poisons past that.

"Keep protesting," she whispered in Marilyn's ear. "Mm, such a sweet orgasm you'll have."

Marilyn could barely hold up her head, but she could still speak.

"You shouldn't bite me," she said weakly. "No, I don't want to be bit!"

Widow had grabbed each of her wrists and roughly yanked her arms behind her.

"Ooh, such a little fighter!"

"Stop! Please don't bind my arms!"

With a poisonous palm on Marilyn's back, holding her into the soft blankets, Widow began wrapping webbing around her wrists, quickly locking them together.

"No, don't! I'll be helpless!"

Widow quickly laid herself back on top of Marilyn, pinning her down.

"Shh, now, precious," she said as she cleared access to her neck. "Such a quarrelsome little girl."

"Let me go! Please!"

"Mm, let me help you relax a little. Mm, your skin is so soft. So soft and juicy."

She bit into her neck and gave her a good dose, and she stayed biting into her until her prey started to go limp.

"Aw, there we go. Such a nicer little girl now. You just lie very still and quiet for me and enjoy that sweetest of orgasms that's only going to get stronger for you."

She leaned over and kissed her cheek, then all over her ear.

"Let's get you tied up pretty just like your little baby sister. Mm, you're both such juicy little things. I do love juicy little twin baby girls."

Marilyn didn't resist while Widow bound her ankles, then pulled her heels up and tied them tight to her wrists.

"Hey, you . . . um . . ."

"Oh my, you're still a talkative little thing, though. Let's make you a quiet little girl for me."

She held a band of webbing near Marilyn's lips and said, "Open up, my precious. Open up."

"Oh, such a good girl," she said when Marilyn parted her lips so that she could work the material into her mouth.

"Mm, just a little bit of cruelty for you, too, my precious little girl."

She pulled back hard on the strap, lifting Marilyn's head up and getting a groan out of her. She fastened it in there, then tied the other end to her wrists.

"Now," Widow said as she lay herself between the two hog-tied twins, "let's see about giving you a very good bite. Oh, yes. Lots of my sweet poisons for you, too, my tender, juicy little baby."

She nudged aside a few blond hairs, then nuzzled in close and bit into the soft skin of Marilyn's neck.

"Mm," she said after backing the sharp teeth out just enough to talk. "You're just the sweetest little thing. Such a precious little-girl sponge for my poisons."

She sank them in again and sucked for a few minutes, sometimes smiling at feeling the body in her arms slumping even more.

"Good for now," she said in a perfectly normal voice and sat up.

She shifted herself around and sat back on her heels between them, facing the same way. In her hands, she held the straps that kept their heads tied up and back, and she pulled them just a bit farther, grinning at them.

"You two grown women thought this was just for fun. And if you weren't having the best, nonstop orgasms of your lives, you'd be screaming that you don't want to be my helpless twin baby girls."

She laughed once and pulled their head straps harder.

"But that's what you are: my precious, twin baby girls. And you're so soft and juicy for me. Helpless."

She tipped her head to listen toward the doorway.

"Hmm, it's gotten so quiet out there. Those beasts have dragged away Risk and that pesky cat too. My sweet baby girls, no one is coming back to save you. A little change of plans. Mm, we have time."

She patted each of them on their bare ass cheeks, rubbed all over them with her fingertips, then reached for the nail clippers on the nightstand.

"Let's just see about those troublesome fingernails of yours, my sweet baby Mare. You won't need them either. Oh, no. Just very nice and soft fingertips."

Chapter 60 – Make Love to Me

"Dammit!"

Risk had his wolf-like hands around the thick, furry neck of the last nearwolf still battling them in the basket as it kept drifting toward the howls and screams of the city.

"Hawken! Hold it steady!"

"I can't! Too damaged!"

"Fuck."

He groaned and gagged as the beast strangled him before he could shift more. On the thing's back, K Kat had her fangs ripping at its neck and into its shoulder, sending blood and furry pieces of skin down onto the basket's floor.

"Steady!"

"I fixed the fire, so up or down!" screamed Hawken. "No sides!"

"Dammit."

The nearwolf let go to get the mad lion off of its back, and Risk took that chance to drive all of his claws into its chest. Then, he dug them in and pulled, tearing loose not just skin and muscle and bone but heart too.

Before the beast could crumple to the floor, he stabbed his claws in again, like a pitchfork.

"Fuck you!" he roared as he tossed it over the side.

They were high enough that he and K Kat had time to look over the side and watch it rip apart on the sharp rocks far below them.

Risk scoffed at the sight, but the lioness only shook her head to clear some blood and gore from her snout.

"What's the problem?"

Up above, Hawken shrugged and said, "Damn wolves. Busted the spout. No steering."

"None at all?"

"Some. Not much."

"Can you fix it?"

"Not without tools."

Risk looked down and said, "Dammit."

He saw that K Kat was gazing up at him, injured in battle.

"Not you. You're a good girl."

She blinked up at him a few times, then got busy licking her wounds.

"Fuck. We need to go back, girl."

Risk looked up and said, "Set it down."

Hawken turned his hawk eyes to look down, past the basket, and saw only packs of nearwolves doing the chasing and crowds and some loners that were busy fleeing. Howls and screams filled the moonlit sky.

"Where? Down there?"

Risk pointed and said, "No. Ham's mountain."

Hawken looked back that way, shaking his head.

"Won't be quick."

Risk waited for him to look back down at him, then said, "Better get started, then."

"Alright."

Risk watched as the navigator tried to hold himself in place with one gloved hand while the other held the wrecked spout. He managed to give it a blast, but it twisted out of his hand like an escaping fire hose.

"Keep trying."

"Alright."

He looked down at the lioness grooming herself, sometimes biting at bits of wolf flesh that got tangled in her short fur, but she didn't look up at him.

Watching Ham's mountain drawing near, slowly and haphazardly, he muttered to himself, "Those girls. Locked alone in that room. Dammit."

* * *

"There we go," Widow said, squeezing Marilyn's hands then letting them go and tossing aside her clippers.

"Just very nice soft little fingertips. So adorable."

Marilyn groaned softly, still hog-tied and lying facedown, then fought to speak around the single tight band pulled deep between her lips.

"Risk . . . Risk will . . ."

Widow leaned over and kissed around her ear.

"Oh, you're so precious. No, little baby. He's very impressive, but there are just too many of those things. He's probably scattered around in tiny pieces by now. That nasty, savage lion too."

Marilyn groaned and turned her eyes enough to see her sister's face. Sophia was still motionless, and even her breasts weren't at all disturbed by any breaths. But Marilyn saw signs that Widow had filled her with enough poisons to sustain an orgasm for her.

Widow's soft hand caressed her, brushing aside stray hairs.

"Hmm, just feel that orgasm that's only getting started."

Marilyn started to moan softly.

"Yes, good girl. Such a good, helpless, tied-up little orgasm girl for me."

Marilyn closed her eyes and her moan turned into a groan, then she fought weakly against all of her bindings.

"Oh, you poor little dear. Don't you worry, you sweet little baby. You'll have more of my delightful poisons swimming all around inside you soon enough. And I know you love orgasms. You'll soon get such a sweet, final one. Mm, so precious."

She patted her ass, then stopped and said, "You want it right now? If you insist."

She giggled as she wiggled a hand under Marilyn near her navel.

"Oh, so very soft. Such a soft little girl."

She reached in farther and lower, then held still with her fingertips at just the right place.

"Oh, there we go. My, you're even softer here. Mm, that's so good. Yes, little girl. Just let yourself enjoy it."

Widow kept rubbing between Marilyn's thighs, and she played with her hair at the same time.

"Mm, juicy little girls are the absolute best. Does that feel nice, sweet baby Mare?"

Marilyn sighed and managed to say, "Uh-huh."

"Hmm, it's only going to get better. Do you know what would help?"

She tried hard to shake her head enough that Widow noticed.

"Oh, you're adorable. I'll tell you: you'll love it so much more if you're as helpless as you can be. Your little baby sister loves that too. Another little bite first can only help."

She kept her hand between Marilyn's thighs, gently rubbing her as she laid herself on top of her, then she slid her fangs into her neck.

"Mm," she said as she sucked on her and gave her more poisons.

Widow fed for a few minutes in the quiet, locked room dug into a mountain beside an abandoned house, then she pulled the pointy teeth back and kissed Marilyn's wounds.

"There we go. You wanted that so you can be a very cooperative little girl."

She watched as Marilyn's breathing slowed and almost stopped.

"Oh, so close. But you can still answer. Mare? How about if we wind a few more tight layers into that pretty mouth of yours? Would you like that?"

Widow had to lean to hear Marilyn say, "Uh-huh."

"Oh, such a good baby. See how much you love all of this with that wonderful orgasm? Yes. Let's do that. Let's fill that pretty mouth."

She stretched the banding material across Marilyn's mouth, which was already locked open, then pulled it in as deep as she could.

"Mm, here we go."

She wound it all around her head, then kept going, giving her a total of five thick bands. All of it was so thick that it was even with her stretched lips.

"Such a good, quiet girl now," Widow said as she tipped Marilyn onto her side, facing Sophia.

"Oh my, you're like your darling little sister: you're both just sweet little babies, but you have such big-girl breasts. Mm, yes, struggle my sweet little thing."

She watched Marilyn's breasts trembling from her efforts to breathe around all the windings deep in her mouth.

"Such teasing nipples you have," she said as she pinched one and tugged it all around before letting it go.

"Yes, you want the other one pinched too. Every littlest touch feels so good, doesn't it?"

Marilyn couldn't answer as Widow pinched the other and jiggled her breast around.

"So adorable. I know what you're both feeling, my sweet little babies. Mm, so nice."

While she was watching Marilyn's breasts closely, her breaths came to a complete stop.

"Aw, there we go. Two very quiet and cooperative little girls for me. Let's just make sure you both stay very quiet. My precious babies won't ever again make another sound."

She reached for the cannister and pulled out the longest piece yet.

"Hmm, both of you are still very juicy for me, though. Oh, so very juicy."

She started with Sophia, wrapping first to cover her mouth, then the rest of her head. But she left her silky black mane hanging out.

"You too, little baby Mare. Oh, let's just hide away that pretty face where no one will ever see it again. Yes, it's dreadful, but it excites you even more."

Widow wrapped Marilyn's head completely in her sticky webbing, leaving only her blond hair hanging out the bottom. Then, she sat back on her short black boots, between them, and patted their bare asses.

"It's just so sweet that both of you, gorgeous blond and brunette twins, like to play at being soft, tender little baby girls. And you both love being helpless but only for a woman."

She reached farther to fluff around both of their hair.

"Yes, only for a woman. It's just so obvious with both of you."

She leaned over and spoke where she knew their ears were, underneath all of the hardening webbing.

"Sweet baby girls, Key S is a myth. It does nothing. You both just love being helpless, pretending to be little girls. But only for a woman."

She kissed each web covered head.

"And now that you're both so utterly helpless for me, it's time for the dreadful things which you both crave. Mm, such tender, juicy little twin baby girls. So juicy for me."

* * *

"Sorry!" Hawken yelled from up on his perch as the balloon drifted and slammed the basket into a large rock on the side of Ham's mountain.

"Easy, alright?"

"It's broke, Risk. Trying!"

The navigator spun the spout, gave it a blast, and felt it fight out of his grasp again. But the wild stream of hot gas served to spin the vessel away from the mountain, leaving it careening toward more jagged rocks.

"We'll crash!"

"I know! Trying!"

The hawk boy strangled the spout and gave it another chance, and it was enough to aim the balloon and its cargo toward a small level area among sharp outcroppings and giant split stones.

"There. Take us there!"

"Trying!"

Risk patted the lioness and rubbed around her ears.

"Be ready."

She swallowed and stared up at him, and he went back to monitoring their progress.

"Now, Risk. Now!"

"Not yet. Hold steady."

"Can't! It's too broken!"

"Dammit."

He shook his hand around over the lion's head, bending her ears every direction.

"You ready, girl?"

She got up and stood by the rail, her heavy paws and claws scraping and hanging on. Risk stood beside her.

"Easy," he said.

"I can't hold it!"

"Easy, girl."

"I'm losing it!"

"Now, K Kat. Jump!"

Risk and his lion clambered over the rail and dropped from too high of a height onto a small patch of bare ground. Risk looked up right away.

"Go! Go higher!"

"I'm going!"

He kept watching only long enough to see intense flames spiraling up above the iron pot. The balloon shivered and stretched and all of the support lines snapped into place.

And the balloon and its basket, and Hawken, left them there.

Risk and K Kat didn't know which direction to guard against when howling erupted all around them.

"Dammit. Fuck."

*　*　*

Marilyn and Sophia lay on their sides, facing each other, with their heads completely wrapped up in Widow's webbing. Her poisons had slowed everything inside them to the point of almost stopping, so even their breathing had ceased.

Each of them had their wrists tied behind them, and a band held their bound ankles close to those wrists. If they could move of their own will, they could grab their spiky high heels.

Under the layers of webbing covering their faces, Sophia's mouth was stretched open with multiple windings of the same material, pulled tight and tied to her wrists, leaving her head tipped back and her throat exposed.

Marilyn had bound her sister that way, and she'd enjoyed the thrill of it. Then, she got tied up the same way.

Widow lay between them, an arm under each trim waist and fondling their asses on and between their cheeks. And she was low enough that their necks and throats were right there for her to bite.

And she did. She bit both of them. Many times, leisurely draining their blood and flooding them with her most potent poisons.

"Mm, you two babies should thank Risk for leaving you here with me. You both know it's where you most want to be. We have so much time for me to enjoy all of your sweet juices. Oh, I do mean all. And you know that the more of my sweet poisons you take in, the stronger those orgasms will be."

She sucked at Marilyn's throat for a minute, then slipped her wet fangs out.

"What's that, Fia? You want a stronger orgasm even if it means more poison inside you, even though it will truly ruin you this time? Hmm, okay. Have some very strong poisons, my little lover girl."

She moaned and turned her head just enough to bite into Sophia's neck, and the only sounds in that quiet room were from Widow sucking at the brunette Killer's throat.

She backed out her fangs, then licked at the two thin trails of blood that Sophia was still offering to her.

"Mm, so sweet. But it's baby Mare's turn. A sweet baby like her wants more poisons too. The little blond baby wants much stronger orgasms. Mm, I do adore my sweet blond lover girl."

Widow turned to face Marilyn and bit deep into her neck. With no sounds from anyone coming to save them, Widow sucked quietly on Marilyn, drawing out her juices and feeding into her yet more of her poisons.

When she finally backed out her two long sharp teeth, she kept her lips on the soft skin of Marilyn's neck until she'd sucked and licked up every tiniest trickle.

"Mm, little twin baby girls are the tastiest."

She fondled around their asses, sometimes slipping her fingers between their cheeks.

She giggled and said, "Just my little twin dolls to play with now. It's all so dreadful, and neither of you even care. You're both so happy to be completely lost in your orgasms."

She gave them each a kiss where she'd been biting them.

"And you both love me. My two sweet little lover girls."

Widow sat up, still between them, and turned herself to face them as she sat back on her heels. She touched Marilyn's hands, flicking around her lifeless fingers. Then, she did the same with Sophia's hands.

"Well, let's just see, my precious little babies. Can you, still? Do you love me enough?"

She rose up onto her knees, stepped her right one to the other side of Marilyn, and lowered herself onto Marilyn's hands.

"Oh, yes. Just like that. Such soft, pretty fingertips for me. Slow, now, blond baby girl. Mm, slow and soft."

She shifted her hips just a little, finding the best place, then shook back her mane while unbuttoning her blouse. She let it drop off of the bed, then took her breasts in both hands.

"Oh, good little girl. Mm, just like that. Help me make my poisons even stronger for both of you."

She looked up and gasped, then pinched her own nipples as she looked down on them again.

"You survived before, dear little babies. Let's give you an even stronger batch. Mm, I'm going to bite and bite and bite."

She looked up and gasped again.

"Mm, yeah. Touch me so softly, my precious blond baby girl."

* * *

Risk faced one way and felt a snapping mountain lion tail hitting him from behind. He heard her growling too.

"Let me," he said. "Just be my backup."

He snarled and roared at the sky as he shifted into the lion that had sliced up so many foes in that madman's stronghold. Long fangs caught traces of the fake light of a fake moon, and he glared and roared at his attackers, two coming straight for him.

They didn't get far. He pounced, leaping high into the air, and landed with his jaws crushing the head of one of the nearwolves. It shrieked for only a second before its brain splattered out of the sides and matted up his snout.

The lion reared up when he faced the other one, swinging one heavy paw, then the other. His claws hooked into everything, never missing, and shredding it all. Pieces of arms and ribs and scalp fell to the ground, then Risk gave one last mighty swipe, interrupted its final scream, and sent its head flying somewhere into the rocks below.

His chest heaving, his eyes burning into the dim light, he snorted and waited for the next target.

But he heard a yip behind him.

Another of the nearwolves had K Kat pinned to the ground, its claws holding her down as she kicked and tried to rip at it. Its snapping jaws were dodging her defenses, looking for a chance at her soft belly.

Risk roared and leaped toward them just as those hideous jaws found K Kat's abdomen. The fangs dug in, and the beast shook, trying to rip parts of the lion loose.

But it died at Risk's hands too soon to bite out a hot feast.

And a ragged beast body without a head slumped back and tumbled quietly down the mountain and into its shadows.

Risk shifted back as quickly as he could and stooped down for the lion.

Only it wasn't the lion. Not K Kat.

Kenzie reached an arm up to him weakly, and he held her sides gently near where blood was escaping and soaking into the soil.

She touched his cheek and said, "Risk. It's me."

His eyes were wet, but he laughed once. Just once.

"Yeah. Kenzie."

She struggled with a few breaths, then said, "Let's finish."

"You mean—"

"Yes. I'm dying."

"No. Not today, you're not."

She shook her head, her eyes wet too.

"Risk. We both know."

He squinted at her, fighting to hold her gaze.

"The lion and me. We know. Make love to me."

"You're hurt. We—"

"Would it take me home?"

"Yeah, but—"

"Take me to Dayzee's. Where you found me. Us."

"Alright."

He let go of her to place his palms on the ground, and he leaned enough to kiss her. Her breaths were short and choppy, some even blowing his black hair aside.

Amid crazed howling all around them and under the fake light of a madman's moon, their lips met.

Chapter 61 – He'll Have to Take Me

"Oh, my, baby girl Fia. Those soft fingertips of yours. Mm . . ."

Widow bucked her hips softly, enjoying the touch of the hands beneath her that were attached to a helplessly bound and poisoned brunette Kildare Killer.

With her left hand, she fondled her own breasts. And with her right, she played with and explored Marilyn's bare ass as she lay next to her, also completely helpless.

Both of them had taken in so much poison, and much stronger poison, that they lay totally still. Not even a shallow breath.

But Widow knew that Sophia had just enough life left to satisfy her in such sweet ways. And she left her breasts alone to reach down and guide Sophia's fingers to just the right places, then push them gently, then slide them along where she wanted them most.

"Oh," she almost laughed, "such a very sweet baby girl. Mm, it's time. My precious little girls are ready for the dreadful things only a cruel woman like me can give them. Things they both want so bad. Mm, they shouldn't pretend to be just little girls if they don't want to be helpless for all of those dreadful things."

She lifted her hips slowly, and Sophia's fingers tried to follow.

"Oh, so slowly. Yes, we can take our time, dear little one. Mm, a little more."

She lowered herself just enough that Sophia's fingertips could barely touch her, two at a time dragging lightly across her.

"Oh, you're so precious!"

With a sigh, she finally got up onto her knees, then swung a leg off of the bed, letting her spiky heel strike the stone floor. While walking toward the door, she made sure that the twins could hear her heels with every step.

A heavy pipe was stashed near the door for any emergency situation. Stout brackets on each side of the doorway matched it perfectly, and Widow lifted it, then dropped it in place.

She turned toward the twins and said, "I'll miss Pauline. We'd spend hours down here, locked together as well as we could bind ourselves. Oh, even that was so nice. All bound up nice and tight, pressed against each other, with nothing for me to do but bite her, give her the poisons that she wanted more than anything, and slowly suck just enough blood out of her to take her close. Very close as her orgasm overwhelmed her."

Standing near the bed, looking down on her trussed-up twin baby girls, Widow smiled and said, "Yes, my juicy little girls are ready."

She untied the bindings holding their legs up, then let them down gently. The tight windings around their ankles were next, and she tossed all of it aside.

Lastly, she loosened the strapping that held their heads back in ways that had made it all that much easier to relax and bite their necks and throats just as many times as she'd wanted.

Their limp bodies lay there, nothing covering any of their skin except for the total wrapping of their heads, the bindings of their arms behind them, and the little bit that their high-heeled shoes covered.

"So gorgeous now. I know you feel that: you're both more gorgeous now than you've ever been before."

She rolled Marilyn over to face up.

She giggled softly and said, "Such big-girl nipples you have, little baby Mare. Mm, I can't resist. You don't want me to."

Leaning over, she sucked in one of Marilyn's stiff nipples and pulled on it with her lips, moaning softly. She let it pop out, then licked it.

She took in the other and tugged it from side to side as she squeezed it between her lips. She let it go, then gave it a long, wet kiss.

"Mm, so precious."

She rolled Sophia over and said, "Yes, you pretend to be a baby girl, but you have a grown-up woman's breasts. And you keep teasing with those nipples. Mm."

She leaned over and sucked on each of them for a minute.

"Mm-hmm. Those are such tasty big-girl breasts. Just adorable."

Widow sighed, studying the naked women lying side by side on the bed in a locked-up basement room. She looked at their trim waists, the soft skin of their bellies, then she let her eyes go even lower.

"Oh, such soft, tender little baby girls. If we weren't concerned about nearwolves interrupting us, or someone named Risk interrupting us, I'd give each of you some very special kisses in your very special places. Mm, such sweet, juicy baby girls."

She looked up at the hoist and pulled down all four straps, each with its own soft, padded loop. Each of those loops found an ankle, then she reached for the button near the webbing cannister.

The motor up above clicked, then started tightening up the straps. Two pairs of Kildare Killer legs, led by their very high spiky heels, were being lifted toward the wood beams above.

Widow scoffed at the sight of the legs getting carried high enough that their bare asses began to leave the blanket, then she shut down the motor. Then, she gave it another run, a short run, lifting them a little more until their lower back areas had lifted too.

"Oh, this is always fun," she said and scooted around to their front sides.

She hit the button again, just a peck, and kept her eyes on their breasts as they began to settle the wrong way.

"Why do I like that so much? Hmm. Who wouldn't?"

She gave the motor another shot, and their bodies were almost straight up, but their shoulders and very high on their backs stayed in contact with the blanket, leaving their web-covered faces pointed up.

She left the motor control to lean down and kiss where two pairs of lips were lost under layers of web.

"Hmm. Soft little babies. Such very good and quiet little girls now."

She gave each pair of breasts a squeeze with both hands, then walked around the bed and got on her knees behind them.

"Mm, so much soft skin. Such perfect little baby girl skin."

She started with Marilyn and reached around her thighs, then kissed the back of each leg. Then, she gave each a little bite.

"Mm, so juicy."

She let one hand drop down to Marilyn's breasts, and the other slipped up between her thighs. Widow paused her biting until she'd done what she wanted with a few of her fingers.

"Mm, just like that. I'll hold you very still."

She held Marilyn like that, sometimes rubbing and playing but mostly just holding her in place, as she sank her fangs into the smooth skin of the back of one thigh.

She leaned away a minute later and watched two very thin trickles of blood seeking the blanket beneath them.

She moaned and bit Marilyn's other leg and sucked out at least as much as the first. And she'd left more poisons with each bite.

"Mm, baby girl Fia. Do you have soft thighs for me? You do? Mm, okay."

She repeated all of it with Sophia, taking her time to be sure that she was holding her in just the right places. Then, she backed away just enough to look at her bite marks, smiling at how the generous expanse of perfect soft skin was marred by her passionate bites.

"You want me to," she said softly. "Both of you. You want to be my helpless babies for whatever dreadful things I want to do to you."

She spread her arms enough to hold them both as they hung from the ceiling, hip to hip.

And she moaned as she bit each of the four soft thighs repeatedly, leaving little red puncture holes from sucking and forcing into them more of her strongest poisons.

* * *

Risk found himself kissing a lion under the light of a phony moon under a rocky ceiling sky.

He sat back and shook his head, checking the lion's wounds. He saw that they were bad.

"Dammit," he said softly.

K Kat lay there on her side, panting and not offended by Risk trying to stop the bleeding, even if with just his palms.

He looked away when he heard growling and howling farther down the mountain but nearby.

After patting the lioness's head once, he walked quietly to the ledge bounding their refuge on the side of the mountain and looked down.

"Fuck."

At least a dozen of the nearwolves were coming, making slow progress but giving no sign of turning back.

He hurried back to K Kat's side.

"Shh," he said as he pried one hand, palm up under the prone lion.

She took deep breaths, quick ones, and only licked at her snout, never complaining as he forced his arm under her.

"I'll carry you."

He stood with the lion in his arms, cradling her, and though her head bounced lightly with his steps, her eyes never wavered from his.

She stayed calm as Risk's steps became choppy and jarring, his boots not easily finding flat areas among the sharp and sloping stones. Yet she never yipped or growled or even took her eyes off of him.

He stopped on a flat outcropping, near a shear drop-off. He felt the warmth of fresh blood soaking out of one beast and onto another.

Looking into the mountain lion's eyes, he said, "We're not done."

He resumed the walk and dared to take his eyes off of the hazardous path to smile at the lion in his arms.

"Kenzie."

*   *   *

Widow kept her fangs in the back of Sophia's thigh and shook her head lightly from side to side, causing the suspended captive to try to spin. But Widow enjoyed holding her in place almost as much as biting her.

"Oh, I could just eat you alive, you precious, juicy little baby girl."

She got down from the bed but stood there for a moment to admire her babies and what she'd done to them.

Their thighs had been bitten so many times that the skin carried tight patterns of tiny puncture marks, many of them still leaking blood. She looked lower, admiring their bare asses.

"Oh my, it'll only take a few minutes. I simply can't resist."

She climbed back onto the bed, knelt behind them, and used both arms to hold them, a hand on each belly.

"Mm," she moaned as she bit into one of Marilyn's ass cheeks, and she sucked at it for a full minute.

"Mm, that's so good."

She bit her other cheek and moaned while sucking juices out through the two tiny punctures, then she backed away to look at what she'd done.

"Your skin is still soft and smooth, dear little blond baby. Aw, you're just all bit up now. Mm, you're just too juicy. You were meant to be bitten."

She gave Sophia the same treatment, leaving bloody bite holes in both of her ass cheeks.

Standing beside the bed again, Widow sighed and fluffed up their long black and blond manes spread out behind them on the blanket.

While reaching for a different cannister of webbing, she glanced at two pairs of large breasts, taking on different appearances from the girls being upside down.

"Oh my, you'd probably love for me to nibble on those too. Mm, so luscious."

She whipped out a long piece of the thicker, wider material and turned back to them. And she let her voice regain a normal tone.

"But I'm no fool. It's possible that Risk will come back for you two. And yes, baby girls, I know all about the sex and death trick that brought you here. You're even hoping to use that to escape the full moon slaughter going on."

She got up close to them, on her knees, and kissed them all over.

"Mm, so nice. If Risk does come back, and if he's desperate to fuck someone, guess who? Yes, me. Not either of you."

She began to wrap Marilyn, feeding it between her thighs first, then tugging it down, getting it jammed in tight.

"Mm, nice and snug. Cruel isn't just for a helpless baby's pretty mouth."

She wrapped the material around Marilyn's hips, weaving it between her thighs often until she'd locked in everything from her navel to halfway down her thighs.

"Oh, and this is a special variety. It sets nice and quick. Locking in all those sweet juicy goodies. If Risk wants to escape, he'll have to take me too."

She smoothed down the end of the very long and careful winding, then shuffled over to kneel in front of Sophia.

"And you, my sweet little baby girl Fia. Let's wrap up all of your tasty little-girl treats too."

Widow finished off Sophia the same way, weaving strands between her thighs, cruelly wedging them in tight, then wrapping all around her many times. Both of the twins were encased in hardening shells that would block any of Risk's amorous attempts at a sex and death rescue.

She'd just finished wrapping up the twins when she heard a commotion outside the heavy door to the hideaway.

"Well, baby girls, that's either more of those horrible wolves or it's Risk. Or could it be both? Hmm."

She checked that the freshest wrapping around their hips and between their thighs was hardening, then she held a breast of each as she turned back toward the door.

"I believe that could be Risk. Those other things would be howling, wouldn't they? Yes, it must be him. Let's give him a sweet view of his only real option to escape."

She hurried quietly to the door, lifted out the heavy pipe blocking it, and turned the lock before keeping her heels from clicking on the wood floor on the way back to the bed.

On the bed, Widow positioned herself on her hands and knees, her face above the covered faces of the girls and her ass end pointed toward the unlocked door.

She shifted her hips around, almost causing her thin, tiny white panties to get wedged in even more deeply.

Speaking to one wrapped face and then the other, she said, "Can you guess what Risk will do with my offer? Of course, you can. Either one of you would take whatever pleasure you could from me. He's no different."

She looked once back over her shoulder but stayed on her hands and knees, pointing her nearly-bare ass toward the door.

"Now," she said, "we wait and see."

She looked away from the door, toward the suspended and bound twins, and said, "Oh, maybe we do have time."

She grinned while looking from one pair of breasts to the other.

"Who's first? Mare. Baby Mare. Mm, such a sweet blond baby girl. With such luscious big-girl breasts for me."

She kept her ass up but leaned enough to get her lips on one of Marilyn's perky nipples.

"Mm, a baby with such sweet, teasing nipples. Just adorable."

She moaned as she resumed her gentle sucking and nibbling, waiting for the door to open.

Chapter 62 – All You Can Do Is Fuck Me

Still carrying the badly injured lion, Risk stomped through the damaged front doorway of Ham's house. A glance around told him that no nearwolves were lurking there, but he also saw that they'd dragged away the bodies of Ham and Pauline.

"Just as well," he said to the lioness, whose eyes were more often closed than open.

While glancing toward the stairs, he said, "Should we even check upstairs?"

K Kat's silence was her answer, and he said, "Yeah. Maybe it's for the better."

He leaned into each of the other rooms just enough that a wolf, if hiding there, would have attacked. There weren't any.

"The girls."

Standing before the heavy wooden door to the hideaway room, he shifted K Kat to support her with one arm, then tried turning the doorknob.

It spun easily, without even a squeak, and he pushed the door in.

"Dammit," he said and lifted the lion higher, letting her rest her head on his shoulder. "What the fuck?"

In the dim light, he saw a bed and a very fine ass—Widow's—with only the thinnest and smallest of white panties stretched tight and covering hardly anything. And she'd aimed it right at him.

She still wore her short black boots, the sharp heels pointing his way, too, and her black mane was fluffed up and laid over her shoulders and back. She wore nothing else and before he could stop himself, he leaned one way to see what he knew were hanging free, pointing unambiguously toward the soft blanket on the bed.

He grumbled at the sight of two pairs of Kildare Killer legs, still wearing their high heels and hooked somewhere near the ceiling.

But his eyes fixed on the mass of webbing each of the girls wore from their navels to halfway up their thighs. The material had set and hardened and gave no hint that it had ever been separate overlapping straps. They appeared to have been dipped in concrete.

At noticing for the first time the soft sucking sounds, he carried K Kat, who was mostly unconscious, to one side and saw Widow's lips gently working at one of Marilyn's nipples. Her cheeks were pumping rapidly, and he saw her throat busy swallowing too.

She turned only her eyes toward him but didn't stop. She only squeezed it tighter between her lips and stretched it as far out as she could, then giggled as she let it slip back out, causing both of Marilyn's breasts to bounce softly before becoming still.

"Dammit. What have you done?"

Widow stayed on her hands and knees and said, "What I do. What I have to do."

He grumbled and said, "Let them down."

"No, silly shifter man."

Before he could speak again, they both heard a nearwolf's howl somewhere outside of Ham's house.

"There's no time," she said, and she still didn't turn herself around. "A big bad wolf will be here soon."

He looked all around the room, saying softly to himself, "Dammit."

Then, he spun around, lion in his arms, and went back to lock the door.

Widow heard it click and said, "The pipe too. Those beasts are too strong for that silly lock."

He grumbled, held K Kat with one arm again, and managed to drop the pipe into its brackets.

She heard it clunk into place and said, "That only buys us some time. They'll still—"

"Us?"

Widow didn't look to confirm that he was watching, but she slowly shifted her hips from side to side, then sighed loudly enough for him to hear.

And she heard his grumbling take a less hostile tone.

She laughed softly and said, "You could say that I'd love them to death. Don't hate me. I didn't ask to become this."

He scanned all around the room again, then focused back on Widow and the bound twins hanging from the ceiling.

"There are too many of them," he said.

"Yes. You're a formidable fighter, but you are just one man. Or something close enough."

He stared, holding the lioness, and waited.

"A man that can take us away from here."

He snarled, even knowing that she couldn't see it.

"By taking . . . me."

He took a step closer to her.

"You killed them?"

"No."

"But you would."

"Yes. Don't hate me. I didn't ask to become this."

Risk grumbled while shifting K Kat to rest her head on his other shoulder.

"You could have found another way."

"Could I? Hmm. Our hungers shape us. Compel us. I've learned to embrace mine."

"You could just kill. Only kill."

"And what of my sexual appetite? Should I cast that aside forever? No, silly man. All of it together is my appetite now."

Widow listened to Risk grumble for a moment, then turned just her head and smiled, saying, "That dying cat would find the blanket soft."

"She's not going to die."

"Hmm. You plan to save her too?"

"Dammit."

Risk shook his head and walked to the bed, then laid K Kat on her side. She'd never moved, but she did open her eyes to blink at him a few times, then she let them close again.

"Your hands are needed here. Slip my panties down for me?"

"I'm not fucking you."

"You mean 'again,' don't you? You'd be fucking me again."

Risk grumbled and said, "One of the twins. It's Sophia's turn."

"Impossible," she said, then she turned to face the twins and leaned forward enough to rub her face across Sophia's breasts. "Oh, she is quite the lovely little thing, though."

"Dammit, no. Not impossible."

"Look," she said. "It's a special recipe of web. You won't break through it quickly enough. Who knew learning chemistry would become so useful?"

Risk studied the thick, solid encasement of the twins. Another howling shot up into the moonlit sky outside the house.

"And these twin girls, all of their . . . openings . . . are locked away. My sweet, tender little baby girls have nothing warm and juicy to offer you."

He grumbled, and she added, "But you, go ahead and play with wolf beasts. My tasty little baby girls still have so much warmth and juice for me. We'll have all sorts of sexual adventures before I'm done with them."

She gave him a moment to respond, but he didn't, so she said, "They'll want to. They love me more than life itself."

"Dammit."

"Fuck is a better word right now, don't you think?"

She didn't wait for an answer. But she did let her voice drip out like a slow stream of honey, thick and sweet and irresistible.

"Just slip down these silly panties of mine. Leave them tight around my thighs. You'll have so much soft skin to enjoy. And I'm already so, so juicy for you."

Risk didn't answer, but he couldn't stop his eyes from locking onto the panties and thighs and soft skin.

"Yes, you remember how soft. Mm, such softness for you."

He stepped closer, until his legs were pressed against the bed.

"So soft," she said. "So wet. Mm, so very wet. Do you want to know why my pussy is so wet?"

He grumbled and said, "Dammit. Why?"

She giggled softly and said, "Because I've taken so much of their juices. My baby girls were so much juicier before we had our most intimate of love affairs."

"You're insane," he said as he got up on the bed, shaking it lightly as he knelt behind her.

"Hmm. Says the shape-shifter who's out of time in a house on a hill and surrounded by nearwolves. My panties are so small and so thin. They shouldn't be in the way like that. Undress me."

Risk groaned and pinched the elastic band with both hands, and he held it there, letting his fingers touch her soft skin.

"Yes. Just like that."

He scowled and pulled the garment halfway down her ass cheeks, then stopped.

"No," he said. "It's not right. It has to be all of us."

She turned herself enough to look at him but not enough to get her panties loose from his hands.

"Mm. Of course. I'll keep these tender little doll girls involved."

She held his gaze for just a second, then added, "Be sure to watch. Just watching feels so good too."

She sighed and turned back around, then started sucking on Sophia's nipples, moving her head and slurping loudly enough for Risk to hear.

"Dammit," he said, knelt behind her, and snapped her panties down to her knees, causing her to gasp softly before returning to Sophia.

"They have to feel it," he said as he was unbuckling his belt.

"Mm, they already are. You should let me give you a good bite. You won't believe what you'd feel."

He snarled and pulled down his zipper.

Widow kept licking and nibbling, and she'd started moaning softly.

Risk laid something hard on Widow, resting it between her ass cheeks.

"Mm," she said while leaning toward Marilyn's breasts. "Such a dangerous man, about to stab me. And I'm just so soft and can't possibly stop him."

Risk snarled and said, "I'm not enjoying it."

She let Marilyn's nipple slip out from the grasp of her wet lips.

"You know that you must. Or we all die."

He grumbled, leaned back just enough, then lowered himself and just broke her softness, letting her get a wet hold on him.

"You would anyway," she said with just a hint of a laugh. "No more talk. I have too many sweet baby girl nipples that I love sucking."

She moaned and resumed licking and sucking on Marilyn's nipples, tipping her head and taking them from every angle.

She kept her cheek pressed into the side of Marilyn's breast and said, "Listen to me sucking their nipples while they're so helpless for me. You know you love even the sound of what I'm doing with them."

Risk, watching her at work on the twins, drove himself in halfway.

"Mm," Widow said, pausing her suckling. "You love it because they're so helpless for us. Helpless baby girls for us together."

He grumbled but tried leaning to watch Widow's lips and tongue. She noticed and came at Marilyn's breasts from the side, giving him a good view.

Then, she leaned to her left while saying, "Mm, little baby girl Fia too. Such sweet nipples she's giving me. Watch my lips sucking the helpless little baby's sweet nipples."

She resumed her loud sucking, and Risk groaned and drove himself all the way in, getting from Widow a groan that was part laugh too.

After gasping up at the ceiling, Risk reached around for K Kat and nudged her jaws closer to his thigh.

She opened her eyes, and he said to her, "Wait. Until."

Blinking was her only response.

"You must be angry," Widow said, her lips still close to Sophia's breasts. "Look what I've done to these delightful twin girls. Ooh, you must be so mad."

Risk groaned and began ramming her, holding her by her hips.

"Oh, I've been so cruel to them. But they're such tasty, helpless little babies for me. Mm, such sweet, juicy little girls."

She kept sucking loudly, never leaving any of their breasts alone for very long and always allowing him to watch as he buried himself in her from behind.

Risk kept pounding her all the way in, his strong hands holding her hips in a grip that she'd never escape even if she'd wanted to.

He didn't look, but he heard K Kat begin to whine softly, and he felt the soft fur of her snout against his leg.

"I bit them both," Widow said. "Oh, Risk, I hung them upside down and bit them so many times. Such sweet, innocent little girls."

Risk slammed himself into her.

"I bit their legs so many times that their smooth skin is ruined forever."

Risk groaned and rammed her harder, and widow sucked and slurped at the captive twins' nipples.

"Even their asses, Risk. Such soft skin, ruined by my cruel fangs. Oh, I bit so deep into their soft asses."

And K Kat had begun gnawing on his leg, her fangs ripping the skin and letting blood out.

"They're so full of my poisons now."

He groaned and drove himself in harder.

"So helpless. Just two very quiet doll babies with adorable nipples for me to suck."

Risk almost roared, almost shifted into something horrible, and got a tighter grip, hammering her from behind.

"Just juicy little treats for me to consume."

Risk saw claws growing from his fingers, and he roared as he dug them into Widow's hips.

"And all you can do is fuck me. You have to fuck me and love it. You see now that you love me too."

She moaned and stretched out one nipple after another, cackling between.

"You see that you love fucking me while we, together, have such helpless, bitten baby girls to enjoy. Mm, lifeless doll babies, Risk!"

Risk called out, "Ah! K Kat, now!"

The lioness sat up, bit into his neck, and used the last of her strength to rip it apart, chewing through skin and muscle and bone.

Widow held both girls with both arms, pulled them closer, and squeezed her face into their breasts.

"Oh, God!" she said.

K Kat roared, her snout a bloody mess, then she clamped her jaws on what was left of his neck and held on tight.

Risk could only gurgle up at the ceiling with a final, deep thrust into Widow.

And he began to sink through the bed, then through the floor and into the mountain rock, taking with him everyone that he could.

Chapter 63 – I Really Didn't Ask for This

Risk's eyes were almost too heavy to keep open, and the brilliant sunlight on his face didn't help. His cheek rested on a rough wood surface that smelled of grease and beer.

He blinked hard a few times, forced one to stay open, then the other, and picked up his head. Still seated, he looked down at the weathered planks and their stains from years of food and drink before he glanced to the left and saw empty bottles and glasses and plates with scraps of food.

Something straight ahead got him to look, and he saw long whiskers twitching, coming up from somewhere below the far edge of the boards. While he was watching, a furry brown snout followed the whiskers up and a second later, K Kat's big eyes blinked slowly as she gazed back at him.

"Good girl," he said with his eyes closing again. "You made it."

"So did I," said someone whose voice he recognized.

Only then did he realize that he was sitting and that there was something on his lap.

So, he looked down.

Widow, her head on his lap, looked up.

She smiled and yawned, then turned onto her side, facing him, and reached around him to snuggle in closer.

"Mm, I like it here."

"Widow," he said.

"Mm-hmm," she said in a normal voice and without looking. "Nice work."

He let out a weak, tired grumble, then rubbed at his eyes. After stretching them open, blinking them a few times, then shaking his head, he looked across the picnic table at a lion that looked back, but only for a second before she looked quickly to her left and right.

He did too.

They both saw trees and grass, more tables with their own clutter, and the back of a weathered brick building with a single door, through which soft classic rock reached out to them.

They saw all of that.

But they didn't see Marilyn or Sophia.

"Get up," he said and reached behind her head, then lifted her and forced her to sit on her own.

She was grinning and still yawning, then tipping, so he held her until she could stay upright on her own.

He looked around again, scowled, then said, "You said they were alive."

Widow stretched her arms out to her sides and yawned again, in no hurry.

She turned to him with a pleasant smile.

"Hmm. Alive enough to feel their best orgasms ever. And to give them. Oh, they gave me some nice ones."

She let him snarl in silence for a second.

"Oh my, but perhaps it was just too much of my delightful poison. Those poor twin baby girls, it seems now, were far more dead than alive."

"Dammit."

"I did try, you know. My lips and tongue couldn't have been more affectionate."

Risk snorted out a breath and held the mountain lion's calm gaze from across the table.

"I'm going back," he said.

Widow laughed and said, "They'll be even more dead by then. No, we're staying here. Wherever the hell this is."

Still gazing into the lion's eyes, he quickly reached to his side and held Widow by her throat.

"No. They're different. They'll recover."

"Hmm. Maybe. You must know that those wolves have probably picked their bones clean by now, though. Two very sweet little bundles of bait, hanging there for them to ravage. Good luck fucking the gristle and bones they've spit up and left behind when—"

He squeezed her throat and said, "We're going back. Me and you."

Turning his head enough to look at her, he said, "Right?"

She couldn't even laugh, so he relaxed his hold on her.

Widow blew out a breath then rubbed her throat before speaking. "I see," she said. "You want to fuck me again."

He kept his hand close, ready to resume his choking.

"I'll fuck you, but only for my lust and amusement here, in this world. I'm never going back."

He squeezed enough to keep her in her seat and with his other arm, he swept the tabletop clean except for one bottle, which he grabbed. A quick glance at K Kat showed a lion panting in what could have been a laugh.

Risk paused while Widow pulled vainly at the hand at her throat, and said to the lion, "Up, girl. Let me see you."

K Kat stood on the bench seat with her front paws on the table. Risk scoffed at the sight of a perfect, lean, muscular lion body.

He looked her in the eyes and said, "Good girl. You can stay. Wait for us."

He lost what little smile he had and lifted Widow by her neck, then quickly dropped her onto the tabletop on her back.

Still squeezing her, keeping her from doing anything but gagging and stammering, he climbed up and got himself between her kicking legs. Holding the bottle in his mouth, Risk undid his belt and zipper, all while Widow was thrashing around, trying to gore him with her sharp heels.

Risk only scoffed at her weak attempts and said, "Try being the victim. You might like it, you mutant bitch."

She scowled and rolled her head, snapping it to each side, and he forced her legs together, then up, leaving them on a shoulder. With a violent pull at her panties, he left the meager bit of fabric as a tight cord around her thighs, near her knees.

He smiled down at her as he was poised to penetrate her, and she held his choking arm with both hands and groaned up at him.

"Yeah," he said, chuckling. "This *is* amusing."

He rammed himself deep into her and watched her eyes close. Then, her hands, which had been ripping at his arm, fell away and lay on the table.

Risk glanced at the lion, who'd watched the entire spectacle. She turned her eyes up to him.

"Damn spiders," he said, laughing just once.

He backed his hand away from her throat, kept it ready, and saw that all she did was open her calm black eyes to look up at him.

She didn't smile when she said, "Told you we'd fuck again."

Then, he snarled, grabbed both of her arms, and plowed into her, forcing her smooth skin roughly across the splintery wooden surface.

Her chest started rising and falling with her deeper breaths, taking her bare breasts up and down while they shook from each of his hard thrusts.

They heard a slamming door and though the cat looked, he and Widow didn't.

"Hey!" a woman yelled. "What the hell? Right here at the Prism?"

Risk broke the bottle against the table's edge and held it out, away from the building and intruder.

"Fucking animals!" she said.

Risk turned and said, "Not now."

"Oh, you're busy," she said. "We can see that. Boss, what the hell is this?"

"I don't know, Dayzee, but it's kind of hot."

Risk heard the woman slap the man that she'd called Boss, then say, "You would think so. If those gorgeous twins were here, they'd—"

Risk didn't stop, but he turned toward the woman and said, "Twins? Marilyn and Sophia?"

"You know them? Who the hell are you?"

"I'm a friend. I'm trying to save them."

"Huh," she said. "Just wonderful. And I'm calling bullshit on that. You don't know them, and there's no way that—"

"Mare," he said, then gave Widow a few more hard jabs.

"What did you say?"

"I said Mare."

"Wait. How did—"

"And Fia."

He kept going at Widow and turned to see the look on Dayzee's face.

"You really do—"

"There's no time. Here."

He handed the broken bottle to her, and she took it.

"What is this? What are you—"

"They'll die if I don't go back. Your mansion was burning."

Dayzee's eyes stretched wide open, and the Boss mostly hid behind her, watching.

"You called someone."

Still, she stared.

"I came. I saved them."

"We, uh, we did try to, um, but the portal, that, uh, it—"

"There's no time! Use the bottle. When I say, cut my throat."

"I'm not cutting anyone's throat! How could that—"

Risk snarled and snatched the sharp piece of glass from her hand, then focused on Widow, giving it to her as deeply and as brutally as he could, and he scoffed at her satisfied smile.

Widow smiled calmly up at him and said, "Mm, I'm cumming. You're making me cum."

He snarled and said, "Dammit. Me too."

With Dayzee and the Boss and K Kat watching, Risk groaned from his sharp climax, then raked the jagged edge across his own throat.

The three of them watched Risk, with hot blood spurting from his neck, and Widow, her back raw from the violent fucking on the rough table, as they sank, and sank, and then were gone.

Dayzee Dazzle shook her head and stared at where they'd been, then looked up at the calm lion.

She squinted at the big cat and said, "Why with the lions all the time?"

* * *

Risk grumbled, his eyes still closed, and felt his body weighted down as he lay on his back. He reached up with both arms and found only soft, warm skin.

He opened his eyes just as Widow was blinking hers, then she pressed her palms against his chest and leaned herself up.

He'd already felt her nipples pressed into his chest, and he forced himself to look only into her eyes.

"Oh," she said. "Back in the wolf pit again."

He tipped his head each way, confirming that they'd made it back. "Good."

"Yes, it was a very good fuck."

He scoffed, looking into her black eyes.

She said, softly and without a hint of a smile, "I really didn't ask for this. You must know that."

He scowled and looked away, but she touched his cheek, turning his head back to face her, and she waited for his answer.

He tipped his head again to glance at the twins.

"They can't hear you," she said, and he looked back up at her.

With a meager scoff, one almost only out of necessity, he said, "Yeah. I get it."

She smiled and said, "With only a slight change in events, that could have been you up there."

He squinted up at her with a scowl.

"For me to feed on. You would have loved being my tasty lover boy."

He shook his head and glared up at her.

"You're already quick to give me some of your hot juices. How many times now?"

She bounced her eyebrows, gave him a quick kiss, and rolled off of him. And he sat up, his eyes fixed on two Kildare Killers, wrapped in Widow's webs and hanging from the ceiling above the bed.

He grumbled and got up on his feet, then looked down at Widow, pointed at her, and said, "Pull up your damn panties."

She did, grinning at him the entire time.

He tipped his head toward the wall and said, "Over there. Go."

She shrugged and went where he'd pointed, then sat on the floor with her back to the wall.

"Stay."

"Hmm. Like a little pet? That you sometimes fuck?"

He snarled and turned away, then stepped up onto the bed. It took only a few seconds to examine the hoist, then he looked around until he saw the control switch on the nightstand.

After a jump to the floor, he held the button, and he guided the girls as he lowered them enough that they could lie flat on their backs.

After a glance back at Widow, he wrestled the loops off of their ankles, scoffing lightly at the difficulty involved from them still wearing spiky high heels.

Feeling around their heads first, he found no edges to peel back. It was like they'd been dipped in something liquid that had hardened up around them.

With a soft roar, he shifted just enough to see long, flat claws with edges like straight razors grow out of his fingertips. After another quick look and a scowl toward Widow, he focused first on the wrapped head with a blond mane.

Working like a surgeon, he cut in enough that he could bend the casing open, then crack it into pieces. He hurried to free the head with a brunette mane too.

He took only a moment to watch their faces, which could have been the faces of dead girls. He slapped each softly, then grinned at the sight and sound of both of them drawing in deep breaths, though neither spoke or even opened her eyes.

Setting to work near their waists, he cut away all of the hardened banding and tossed it to the floor. Some of the harder pieces he threw toward Widow, saying, "Damn webs," but she only scoffed, then smiled.

"I'm staying. Like you ordered."

With a grumble, he turned back to the twins and rolled them over.

He froze at the sight of their legs with all of the tiny punctures in the backs of their thighs.

"Dammit," he said, glaring at Widow.

She only shrugged, then said, "They're very tasty little babies. Try a nibble yourself. You know you want to."

"Just shut up."

He kept glancing at Widow as he untied their arms, which had the less severe banding material.

Sophia was nearest, so he touched the back of her thigh softly.

"Damn world," he said. "Damn Below the Bay."

He'd just rolled them over to face up again when he stopped at mad howling coming from inside the house. Staying still, he and Widow listened and heard claws scraping across the floor, tables being overturned, and determined, hungry growling.

Outside the door, there was one loud, angry howl, then something heavy rammed the door. Then, another heavy thing. Then, two things together.

The bracket holding the pipe at the door's swinging side bent, then got pried and hung there, useless, as the pipe fell and rolled out of the way.

A hard strike sent the door swinging in, and two nearwolves, baring their teeth and with thick drool hanging from their chins, stared into the room.

"Fuck."

* * *

Running toward the door, Risk said to himself, "I don't have time for this, dammit."

With every step, he became more of a gorilla. Short black fur clung to thick, rippled muscles everywhere on his legs and arms, his chest, and his shoulders and back. Even his neck swelled into a thick post.

But the wolves didn't hesitate. They rushed in to meet him halfway, snarling and snapping and swiping with their long claws.

The gorilla roared and accepted the damage. He'd never slowed and, bleeding badly, he leaned over to ram a shoulder into the abdomen of one, then he lifted it off of the ground.

Holding that beast high, taking more wounds from claws furiously raking across his back, the gorilla took hold of the other beast by its throat and lifted it up, leaving its legs kicking.

Then, he lifted it higher, quickly, ramming its head into the heavy boards holding up the floor above them.

A shower of blood hit the floor first, then the enraged ape slammed down what was left, splashing the blood and brains out to the sides.

Bleeding badly, his back a maze of rips and tears and red lines clogging up the black fur, the gorilla reached around the desperate, clawing nearwolf with his other arm.

And with an angry roar to the ceiling, he squeezed that thing as it wiggled and screamed then fell to the ground.

In front of the gorilla.

And behind him too.

Risk shifted back quickly and looked out through the door which had been damaged too badly to stop any more of the beasts.

The house was clear, but he heard more coming.

"Dammit."

He spun around, took a step toward the bed, then stopped.

"Oh, fuck."

Marilyn and Sophia were with Widow, and they lay with her on the bed, each under one of Widow's arms.

Widow gazed at Risk, and smiled when she could, as she took turns kissing each of them while they rubbed her breasts, then her belly, then lower, between her thighs.

Her black eyes were almost closed as she grinned and blew him a kiss.

Chapter 64 – We Can't Let Her Die

Risk staggered back toward the bed, his back shredded and leaving a red trail behind him. Only Widow noticed him returning, and he scowled at her for only a second before grabbing her arm and jerking her up from between the twins.

"Hey," said Sophia, her eyes still struggling, "she . . . wasn't hurting us."

Risk grumbled as he dragged Widow away and said, "She will."

He shoved her down into a corner and added, "Again."

Widow smiled up at him, and he gave her a quick scowl before returning to the bed. Along the way, he picked up the girls' two burlap blankets.

"We think . . . she means well," Marilyn said, and she'd taken her sister's hand.

Risk shook his head at both of them and tossed the blankets to them.

"Use these."

Then, he half collapsed forward to support himself on the bed.

"Oh, Risk, you're hurt!"

"Yeah, Mare. I need to lie down."

He rolled himself slowly onto his back near the edge of the bed, and he didn't stop his eyes from closing.

Until they all heard a pack of nearwolves howling as they scaled the rock mountain, coming closer to Ham's house.

Without opening his eyes, he said, "Dammit. More fucking wolves."

"Risk, we have to leave."

"Yeah, Fia."

Marilyn tried shaking him and said, "Now, Risk! Sissy and I are kind of, sort of better. We think."

"We're ready if you are," Sophia said with a tired smirk. "Look at us. You'll see."

He opened his eyes and looked at the twins sitting back on their heels beside him. Both were entirely naked except for bits of sticky webbing in odd places. But they'd fluffed up their hair and despite their eyes threatening to close, he fixed his eyes on their lips, which were full, and wet, and kind of red, and getting farther away every . . .

"Risk!" Marilyn yelled. "You have to stay awake!"

Sophia smirked and said, "Part of you anyway."

"That's funny, Sissy. But not really because the monsters are coming!"

"Sis is right," Sophia said as she reached for his pants.

"He's smiling, Sissy. He's going to be okay."

"Huh. No, Sis. He'll be better than okay. Help me."

She finished loosening it all and with Marilyn's help, they pulled his pants down to his knees.

"Oh my goodness," said Marilyn. "Even after killing those things and being a gorilla and all that?"

"Like he said, Sis. It's his ass to risk."

"Funny, Sissy. Oh, he did say that it was your turn, remember?"

"Mm, I do remember."

With Marilyn holding both of her hands, Sophia swung a leg over and straddled him.

Marilyn giggled and said, "Let me help, Sissy," then let go of one of her sister's hands to aim something straight up for her.

"Have a seat, Sissy."

She did, saying, "Mm, that's nice. Thanks. I couldn't hardly miss."

"Sissy, that's funny but not really."

Sophia bounced a few times, then stayed seated, anchored.

"Sis. Have a seat," Sophia said, grinning.

"Oh, should I?"

"Well, you have to. Remember how this works? It has to be everyone."

"Oh. I do now."

She giggled and added, "Even if there's a lioness too."

"Yep. Even then. Here, I'll help you."

Sophia held her sister's hands until she'd placed a knee on each side of Risk, near his waist, and knelt there, still holding her sister's hands.

"Um, is he awake enough, Sissy?"

Sophia let her go to push down on her shoulders and said, "He will be. I would."

Marilyn giggled and said, "Sissy, you're silly. I believe that's true, though."

Sophia was already feeling it, and she gave her sister a smile.

"Okay, Sissy."

Marilyn lowered herself down, aiming for Risk's mouth with what she knew wanted the most attention.

"Oh, Sissy," she said, looking up at the ceiling.

"He's awake?"

"Mm-hmm. Very much so. Yes."

Sophia started a steady, gentle bounce, and Marilyn wiggled her hips, making subtle adjustments for the bleeding and almost knocked-out man beneath her.

But they stopped at the sounds of nearwolves, so close that they could have been on Ham's patio.

Sophia looked toward Widow, who was holding her gaze with no expression. She looked back at Marilyn.

"She knows she's going to die, Sis," she whispered. "She can't fight those things."

Marilyn gave Widow a glance, then leaned closer to her sister and whispered, "Uh-uh, Sissy. We can't let her die."

"You, uh, you think we—"

Marilyn smiled as she silenced Sophia with one finger to her lips. And they both noticed that it was a very soft fingertip, with no sharp nails to interfere with anything asked of it.

She leaned forward and gave Sophia a quick kiss, then looked toward Widow and mouthed the words, "Come here!"

Widow tipped her head and mouthed her own word.

"Really?"

Marilyn nodded with a grin, then tipped her head, inviting the woman to come join them.

While Widow was getting up onto her short black boots, Sophia held a finger up to her own lips and mouthed, "Shh!"

Widow tiptoed to the far side of the bed, then climbed up as quietly as she could and shook the bed as little as possible.

All eyes were on Risk, but he seemed to have only enough strength to service Marilyn and Sophia and was oblivious to everything else. Widow crawled closer and stayed on her hands and knees near the three of them.

Marilyn sighed and smiled at her sister, who only nodded to her with her own tired smile.

"It has to be all of us, Sis."

"Oh, that's true," she whispered. "Well, since we have no choice . . ."

Marilyn gestured for Widow to come closer, and she waited with her eyebrows up, then she looked to Sophia.

Sophia nodded and whispered, "Get closer. Right next to us."

Shaking her head but smiling, too, Widow got close, her knee touching Marilyn's leg where she'd leaned herself down to cover Risk, and her hand on Sophia's thigh where she sat on his lap, snugly.

Then, Marilyn reached over and rubbed Widow's ass, patting it a few times then reaching under her panties, while Widow looked up at Sophia with an equally tired smile.

Sophia kept riding Risk, and she held Marilyn's gaze as she tipped her head toward Widow and said, "Not acting, Sis, remember?"

"Oh, I do now. Yes."

Marilyn looked down just as Widow turned her head enough to look into her eyes and purse her lips, then smile.

With a deep sigh, being attended to by Risk between her thighs, Marilyn gently rubbed her way down Widow's ass, then farther, between her thighs and found the part of her she sought.

Widow gasped while looking up at Sophia, who lightly brushed back her thick black hair. Then, she took a gentle hold of Widow's chin and guided her closer toward her breasts.

And Widow never broke her gaze into Sophia's eyes as she closed her lips on one of her very excited nipples. Sophia nodded, caressed Window's ear a few times, then played with her hair while holding her mouth to her breast.

Sophia looked again at her sister, whose breasts were shaking lightly with every tremor she felt from Risk, and said, "Us, too, Sis. All of us."

"Mm-hmm, Sissy."

She grinned as she drove a few fingers deeper into Widow, who gasped but quickly recovered and resumed her steady suckling of Sophia.

"Kiss me, Sis. I'm so close."

"Oh, Sissy, I think I'm already there."

They kissed, a deep kiss, and each of the girls placed a hand over Risk's heart.

Sophia kept bouncing and shifting her hips, grinding into him.

Marilyn was mostly still, letting the dying man beneath her do his job.

Widow, on her hands and knees beside all three of them, began shaking as her orgasm was just about to hit her, and she moaned softly from Marilyn's skillful fingers moving slowly and gently, the way she'd learned that Widow wanted it, and from Sophia holding her so that she couldn't stop sucking at her breast.

The twins felt the man from Below the Bay begin to shake, too, and they paused their kiss only long enough to see his ab muscles tightening and relaxing.

Marilyn whispered, "Now, Sissy."

"Mm-hmm. Let's get the fuck out of here, Sis."

"Oh, Sissy, that's kind of . . . funny . . . and, oh my goodness!"

The Kildare Killers heated up their hands, even in the throes of ecstasy that hit the three women at the same time, and the room filled with the stench of burning flesh as they sent their hands all the way through Risk's chest.

The room around them became mountain rock around them.

And all of them, each at the peak of their orgasms, vanished from the attacking nearwolves in Ham's house on a mountain in a place that they'd named Below the Bay.

Chapter 65 – I Still Have to Go Back

Risk took a deep breath when he felt his cheek again flat against a wooden plank, but there was no one's head on his lap.

He heard a voice. A somewhat familiar one.

"You're back? Where did you just go?"

He squeezed his eyes harder shut and reached one hand to rub them.

"And why does this lion seem so familiar?"

Only then did he feel a warm body slumped against his side. He picked his head up, shook it a few times, and looked across the table at Dayzee Dazzle.

She squinted at him, then looked at the Boss, to her left, then at K Kat, seated on the bench to her right. The lion gave her cheek a wet lick, causing her to scrunch up her face, then she stared at Risk too.

Risk blinked a few times, then shook his head again.

He saw Dayzee's eyes glance beside him, then back into his eyes.

"Are you going to rape her again?"

"Dammit," he said, then turned toward Widow, and the motion upset her balance, causing the unconscious woman to slump across his lap.

He looked up at Dayzee and said, "The twins. Mare and Fia. Are they here?"

"Not since you rescued them from under my burning mansion. Or so you said. Just who the hell are you anyway?"

"Risk. You're Dayzee?"

"Yeah, that's me."

"They talked about you."

"Good things, I hope. You said you were going to go somewhere and bring back those gorgeous—"

She snapped her head to look to one side.

"There they are!"

She waved a hand and yelled, "Mare! Fia! Over here!"

The twins stumbled toward the table, each rubbing their eyes with one hand and holding her sister's waist with the other.

Each had a loose burlap blanket over their shoulders, and they stabbed the asphalt parking lot with their high heels.

"Um, it might be a little early for that look, girls. Really cute. Alright, maybe not burlap, though."

"Oh, Dayzee," said Marilyn, "it's so good to see you. It's been so long."

"It has? The Boss and I haven't even left Earth yet. What are you talking about?"

Sophia smirked at her and said, "Since we left here, it's been the longest month of our lives."

"Huh?"

Both girls noticed Widow reclined across Risk's lap, but they ignored her for the moment.

"Risk, it worked," said Marilyn. "You brought us back."

"We all did, Mare."

"Hey," said Dayzee, "you really do call her that."

"He calls me Fia, too, Dayzee."

"You two," Dayzee said, shaking her head.

"What's she doing here?" Sophia said, pointing at Widow, who was stretching her arms out and yawning.

"Oh, Sissy," said Marilyn. "Try to remember."

"Oh. Yeah. We, um, that's our fault."

"I can't believe I ever liked her. Why did we want her to come back with us?"

"Sis, we loved her and all the things she did. Right now, I have no idea why."

"It cures you," Risk said, and he turned enough that they could see his back.

His vest was shredded but the skin beneath it was perfect.

"Your legs," he said to the twins. "They should be okay now."

"Oh, Sis, I remember that now. When we were leaving, the backs of—"

"Leaving," Marilyn said with a giggle. "Sissy, you make it sound like we caught a cab."

"Hell of a cab ride, Sis. Anyway, do you remember that? Were your legs hurting too?"

"Oh. I remember that now. Yes, all sorts of little pinches."

They both stood enough, and held away their blankets enough, that they could examine the backs of the other's thighs.

"Perfect, Sis. Your legs are gorgeous again."

"Yours, too, Sissy. Oh, that Widow."

They both glared down at Widow as she lay, still unconscious, across Risk's lap.

Widow opened her eyes and looked up at Risk, saying, "Hmm, here we are again."

He forced her up and pushed her to sit at the far end of the table. She stretched her arms to her sides and held a long, relaxed yawn.

"I heard both of you," she said. "I won't apologize for what I've become. And you two really are tasty and delightful."

The girls looked at each other, grinning.

"You are, Sis. Can't blame her."

"I'd bite you, too, Sissy. Oh yeah."

Marilyn turned toward Risk and said, "I get it. That fixed us. I don't know what I think about her now."

Risk was turned away from her, glaring at Widow.

"I didn't bring you," he said to her.

Widow grinned, holding his gaze, and tipped her head toward the twins.

"No. They did. It was quite nice too."

"You don't belong here," he told her.

Widow smirked and said, "And you do?"

"I'm not staying. I have to stop Archie from—"

"Archie?" said Dayzee. "What a coincidence. There's some bloody guy swilling booze inside. Said his name was Archie."

*　*　*

"No," said Risk. "Archie? It can't be."

"I told you he might come here," Marilyn said with a tired but still pleasant smile.

"Sis did say that, Risk," Sophia said as she and her sister sat beside him, on the opposite side from Widow.

Risk looked around and said, "This is West Hollywood?"

Dayzee grinned at the twins, shaking her head.

"We're off to a good start—he knows his maps and stuff. That calls for a drink."

"No," he told her. "Not for me. I still have to go back."

"Because of that plan?" said Sophia. "Those wolves have probably killed everything already."

"Oh, Sissy, maybe that fake moon burned out. They might just be normal freaks again by now."

"Normal freaks, Sis? Like those zombeings? Listen to yourself."

Marilyn looked down with a smile.

"That is kind of funny, Sissy."

Dayzee had been looking from one to the other and blurted out, "Seriously, what on Earth are you two talking about?"

Sophia smirked and said, "That's always going to be funny, Dayzee."

Before Marilyn could comment, she pointed at Risk and said, "Where have you been with these girls? You said you took them? Where? Up the coast?"

"Huh," said Sophia. "You're not entirely wrong with that."

"What, Fia?"

"It was more like down," Marilyn said with a giggle. "Kind of up *and* down."

"What, Mare? And who is she?" Dayzee said while pointing toward Widow. "And why are we always surrounded by lions?"

"Oh, Dayzee," Marilyn said with a pleasant smile. "It's only just one. She's K Kat."

"K who? Somebody really should start—"

"There's no time," Risk said. "Archie can stay, but I have to go."

"I don't know why you want to go so bad, Risk."

"I have to keep trying, Fia."

"Oh," said Marilyn. "It's all about being good? Being a better man?"

He looked up into the trees and said, "If I can do it there, then—"

"Below the Bay."

"Yeah, Fia. If I can be good there, Topside would be easy."

"Topside?" said Dayzee. "Is that the new restaurant on Wilshire? Really, what are you all talking about?"

"Here," said Sophia, pointing in a couple of directions. "This is Topside. Risk, if you're going back, I'll go, too, then."

"Sissy, really?"

Sophia nodded and said, "He saved our asses a lot of times, Sis."

"Oh, very true, Sissy."

She giggled and added, "He risked his ass many times for us."

Sophia pointed at her sister and said, "Well, Sis, it was his ass to—"

"I'll go back too," Widow said from the far end of the table. "I have to."

All eyes turned to her.

"I died to leave this world,"—she held her arms out and smirked as she gave it all a glance—"and even you, Risk, can't fix that."

He nodded and said, "You died here."

She frowned and said, "Yes. Here, I'm just dead. I thought you being different would fix it somehow."

Risk nodded and said, "You already feel it."

Widow looked down, sighed, and said, "Yeah. I'm dying. For real, this time."

Marilyn, still looking toward Widow, heard her sister sigh behind her.

"Oh, okay," she said. "I'll go back too. So, Risk, Sissy and I are with you, if you insist on going back to that horrible place."

Sophia said, "Kenzie too."

Dayzee looked around and said, "Whatever happened to her?"

"Um, she's around," said Sophia.

"That's funny, Sissy. True, too, though."

Widow cleared her throat, getting them all to look her way.

"I'd rather return than be dead."

"Um," said Sophia, "you'd still be a, um, you'd be—"

She held Sophia's gaze and said, "I am even now."

Sophia giggled softly and looked at her lap. Widow smiled at the sight of it, then held Risk's gaze.

"You know that I didn't ask for this."

"Yeah. I know."

"And you know that I've embraced it. It's who I am now."

"Yeah."

She smiled at each of them, then looked into Sophia's eyes when she said, "And none of you would have me any other way."

"Well," said Marilyn, causing Risk to turn toward her, "there you have it. All of us are going with you."

He squinted at her, even though she was sitting so close that they were rubbing up against each other.

He snapped his head around to see Widow, and she only smiled as she shrugged, causing him to snarl.

He spun around again to check Sophia, and he saw that she was leaning forward, looking past him at Widow. With a silly smile.

Grumbling, he looked across the table at Dayzee Dazzle.

She pointed at him, laughing, and said, "Who's taking whom, huh?"

He let a heavy breath rasp out, then looked up into the trees behind the Prism bar on Sunset Boulevard.
"Dammit."

Enjoy the Story?

Thank you for reading! Please consider leaving a review and/or a rating at your favorite bookseller or with your favorite book club. Help your fellow readers meet Risk and the Killers!

For more about Edward Allen Karr and his books, visit:

www.LakesideLetters.com

What's Next for Risk and the Killers?

Dying to be Widow
Risk and the Killers Book Two

Before Risk and the Kildare Killers used a wild sex and death escapade to flee the raging flames beneath Dayzee Dazzle's mansion in Beverly Hills, bringing them to a dark, burning, nightmare world . . .

WIDOW WAS ALREADY THERE

The shy, prudish woman had earned her passage to Below the Bay like all the rest: she died at a peak moment of ecstasy. In that hellish landscape below the San Francisco Bay, in shock and losing her mind, she started mutating from a blast of nasty radiation, got violently and cruelly raped, then got cast out into the savage city, still gagged and bound.

Was it her fate to perish at the claws and fangs of whichever beast found her first? Not a chance. She learned to embrace that world, celebrate the gorgeous but monstrous thing she'd become, and reject any boundaries between sex and death and love and consumption.

Content advisory: This book is intended for a mature audience.

Below the Bay

Is Book One in the series
Risk and the Killers

Which is the sequel series to
Thrills N Kills in the Hills

Dayzee Dazzle and her best friends, the Kildare Killers, are famous and gorgeous. They're too captivating to be from this planet, and they like it that way. Earthmen can't resist them and rarely survive encounters with them.

They find humor in horror, confront the ghastly with laughter and loss of clothing, and leave dead bodies and satisfied smiles in their wake.

Dayzee Dazzle and the Kildare Killers – Book One
Dayzee Dazzle and her Manic Mansion – Book Two
Dayzee Dazzle and the On-Set Onslaught – Book Three
Dayzee Dazzle and the Cadaver Collectors – Book Four

Have You Met Lin Finity?

She's the powerful star of her own series titled Fringes of Infinity. In the beginning, she's forced to learn how to control the unstoppable, magical power she earned at age fifteen. After killing her abusive uncle with her deadly new ability, she locked it away inside herself. Now, she's in her forties, and it's back. She calls it *Mayhem*. And it's done waiting.

Book One and the Novella are free in e-book format. Just visit https://www.LakesideLetters.com

Lin Finity and her Mayhem Rising
Lin Finity in Holding On

About the Author

Edward Allen Karr was born, raised, and continues to reside in Ohio, USA. His adult life has followed a meandering path, ranging from working an automotive assembly line to designing space flight hardware. And through all of it, he's seen that life is a captivating and ultimately unexplainable endeavor. His writing seeks to add a splash of wonder to a world already awash in it.

*   *   *

For more information, please visit:

www.LakesideLetters.com